nowledge. 知識工場

Knowledge is everything！

nowledge. 知識工場

Knowledge is everything！

一聽
忘不了！

A Self-training Class
for **Listening.**

張翔 / 著

兩段速英語
精聽精練

漸進式聽法 ➕ 爆量練習題 ＝ 突破英聽無極限

分數 NO.1 **考場題型一個不漏**

上考場前的第一本自救書。囊括**各大英檢必考**的三大題型，藉書熟練，答題就能**又快又準**。

效果 NO.1 **最狂兩段變速特訓**

用「**兩段速聽法**」打垮過去的「盲聽瞎練」。**由慢漸快**，真正聽得懂，打造**英語金耳朵**。

臨場感 NO.1 **擬真試題＆解析**

精選**日常＆考場**必見的8大主題，編寫試題與解析。**練習爆量、解析到位**，不知不覺就搞定聽力。

User's Guide

使用說明

STEP 1　情境分類，架構最清晰

本書以**情境式分類**，將生活 & 考試常見的主題分為八章。此外，標題的右下角會註明「本單元內容常在什麼情境中出現」，以幫助讀者了解**應用範圍**。

STEP 2　難易度燈泡，一眼掌握

題目依照**單字難易度 & 選項混淆度**，分成 **1 ～ 5** 級。1 級題目為答題率偏高的基礎題，5 級題目則為學習者容易選錯的進階題，測驗、複習時都能參考。

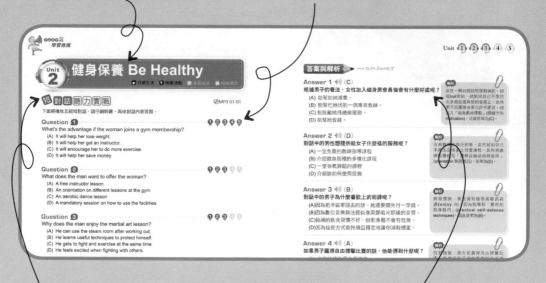

STEP 3　聽力實戰，模擬度破表

依照各章主題，提供符合**英文檢定考難度**的題目。並以「**實用度**」為考量，囊括各大檢定考常見的「**短對話 / 長對話 / 短文**」三大題型，考什麼都上手。

STEP 4　中譯與解析，深度解題

除了題目與選項的**中文翻譯**外，另外會在**解析**內點出每一題的**解題關鍵**，並解釋關鍵單字與片語的意思，看了就能掌握核心。

中英文內容，一看就通

✈ 中英文內容　　　　　　　⊙慢速MP3 02-02　◎正常速MP3 02-03

💬 短對話 **1** *Conversation*

Merry: Have you been to the new bar, "Heaven"?
梅莉： 你去過那家新開的酒吧「天堂」嗎？
Alvin: Yes. The owner used to be the head bartender in another bar; he then opened up and now runs "Heaven".
亞文： 去過，老闆以前是另一間酒吧的首席酒保，後來自己開了「天堂」。

💬 短對話 **2** *Conv*

Chris: I had too ma

✈ 中英文內容　　　　　　　⊙慢速MP3 02-05　◎正常速MP3 02-06

Kathy: How about we go for some afternoon tea?
凱西： 我們去吃下午茶怎麼樣？

Chris: Only if the food is good. I'd rather starve than spend money on very average food.
克里斯：好吃才要去，我寧願餓肚子也不要在沒什麼特別的食物上浪費錢。

✈ 中英文內容

📝 短文 **1**　　　　　　　　⊙慢速MP3 04-09　◎正常速MP3 04-10

Most people associate pigeon with racing and annoying flocks of birds on the road. However, pigeon can also make a rather tasty poultry for cooking. Pigeon meat is most suitable for grilling and roasting. Also, timing is critical in cooking pigeon because as soon as you overcook it, the meat becomes extremely leathery and tough. You don't need to be an expert chef to make a nice grilled pigeon. Anyone with general cooking experience can make it. It is delicious just served with a pinch of salt and pepper.

大多數人會將鴿子與賽鴿活動及路上討厭的鴿群聯想在一起。但是，鴿子其實也是種美味的烹飪類禽肉，鴿肉最適合的烹調方式為燒烤或炙烤。同時，時間控制也非常重要，因為只要你一煮過頭，鴿肉馬上就會變得又老又硬。就算不是專業的廚師，也能烤出美味的鴿肉，任何有點烹飪經驗的人都做得到，只要撒些鹽和胡椒粉上去就很美味了。

📝 短文 **2**　　　　　　　　⊙慢速MP3 04-11　◎正常速MP3 04-12

每一題型都將補充完整的**中英文內容**，並以**顏色標註**解題的關鍵字與句子，不管是想專注在解題關鍵上，還是想要隨著專業外師朗誦，都非常方便。

兩段速MP3，訓練紮實

題目以正常速朗讀，模擬檢定考的實況。中英文內容則以「⊙**慢速**→◎**正常速**」的兩段式朗讀法，以慢速「聽懂內容」，再以正常速「熟悉速度」，提高跟聽能力。

進階英聽自救網站

附錄的**好康大補帖**將補充**免費**的聽力訓練網站。會介紹每個網站的**特色**，標註**實用度**與**難易度**，讀者可按自己的程度與需求挑選。

好康大補帖 ～自學急救 must-see 網站

👤 **優質影片訓練網站** 👤

🎧 TED: Ideas worth spreading

💻 http://www.ted.com/

這個網站蒐集了許多很棒的演講內容，在觀賞影片時能選擇字幕（但並非每部影片都附上多種語言字幕），想自我訓練的人可以看無字幕版。更棒的是，每個影片都會附上完整的英文內容（transcript），而且會隨著演講者讀到的句子，一句句標註出來，所以聽不懂的學習者可以跟著文字邊聽邊讀，甚至記錄自己不懂的單字與片語。

自學實用度 ★★★★★　　　　　內容難度 ★★★★☆

這樣訓練聽力，真的受用一輩子

　　一般來說，英語的「聽、說、讀、寫」四大領域應該要並進學習，可惜的是，大部分的亞洲學生多半專注於「讀與寫」的能力，整體而言，「聽與說」的能力相對較弱。甚至於我教過的學生裡，幾乎人手一本單字書，但問起「聽與說」的訓練，多半顯得毫無頭緒。

　　之前看到一則新聞，點出高中學生的英聽成績，和以往相比，「幾乎完全聽懂」的比例在下降，其實這是個滿值得我們深思的現象。許多考生著重的，是「單字為基礎」這個觀念，這點我也認同，但過猶不及，一旦過度強調「單字」，學生就會以為「只要我單字背得多，就算聽與說差一點，也沒關係」。過去，這樣偏頗的學習方向或許並沒有造成什麼大問題，但在現今，我們已經不能無止盡地沿用這種「啃單字書、背字典」的學習方式了。僅僅是各大英文檢定考，也已經有越來越多開始注重「聽力」與「口說」的能力，希望能讓學生跳脫以往的學習窠臼。

　　就我教學的經驗來說，有心的學生在單字量上的差距並不大，令人驚訝的是，聽力測驗往往成為關鍵的決勝點。我曾經教過一位學生，她非常用心，不僅是我上課教的單字，各大模擬考、課外文章她都沒有少閱讀。每次我看到她的學習本，上面密密麻麻的都是單字與片語，令人佩服。事實上，不管遇到什麼考試，她的閱讀測驗、克漏字等等都絕不輸人，但當她的英文檢定考成績下來時，我卻發現那頂多只能算中上的成績，對學生來說，那無疑是一大打擊。檢討時，很容易就

看出她的問題出在「聽力」。因為不習慣外國人說話的速度，所以即便都是她理解的單字，一變成聽力的題目，她就幾乎聽不懂了。

我一直覺得，這樣是很可惜的一件事，你說學生程度不好？倒也不是，純粹只是因為平日不注重聽力訓練，所以才失分至此。對亞洲學生而言，最不容易克服的，其實是「對聽力的恐懼感」。如果我跟你保證，聽力測驗 80% 以上的內容，都不會涉及多艱澀的用字，你是否會感到驚訝呢？如果會的話，請務必給自己一個機會，掌握這些你原本就聽得懂的英文。

在編寫本書之前，我參考了各大檢定考的常見題型，決定把「短對話 / 長對話 / 短文」三大類一併囊括在本書中。除此之外，編寫時也考量題目的難易度 & 生活中常見的幾個話題，融合之後，才決定了每個單元的內容。我希望這不僅僅是一本有關聽力訓練的書，還能是最生活化、最實用的英文工具書。

在構想本書時，我就已經想好，除了一開始的題目之外，後面要以「⊙慢速→◉正常速」的兩段式朗讀法，帶領讀者熟悉各單元內容。這種設計的優勢在於，能讓讀者先以慢速「聽懂內容」，再回到正常速「熟悉速度」。對我來說，不斷重複根本聽不懂或跟不上的英文內容，並不會比循序漸進的學習法要有效率。如果讀者能先習慣慢速朗讀，對他們來說不僅是聽懂，同時還能降低他們對「聽」的恐懼，進而享受聽英文的過程。如此，不管是面對什麼樣的考題變化，或者是什麼樣的外國人，學習者都能敞開心胸去聽，而這一點，其實才是聽力能不斷進步的關鍵！

張 翔

CONTENTS 目錄

PART 1

飲食與美味

★★食物喜好、推薦美食，通關聽力的第一課，就從飲食開始！★★

PART 2

流行與逛街

★★撿便宜、引領流行，身家必備的打扮儀容，怎麼聽就是這些！★★

PART 3

運動與休閒

★★活動身體、娛樂放鬆，提升身心健康，熱門話題不可少！★★

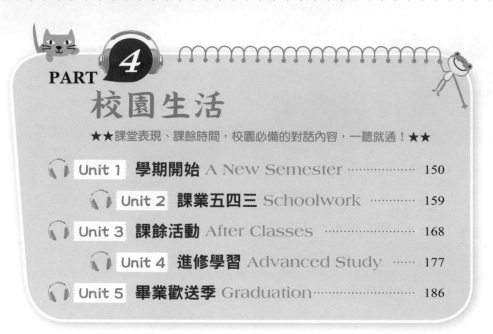

PART 8

社會議題

★★深度對談、意見交流，搞定專門領域，聽力K.O沒問題！★★

PART 1

飲食與美味

食物喜好、推薦美食，通關聽力的第一課，
就從飲食開始！

Unit 1 在餐廳中 Go Dining

日常生活　娛樂活動　意見交流　特殊場合

MP3 01-01

下面將播放五組短對話，請仔細聆聽，再依對話內容答題。

Question 1

What time did the man suggest?

 (A) 7:45
 (B) 6:45
 (C) He didn't say.
 (D) 8:15

Question 2

How many paying customers are there in total?

 (A) Four
 (B) Two
 (C) Five
 (D) Six

Question 3

What dish does the man want to begin his meal with?

 (A) Salad
 (B) Steak
 (C) Soup
 (D) Something lighter

Question 4

What soup will the man have?

 (A) Clam chowder
 (B) Beef and tomato soup
 (C) No soup; it ran out.
 (D) A special soup

Question 5

Who is paying for this meal?

 (A) The woman
 (B) The man
 (C) Both are paying for their own orders
 (D) The Dutch

答案與解析 ~answer

Answer 1 (B)
男性建議的時間是什麼時候？

(A) 七點四十五分
(B) 六點四十五分
(C) 他沒有說。
(D) 八點十五分

> **解析**
> 題目問的是餐廳員工的建議時間，而非女性想要的時間。女性一開始說她要訂 7:45 (a quarter to eight)，但因為那個時間已經沒位子，所以餐廳員工建議她提前一個小時來，正確答案為(B)的6:45。

Answer 2 (C)
需要付費的客人總共有幾位呢？

(A) 四位
(B) 兩位
(C) 五位
(D) 六位

> **解析**
> 聽到服務生的詢問，女性一開始就回答了總人數六人(six)，但提到其中一位為嬰兒；這題的另一個關鍵在服務生的回答，他提到「嬰兒不會算為付費客人」(The baby won't count as...)，正確答案為(C)。

Answer 3 (A)
男性想從哪一道餐點開始品嚐？

(A) 沙拉
(B) 牛排
(C) 湯品
(D) 較清淡、無負擔的食物

> **解析**
> 討論要從哪道菜先吃起時，男性說他想從清淡點的菜色，像是沙拉之類的 (something light like salad)開始享用。要注意的是對話中的something lighter並非菜色，而是形容沙拉的詞彙而已，因此最佳答案為(A)。

Answer 4 (B)
對話中的男性點的湯會是什麼呢？

(A) 蛤蜊濃湯
(B) 牛肉番茄湯
(C) 沒點湯，因為賣完了。
(D) 一種特別的湯品

> **解析**
> Today's Special是餐廳的「當日限定菜色」，而非字面「特殊」的意思，所以不能選(D)。服務生解釋原本的例湯(clam chowder)已經賣完，因此被換成牛肉番茄湯(beef and tomato soup)，正確答案為(B)。

Answer 5 (C)
誰會付帳單呢？

(A) 對話中的女性
(B) 對話中的男性
(C) 各付各的
(D) 荷蘭人

> **解析**
> 對話中的女性原本準備一起買單，但是男性又堅持要請她，所以她最後提議以 (go Dutch)「AA制；平均分擔」的方式買單，因此答案為(C)。

 中英文內容

◎慢速MP3 01-02　　◎正常速MP3 01-03

短對話 ① Conversation

Anna: Hello, I'd like to book a table at your restaurant, around a quarter to eight.

安娜： 您好，我要預訂晚上七點四十五分左右的桌位。

Bob: May I suggest you **come an hour earlier**? We are currently fully booked for your preferred time.

鮑伯： 請問您是否願意提早一個小時前來？因為您想要的時間已經客滿了。

短對話 ② Conversation

Waiter: How many of you are there, please?

服務生：請問你們一共有幾位呢？

Jill: **Six. But one is only a baby**, so I'm not sure if she counts as one.

吉兒： 六位，可是有一個是嬰兒，我不知道她算不算一位。

Waiter: **The baby won't count as a paying customer** for our buffet.

服務生：嬰兒不會算為吃到飽的付費客人。

短對話 ③ Conversation

Susie: What a selection they have! What are you going to start with?

蘇西： 這裡的菜色選擇真多呢！你要先吃哪道菜？

Colin: The steak looks delicious. But I'll start with **something lighter like salad**.

科林： 牛排看起來很美味，但我想從清淡點的沙拉吃起。

短對話 ④ Conversation

Frank: I would like to have "Today's Special" for the soup. What is it anyway?

法蘭克：我要一份「今日例湯」，今天的湯是什麼呢？

Donna: The special is clam chowder, but it has just run out. It has been **replaced by beef and tomato soup**.

唐娜： 原本的例湯是蛤蜊濃湯，但剛剛供應完了，所以用牛肉番茄湯替換。

短對話 ⑤ Conversation

Betty: It's my treat today.

貝蒂： 今天我買單。

Sam: No. I really should buy you this meal for your help.

山姆： 這怎麼行，我才應該請你這一頓，感謝你的幫忙。

Betty: If you insist, then **let's just go Dutch**. Otherwise, we'll be here all night fighting for the bill.

貝蒂： 如果你堅持，那還是各付各的吧，免得整晚在這裡搶帳單。

長對話聽力實戰

請仔細聆聽下面的長對話，再依對話內容選擇正確答案。

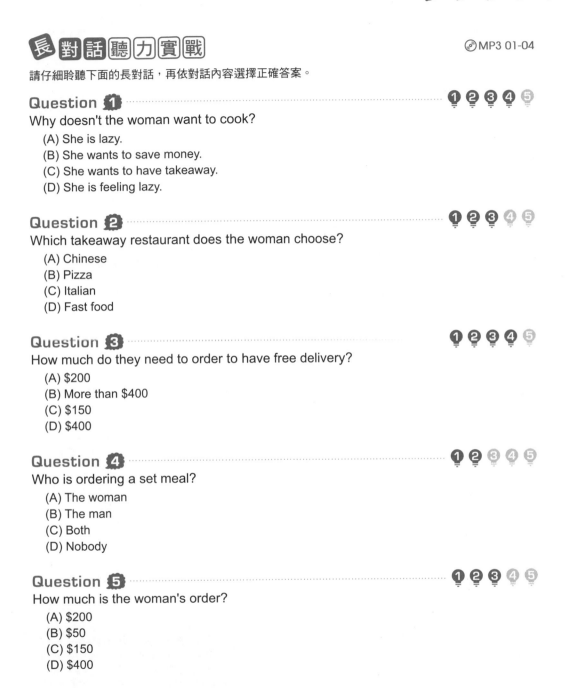

Question 1

Why doesn't the woman want to cook?

(A) She is lazy.
(B) She wants to save money.
(C) She wants to have takeaway.
(D) She is feeling lazy.

Question 2

Which takeaway restaurant does the woman choose?

(A) Chinese
(B) Pizza
(C) Italian
(D) Fast food

Question 3

How much do they need to order to have free delivery?

(A) $200
(B) More than $400
(C) $150
(D) $400

Question 4

Who is ordering a set meal?

(A) The woman
(B) The man
(C) Both
(D) Nobody

Question 5

How much is the woman's order?

(A) $200
(B) $50
(C) $150
(D) $400

答案與解析 ~answer

Answer 1 (D)
對話中的女性為何不想煮飯？

   (A) 因為她很懶惰。
   (B) 因為她想省錢。
   (C) 因為她想叫外送。
   (D) 因為她懶得煮飯。

解析
莎朗在解釋為何不想煮飯時說她懶得煮飯(feeling too lazy to cook)，選項(A)的She is lazy「她很懶惰」是用來形容一個人的個性，跟用現在式的feeling lazy「感覺懶懶的」不同，正確答案為(D)。

Answer 2 (A)
對話中的女性最後決定叫哪一家餐廳的外送呢？

   (A) 中國餐廳
   (B) 披薩店
   (C) 義大利餐廳
   (D) 速食店

解析
針對選擇哪間外帶餐廳，男性給了女性「轉角」(round the corner)的中國餐廳和「隔兩條街」(two streets away)的披薩店兩個選項，女性回答「越近的越好」(the closer the better)，正確答案為(A)。

Answer 3 (D)
兩人共須點多少元的餐點，才能享有免費外送的服務呢？

   (A) 兩百元
   (B) 四百元以上
   (C) 一百五十元
   (D) 四百元

解析
男性解釋菜單上說四百元或是更多的消費(order of $400 or more)就可享有免費外送的服務，不一定要超過四百元，正確答案為(D)。

Answer 4 (C)
誰點了套餐呢？

   (A) 對話中的女性
   (B) 對話中的男性
   (C) 兩人
   (D) 沒有人

解析
女性一開始只點了份炒飯，後來她又加價把原本的單點改成套餐(make it into a set for an extra...)，這裡的set就是等同於set meal的「套餐」。男性則直接說他要五號餐 (set meal number 5)，所以他們兩人都點了套餐，答案為(C)。

Answer 5 (A)
對話中女性點的餐是多少錢？

(A) 兩百元
(B) 五十元
(C) 一百五十元
(D) 四百元

解析
女性一開始點的炒飯只有$150元(that is $150 only)，結果她又用「額外的」五十元將她的餐點變成一個套餐(a set for an extra $50)，兩者加總起來，她的套餐是兩百元，答案為(A)。

 中英文內容

David: What are you cooking for dinner tonight?
大衛： 今天的晚餐你打算煮什麼？

Sharon: I have Italian pasta ingredients, but **I'm feeling too lazy** to cook.
莎朗： 我有煮義大利麵的食材，但我懶得煮。

David: How about going out for dinner?
大衛： 那出去吃晚餐怎麼樣？

Sharon: What choices are there?
莎朗： 有什麼選擇？

David: There's a Chinese restaurant just round the corner and pizza place two streets away.
大衛： 轉角就有家中國餐館，隔兩條街有間披薩店。

Sharon: **The closer the better.** Do they deliver?
莎朗： 越近的越好，他們能外送嗎？

David: I thought you chose the closer one because you don't want to walk too far.
大衛： 我以為你是因為不想走太遠，所以才選近的。

Sharon: I don't want to step out at all.
莎朗： 我完全不想出門。

David: Let me see...it says **free delivery for orders of $400 or more.**
大衛： 讓我看看，上面說滿四百元就可以免費外送。

Sharon: I want a portion of fried rice. **That is $150 only.** Wait. I also want to get sweetcorn soup and a coke, which will **make it into a set for an extra $50.**
莎朗： 我要一份炒飯，這樣才一百五十元。等等，我要再加點玉米濃湯和可樂，加五十元升等成套餐。

David: And I will **have a set meal number five.**
大衛： 那我要點一個五號餐。

短文聽力實戰

◉MP3 01-07(短文1)　◉MP3 01-08(短文2)

請仔細聆聽下面兩段短文，並分別回答Q1~Q2&Q3~Q5兩大題。

Question 1

What do people look for in restaurants now apart from good food?

(A) Good atmosphere
(B) Great taste
(C) Superhero characters
(D) Live bands

Question 2

What makes people visit a restaurant repeatedly?

(A) Cheap meals
(B) Good food and taste
(C) Live bands
(D) Creative menus

Question 3

What are the reasons that make it so difficult to stay healthy?

(A) Obesity and junk food
(B) Junk food and a busy lifestyle
(C) People don't want to eat healthily.
(D) People don't like healthy food.

Question 4

What does a healthy balanced diet give you?

(A) A better body shape
(B) A better lifestyle
(C) More energy
(D) Less fat

Question 5

Apart from exercise, what else cannot completely replace a balanced diet?

(A) Extreme diet
(B) Energy bar
(C) More exercise
(D) Junk food

答案與解析 ~answer

Answer 1 (A)

除了美味的餐點之外，現代人還重視餐廳的什麼特色？

(A) 絕佳氣氛
(B) 美味的餐點
(C) 超級英雄的角色
(D) 樂團的現場表演

解析

關於人們對餐廳的要求，除了美味的餐點(good food)之外，就是第一段提到人們追求(sought after)的「絕佳氣氛」(good ambiance)。選項(C)和(D)雖然都能製造良好氣氛，但不一定每間餐廳都有這些元素，因此答案為(A)。

Answer 2 (B)

什麼能讓顧客一再光顧同一家餐廳呢？

(A) 便宜的餐點
(B) 美味的菜色
(C) 現場表演的樂團
(D) 有創意的菜單

解析

文中說到要讓顧客一再上門，餐廳須要提供「美味的菜色」(provide good food and taste)。選項(C)和(D)都是吸引人的元素，但並非鞏固顧客群的核心元素，最基本的(most basic)還是美味的食物，因此選(B)。

Answer 3 (B)

什麼原因讓維持健康這件事變得困難呢？

(A) 肥胖與垃圾食物
(B) 垃圾食物與忙碌的生活型態
(C) 人們不想吃得健康。
(D) 人們不喜歡健康的食品。

解析

文中提到隨處可見的垃圾食物(junk food)與忙碌的生活型態(busy lifestyles)是增加維持健康難度的主因(make it very challenging to stay healthy)，challenging指「困難的」，答案選(B)。

Answer 4 (C)

一個營養均衡的飲食能讓你得到什麼呢？

(A) 好身材
(B) 更好的生活型態
(C) 更充沛的精神
(D) 變得不那麼胖

解析

文章提到一個均衡的飲食能讓你充滿精神(feel more energized)，因此，正確答案為(C)。

Answer 5 (A)

除了運動之外，另一項無法完全取代均衡飲食的方式為何？

(A) 極端的減肥
(B) 能量棒
(C) 更多的運動
(D) 垃圾食物

解析

文中提到均衡的飲食不能單純用運動(exercise)或「激烈的減肥方式」(drastic dieting)取代，關鍵字為replace(取代)，正確答案為(A)。

中英文內容

短文 1

⊙慢速MP3 01-09   ◎正常速MP3 01-10

Nowadays, good food is no longer the only thing consumers look for in restaurants; **good ambiance is now sought after** as much as great taste. Many restaurants now have a distinct theme and creative menu. For example, there are dishes inspired by superhero characters such as Hulk or Superman. When you go to a restaurant, sometimes you even have a live band playing. Of course, competitors copy very fast, so to make customers come time after time, a restaurant must find its true uniqueness that cannot be easily copied. By that, we are talking about providing **good food and taste**, which are the most basic things, but they are also the most difficult things to achieve and maintain.

在現今，消費者對餐廳的要求不再只有美味的餐點，現代人所追求的絕佳氣氛不比對食物的要求來的少。許多餐廳現在都主打各種不同的主題和極富創意的菜單，像是以綠巨人浩克或超人等超級英雄角色為靈感的菜色。踏進一家餐廳時，有時候甚至有樂團的現場演唱。當然，市面上的競爭者模仿的速度非常快，因此，為了確保顧客會一再上門消費，餐廳必須找到自己真正難以複製的獨特性；也就是提供美味的餐點，這是最基本的，同時也是最難達到和維持下去的事。

短文 2

⊙慢速MP3 01-11   ◎正常速MP3 01-12

Obesity is becoming one of the most common and serious problems among modern youth. Even though we constantly remind people to eat healthily, the amount of **junk food** out there and people's **busy lifestyles** make it very challenging to stay healthy. We always hear doctors and nutritionists talk about the importance of having **a healthy balanced diet**, which makes you feel **more energized**. If you are not careful about what you eat, you will very likely suffer the consequences later in life. A balanced diet cannot be simply replaced by **exercise** and **drastic dieting**; you must remember that being in shape and not being overweight do not equal being healthy.

肥胖是現代年輕人最常見、最嚴重的問題之一。就算我們不斷提醒民眾要吃得健康，但隨處可見的垃圾食物以及忙碌的生活型態卻讓維持健康這件事變得很困難。我們常聽到醫生和營養師提倡營養均衡的飲食有多重要，因為均衡的飲食能讓你感到精神充沛。如果不多加注意自己的飲食習慣，上了年紀後就會嚐到負面的影響。均衡的飲食不能單純以運動和激烈的減肥方式取代，記住，維持身材和體重不超重並不等於身體健康。

Unit 2 在酒吧 At The Bar

📖 日常生活　🎭 娛樂活動　✏ 意見交流　🔰 特殊場合

短對話聽力實戰

🎧 MP3 02-01

下面將播放五組短對話，請仔細聆聽，再依對話內容答題。

Question 1

1 2 3 4 5

What was the owner before he ran "Heaven"?

(A) A bartender
(B) A waiter
(C) An owner
(D) A regular customer

Question 2

1 2 3 4 5

What is the disadvantage of a "buy-one-get-one free" deal?

(A) You actually buy more drinks than usual.
(B) You can only have Long Island Ice Tea.
(C) It makes you want to spend more.
(D) You drink more and get drunk more easily.

Question 3

1 2 3 4 5

Who taught the girl to play jazz piano?

(A) A piano teacher
(B) Herself
(C) A consultant
(D) A professional trainer

Question 4

1 2 3 4 5

What does the man's friend do?

(A) He's the restaurant owner.
(B) He's an artist.
(C) He plays in a band.
(D) He's a singer.

Question 5

1 2 3 4 5

Why didn't the boy ask Sheila to go to the prom?

(A) Because he is out of her league.
(B) Because Sheila is dating someone.
(C) Because he thought Sheila already had a date.
(D) Because Sheila does not want to go to the prom.

答案與解析 ~answer

Answer 1 (A)

「天堂酒吧」的老闆在開業前做過什麼工作？

(A) 酒保
(B) 服務生
(C) 老闆
(D) 一名常客

解析
男子在介紹酒吧的老闆時，說他曾經是另一家酒吧的酒保，但並沒有強調他現在是酒保，重點單字為「曾經」(used to be)，最佳答案為(A)。

Answer 2 (D)

「買一送一」的促銷有什麼缺點呢？

(A) 你會買得比平常多。
(B) 你只能買長島冰茶。
(C) 這種促銷手法會讓你想花更多錢。
(D) 你會喝得更多，很容易就醉了。

解析
對話中提到這種促銷優惠的「缺點」(drawback)之一是因為它會讓你覺得比平常花得少，容易喝太多。選項(A)是過程，但對話強調的缺點是喝太多而醉倒這個最終的結果，最佳答案為(D)。

Answer 3 (B)

誰教會女孩彈爵士鋼琴的？

(A) 一名鋼琴老師
(B) 她自己學會的
(C) 一名顧問
(D) 一名專業教練

解析
女孩解釋說她在比賽前有「詢問」(consulted)過老師的意見，但是沒有說這個老師教她演奏爵士鋼琴。她接著解釋自己其實算是「無師自通」的鋼琴家(self-taught pianist)，正確答案為(B)。

Answer 4 (A)

男性的朋友是做什麼的？

(A) 他是餐廳老闆。
(B) 他是一名藝術家。
(C) 他在樂團演奏。
(D) 他是一名歌手。

解析
聽完女性的話，男性特別提到他有個「開餐廳的朋友」(a restaurant-owner friend)正在找表演者，重點在男性一開始提到的朋友身分，後續的表演者則與本題無關，正確答案為(A)。

Answer 5 (C)

男孩為何沒有邀請希拉做他的舞會女伴呢？

(A) 因為希拉配不上他。
(B) 因為希拉與其他人交往。
(C) 因為他認為希拉已經有舞伴了。
(D) 因為希拉不想去參加舞會。

解析
男孩認為希拉已經有伴了(already had a date)，正確答案為(C)。至於(B)的date someone意指「交往」，跟舞會的date「男伴/女伴」不同。

 中英文內容

短對話 1 Conversation

Merry: Have you been to the new bar, "Heaven"?

梅莉： 你去過那家新開的酒吧「天堂」嗎？

Alvin: Yes. The owner **used to be the head bartender** in another bar; he then opened up and now runs "Heaven".

亞文： 去過，老闆以前是另一間酒吧的首席酒保，後來自己開了「天堂」。

短對話 2 Conversation

Chris: I had too many of the "buy-one-get-one free" Long Island Ice Teas.

克里斯：那個「買一送一」的優惠害我喝了太多長島冰茶。

Vicky: That's one **drawback** of promotional deals like this.

緋琪： 這是這類促銷優惠的缺點之一。

Chris: That's right. You think you are not spending that much, so you **end up drinking much more**. Before you know it, you are **drunk**!

克里斯：對啊，覺得花的錢變少，就喝得更多，一不小心就醉了！

短對話 3 Conversation

Ben: Congratulations on winning the competition! Who taught you to play jazz?

班： 恭喜你贏得比賽！是誰教你彈爵士樂的啊？

Kate: I consulted a piano teacher before, but I'm actually **a self-taught pianist**.

凱特： 我有詢問過一名老師的意見，但我其實算是無師自通。

短對話 4 Conversation

Susan: Do you happen to know anyone who is looking for musicians to perform?

蘇珊： 你剛好知道有誰在找音樂家表演的嗎？

Leo: I have **a restaurant-owner friend** who is looking for various artists to perform live at his restaurant.

里歐： 我有個開餐廳的朋友正在找各種表演者在他餐廳做現場表演。

短對話 5 Conversation

Leila: You should ask Sheila to go to the prom with you.

莉拉： 你應該邀請希拉做你的女伴，一起去舞會。

Billy: I thought **she already had a date**. Besides, I think she is out of my league.

比利： 我覺得她已經有伴了，而且我覺得我配不上她。

Leila: She's not going with anyone yet. Seize the opportunity!

莉拉： 她還沒有男伴，快把握機會！

長對話聽力實戰

⊘MP3 02-04

請仔細聆聽下面的長對話，再依對話內容選擇正確答案。

Question 1

Why does the man agree to go and have afternoon tea?

- (A) Because he is hungry.
- (B) Because the woman assures him the food is good.
- (C) Because he wants to have afternoon tea.
- (D) Because he does not want to eat dinner.

Question 2

What kind of afternoon tea menu does the restaurant provide?

- (A) British afternoon tea
- (B) Italian dessert
- (C) Cheap dishes
- (D) Freshly made dishes

Question 3

What deal does the restaurant currently offer?

- (A) 80% off
- (B) 10% off
- (C) Buy one, get one free
- (D) 20% off

Question 4

Which dish/dishes does the woman most recommend?

- (A) Scones
- (B) Jam and cream
- (C) Pies
- (D) Sandwiches

Question 5

What does the man say he will try?

- (A) The instant coffee
- (B) The freshly made coffee
- (C) The pie
- (D) The scone

答案與解析 ～answer

Answer 1 ◀᯼ (B)

男性為什麼答應去吃下午茶？

(A) 因為他很餓。

(B) 因為女性向他保證茶點很美味。

(C) 因為他自己想吃下午茶。

(D) 因為他不想吃晚餐。

解析

女性提出下午茶的主意後，男性強調要食物好吃他才去(Only if the food is good.)，不然他寧願餓肚子，女性後來提到那家店提供「美味的」(fantastic)英式下午茶，正確答案為(B)。

Answer 2 ◀᯼ (A)

這家餐廳提供什麼類別的下午茶餐點呢？

(A) 英式下午茶

(B) 義式甜點

(C) 便宜的點心

(D) 新鮮的茶點

解析

解題重點在女性提到的「英式下午茶點」(British afternoon tea dishes)，雖然後續介紹了其他甜點(如司康)，但問起「類別」，還是必須回到大範圍的英式下午茶，正確答案為(A)。

Answer 3 ◀᯼ (D)

這家餐廳目前提供什麼樣的優惠呢？

(A) 兩折的優惠

(B) 九折的優惠

(C) 買一送一

(D) 八折優惠

解析

女性說這家餐廳目前有打八折的優惠(They have a 20% off deal at the moment.)。選項(B)的九折是她上次去的優惠，關鍵字at the moment和last time區別「目前」與「之前」，正確答案為(D)。

Answer 4 ◀᯼ (A)

女性最推薦的是什麼餐點呢？

(A) 司康餅

(B) 果醬與奶油

(C) 派

(D) 三明治

解析

當男性問起推薦的餐點時，女性說她「每次都會點一份司康餅」(I always order a scone)，可見她最愛、最推薦的餐點是司康餅，因此選(A)。

Answer 5 ◀᯼ (B)

男性說他一定會點來嚐嚐的是什麼呢？

(A) 即溶咖啡

(B) 現磨現泡的咖啡

(C) 派

(D) 司康餅

解析

雖然女性最推薦的是司康餅，但是男性並沒有明說會點司康餅。反倒是討論到現磨現沖的咖啡時，提到他「一定要點來嚐嚐」(definitely going to try it out)，因此答案選(B)。

中英文內容

⊙ 慢速MP3 02-05　　⊙ 正常速MP3 02-06

Kathy: How about we go for some afternoon tea?
凱西：　我們去吃下午茶怎麼樣？

Chris: **Only if the food is good.** I'd rather starve than spend money on very average food.
克里斯：好吃我才要去，我寧願餓肚子也不要在沒什麼特別的食物上浪費錢。

Kathy: They do all kinds of fantastic **British afternoon tea dishes**.
凱西：　他們提供很多好吃的英式下午茶點。

Chris: Sounds good.
克里斯：聽起來不錯。

Kathy: Plus, they have a **20% off** deal at the moment, which is much better than the 10% off deal I had last time.
凱西：　而且，他們目前有打八折的優惠，比我上次去的九折優惠好很多。

Chris: Even better, any particular recommendations?
克里斯：這點就更棒了，你有什麼特別推薦的嗎？

Kathy: I **always order a scone.** It is a match in heaven with the jam and cream.
凱西：　我每次都會點司康餅，和果醬和奶油簡直是絕配。

Chris: My mouth is watering already. Do they have **freshly ground and made coffee**?
克里斯：我都口水直流了。那他們有提供現磨現沖的咖啡嗎？

Kathy: Of course. Instant coffee cannot compare with what they have.
凱西：　那當然，即溶咖啡完全不能跟他們的相比。

Chris: I'm **definitely going to try it out.** What are we waiting for? Let's go!
克里斯：我一定要點來嚐嚐，那我們還在等什麼？快走吧！

短文聽力實戰

MP3 02-07（短文1）　　MP3 02-08（短文2）

請仔細聆聽下面兩段短文，並分別回答Q1~Q2&Q3~Q5兩大題。

Question 1

Why did the man get drunk so quickly?

(A) He didn't eat anything.
(B) He vomited everything he ate.
(C) He started drinking before the meal.
(D) He only ate a little.

Question 2

Why is the man's memory of his birthday celebration not so good?

(A) He vomited everything.
(B) He had a very bad hangover afterwards.
(C) He didn't like the food.
(D) He wasted food.

Question 3

How many times is the girl asked to perform at the restaurant?

(A) Once a week
(B) It is not stated.
(C) Twice a week
(D) Every weekend

Question 4

What helped the girl get the job at the restaurant?

(A) Winning the competition
(B) Her willingness to perform for free
(C) Her friend recommended her.
(D) Her great talent

Question 5

How many times has the girl performed at the restaurant?

(A) Once
(B) Twice
(C) Never
(D) Many times

答案與解析 ～answer

Answer 1 ◀» (C)

男性為什麼很快就醉倒了？

(A) 因為他沒有吃東西。
(B) 因為他吐光了所有吃的食物。
(C) 因為他在吃飯前就喝酒。
(D) 因為他只吃了一點點東西。

解析

男性說他們在開始吃飯前就已經喝了太多(before we started eating, we had already had too much alcohol)，接著說「因此」(Hence)他很快就醉了，正確答案為(C)。

Answer 2 ◀» (B)

為何男性對這次慶生活動的印象不是很好呢？

(A) 他吐光了所有東西。
(B) 他之後有嚴重的宿醉。
(C) 他不喜歡餐廳的食物。
(D) 他浪費食物。

解析

選項(A)是喝醉酒的後果(吐光吃下肚的食物)，但男主角之所以產生不好的印象，主因還是隔天的嚴重宿醉(terrible hangover)，因此最佳答案為(B)。

Answer 3 ◀» (C)

女性被要求到餐廳表演的頻率或次數為何？

(A) 一週一次
(B) 沒有提到。
(C) 一週兩次
(D) 每個週末

解析

女性提到餐廳老闆在尋找表演者，要在他的餐廳做「一週兩次」的(twice a week)現場表演，答案為(C)。英文中的一次通常用once表達，兩次則為twice，兩次以上才用一般數字(three times, four times...etc.)描述。

Answer 4 ◀» (C)

什麼因素幫助女生取得餐廳的工作？

(A) 贏得比賽
(B) 願意免費表演
(C) 她朋友的引薦
(D) 她優異的天分

解析

女生提到如果沒有她朋友的引薦(without Ben's referral, I don't think I would...)，她應該沒那麼容易得到工作機會。選項(A)與(B)是「可能」被錄取的原因，但未經證實，最佳答案為(C)。

Answer 5 ◀» (A)

女生目前為止到那家餐廳表演了幾次？

(A) 一次
(B) 兩次
(C) 還沒有表演過
(D) 很多次

解析

女生提到昨晚是她第一次表演(Last night, I had my first appearance)，而且她迫不及待想再次上台表演(cannot wait表示對某件事的期待)，因此可推論出她目前只表演過一次，正確答案為(A)。

◎慢速MP3 02-09　◎正常速MP3 02-10

It was my birthday last weekend. My friends booked us a table at an expensive restaurant. We arrived way too early, so we went to their bar and started drinking. And **before we started eating, we had already had too much alcohol!** Hence, I got drunk very quickly. And my friends continued to buy me drinks throughout the meal. Even though the meal was delicious, I vomited everything I had eaten afterwards! It could have been a great birthday celebration, but **my terrible hangover the next day** spoiled my memory of it.

上個週末是我的生日，我的朋友訂了一間名貴的餐廳慶祝。我們那天太早抵達，就先去餐廳的酒吧喝酒，結果在開始吃飯前，我們就已經喝了太多！所以我很快就醉倒，而且我的朋友在吃飯時還不斷請我喝酒，雖然那餐飯很美味，我之後卻把所有吃下去的食物都吐光了！本來應該是美好的慶生活動，但隔天的宿醉完全毀了我對這次慶生的回憶。

◎慢速MP3 02-11　◎正常速MP3 02-12

My friend Ben came to see me perform at the jazz piano competition. I was thrilled to have won. Moreover, I now have a great opportunity. Ben's friend owns an Italian restaurant, and was looking for artists to perform live at the restaurant **twice a week**. Even though I won a competition and was willing to do my first performance for free, I don't think I would have got the job quite so easily **without Ben's referral**. **Last night, I had my first appearance** and received really good feedback from the customers. I'm really pleased and **cannot wait to perform there again!**

我的朋友，班，來看我的爵士鋼琴比賽表演。贏得比賽讓我很高興，更開心的是，還因此得到了一個很棒的表演機會。班的朋友是間義大利餐廳的老闆，正在尋找一週能到他餐廳表演兩次的表演者。雖然贏得比賽，我也願意無償演出第一場，但如果沒有班的引薦，我想也沒那麼容易就得到這個工作機會。昨晚是我在餐廳的第一場表演，從餐廳客人那裡得到許多很棒的迴響，這讓我感到很開心，等不及想再到那裡表演呢！

Unit 3 食物喜好 The Food

日常生活　娛樂活動　意見交流　特殊場合

短 對 話 聽 力 實 戰

MP3 03-01

下面將播放五組短對話，請仔細聆聽，再依對話內容答題。

Question 1

What kind of restaurant is the man looking for?

(A) A vegan restaurant
(B) A restaurant with vegetarian dishes
(C) A restaurant with vegan dishes
(D) Any restaurant

Question 2

What can the man eat as a vegan?

(A) Anything with dairy in it
(B) Only food with eggs and butter
(C) Anything apart from dairy products
(D) Food without meat or dairy

Question 3

Why does the girl offer the boy apples?

(A) The boy says it is not the best time for watermelon.
(B) The boy says he does not like watermelon.
(C) The girl likes apples more.
(D) The girl did not buy watermelon.

Question 4

What time is brunch available at the restaurant?

(A) After 11:30
(B) After 9:00
(C) After 10:00
(D) Before 9:00

Question 5

Why doesn't the woman want to have a buffet lunch?

(A) It is too expensive.
(B) She won't get her money's worth.
(C) They only have ten dishes to choose from.
(D) She wants to order a single dish.

答案與解析 ~answer

Answer 1 (B)

男性想找的是什麼類型的餐廳呢？

(A) 全素食的餐廳
(B) 有提供蛋奶素餐點的餐廳
(C) 有提供全素飲食的餐廳
(D) 任何餐廳都可以

解析

男性要找提供「素食餐點」(vegetarian dishes 蛋奶素的餐點)的餐廳，而後女生推薦一間「全素餐廳」(vegan restaurant)。但是，男性並沒有特別強調要吃全素，重點還是一開始男子所說的vegetarian dishes，因此選(B)。

Answer 2 (D)

身為吃全素的素食者，男性可以吃的食物為何？

(A) 乳製品
(B) 只能吃摻有蛋與奶的食品
(C) 不摻乳製品的食物
(D) 不含肉類或乳製品的食物

解析

男性提到自己除了肉類之外，也不吃乳製品(dairy products)，注意題目所問的vegan，指的是嚴格吃素者，和一般吃蛋奶素的人(vegetarian)不同，因此答案為(D)。

Answer 3 (A)

對話中的女孩為何會給男孩蘋果呢？

(A) 男孩說現在並非產西瓜的季節。
(B) 男孩不喜歡西瓜。
(C) 女孩更喜歡蘋果。
(D) 女孩沒有買西瓜。

解析

女孩一開始問男孩是否要吃西瓜，男孩反問西瓜是否為「當季的」(in season)水果(因為他認為不是)，被這樣一問，女孩才改提議請男孩吃蘋果，因此答案為(A)。

Answer 4 (C)

這家餐廳從幾點開始提供早午餐呢？

(A) 十一點半之後
(B) 九點之後
(C) 十點之後
(D) 九點之前

解析

解題關鍵在男性提到的available only after 10(十點過後才有供應)，選項(B)與(D)中提到的9:00是女生要約的時間，但這時只有普通的早餐，因此答案為(C)。

Answer 5 (B)

女性為何不想吃自助式的午餐呢？

(A) 因為太貴了。
(B) 因為她覺得划不來。
(C) 因為那個自助吧只有十樣菜可選。
(D) 因為她只想點一道餐點而已。

解析

女性說自己吃自助式的「划不來」(I don't think I'll get my money's worth)，因而決定單點，雖然男性有提到價格，但女性最主要的考量還是自己吃不多，正確答案為(B)。

◉慢速MP3 03-02　　◉正常速MP3 03-03

短對話 1　Conversation

Stan: A vegetarian friend is visiting me tonight, and I'm looking for **a restaurant that provides a good selection of vegetarian dishes**.

史丹： 我有個吃素的朋友今晚要來找我，我正在找有提供美味蛋奶素餐點的餐廳。

Patty: I know of a very nice vegan restaurant.

派蒂： 我知道一家非常棒的全素餐廳。

短對話 2　Conversation

Fred: **Besides meat, I don't eat dairy products with eggs and butter**.

弗雷德：除了肉類之外，我也不吃含蛋類和奶油的乳製品。

Sue: Wow! So you are **a vegan** then.

蘇： 哇！所以你吃全素耶。

短對話 3　Conversation

Emily: I just bought a lot of fruit. Do you want some watermelon?

艾蜜利：我剛才買了很多水果，你想吃西瓜嗎？

Greg: **Are they in season now?** I thought not.

葛瑞格：現在是產西瓜的季節嗎？我以為不是。

Emily: Really? That's a shame. How about some apples?

艾蜜利：真的嗎？那太可惜了。要不然來些蘋果如何？

短對話 4　Conversation

Becky: Let's meet at 9a.m. tomorrow and have brunch together.

貝琪： 我們明天早上九點一起去吃早午餐吧。

Kevin: But the brunch menu is **available only after 10**. We can only have the normal breakfast menu at 9.

凱文： 但十點過後才供應早午餐，九點去吃就只能點普通的早餐。

短對話 5　Conversation

Peter: The buffet costs NT$499 per person. They offer ten dishes to choose from.

彼得： 這個自助吧一個人499元，他們供應十道吃到飽的餐點。

Cherry: I don't think I'll get my money's worth because **I can't eat that much**. I'll just order a single dish.

雀芮： 我吃不了那麼多，吃自助式的划不來，我還是單點就好。

長 對 話 聽 力 實 戰

🎧 MP3 03-04

請仔細聆聽下面的長對話，再依對話內容選擇正確答案。

Question 1

What problem does the girl's American classmate have?

(A) He has an addiction.
(B) He has a passion.
(C) He is a dessert lover.
(D) He likes to have dessert after meals.

Question 2

Why does the man call himself a "dessert lover", too?

(A) He eats dessert after every meal.
(B) He eats dessert after most of his meals.
(C) He eats dessert for breakfast.
(D) He always orders dessert when he goes out.

Question 3

How does the girl's classmate feel if he doesn't eat dessert?

(A) He feels agitated and annoyed.
(B) He feels sad.
(C) He feels happy.
(D) He feels lonely.

Question 4

How does the man describe the American classmate's love for dessert?

(A) He can eat dessert without dinner.
(B) He only needs to eat dessert and nothing else.
(C) He can eat three desserts a day.
(D) He can live without dessert.

Question 5

Why does the girl disagree with her classmate's addiction?

(A) Eating dessert three times a day is too much.
(B) It is strange.
(C) It is bad for his health.
(D) Eating dessert that much would be too expensive.

答案與解析 ~answer

Answer 1 (A)

女孩的美國同學有什麼樣的問題？

(A) 他有上癮症狀。
(B) 他有一股熱情。
(C) 他是甜食愛好者。
(D) 他餐後喜歡吃甜點。

解析

一問到有什麼問題，答案應該是較負面的，所以可以排除(B)(C)(D)這種無特別好壞的選項。對話中，女性認為美國同學的狀況比較像是「上癮(症狀)」，而不只是單純的「熱愛」(an addiction than passion)，答案為(A)。

Answer 2 (B)

男性為什麼說自己也是一位「甜食愛好者」呢？

(A) 因為他每餐飯後都吃甜點。
(B) 因為他幾乎每餐飯後都會吃甜點。
(C) 因為他吃甜點當早餐。
(D) 因為他出門一定會點甜點。

解析

男性說那位美國同學聽起來的確是個甜食愛好者，和他差不多，因為他本身「幾乎每餐都會吃甜點」(have dessert after most of my meals)，關鍵字是「幾乎」(most)，並非every或always，正確答案為(B)。

Answer 3 (A)

女孩的同學如果沒吃到甜點，情緒會如何？

(A) 他會感到情緒煩躁。
(B) 他會感到難過。
(C) 他會感到愉悅。
(D) 他會感到寂寞。

解析

女孩說那位美國同學如果「一餐沒吃甜點」就會「感到煩躁」(gets frustrated)，從frustrated這個單字可知對方的情緒偏向低落的狀態，最佳答案為(A)。

Answer 4 (B)

男性如何形容那名美國同學對甜食的熱愛呢？

(A) 他能以甜食取代晚餐。
(B) 他只須要吃甜食，其他什麼都不用。
(C) 他一天能吃三次甜點。
(D) 他可以不吃甜食過活。

解析

聽到女孩對美國同學的描述後，男子回應對方似乎能「吃甜點為生」(live on desserts)，live on是「靠某物過活」之意，整句翻譯為「只要有甜點就好」，正確答案為(B)。

Answer 5 (C)

女孩為何不認同她同學對甜食的上癮症狀呢？

(A) 因為照三餐吃甜食太多了。
(B) 因為很奇怪。
(C) 因為那對健康有害。
(D) 因為那樣吃甜點的開銷很大。

解析

女孩說「這肯定對身體有害」(bad for your body)，表示她不能認同美國同學過量吃甜食的行為。選項(A)提到一天吃三次甜點，但是美國同學一天「至少」吃三次甜點，因此最佳答案為(C)。

中英文內容

⊙ 慢速MP3 03-05   ◎ 正常速MP3 03-06

Betty: My American classmate is a real dessert lover. He always orders dessert when we go to restaurants.
貝蒂： 我的美國同學真是個甜品愛好者，每次去餐廳他必點甜點。

Ryan: It sounds like he is a dessert lover, just like me.
萊恩： 他聽起來的確是個甜食愛好者，和我差不多。

Betty: I think it is **more an addiction than a passion** though.
貝蒂： 但我覺得他的狀況比較像是上癮，而不是單純的熱愛耶。

Ryan: Why do you say that?
萊恩： 為什麼這麼說？

Betty: Well, he has dessert after meals.
貝蒂： 他飯後必吃甜點。

Ryan: I **have dessert after most of my meals**, too.
萊恩： 我飯後也幾乎都會吃甜點啊。

Betty: But he eats dessert at every meal. And he **gets frustrated** if he goes through just one meal **without dessert**!
貝蒂： 但是他餐餐都要吃甜點。如果有一餐沒吃到甜點，他就會感到煩躁！

Ryan: Sounds like he **can live on desserts**.
萊恩： 聽起來他都可以吃甜點為生了。

Betty: At least three desserts a day! That is definitely **bad for your body**.
貝蒂： 一天至少吃三次耶！這種吃法肯定對身體有害。

Ryan: I'm a dessert lover, but I totally agree with you.
萊恩： 我是甜食愛好者，但我完全同意你的看法。

短文聽力實戰

@MP3 03-07(短文1) @MP3 03-08(短文2)

請仔細聆聽下面兩段短文，並分別回答Q1~Q2&Q3~Q5兩大題。

Question 1

What is cooking to Nigella?

(A) A career

(B) Something she doesn't mind

(C) Something she likes but doesn't share with others

(D) Her sole hobby

Question 2

Why does Nigella enjoy making dessert?

(A) Her desserts make people fat.

(B) Her desserts make people happy.

(C) Her desserts make people try cooking.

(D) Her desserts make people eat more.

Question 3

Why does the woman find it annoying to eat out with Barry?

(A) He always forces her to order dessert.

(B) It is hard to resist having dessert when Barry orders one.

(C) She doesn't like dessert.

(D) Barry doesn't order dessert for her.

Question 4

Speaking of having dessert, what becomes the woman's worry now?

(A) She puts on weight.

(B) She feels guilty afterwards.

(C) She doesn't like the taste of desserts.

(D) She thinks desserts are too expensive.

Question 5

What does the woman say she should do if Barry invites her again?

(A) Decline

(B) Accept

(C) Invite other friends

(D) Make Barry stay home and cook

答案與解析 ～answer

Answer 1 ◀ᴺ (D)
對奈吉拉來說，烹飪有什麼意義呢？

(A) 是一種職業
(B) 是一個她不介意的事
(C) 她喜歡，但不會與人分享的事
(D) 她唯一的嗜好

解析
文中一開始就說了奈吉拉「唯一的休閒娛樂」(only recreation)就是烹飪，若沒有聽清楚關鍵字recreation，也可以由後面的something she truly enjoys推知答案為(D)。

Answer 2 ◀ᴺ (B)
為什麼奈吉拉喜歡做甜點呢？

(A) 她的甜點能讓人發胖。
(B) 她的甜點讓人愉悅。
(C) 她的甜點能激發人們嘗試烹飪。
(D) 她的甜點能增進人們食慾，吃很多。

解析
針對為什麼奈吉拉喜歡做甜點，文中有解釋說是因為她「愛看人們帶著微笑品嚐她的甜點」(loves the smile it puts on everyone's face)，正確答案為(B)。

Answer 3 ◀ᴺ (B)
女性為何不喜歡和巴瑞一同出去吃飯呢？

(A) 他會強迫她點甜點。
(B) 當巴瑞點了甜點，她很難抗拒。
(C) 她不喜歡甜點。
(D) 巴瑞不會幫她點甜點。

解析
每當巴瑞點甜點時，女性就「很難不被誘惑」(hard not to be tempted)。(C)選項完全沒有被提及，(A)與(D)雖然都提到order這個單字，但巴瑞並沒有強迫她，更沒有出現doesn't order(不點)的情況，正確答案為(B)。

Answer 4 ◀ᴺ (A)
講到吃甜點，什麼成為女性擔憂的事情呢？

(A) 她變胖了。
(B) 之後她會產生罪惡感。
(C) 她不喜歡甜點的口感。
(D) 她覺得甜點太貴了。

解析
這裡問的是女性的「憂慮」(worry)，與此有關的內容，就是最後兩句所提到的「體重上升」(gaining weight)，正確答案為(A)，雖然(B)也有可能發生，但選擇時請以文中明確提到的內容為準。

Answer 5 ◀ᴺ (A)
如果巴瑞再來邀請女性的話，她想要怎麼做？

(A) 拒絕
(B) 接受
(C) 邀請其他朋友
(D) 讓巴瑞待在家煮飯

解析
本題線索在文章最後，女性談到自己體重飆升的問題，說她必須要開始「拒絕」巴瑞的邀約(refusing Barry's dessert tasting invitation)，正確答案為(A)。

 中英文內容

 短文 1

⊙慢速MP3 03-09　⊙正常速MP3 03-10

Nigella's **only recreation** is cooking. It is not just something she has to do but something she truly enjoys. She cooks all kinds of wonderful food, but she has a particular talent for making desserts. Nigella enjoys making desserts because **she loves the smile it puts on everyone's face who tastes them.** She is constantly experimenting and developing recipes. She has developed no fewer than ten different recipes just for Tiramisu alone! Nigella understands the importance of nutrition as well as taste; therefore, she tries to minimize artificial additives in her cooking. I really wish I could be as talented as her.

　　奈吉拉唯一的休閒娛樂就是烹飪。她不是單純地「必須煮飯」，而是真正享受烹飪的樂趣。她會烹調許多美味佳餚，但甜點是她特別的強項。奈吉拉很愛看人們帶著笑容品嚐她的甜點，所以她很喜歡製作甜點。她不斷實驗，創新食譜，光是提拉米蘇，她就已經創出不下十種食譜了呢！除了美味與否外，奈吉拉也懂得營養的重要性，所以她的食譜都會盡量少用人工添加劑，真希望我能像她那樣有天分。

 短文 2

⊙慢速MP3 03-11　⊙正常速MP3 03-12

It is dangerous having a friend who is a dessert connoisseur. My friend Barry not only loves dessert, but will put in a great deal of effort to find some special dessert shops. He loves trying out different desserts everywhere. And I **find it slightly annoying** eating out with him because **it is so hard not to be tempted by the desserts he orders!** I sometimes tell myself,"Just one bite", but as soon as I take one bite, Barry persuades me to have more! Thanks to him, I now need to worry about **gaining weight**. I really have to **start refusing Barry's dessert tasting invitation**.

　　有個甜點行家的朋友真是件危險的事。我的朋友巴瑞不僅熱愛甜點，還會花很多心思去尋找特別的甜點店家。他喜歡到處品嚐不同的甜點，但對我來說，跟他一起出去吃飯有點討厭，因為我很難不被他點的甜點誘惑！有時候，我會告訴自己「就只吃一口」，但當我嚐了一口後，巴瑞就會說服我繼續吃！也因為他，我現在得擔心體重飆升的問題了，說實話，我真的得開始拒絕他有關品嚐甜點的邀約了。

Unit 4 特色小吃 Taiwanese Food

📷 日常生活　🎤 娛樂活動　✏️ 意見交流　🚩 特殊場合

短對話聽力實戰

🎧 MP3 04-01

下面將播放五組短對話，請仔細聆聽，再依對話內容答題。

Question 1

What Taiwanese food does the man dislike?

(A) Beef noodles
(B) Crispy fried chicken
(C) He doesn't say.
(D) All Taiwanese food

Question 2

What Taiwanese food won't the woman try?

(A) Pig's blood rice pudding
(B) Crispy fried chicken
(C) Black marble eggs
(D) Stinky tofu

Question 3

What dish does the woman want to have?

(A) Pearl milk tea
(B) Crab
(C) Shaved ice
(D) Oyster omelets

Question 4

What does the man say a wedding "Bun Dough" is?

(A) A backyard BBQ
(B) An outdoor wedding reception meal
(C) A wedding reception
(D) An outdoor buffet

Question 5

Why does the woman find "Bun Dough" a very different experience?

(A) Because of the special mobile trailer stage performance
(B) Because of the amount of people there
(C) Because of the sit-down meal
(D) Because it was a Taiwanese tradition.

答案與解析 ～answer

Answer 1 (C)
男性不喜歡吃的臺灣食物是什麼？

(A) 牛肉麵
(B) 鹽酥雞
(C) 沒有提到。
(D) 所有的臺灣食物

> **解析**
> 題目問的是這個男性「不喜歡」吃什麼臺灣食物，解題的重點就在這裡。他提到自己喜歡的兩道小吃，不喜歡的則完全沒有提到，正確答案選(C)。

Answer 2 (C)
女性不會嘗試的臺灣食物是什麼？

(A) 豬血糕
(B) 鹽酥雞
(C) 皮蛋
(D) 臭豆腐

> **解析**
> 當女性被問到是否吃過皮蛋時，她提到不知為何，就是沒辦法「嘗試皮蛋」(can't bring myself to try)，因此答案為(C)。bring oneself to是「某人(下決心)強迫自己做某事」的意思。

Answer 3 (D)
女性想吃什麼呢？

(A) 珍珠奶茶
(B) 螃蟹
(C) 刨冰
(D) 蚵仔煎

> **解析**
> 當女性提議要去夜市時，她提到自己「好想吃」蚵仔煎(a craving for oyster omelets)，因此答案為(D)。have a craving for/to do...是「有強烈想要擁有某物/做某事」的意思。

Answer 4 (B)
男性如何解釋「辦桌」婚宴呢？

(A) 一種在後院烤肉的形式
(B) 戶外舉辦的婚禮宴席
(C) 婚禮宴席
(D) 戶外的自助吧

> **解析**
> 男性解釋「辦桌」(Bun Dough)婚宴是種「戶外舉辦的婚禮宴席」，關鍵字為outdoor(戶外的)，正確答案為(B)。注意選項(A)的backyard BBQ與選項(D)的buffet是誤導的選項。

Answer 5 (A)
女性為什麼覺得去吃「辦桌」是個很特殊的體驗？

(A) 因為行動舞台的表演
(B) 因為有大量的人群
(C) 因為大家圍桌坐著吃
(D) 因為那是臺灣的傳統。

> **解析**
> 題目詢問辦桌「非常不同」(very different)的地方，與女性最後提到的「行動舞台車的歌舞表演」相呼應，關鍵字為unexpected(出乎意料的)，正確答案為(A)。

短對話 ❶ *Conversation*

Cindy: What do you like most about Taiwanese food?

辛蒂： 你最喜歡什麼臺灣食物呢？

Stuart: Beef noodles are my firm favorite. But crispy fried chicken is pretty delicious, too.

史都華：牛肉麵無庸置疑是我的最愛，但鹽酥雞也非常美味。

短對話 ❷ *Conversation*

Joey: Have you tried black marble eggs?

喬伊： 你有吃過皮蛋嗎？

Fay: It's strange. I wouldn't say no to pig's blood rice pudding. But for some reason, I **can't bring myself to try those eggs**.

菲： 很奇怪，我不介意吃豬血糕，但不知為何，就是無法去吃那個蛋。

短對話 ❸ *Conversation*

Eve: Let's try some authentic Taiwanese snack foods in the night market! I **have a craving for oyster omelets**.

伊芙： 我們去夜市品嚐道地的臺灣小吃吧！我好想吃蚵仔煎。

David: Shaved ice has also been recommended to me as something I should try.

大衛： 也有人和我推薦刨冰，說我一定得試試。

短對話 ❹ *Conversation*

Ivy: Ann invited me to her "Bun Dough" wedding reception. What is a "Bun Dough"?

艾薇： 安邀請我參加她的「辦桌」婚宴，什麼是「辦桌」啊？

Larry: It's a wedding banquet meal **you hold outdoors**. It's quite different from a backyard BBQ or buffet.

賴瑞： 那是一種辦在戶外的婚禮宴席，和在院子烤肉或自助吧的感覺相當不同喔。

短對話 ❺ *Conversation*

Beth: I went to a "Bun Dough" last night. What a different experience!

貝絲： 我昨晚去吃辦桌，感覺好新奇喔！

Matt: What made it so different?

麥特： 那個有什麼特別啊？

Beth: Everything was prepared outdoors. Besides, **the mobile trailer stage with all the singing and dancing** was unexpected!

貝絲： 餐點直接在戶外準備，除此之外，行動舞台車的歌舞表演太令人意外了！

長 對 話 聽 力 實 戰

⊘MP3 04-04

請仔細聆聽下面的長對話，再依對話內容選擇正確答案。

Question 1

❶❷❸❹❺

How does the man describe a night market?

(A) An outdoor area with many food shops
(B) A shopping mall
(C) A fairground
(D) An outdoor supermarket

Question 2

❶❷❸❹❺

What can you do at a night market except eating?

(A) Shop for ingredients
(B) Play fairground games
(C) Shop and play games
(D) Window shop

Question 3

❶❷❸❹❺

What kinds of food you can get at a night market?

(A) International food
(B) Local food
(C) Local and international food
(D) Taiwanese and German food

Question 4

❶❷❸❹❺

In the man's opinion, what do night markets nowadays also cater to?

(A) Their selling volume
(B) Some popular food
(C) The domestic tourists
(D) The increasing tourists

Question 5

❶❷❸❹❺

Why does the woman like night markets?

(A) You can get German pork knuckle.
(B) You can play games.
(C) You can get all kinds of food in the same place.
(D) You can get international foods.

答案與解析 ~answer

Answer 1 (A)
男性如何形容夜市呢？

(A) 有許多美食店家的戶外區域

(B) 購物商場

(C) 露天商展的場地

(D) 戶外的超市

> **解析**
> 男性一開始以為夜市是一種「露天的美食廣場」(open-air food courts)，這跟答案(A)的「有許多美食店家的戶外區域」(An outdoor area with many food shops) 最接近。

Answer 2 (C)
在夜市裡除了吃以外，還能做些什麼呢？

(A) 購買食材

(B) 玩園遊會的遊戲

(C) 購物和玩遊戲

(D) 只逛不買的逛街

> **解析**
> 女性解釋去夜市不只可以吃到許多美食，同時還能「購物和玩遊戲」(go shopping and play games)；雖然有提到其性質與園遊會有點像，但並沒有提到會玩園遊會的遊戲，正確答案為(C)。

Answer 3 (C)
在夜市裡可以吃到什麼樣的食物呢？

(A) 世界各國的食物

(B) 當地美食

(C) 當地與國際美食

(D) 臺灣與德國的美食

> **解析**
> 女性提到夜市的美食並不限於臺灣 (Taiwanese cuisine)，還包括「世界各地的美食」(food from around the world)，正確答案為(C)。選項(D)只是用臺灣和德國食物舉例，但並不限於這些。

Answer 4 (D)
就男性而言，現在的夜市也會顧及什麼呢？

(A) 銷售量

(B) 一些受歡迎的食品

(C) 本國觀光客

(D) 日漸增加的觀光客

> **解析**
> 針對女性說夜市現在提供許多臺灣與世界各地美食，男性回應說現在夜市還「顧及」(cater for)「日漸成長的觀光客市場」，但並沒有特別說是「本國觀光客」(domestic)還是「國際觀光客」(international)，因此選(D)。

Answer 5 (C)
女性為什麼喜歡夜市？

(A) 你可以吃到德國豬腳。

(B) 你可以玩遊戲。

(C) 你可以在同一處吃到各式各樣的美食。

(D) 你能品嚐國際美食。

> **解析**
> 女性特別解釋，對她來說，夜市「最吸引人」之處(most attractive thing)就是可以在「同一個地方吃到許多不同的美食」(all kinds of food...in just one place)，正確答案為(C)。

⊙ 慢速MP3 04-05　　◎ 正常速MP3 04-06

Leo: What would you say is one thing I must try in Taiwan?
里歐：　就你而言，有什麼東西是我來臺灣一定要嘗試的？

Tina: I'd definitely say night markets.
蒂娜：　那肯定是夜市囉。

Leo: Why? Aren't they just **open-air food courts**?
里歐：　為什麼？那不就是一種露天的美食廣場嗎？

Tina: Food is a major part of it. But you can also **go shopping and play games**. It's a bit like a fair, but with a much better selection of food.
蒂娜：　美食當然是主要的賣點，但你還可以購物和玩遊戲，感覺有點像園遊會，但食物的選擇更多元。

Leo: Sounds like there are many things to see at a night market.
里歐：　聽起來夜市有很多東西值得看。

Tina: You will find **not only Taiwanese cuisine there but also food from around the world**.
蒂娜：　那裡不只有臺灣美食，還吃得到世界各地的特色食物。

Leo: So they **cater to the growing tourist market** then.
里歐：　所以夜市現在也顧及到日漸成長的觀光客市場了。

Tina: The most attractive thing about night markets is you can try **all kinds of food**, authentic local snacks or international food, **in just one place**.
蒂娜：　夜市最吸引人的就是可以吃到各種美食，不管是道地小吃或是國外美食，都可以在同一個地方吃到。

Leo: Like what?
里歐：　比方説有什麼？

Tina: There are so many types, from kumquat lemon tea with jelly to German pork knuckle. You'll definitely find something you enjoy.
蒂娜：　要舉例的話太多了，從金桔檸檬愛玉到德國豬腳都有，你肯定能找到愛吃的。

短文聽力實戰

◎MP3 04-07（短文1）　◎MP3 04-08（短文2）

請仔細聆聽下面兩段短文，並分別回答Q1~Q2&Q3~Q5兩大題。

Question 1

What is the best way to cook pigeon meat?

(A) Boiled and baked
(B) Grilled and roasted
(C) Pan fried
(D) Grilled and pan fried

Question 2

What do you need to have to cook a nice grilled pigeon?

(A) A bit of general cooking knowledge
(B) A professional chef
(C) A leathery and tough pigeon
(D) A BBQ chef

Question 3

What did the speakers go to the night market to experience?

(A) Taiwanese culture
(B) Taiwanese food
(C) Stinky tofu
(D) Nightlife

Question 4

Why didn't the girl want to try stinky tofu at first?

(A) Because it smelt bad.
(B) Because it was disgusting.
(C) Because she doesn't like the thought of fermented tofu.
(D) Because it was not cooked.

Question 5

Why was the girl surprised after she tasted stinky tofu?

(A) It tasted delicious.
(B) It tasted better than she expected.
(C) It tasted better than fermented tofu.
(D) It tasted better than normal tofu.

答案與解析 ～answer

Answer 1 (B)
鴿肉最佳的烹調方式為何？
- (A) 水煮與烤
- (B) 燒烤和烘烤
- (C) 用平底鍋煎
- (D) 燒烤加用平底鍋煎

解析
解題關鍵在文中的is most suitable for(最適合)，後面所提到的燒烤和烘烤(grilling and roasting)就是男性所推薦的烹調方法，正確答案為(B)。

Answer 2 (A)
想要烤出美味的鴿肉，你需要擁有什麼？
- (A) 一點基本的烹調知識
- (B) 一位專業主廚
- (C) 一隻像皮革般硬的鴿肉
- (D) 一位BBQ的主廚

解析
根據文章的內容，「有點煮飯經驗的人都做得到」，重點在with general cooking experience，正確答案為(A)。注意選項(B)的意思為「必須有專業主廚才能料理」。

Answer 3 (A)
兩位說話者去夜市是為了體驗什麼？
- (A) 臺灣文化
- (B) 臺灣食物
- (C) 臭豆腐
- (D) 夜生活

解析
文中一開始，女生就提到她與朋友一起去夜市去體驗「臺灣本地文化」(local cultures of Taiwan)，雖然後續提到很多關於食物的內容，但重點在題目當中experience(體驗)這個字，所以最佳答案為(A)。

Answer 4 (C)
女生為何一開始不想嘗試臭豆腐呢？
- (A) 因為臭豆腐的味道很臭。
- (B) 因為臭豆腐很噁心。
- (C) 因為一想到發酵豆腐，她就受不了。
- (D) 因為臭豆腐沒煮過，是生的。

解析
文中雖然提到臭豆腐的味道很臭，但女生不想嘗試的主因是她不喜歡「將生豆腐發酵」的過程，這讓她覺得好像在「吃壞掉的東西」(eat something off)，正確答案為(C)。

Answer 5 (B)
在嚐過臭豆腐之後，女生為什麼感到驚訝？
- (A) 因為很美味。
- (B) 因為比她預期的好吃。
- (C) 因為比發酵後的豆腐好吃。
- (D) 因為比普通的豆腐好吃。

解析
女生最後還是嚐了臭豆腐，並說「讓人驚訝的是」(關鍵字為Surprisingly)，臭豆腐「吃起來比聞起來要美味」(tasted better than it smelt)，代表臭豆腐比她預期的還好吃，因此選(B)。

 短文 1

⊙慢速MP3 04-09　　◎正常速MP3 04-10

Most people associate pigeon with racing and annoying flocks of birds on the road. However, pigeon can also make a rather tasty poultry for cooking. Pigeon meat **is most suitable for grilling and roasting**. Also, timing is critical in cooking pigeon because as soon as you overcook it, the meat becomes extremely leathery and tough. You don't need to be an expert chef to make a nice grilled pigeon. Anyone **with general cooking experience** can make it. It is delicious just served with a pinch of salt and pepper.

　　大多數人會將鴿子與賽鴿活動及路上討厭的鴿群聯想在一起。但是，鴿子其實也是種美味的烹飪類禽肉，鴿肉最適合的烹調方式為燒烤和烘烤。同時，時間控制也非常重要，因為只要你一煮過頭，鴿肉馬上就會變得又老又硬。就算不是專業的廚師，也能烤出美味的鴿肉，任何有點煮飯經驗的人都做得到，只要撒些鹽和胡椒粉上去就很美味了。

 短文 2

⊙慢速MP3 04-11　　◎正常速MP3 04-12

Yesterday, my classmate Alfred and I went to the night market near our university to experience **the local cultures of Taiwan**. I had been previously warned about the potent smell of certain foods, and it's exactly what stinky tofu is about! Alfred asked me to try it, but I refused at first. I didn't like the idea that **tofu had fermented** before it was cooked. It seems that you are **eating something off**. However, he managed to convince me to take a bite. Surprisingly, **it tasted better than it smelt**. I cannot say it's something I love, but I have certainly become more open-minded about trying different foods.

　　昨天，我的同學艾佛瑞和我一起去大學附近的夜市，體驗臺灣本地文化。之前有其他人告訴我，有些食物的味道非常強烈，臭豆腐的味道真不是蓋的！艾佛瑞叫我嚐嚐看，但我最初拒絕了，我不喜歡這道小吃煮熟前將豆腐先發酵的這個過程，那讓我覺得好像在吃壞掉的食品。但最後艾佛瑞還是說服我嚐了一口，讓人驚訝的是，臭豆腐吃起來比聞起來要美味，雖然我不能說我愛臭豆腐，但至少我現在比較願意嘗試不同的食物了。

Unit
5

其他餐點 Other Foods

📋 日常生活　　🎤 娛樂活動　　✏️ 意見交流　　🚩 特殊場合

🎧 MP3 05-01

下面將播放五組短對話，請仔細聆聽，再依對話內容答題。

Question 1

How does the man find the dish escargot?

(A) It tastes disgusting to him.
(B) It sounds disgusting. He doesn't want to try it.
(C) He is disgusted by the look of it.
(D) He likes the taste of it.

Question 2

How does the man describe snails and Taiwanese whelk as being similar?

(A) The seasoning
(B) The look
(C) The texture
(D) The way they are cooked

Question 3

Why doesn't the woman want to go to KFC?

(A) She has it too often.
(B) She had it last week.
(C) She doesn't want to eat fried chicken.
(D) She doesn't like chicken.

Question 4

What is the man eating in the fast food restaurant?

(A) A Happy Meal
(B) A set meal
(C) Chicken nuggets
(D) Just a Coke

Question 5

Why does the man think it's OK to eat fast food sometimes?

(A) Because they now serve healthy dishes, too.
(B) Because he didn't have it last week.
(C) Because he thinks fast food in moderation is okay.
(D) Because the woman says he can eat it.

答案與解析 ～answer

Answer 1 (B)
男性對蝸牛餐點的看法為何？

(A) 吃起來很噁心。

(B) 聽上去很噁心，他不想吃。

(C) 看到菜的模樣，他感到噁心。

(D) 他喜歡嚐起來的味道。

解析
escargot就是法文的「蝸牛」(snail)。解題重點在男性回應的It sounds disgusting(聽起來很噁心)。而女性回應if you had tried it(如果有吃過的話)，由此可推斷男性沒吃過這道菜，所以選(B)。

Answer 2 (C)
男性覺得蝸牛和臺灣田螺哪裡相似？

(A) 調味(料)

(B) 看上去的模樣

(C) 口感

(D) 烹調方式

解析
男性覺得蝸牛滿像臺灣的田螺肉，接著解釋「調味可能不盡相同」，但是「口感很類似」，正確答案為(C)。texture為「(物的)質感」，描述食物時，講的就是咬起來的「口感」。

Answer 3 (C)
女性為什麼不想吃肯德基呢？

(A) 她太常吃肯德基了。

(B) 她上週才吃過肯德基。

(C) 她不想吃炸雞。

(D) 她不喜歡雞肉。

解析
解題關鍵在女性本身對吃速食的想法，她首先提到男性前一天才吃過，這與她本身是否想吃無關；重點在後面提到的「不想吃炸雞」(don't fancy fried chicken)，正確答案為(C)。

Answer 4 (B)
男性在速食餐廳裡吃什麼？

(A) 快樂兒童餐

(B) 套餐

(C) 雞塊

(D) 只有點一杯可樂

解析
服務生問男性他點的「套餐」是否要內用時，他給予了yes的回答，此為解題關鍵，正確答案為(B)。至於另外多點的雞塊要「外帶」(take a portion of the chicken nuggets away)，與題目無關。

Answer 5 (C)
男性為何覺得偶爾吃速食是可以接受的呢？

(A) 因為速食餐廳現在也供應健康的餐點。

(B) 因為他前一週沒有吃速食。

(C) 因為他覺得適度地吃一些是可以接受的。

(D) 因為女性允許他吃速食。

解析
女性一開始就說速食對身體不好，此時男性回應「任何事適度就好」(everything is fine in moderation)，聽懂moderation為「適度」之意，就明白他認為偶爾吃不為過，答案選(C)。

 中英文內容　　　　　　　⊙慢速MP3 05-02　　◎正常速MP3 05-03

短對話 ❶ *Conversation*

Jessie: I'm going to a French restaurant tonight, and I'll try escargot!

潔西：　我今晚要去法國餐廳吃飯，我想嘗試法式田螺！

Ted:　Snails! Why would you want to eat that? **It sounds disgusting**.

泰德：　蝸牛！你怎麼會想吃那種東西？聽起來真噁。

Jessie: If you had tried it, you would not say that.

潔西：　如果你吃過的話，就不會這樣說了。

短對話 ❷ *Conversation*

Eddie:　I really enjoyed the snails. They're like the whelks we have in Taiwan. Maybe not so much the flavor of the seasoning, but **the texture is certainly familiar**.

艾迪：　我很喜歡剛才的蝸牛，嚐起來很像我們在臺灣吃的螺肉。調味可能不盡相同，但口感很類似。

Amy:　I thought French food would be totally different from Taiwanese food.

愛咪：　我還以為法國菜跟臺灣菜完全不同呢。

短對話 ❸ *Conversation*

Jack:　I fancy fast food. How about having lunch at KFC?

傑克：　我想吃速食，中午吃肯德基怎麼樣？

Lucy:　Didn't you have that yesterday? Besides, **I don't fancy fried chicken today**.

露西：　你昨天不是才吃過？況且，我今天不想吃炸雞。

短對話 ❹ *Conversation*

Phil:　I'd like **a number 1 with a Coke**, please.

菲爾：　我要點一號餐，飲料配可樂，謝謝。

Waitress: Are you eating in, sir?

女服務生：請問您是內用嗎，先生？

Phil:　Yes, but I'd also like to take a portion of the chicken nuggets away.

菲爾：　對，但是我要另外外帶一份雞塊。

短對話 ❺ *Conversation*

Tina:　Fast food like McDonald's is really bad for your health.

蒂娜：　像麥當勞這種速食對身體真的有害。

Henry:　But I think **everything is fine in moderation**. Having it every now and then is okay to me.

亨利：　但任何事適度就好，所以我覺得偶爾吃吃不為過啦。

長對話聽力實戰

◎ MP3 05-04

請仔細聆聽下面的長對話，再依對話內容選擇正確答案。

Question 1

What hasn't the woman tried before?

(A) Fresh pasta
(B) Dried pasta
(C) Pasta
(D) Italian pasta

Question 2

Apart from flour, what are the other ingredients?

(A) Onions
(B) Eggs and water
(C) Onions and tomatoes
(D) Water

Question 3

What do you need to make sure about the dough before rolling?

(A) It is al dente.
(B) It is smooth.
(C) It is big.
(D) It is flat.

Question 4

Based on the man's explanation, what does "al dente" mean?

(A) It is hard.
(B) It is soft.
(C) It is overcooked.
(D) It is firm to the bite.

Question 5

Why does the woman want to have late-night snacks?

(A) Because she doesn't want to give it up.
(B) Because the man made her hungry by talking about pasta.
(C) Because she doesn't like pasta.
(D) Because she is staying up late.

PART 1
飲食與美味

答案與解析 ~answer

Answer 1 ◀)) (A)
對話中的女性沒有嘗試過什麼？
- (A) 新鮮手工的義大利麵
- (B) 乾燥的義大利麵
- (C) 義大利麵
- (D) 義式義大利麵

解析

本題的關鍵在對話一開始，女性表示她只吃過「乾燥的義大利麵」(dried pasta)，所以只單純提及義大利麵的選項都要刪除(因為她吃過，只是並非新鮮手工製)，正確答案為(A)。

Answer 2 ◀)) (B)
除了麵粉之外，還需要什麼其他的材料？
- (A) 洋蔥
- (B) 蛋和水
- (C) 洋蔥和番茄
- (D) 水

解析

男性在談到揉麵糰的材料時，提到了麵粉、蛋、以及水，所以選(B)。注意選項(A)和(C)的洋蔥和番茄是醬汁可選擇性加入的食材，並非正確答案。

Answer 3 ◀)) (B)
在桿麵之前，你必須要確定麵糰呈現什麼樣的狀態？
- (A) 口感很有彈性。
- (B) 呈光滑狀。
- (C) 麵糰夠大。
- (D) 麵糰已經壓平了。

解析

男性在解釋如何做新鮮手工義大利麵的麵條時提到，桿麵之前要確保麵糰已經呈「光滑狀」(smooth)，正確答案為(B)。選項(A)的al dente是在說「煮」義大利麵時需要注意的事項。

Answer 4 ◀)) (D)
根據男性的解釋，al dente是什麼意思呢？
- (A) 很硬。
- (B) 很軟。
- (C) 煮過頭。
- (D) 彈牙的口感。

解析

al dente為義大利文，意思是「保有彈牙的口感」(keep it firm to the bite)，firm形容物體「結實的」，可由其意推斷並非煮過頭，容易咬斷的軟麵條；而(A)的hard形容硬梆梆的質感，不適合形容麵條，因此選(D)。

Answer 5 ◀)) (B)
對話中的女性為什麼想吃消夜呢？
- (A) 因為她不想戒除吃消夜的習慣。
- (B) 因為男性一直談論義大利麵，害她餓了。
- (C) 因為她不喜歡義大利麵。
- (D) 因為她要熬夜。

解析

兩人討論到最後，女性怪男性一直「講義大利麵」(all that talk of pasta)，害她都餓了，因此她想來點消夜。這裡的talk of有「談到；至於」的意思，正確答案為(B)。

⊙ 慢速MP3 05-05　　◎ 正常速MP3 05-06

Peggy: I've **only had dried pasta**. Is it easy to make fresh handmade pasta?
佩姬：　我只有吃過乾燥的義大利麵，新鮮的容易做嗎？

Jack: Regardless of the kneading, the ingredients are simple.
傑克：　先不論揉麵，材料很簡單。

Peggy: What do you need to make it?
佩姬：　你需要什麼食材？

Jack: Flour, **eggs, and water**. That's it. Of course, you can add whatever you like to the sauce, like onions and tomatoes.
傑克：　麵粉、蛋、以及水，就這樣而已。當然，你可以隨心所欲地把喜歡的食材加入醬汁，比如洋蔥和番茄。

Peggy: What's your tip for cooking pasta?
佩姬：　那你煮義大利麵時的祕訣是什麼？

Jack: Make sure **the dough is smooth before rolling**. And when you cook it, keep it al dente.
傑克：　桿麵之前，要確保麵糰已經呈光滑狀，在煮的時候則必須保持麵條al dente的口感。

Peggy: What does "al dente" mean?
佩姬：　al dente是什麼意思？

Jack: It means you keep it **firm to the bite**. Don't overcook it.
傑克：　意思是要讓麵條保有彈牙的口感，不要煮過頭。

Peggy: Sounds good. Now, I'm going to get some late-night snacks.
佩姬：　聽起來很不賴，現在呢，我得來點消夜。

Jack: Didn't you say you wanted to stop eating late at night?
傑克：　你不是說要戒除吃消夜的習慣嗎？

Peggy: I do, but **all that talk of pasta has made me hungry**!
佩姬：　我是啊，但你一直講義大利麵，害我都餓了！

短 文 聽 力 實 戰 　　🎧 MP3 05-07(短文1)　🎧 MP3 05-08(短文2)

請仔細聆聽下面兩段短文，並分別回答Q1~Q2&Q3~Q5兩大題。

Question ❶ ·· ❶❷❸❹❺

Who did the food shopping for the dinner party?

    (A) The man

    (B) His friend, Cathy

    (C) Both of them

    (D) Nobody

Question ❷ ·· ❶❷❸❹❺

What did Cathy find fascinating during the process of cooking?

    (A) They cooked very different dishes.

    (B) They used different ingredients.

    (C) She cooked very slowly, and he cooked very fast.

    (D) The way they cooked and cookware they used were very different.

Question ❸ ·· ❶❷❸❹❺

How does the girl find cooking for herself?

    (A) The food doesn't taste good.

    (B) It's too much trouble for one person.

    (C) It's boring because you can only have one dish.

    (D) It's difficult to buy so few ingredients.

Question ❹ ·· ❶❷❸❹❺

What did the girl demonstrate to her classmates?

    (A) How multipurpose a rice cooker is.

    (B) How to cook many different dishes.

    (C) How to cook rice using a rice cooker.

    (D) How to make stewed pork in a rice cooker.

Question ❺ ·· ❶❷❸❹❺

What did the girl's classmate ask her?

    (A) Where she kept her rice cooker.

    (B) Where they can get the dishes from.

    (C) Where she bought her rice cooker.

    (D) Where she got her ingredients.

答案與解析 ~answer

Answer 1 (C)

誰去購買了晚餐聚會要用的食材呢？

(A) 男性
(B) 他的朋友凱西
(C) 男性與凱西兩人
(D) 沒有人

解析

根據文章的內容，男性提到他與凱西「各自買了自己要用的食材」(We each bought our own ingredients)，因此正確答案為(C)。

Answer 2 (D)

在煮飯的過程中，讓凱西感到訝異的現象是什麼？

(A) 他們兩人煮的菜完全不同。
(B) 他們使用不同的食材煮飯。
(C) 凱西煮了很久，而男性很快就完成了。
(D) 兩人煮飯的方法和用的鍋具相當不同。

解析

男性提到自己只需要「用一個炒鍋就搞定所有菜」(cook everything in the same wok)，這讓使用了「五、六個不同的燉鍋、平底鍋」的凱西感到驚訝，正確答案為(D)。

Answer 3 (B)

女生對「煮給自己吃」這件事有什麼樣的想法呢？

(A) 食物不怎麼好吃。
(B) 準備一人份的菜實在太麻煩了。
(C) 因為只能準備一道菜，所以很無趣。
(D) 要買少量的食材很困難。

解析

女生一開始就說她覺得煮給自己吃滿難的，進一步解釋臺灣典型的多道配菜吃法，給的結論是「每道菜的份量只準備一點點實在很麻煩」。關鍵字為文中的troublesome(麻煩的)，因此選(B)。

Answer 4 (A)

女生展示了什麼給她的同班同學看呢？

(A) 電鍋有多萬能。
(B) 如何烹調各種料理。
(C) 如何用電鍋煮飯。
(D) 如何用電鍋完成蒸豬肉。

解析

解題重點在於文中提到的show my classmates...，句中的show等同於問題的demonstrate，因此最佳答案為(A)。選項(C)與(D)雖然都有被提到，但那只是女生在展示電鍋有多「萬能」(versatile)的例子而已。

Answer 5 (C)

女生的同班同學問了她什麼？

(A) 她把電鍋放在哪裡。
(B) 去哪裡能買到那些菜餚。
(C) 她在哪裡買的電鍋。
(D) 她的食材是在哪裡買的。

解析

本題答案在女生的同學見識到電鍋有多麼的萬能後，感到很吃驚，問她電鍋是從哪裡買的(where I got the cooker from)，因此選(C)。to get...from...這個片語為「從…取得…」之意。

中英文內容

短文 **1**

◉慢速MP3 05-09　　◉正常速MP3 05-10

Cathy and I got together last weekend to do some cooking. **We each bought our own ingredients** and cooked typical cuisine of our countries. I made Taiwanese food, and Cathy cooked British food. Cathy found it fascinating to **see me cooking everything in the same wok**, whereas **she used about five or six different saucepans and pans** for all the different side dishes. It took her a long time to roast a whole chicken in the oven. On the other hand, even though the chopping of the ingredients took me a while, my dishes were quickly ready after I started stir-frying.

　　凱西和我上個週末一起煮飯。我們各自買了自己要用的食材,煮自己國家的典型美食。我準備了臺灣菜,凱西則準備英國菜。看到我只需要一個炒鍋就搞定所有菜式,凱西覺得很神奇,因為她用了五、六個不同的燉鍋和平底鍋來準備不同的小菜,她還花了很多時間準備一隻烤全雞;反之,雖然我切菜花了點時間,但一旦開始炒菜,我很快就完成了。

短文 **2**

◉慢速MP3 05-11　　◉正常速MP3 05-12

I love cooking with friends because I find it hard to cook just for myself. In Taiwan, we tend to eat rice with several different dishes. Therefore, to prepare and **cook a little bit of each dish is troublesome**. On the other hand, when you cook with friends, you won't have this problem since you can share with others. Yesterday, I showed my classmates **how versatile a rice cooker can be**. Not only did I cook rice in it, but I also made some stewed pork. My friends were totally amazed and asked me **where I got the cooker from**. Because of this great experience, we decided to cook together again this weekend. I just can't wait!

　　我喜歡和朋友一起煮飯,因為只煮給自己吃是件滿困難的事。我們在臺灣的飲食習慣一般都是吃飯配好幾道菜,每道菜的份量如果只準備一點點,實在很麻煩。反之,當與朋友一起煮飯時,因為能與其他人分享菜式,所以根本就不會有這個問題。我昨天讓同學見識電鍋有多麼的萬能,我不只用它煮飯,還做了燉豬肉,我的朋友都很吃驚,問我那個電鍋是從哪裡買的。因為這次開心的經驗,所以我們決定這個週末再聚在一起煮菜,真讓人期待呢!

2 PART

流行與逛街

撿便宜、引領流行，身家必備的打扮儀容，
怎麼聽就是這些！

討論儀容 Appearance

Unit 1

📋日常生活　　💡娛樂活動　　✏意見交流　　🏁特殊場合

短 對 話 聽 力 實 戰

🎧 MP3 06-01

下面將播放五組短對話，請仔細聆聽，再依對話內容答題。

Question 1　　1 2 3 4 5

What appointment is the woman booking?

(A) A wash and cut appointment
(B) A scalp massage appointment
(C) A scalp massage and styling appointment
(D) A haircut appointment

Question 2　　1 2 3 4 5

What is the woman definitely going to do to her hair?

(A) Have a cut and perm
(B) Have a perm
(C) Have her hair cut short
(D) Grow her hair long

Question 3　　1 2 3 4 5

Why is the woman going to the annual sale?

(A) To find some accessories
(B) To get a new dress
(C) Because they have a 40% off sale.
(D) Because the man encourages her to go.

Question 4　　1 2 3 4 5

Why does the man advise the woman not to bring her credit card?

(A) Because she will get some good offers.
(B) Because she would spend too much if she uses her credit card.
(C) Because she cannot use her credit card for the sale.
(D) Because he doesn't want her to go to the annual sale.

Question 5　　1 2 3 4 5

What is the girl's problem with the annual sales?

(A) She becomes a practical shopper.
(B) She spends too much money.
(C) She buys things that become outdated quickly.
(D) She makes rushed purchasing decisions.

答案與解析 ～answer

Answer 1 🔊 (A)
對話中的女性要預約什麼服務？

(A) 洗髮與剪髮的服務

(B) 頭皮按摩的服務

(C) 頭皮按摩與剪後造型的服務

(D) 剪髮的服務

解析

女性一開始說她要預約剪髮，在設計師詢問是否要洗髮時，她回答sure，表示要一併預約洗髮，因此此選(A)。選項(B)跟(C)提到的頭皮按摩和剪後的造型服務是女性問是否包含在內的額外服務，並非她的預約項目。

Answer 2 🔊 (C)
對於頭髮，女性百分之百會做的造型是什麼？

(A) 剪髮與燙髮

(B) 燙髮

(C) 剪短頭髮

(D) 把頭髮留長

解析

因為題目問的是「絕對」(definitely)這個字，所以要選的是女性已經打定主意要做的造型，即have my hair cut short(剪短頭髮)，燙髮(perm)只是她在考慮的可能性，尚未確定要做，最佳答案為(C)。

Answer 3 🔊 (A)
女性為什麼打算去百貨公司的週年慶呢？

(A) 為了買飾品

(B) 為了買件新洋裝

(C) 因為百貨公司打六折。

(D) 因為男性鼓勵她去。

解析

女性要去百貨公司的週年慶，是因為她需要「飾品」(accessories)來「搭配新洋裝」(match my new dress)，因此答案為(A)。

Answer 4 🔊 (B)
男性為什麼建議女性不要帶信用卡呢？

(A) 因為她能取得一些好優惠。

(B) 因為她一刷卡，就會花太多。

(C) 因為她無法在週年慶的時候刷卡。

(D) 因為他不希望她去週年慶。

解析

從對話的第一句就能聽出男性不希望女性帶信用卡去週年慶，當女性反問原因時，男性回話的關鍵字overspend(超支)就是答案，因此選(B)。

Answer 5 🔊 (D)
女生一遇到週年慶，就會有什麼問題？

(A) 她就會變成一個理性的消費者。

(B) 她會花太多錢。

(C) 她會買一些很快就退流行的東西。

(D) 她會做倉促的購買決定。

解析

題目問的是女生的問題，所以不妨專注於她的談話內容。她提到自己一遇到週年慶她就容易「衝動購物」(impulse buying)，答案為(D)。選項(B)有可能是衝動購物的結果，但對話中沒有直接提及。

短對話 1　Conversation

Carol: Hi, I'd like to **book an appointment for a haircut**.
卡蘿： 嗨，你好，我要預約剪髮。

Hairdresser: Would you like to **have a wash**, too?
美髮造型師： 請問您要順便洗髮嗎？

Carol: **Sure**. I will also get a scalp massage and my hair styled afterwards, right？
卡蘿： 好啊，那會包含頭皮按摩和剪後的造型服務吧？

短對話 2　Conversation

Tessa: I've booked an appointment to **have my hair cut short**. I'm even thinking about a perm.
泰莎： 我已經預約好要剪髮了，我甚至在考慮燙頭髮。

Wayne: That'll be very different from the long hair you have now.
韋恩： 那會和你目前的長髮造型很不同耶。

短對話 3　Conversation

Vicky: I'm going to the department store's annual sale. I need some **accessories** to match my new dress.
薇琪： 我要去百貨公司的週年慶，我需要飾品來搭配我的新洋裝。

Troy: You should be able to get some good deals.
特洛伊： 你應該能找到不錯的好康。

短對話 4　Conversation

Ben: If you are going to the department store's annual sale, I don't think you should take your credit card with you.
班： 如果你要去百貨公司的週年慶，那最好不要帶信用卡。

Peggy: Why not? I can use it to get some nice offers.
佩姬： 為什麼？刷卡可以有一些好優惠耶。

Ben: But you often **overspend** when you take it!
班： 可是你一拿出卡，就經常超支啊！

短對話 5　Conversation

Dana: I suffer from **impulse buying** when I go to annual sales.
黛娜： 只要一碰上週年慶，我就很容易衝動購物。

Zac: I guess I'm more of a practical shopper.
查克： 我應該算是比較理性的消費者吧。

長對話聽力實戰

MP3 06-04

請仔細聆聽下面的長對話，再依對話內容選擇正確答案。

Question 1

What kind of information is the woman looking for?

(A) Plastic surgeons in her area
(B) Types of plastic surgery
(C) Plastic surgeons abroad
(D) The cost of having plastic surgery

Question 2

What does the woman want to change?

(A) Her figure
(B) Her facial features
(C) Her legs
(D) Her style

Question 3

What issue does the woman mention is due to how she looks?

(A) She feels unhappy.
(B) She cannot find her dream man.
(C) Her nose is too flat.
(D) She feels bad about her future.

Question 4

What does the man say is the biggest problem with surgery?

(A) It is very expensive.
(B) It is very painful.
(C) It will not work.
(D) It has risks.

Question 5

Why does the man suggest using make-up more instead of having surgery?

(A) Make-up is less dangerous.
(B) It gives better results.
(C) He knows a lot about make-up.
(D) It is more expensive.

答案與解析 ～answer

Answer 1 (A)
女性在尋找什麼類型的資訊呢？

(A) 她居住區域中的整型醫師
(B) 整型手術的種類
(C) 國外的整型醫師
(D) 動整型手術的花費

> **解析**
> 男性問女性她在看什麼，女性回答說覺得她在找「本地的」整型醫師(local plastic surgeons)，沒有提到在找尋其他資訊，正確答案為(A)。

Answer 2 (B)
女性想要改變的部位是哪裡？

(A) 她的身材
(B) 她的五官
(C) 她的腿
(D) 她的風格

> **解析**
> 被問及想要做什麼整型，女性回答自己對「身材不滿意」(not happy with my figure)，但並沒有說要改變身材，反而說她最「急迫」(most desperate)的是「讓五官更好看」，正確答案為(B)。

Answer 3 (B)
女性認為自己的長相影響到什麼？

(A) 她感到不快樂。
(B) 她遇不到夢中情人。
(C) 她的鼻子太塌了。
(D) 她對自己的未來感到不安。

> **解析**
> 要找出題目所提到的「問題」(issue)，就要找出對話中與長相有因果關係的內容，即女性認為她不好看的五官(特別是塌鼻子)是她一直「找不到夢中情人的原因」(it's why I can't find my dream man)，答案為(B)。

Answer 4 (D)
根據男性的話，整型手術最大的問題是什麼呢？

(A) 花費會很貴。
(B) 動手術時很痛。
(C) 整完也沒差。
(D) 整型有風險。

> **解析**
> 解題關鍵句為What I care most...，這裡點出男性認為最大的問題在於手術有「很大的風險」(the great risks)，正確答案為(D)。

Answer 5 (A)
和整型手術相比，男性為何比較推薦化妝呢？

(A) 因為化妝風險比較低。
(B) 因為化妝的效果比較好。
(C) 因為他很懂化妝。
(D) 因為化妝的花費更高。

> **解析**
> 在選項當中，可先剔除完全沒提到的(C)與(D)。請注意選項(B)，雖然男性在對話中肯定化妝會有幫助，但他並沒有比較化妝與整型的效果，最佳答案為(A)，關鍵字在...much cheaper and safer，表示男性認為化妝安全許多。

⊙慢速MP3 06-05　⊚正常速MP3 06-06

Tom: What are you reading?
湯姆： 你在看什麼？

Nikki: I'm researching **local plastic surgeons**.
妮琪： 我在找本地整型醫生的相關資訊。

Tom: Why? What are you thinking of having?
湯姆： 為什麼？你想要做哪方面的整型手術啊？

Nikki: I'm not happy with my figure, but I'm most desperate to **make my facial features prettier**.
妮琪： 我不滿意自己的身材，但我現在最急迫想要的，是讓五官更好看。

Tom: Don't be silly. You look lovely.
湯姆： 別傻了，妳目前看起來就很好啦。

Nikki: I don't think so, especially with my flat nose. I think it's why I **can't find my dream man**.
妮琪： 我不這麼認為，尤其是我的塌鼻子，我覺得這是我找不到夢中情人的原因。

Tom: **What I care most** about, though, is that you realize **the great risks** attached to such surgeries.
湯姆： 我最在意的是，你確實了解這類手術伴隨著很大的風險。

Nikki: Yes, I have been told. That's why I have to find a good surgeon.
妮琪： 有，其他人有和我說過，這也是為什麼我必須找到一個好醫師。

Tom: Why don't you start wearing make-up? That can make a big difference.
湯姆： 你為什麼不開始化妝呢？那能讓你有很大的改變。

Nikki: Do you really think that'll help?
妮琪： 你真的認為化妝有幫助？

Tom: Absolutely. Besides, it's much **cheaper and safer** than having surgery.
湯姆： 肯定會，而且化妝比整型便宜，也安全多了。

短文聽力實戰

MP3 06-07(短文1)　　MP3 06-08(短文2)

請仔細聆聽下面兩段短文，並分別回答Q1~Q2&Q3~Q5兩大題。

Question 1

Why are certain diets "fashionable"?

(A) Because they are endorsed by famous people.
(B) Because they are very effective at keeping weight off.
(C) Because we always want to try new diets.
(D) Because they make you lose weight very steadily.

Question 2

Based on the article, what is losing weight not about?

(A) It's not about a balanced diet.
(B) It's not about a change in lifestyle.
(C) It's not merely monitoring your weight.
(D) It's not about being healthier.

Question 3

How do certain too-perfect models influence teenagers?

(A) They tell teenagers they are fat.
(B) They force teenagers to go on extreme diets.
(C) They make teenagers think they are thin enough.
(D) Indirectly, they make teenagers feel fat.

Question 4

What kind of diets some girls adopt is bad for their health?

(A) Low-fat diets
(B) Extreme diets
(C) Diets full of unhealthy foods
(D) Strictly controlled diets

Question 5

Based on the article, which statement below is true?

(A) Being thin often means you are healthy.
(B) A positive self-image is equally important as being in shape.
(C) Extreme diets are bad but not dangerous for the body.
(D) Doctors say diets are all about losing weight.

答案與解析 ～answer

Answer 1 (A)
為什麼有些減肥方式特別流行呢？
- (A) 因為這些方式有名人的背書。
- (B) 因為這些方式很有減肥效果。
- (C) 因為我們總是想要嘗試新的減肥方法。
- (D) 因為這些方式能持續且穩定地讓你減輕體重。

解析
題目中的fashionable(流行的)對應到文中的第一句fashion(流行)，就能知道特定減肥方式之所以會流行，與「明星」(celebrities)有關，因此選答案(A)。

Answer 2 (C)
根據文章的內容，減重與什麼無關呢？
- (A) 與均衡飲食無關。
- (B) 與改變生活型態無關。
- (C) 與只專注於體重計上的數字無關。
- (D) 與活得更健康無關。

解析
解答本題之前，一定要注意題目問的是與什麼「無關」(not about)。文中提到Losing weight is not just about tracking numbers，此處的number指的是體重，正確答案為(C)。

Answer 3 (D)
那些過度完美的模特兒對青少年有什麼樣的影響呢？
- (A) 他們告訴青少年他們太胖了。
- (B) 他們強迫青少年用極端的方式減肥。
- (C) 他們讓青少年覺得自己夠瘦了。
- (D) 間接地讓青少年覺得自己太胖。

解析
解題的關鍵句在indirectly(間接地)帶出的...think they are overweight(那些過度完美的模特兒讓青少年覺得自己過胖)，因此答案選(D)。

Answer 4 (B)
一些女孩所採用的什麼飲食對健康有害呢？
- (A) 低脂飲食
- (B) 極端的飲食
- (C) 充斥不健康食物的飲食
- (D) 嚴格控管的飲食

解析
有些女孩會將模特兒的身材視為標準，採用「極端」(extreme)的飲食來減肥，關鍵字為extreme，答案為(B)。注意(A)(D)不一定會對健康有害，而(C)則是因為沒有直接提到，所以不選。

Answer 5 (B)
根據本文的內容，以下哪一句敘述為真？
- (A) 維持瘦瘦的身材通常就代表很健康。
- (B) 一個正面的自我印象和維持身材同樣重要。
- (C) 極端的飲食習慣不好，但對身體不會有危險。
- (D) 醫生說控制飲食就是為了減重。

解析
本文最後提到建立良好正面的自我印象與維持身材「同樣重要」(just as important as)，答案為(B)。比較需要注意(C)，因為文中提到極端的手段對健康有害，可推知說話者不認同這種方式，因此可剔除這個選項。

中英文內容

短文 1

⊙慢速MP3 06-09　◎正常速MP3 06-10

The word "fashion" also applies to diets. **Celebrities** are known for various extreme diets that help them look the way they are; hence, **those diets become fashionable for a period of time**. However, it has been proven that no matter how effective a particular diet is, nothing beats the good old-fashion balanced diet and exercise. Losing weight is **not just about tracking numbers**. A balanced diet and regular exercise keep your mind clear and your body fit. In order to keep your motivation up, think about making your lifestyle healthier rather than focusing on the numbers on the scale.

「流行」一詞現在也可以應用在減肥上了。明星們會用極端的減肥方式維持身材；因此，有些減肥法會有一陣子特別流行。但是，實際的證據顯示，不管特殊的減肥法多麼有效、快速，最終敵不過均衡飲食和運動。減重不應該只注意體重數字的增減而已，均衡的飲食和規律的運動能讓人頭腦清醒、身材更好，為了讓自己保有持之以恆的動力，記得不要把重心放在體重計上顯示的數字，而要讓自己活得更健康。

短文 2

⊙慢速MP3 06-11　◎正常速MP3 06-12

More and more people seem to suffer from having a negative self-image. Teenagers are particularly susceptible to the subconscious pressure added by too-perfect models in magazines, which **indirectly** make them **feel they are overweight**. Some girls even see models as the standard and **go on extreme diets** that are bad for their health. To solve this problem, many doctors start to promote that healthy diets are not just about losing weight. It is important to understand that being thin does not mean you are healthy. And we should also know that developing **a positive self-image is just as important as keeping in shape**.

越來越多人似乎對自己產生負面的印象。青少年尤其容易受到影響，像是雜誌裡面那些看起來過度完美的模特兒就帶給他們潛在壓力，間接讓許多青少年覺得自己過胖。有些女孩甚至會將模特兒視為標準，採用極端、對身體造成危害的減肥方式。為了解決這個問題，許多醫生開始提倡「健康的飲食不再只是減重」的觀念，理解身材瘦並不代表健康很重要，我們也必須了解，建立良好正面的自我印象與維持身材一樣重要。

上網購物 Via The Internet

日常生活　娛樂活動　意見交流　特殊場合

短對話聽力實戰

◎ MP3 07-01

下面將播放五組短對話，請仔細聆聽，再依對話內容答題。

Question 1

What's the advantage of the virtual make-up software?

(A) It helps customers find whatever make-up they need online.
(B) It helps make online shopping less expensive.
(C) It helps women see what they look like without the make-up.
(D) There is a smaller chance of buying unsuitable things.

Question 2

What trend tells us that the online market is big?

(A) Revenue of online shops is sometimes greater than the in-store's.
(B) Customers do not go to stores for shopping anymore.
(C) All brick-and-mortar shops now also have online shops.
(D) More and more customers tend to shop online.

Question 3

Why does the girl like shopping on the particular website?

(A) The shipping is free.
(B) She can get her money back if the clothes don't fit.
(C) She can buy clothes from the States.
(D) She can get a 100% discount.

Question 4

Why does the man have doubts about online shopping?

(A) Because you cannot touch the products.
(B) Because he doesn't like taking risks.
(C) Because the image and the real thing could be very different.
(D) Because he has never tried online shopping.

Question 5

Why wouldn't the woman send back the dress?

(A) Because she might not get a refund.
(B) Because she can earn more by selling the dress online.
(C) Because she needs to spend money to post it back.
(D) Because the dress is non-refundable.

答案與解析 ~answer

Answer 1 (D)

虛擬上妝軟體有什麼優點？

(A) 幫助消費者找到自己需要的產品。

(B) 能減低線上購物的花費。

(C) 能讓女性看到自己素顏的樣子。

(D) 買到不適合自己的化妝品的機率較小。

解析

聽到女性說明虛擬上妝軟體的作用後，男性提到這樣能「減少買到不適合自己化妝品的風險」，關鍵字為reduce the risk of...，正確答案為(D)。注意選項(A)雖然也有可能發生，但並非對話中明確提到的內容。

Answer 2 (A)

哪種趨勢能顯示出網路市場的廣大呢？

(A) 線上商店的營業額有時比實體商店的還要多。

(B) 顧客已經不再去商店購物了。

(C) 現在的實體商店都會設立自己的線上商城。

(D) 越來越多人在網路上購物。

解析

解題必須「以實際提到的內容為準」。從男子第一句提到的「發展旺盛」，或許能聯想到(B)(C)(D)，但這都只是推論出來的結果，最佳答案為(A)。(C)選項的brick-and-mortar和in-store都是「實體商店」的形容詞。

Answer 3 (B)

女孩為什麼喜歡在特定的網站上購物呢？

(A) 因為購物免運費。

(B) 因為如果衣服不合身，她可以退費。

(C) 因為她能從美國買衣服。

(D) 因為她可以得到全額折扣。

解析

針對本題，必須選擇女孩自己提到她愛在該網站購物的原因。雖然有提到免運費，但這只是回答男生的問題。真正的答案在女孩最後提到I love shopping on their website because...後面的原因，正確答案為(B)。

Answer 4 (C)

男性為什麼會對網購持以懷疑的態度呢？

(A) 因為你無法觸碰商品。

(B) 因為他不喜歡冒險。

(C) 因為照片和實物有時可能會有很大的差異。

(D) 因為他從來沒有用網路購物過。

解析

當女性說她網購的鞋子不合腳，而且顏色與照片看起來也不同時，男性才說他對於網路購物採「保留態度」(skeptical懷疑的)，因為有時候你看到的跟實品「有很大的落差」，正確答案為(C)。

Answer 5 (A)

女性為什麼不把洋裝寄回店家，辦理退貨呢？

(A) 因為她可能拿不到退費。

(B) 因為上網賣掉洋裝的話，她賺的更多。

(C) 因為把洋裝寄回去的話，她還要額外付一筆錢。

(D) 因為那件洋裝不接受退貨。

解析

女性提到自己把衣服的標籤剪了，寄回去後店家可能因為沒有標籤而不接受退貨(I don't know if it is refundable)，答案為(A)。注意(D)與(A)的差別在(D)確定店家不退貨，但女性其實不確定，所以不能選(D)。

 中英文內容

⊙慢速MP3 07-02　　⊙正常速MP3 07-03

短對話 1 Conversation

Fanny: Look! This online shop uses virtual make-up software. You can see how you'll look like with their make-up.

芬妮： 你看！這家網路商店有虛擬上妝軟體，你可以看到自己用了他們家化妝產品後的模樣。

Paul: That should **reduce the risk** of **buying make-up that doesn't fit** you.

保羅： 這樣應該可以減少買到不適合自己的化妝品的風險。

短對話 2 Conversation

Manny: E-commerce is really booming now.

曼尼： 電子商務現在的發展真是旺盛啊。

Linda: That's right. Online sales revenue sometimes even **surpasses the in-store revenue**.

琳達： 對啊，線上商店的營業額有時候甚至還超越實體商店的呢。

短對話 3 Conversation

Chloe: I'm buying some clothes from an online shop based in the States.

克蘿伊：我在這個美國的線上商城買衣服。

Terry: Isn't overseas shipping expensive? And what if it doesn't fit?

泰瑞： 國外的運費不是很貴嗎？而且如果衣服不合身怎麼辦？

Chloe: Shipping is completely free now. I love shopping on their website because they have **a 100% refund policy**, too.

克蘿伊：他們現在都免運費。我很愛在他們的網站上購物，因為他們提供全額退費的服務。

短對話 4 Conversation

Phoebe: These shoes I bought online don't fit me. Besides, the actual color looks different from the pictures.

菲比： 我在網路上買的這雙鞋子不合腳，而且，鞋子的實際顏色跟照片看起來不同。

Ian: That's why I'm a bit **skeptical** about online shopping. There's sometimes **a large gap** between **what you see in the pictures and what you get**.

伊恩： 這就是我之所以對網購採保留態度的原因，有時候你看到的圖片跟實際拿到的產品有很大的落差。

短對話 5 Conversation

Kevin: Why don't you get a refund on the dress since it doesn't fit you?

凱文： 既然這件洋裝不合身，你為什麼不退貨呢？

Emily: Because I've cut off the tag. I **don't know if it is refundable** without the tag.

艾蜜莉：因為我已經把標籤剪掉了，不確定店家還接不接受退貨。

長對話聽力實戰

◎MP3 07-04

請仔細聆聽下面的長對話，再依對話內容選擇正確答案。

Question 1 ①②③④⑤

What's the actual price the woman paid for her dress?

(A) $200
(B) $60
(C) $80
(D) $160

Question 2 ①②③④⑤

Why did the woman choose the particular dress?

(A) Because everything about the dress is what she wants.
(B) Because it was a good bargain.
(C) Because it is a designer brand.
(D) Because it was the last one in the shop.

Question 3 ①②③④⑤

Why does the man want the woman to go shopping with him?

(A) Because he needs her to give him her opinion.
(B) Because the woman can find a good bargain.
(C) Because the woman will find some styles he has not tried yet.
(D) Because the woman always makes the right decision.

Question 4 ①②③④⑤

What does the man say the woman might find for him?

(A) A better bargain
(B) Suit styles that he hasn't tried
(C) A designer suit
(D) A style people like

Question 5 ①②③④⑤

Where will the woman take the man to look for his suit?

(A) Some shops she has not been to
(B) A department store
(C) A designer dress shop
(D) The same shop where she purchased her dress

答案與解析 ～answer

Answer 1 (B)
女性買洋裝實際付的錢是多少呢?
- (A) 200美元
- (B) 60美元
- (C) 80美元
- (D) 160美元

解析

歐美國家對折扣的形容方式與我們不同。文中提到的70% off就是中文「打三折」之意,所以$200*0.3=$60,答案選(B)。但本題其實並不需要複雜的運算,因為就在女生提到折扣後,男性立刻驚訝地提到$60的價格。

Answer 2 (A)
女性為什麼會選擇這一件洋裝呢?
- (A) 因為這件洋裝完全符合她想要的樣式。
- (B) 因為價格很划算。
- (C) 因為是一件設計師的品牌。
- (D) 因為店裡只剩下最後一件。

解析

選項(C)與(D)在對話中都沒有提到,所以可以剔除,比較容易混淆的是(A)與(B)的選項,解題的關鍵句在女性提到禮服的設計、布料和顏色都是她想要的,親民的價格為額外優點(extra benefit),由此可知她最主要的考量為(A)。

Answer 3 (A)
男性為何會希望女性陪他去購物呢?
- (A) 因為他需要她給予意見。
- (B) 因為女性能找到便宜划算的西裝。
- (C) 因為女性會找到他尚未試過的款式。
- (D) 因為女性總是能做出對的決定。

解析

男性提到自己之所以還沒買西裝,是因為他無法決定,所以需要女性給他「意見」(opinions),答案選(A)。注意選項(C)是肯定女性能找到他沒試過的款式,但對話中是用might,僅表達可能性而已。

Answer 4 (B)
男性認為女性能替他找到什麼呢?
- (A) 更便宜划算的西裝
- (B) 他沒有試過的款式
- (C) 有設計師品牌的服裝
- (D) 大家會喜歡的樣式

解析

雖然對話前面有提到優惠的價格與服裝的設計,但這些都是用來形容女性買到的禮服。說到男性的西裝時,他說女性可能會找到他「沒試過的款式」(find some styles that I haven't tried),因此選(B)。

Answer 5 (D)
女性將會帶男性到哪裡物色西裝呢?
- (A) 她沒有去過的一些店家
- (B) 百貨公司
- (C) 某設計師的服裝店
- (D) 她買洋裝的那家店

解析

在對話最後,女性說她打算先帶男性到「她買禮服的那家店」(where I bought my dress)看看,因為那家店的男士服裝部的選擇很多,正確答案為(D)。

 中英文內容

◎ 慢速MP3 07-05　　◎ 正常速MP3 07-06

Mark: Have you got a dress for the prom yet?
馬克： 你買了舞會要穿的禮服了嗎？

Sharon: Definitely. Let me show you. I am really happy with this dress.
莎朗： 當然，你來看看，我對這件禮服非常滿意。

Mark: It's gorgeous! You must have spent a fortune on it.
馬克： 實在是太美了！你一定花了不少錢吧？

Sharon: Not really. **Originally, it cost $200** dollars, but I got it for **70% off the original price.**
莎朗： 其實沒有耶，這件洋裝原本要200美元，但我用三折買下的。

Mark: Only **$60 dollars** for that?! You got yourself a real bargain.
馬克： 才花60美元嗎？！你真是賺到了。

Sharon: Its design, material and color are **all what I was looking for**. The bargain price, of course, was a nice **extra benefit**. How about your suit?
莎朗： 禮服的設計、布料和顏色都符合我在找的樣式，當然，親民的價格也是個很棒的額外優點。那你的西裝準備得怎麼樣了？

Mark: I **can't seem to decide among the choices**. I was wondering if you could go shopping with me and give me **your opinion**.
馬克： 要在眾多選擇中挑出一件好困難，我正想問你可不可以跟我一起去挑，給我意見。

Sharon: Sure. I'd love to.
莎朗： 好啊，樂意至極。

Mark: You **might find some styles that I haven't tried** yet.
馬克： 也許你能找到一些我還沒試過的款式。

Sharon: I'll take you to **the shop where I bought my dress**. They have a large men's section.
莎朗： 那我先帶你到我買禮服的那家店看看，他們男士服裝部的選擇很多。

短文聽力實戰

◎MP3 07-07(短文1)　◎MP3 07-08(短文2)

請仔細聆聽下面兩段短文，並分別回答Q1~Q2&Q3~Q5兩大題。

Question ❶
Why is the modern society attracted to online shopping?

    (A) Because going to a store is old-fashioned.
    (B) Because almost everyone owns a computer.
    (C) Because of the increase in convenience and privacy.
    (D) Because everything is just a mouse click away.

Question ❷
Where can we do online shopping now?

    (A) On the bus
    (B) In an air-conditioned office
    (C) In a store
    (D) Almost wherever we like

Question ❸
Software such as Photoshop has made what more difficult?

    (A) Tell if a product photo is truthful
    (B) Digitally edit product photos
    (C) Imagine what the product actually looks like
    (D) Realize what we are paying for in a product

Question ❹
When we shop online, what is quite common to see?

    (A) Product-enhancing software
    (B) Digital products
    (C) Product photos digitally taken
    (D) Product photos digitally improved

Question ❺
What's the negative result of the over-edited photos?

    (A) They may mislead consumers.
    (B) Consumers will be more willing to shop online.
    (C) They may confuse consumers.
    (D) Products might look fake.

答案與解析 ✏️ ~answer

Answer 1 🔊 (C)
為什麼現代社會的大眾會被網路購物吸引呢？

(A) 因為去店裡消費已經落伍了。

(B) 因為幾乎每個人都有電腦。

(C) 因為其帶來的便利性與隱私更高。

(D) 因為只須要按幾下滑鼠就能完成購物。

> **解析**
> 文中説大眾被網路購物「吸引」的原因是因為它提供了更多的「方便性」與「隱私」(greater convenience and privacy)。注意選項(D)雖然有被提到，但這是舉例時所提到的細節，會因人而異，不能代表大眾，最佳答案為(C)。

Answer 2 🔊 (D)
我們現在可以在何處上網購物呢？

(A) 在公車上

(B) 在開著冷氣的辦公室

(C) 在店家裡

(D) 幾乎所有的場所

> **解析**
> 雖然文中有提到在開著冷氣的辦公室內與公車上都可以購物，但如此(A)與(B)都變成能選的答案，此時要選能包含這兩個選項的最佳答案，也就是(D)。

Answer 3 🔊 (A)
Photoshop這一類的軟體讓什麼事情變得越來越困難呢？

(A) 分辨產品的照片是否真實

(B) 以數位後製的技術處理相片

(C) 想像產品實際看起來的樣子

(D) 了解我們購買的產品是什麼

> **解析**
> 解題關鍵在文章一開始，提到這類軟體讓人越來越難分辨產品照片的「真實性」(genuineness of product images)，因此選(A)。其他三個選項都與「變得困難」的概念無關，所以剔除。

Answer 4 🔊 (D)
當我們上網購物時，很常看到什麼樣的現象呢？

(A) 產品優化軟體

(B) 數位產品

(C) 用數位相機拍攝的產品照片

(D) 經過數位後製技術處理的照片

> **解析**
> 文章內提到，沒經過「數位處理優化」(digitally enhanced)的產品照片幾乎找不到，正確答案為(D)。注意選項(C)，雖然這是有可能發生的現實，但文章中並未直接提到這一點，所以不適合選。

Answer 5 🔊 (A)
根據本文，過度修片會造成什麼不良後果呢？

(A) 會誤導消費者。

(B) 消費者會更願意上網購物。

(C) 會讓消費者感到困惑。

(D) 產品看起來可能像假的。

> **解析**
>
> 文中最後提到廣告業者有時會過度修片，因而「誤導消費者」(mislead consumers)，正確答案為(A)。注意答題時必須選文章確實有提到的內容，比如選項(C)，文章提到的是消費者會失望(disappointed)，所以不能選。

⊙慢速MP3 07-09　◎正常速MP3 07-10

The evolvement of modern technologies such as 3G/4G Internet and mobile devices and applications have dramatically changed the way we shop. Modern society **is drawn to online shopping** because of **the greater convenience and privacy** it offers. For example, if you suddenly think of something to buy at 3a.m., almost whatever you want is simply a mouse click away when you shop online. Instead of rushing to a store to buy something during your one-hour lunch break, you can shop on your computer in the comfort of an air-conditioned office, or even on the phone when you are on the bus. Thanks to technology, we are **no longer restricted by where we are**.

現代科技的發展，比如3G/4G網路、行動裝置和應用程式等，都大幅改變了我們的消費模式。現代社會的大眾之所以會被網路購物吸引，是因為它提供了更多的方便性與隱私。舉例來說，如果你在凌晨三點突然想到要買某樣東西，只要動動手指、按幾下滑鼠就能完成線上購物，幾乎什麼都買得到。和在一個小時的午休時間內跑去店家買東西相比，你只要舒適地待在開著冷氣的辦公室內，就能用電腦購物，甚至連坐公車的時候都能用手機購物，感謝科技的發展，我們不再受地點侷限了。

⊙慢速MP3 07-11　◎正常速MP3 07-12

With advanced technologies and software such as Photoshop, it is becoming increasingly difficult to judge **the genuineness of product images**. The computer has brought us digital effects, which has advanced so much over the last few decades that images can be manipulated beyond our imagination. It is almost impossible not to encounter **digitally enhanced photos** of products sold online. Advertisers will defend themselves by saying that they edit the images to emphasize the good features of their products. However, advertisers sometimes over-edit the photos to **mislead** consumers. In those cases, buyers usually end up being disappointed when they get the products.

Photoshop這一類的高科技軟體讓人越來越難分辨產品照片的真實性。電腦為我們帶來了數位後製，這種技術在這幾十年間飛快進展，到現在，影像處理的技術已經超越我們的想像。沒經過數位處理優化的網購照片幾乎找不到。針對這件事，廣告業者會為自己辯護，說他們修照片是為了強調產品的優點，但他們有時會過度修片，誤導消費者，遇到這種情況的話，購買者最終拿到產品時，通常會很失望。

Unit 3 逛街血拚 Go Shopping

📱 日常生活　🎤 娛樂活動　📝 意見交流　🚩 特殊場合

短對話聽力實戰

 MP3 08-01

下面將播放五組短對話，請仔細聆聽，再依對話內容答題。

Question 1

How are the buyers of the limited bag chosen?

(A) The buyers who pay the deposit will be chosen.
(B) They are chosen in the order of registration.
(C) They'll be chosen by random selection.
(D) The buyers need to vote for it.

Question 2

What does the woman say limited-edition items make people feel?

(A) They feel somehow better than others.
(B) They feel more powerful than others.
(C) They feel richer than others.
(D) They feel more excited.

Question 3

What does the woman suggest the man get for his daughter's birthday?

(A) Cash
(B) A supermarket voucher
(C) A voucher from a shop
(D) Some clothes she likes

Question 4

What does the man ask the clerk to do?

(A) Remove the price tag and wrap the gift
(B) Take off the price tag
(C) Give him a gift bag
(D) Give him a gift bag and remove the price tag

Question 5

What does the man suggest the woman do?

(A) Remove the price tag and keep the receipt
(B) Keep the receipt and check if the price tag can be removed
(C) Ask for Lisa's size
(D) Exchange the top for something else

答案與解析 ~answer

Answer 1 (C)
限量包的買家是如何被決定的呢？
- (A) 付訂金的買家就會被選中。
- (B) 根據註冊的順序選擇買家。
- (C) 最後的買家是隨機挑選的。
- (D) 買家必須投票。

解析
女性在解釋限量包搶購的過程中提到，登記時要先付一筆訂金，這是必要的程序，然後才「隨機抽選買家」(they'll randomly pick the buyers)，因此選 (C)。(randomly 隨機地)

Answer 2 (A)
限量版的物品會讓人們產生什麼樣的感覺？
- (A) 覺得他們比其他人優越。
- (B) 覺得他們比其他人有權力。
- (C) 覺得他們比其他人有錢。
- (D) 他們會感到更興奮。

解析
男性不理解會為衣服或包包排隊的心理，此時女性回答，成功取得限量版的物品會讓人產生「優越感」(superior 優越的)，最接的答案為(A)。(B)與(C)的確可能是優越感裡所包含的心情，但還是必須選擇與superior最接近的意思。

Answer 3 (C)
女性建議男性送什麼禮物給他的女兒？
- (A) 現金
- (B) 超市的禮券
- (C) 商店的禮券
- (D) 女兒喜歡的服飾

解析
作為生日禮物，女性建議男性送「服飾店的禮券」(a voucher from a clothes store)，讓她自己挑，正確答案為(C)。

Answer 4 (B)
對話中的男性要求店員什麼呢？
- (A) 把價格標籤拿掉，再包裝禮物
- (B) 把價格標籤撕掉
- (C) 給他一個裝禮物的袋子
- (D) 給他裝禮物的袋子，並拿掉標籤

解析
本題的答案在對話的最後一句，男性請對方剪掉產品的標價(remove the price tag)，但不用包裝，答案為(B)。另外也可以從連接詞but得知前後兩件事隱含相異的作法，所以如果只聽到前半句，也能合理推測禮物無須包裝。

Answer 5 (B)
男性建議女性做什麼？
- (A) 拿掉價格標籤並保留收據
- (B) 保留收據，再確認價格標籤能不能拿掉
- (C) 問清楚麗莎她的尺寸
- (D) 將上衣換成其他商品

解析
男性建議女性「確定她能不能拿掉價格標籤」(check if the price tag can be removed)，正確答案為(B)。另外須注意男性提到用「收據」換貨，所以收據(receipt)很顯然必須保留。

中英文內容

⊙慢速MP3 08-02　　◎正常速MP3 08-03

短對話 1 Conversation

Ewan: If you really want this limited edition bag, just go and get it!

伊旺： 你如果這麼想要這個限量包，那就去買啊！

Dora: But a deposit is required when you register, and they'll **randomly pick the buyers**. I'll be really disappointed if I don't get it after all that.

朵拉： 可是你登記時要先付訂金，然後他們再隨機抽選買家。如果這麼努力之後還買不到，我肯定會很失望。

短對話 2 Conversation

Michael: I don't understand why people would queue for hours for clothes and bags.

麥可： 我不理解為何有人願意排好幾個小時的隊，就為了買衣服和包包。

Tara: That's the power of brand. If you manage to get a limited-edition item, it somehow makes you **feel superior**.

塔拉： 這就是品牌的力量。如果你取得限量版產品，就會產生優越感。

短對話 3 Conversation

Craig: My daughter's birthday is coming, but I'm terrible at picking clothes.

克雷格：我女兒的生日快到了，但我很不會挑衣服。

Linda: Why don't you get her **a voucher from a clothing store**? Then she can buy what she likes.

琳達： 你為什麼不直接送她服飾店的禮券呢？這樣她就能自己買喜歡的東西。

短對話 4 Conversation

Fred: I'm buying this as a gift for a friend.

弗雷德：我要買這個送朋友當禮物。

Clerk: Shall I cut off the price tag and wrap it up for you?

店員： 那我是否該幫您剪掉價格標籤，包裝起來呢？

Fred: Please remove the price tag, but there's **no need to wrap it**. Thank you.

弗雷德：請幫我將標籤拿掉，但不用包裝，謝謝。

短對話 5 Conversation

Emma: How do I buy a top for Lisa as a gift if I'm not sure about her size?

艾瑪： 如果我不確定麗莎的尺寸，要怎樣買上衣當她的禮物啊？

Peter: I think you can **get it exchanged with the receipt** if the top doesn't fit. But you should **check if the price tag can be removed** first.

彼得： 上衣如果不合的話，拿收據應該就可以換貨。但你得先確定能不能拿掉價格標籤。

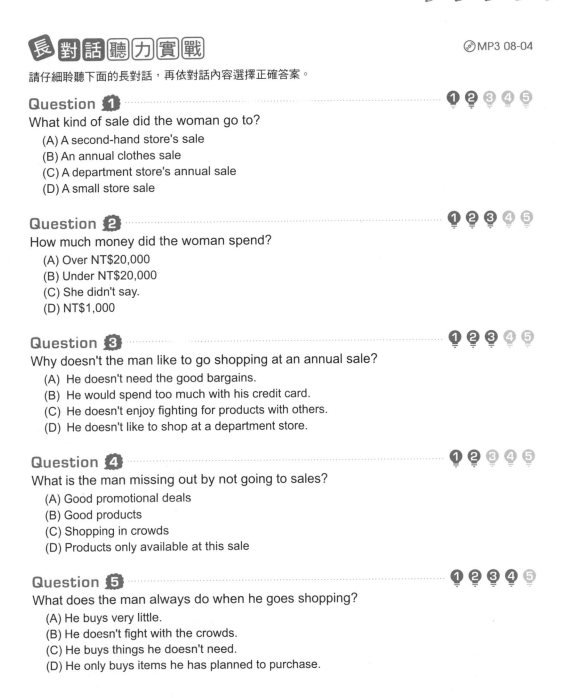

長對話聽力實戰 　　　　　　　　　　　　　　⚙MP3 08-04

請仔細聆聽下面的長對話，再依對話內容選擇正確答案。

Question ❶ ⋯⋯⋯⋯⋯⋯⋯⋯⋯⋯⋯⋯⋯⋯⋯⋯⋯⋯ ❶ ❷ ❸ ❹ ❺

What kind of sale did the woman go to?

(A) A second-hand store's sale
(B) An annual clothes sale
(C) A department store's annual sale
(D) A small store sale

Question ❷ ⋯⋯⋯⋯⋯⋯⋯⋯⋯⋯⋯⋯⋯⋯⋯⋯⋯⋯ ❶ ❷ ❸ ❹ ❺

How much money did the woman spend?

(A) Over NT$20,000
(B) Under NT$20,000
(C) She didn't say.
(D) NT$1,000

Question ❸ ⋯⋯⋯⋯⋯⋯⋯⋯⋯⋯⋯⋯⋯⋯⋯⋯⋯⋯ ❶ ❷ ❸ ❹ ❺

Why doesn't the man like to go shopping at an annual sale?

(A) He doesn't need the good bargains.
(B) He would spend too much with his credit card.
(C) He doesn't enjoy fighting for products with others.
(D) He doesn't like to shop at a department store.

Question ❹ ⋯⋯⋯⋯⋯⋯⋯⋯⋯⋯⋯⋯⋯⋯⋯⋯⋯⋯ ❶ ❷ ❸ ❹ ❺

What is the man missing out by not going to sales?

(A) Good promotional deals
(B) Good products
(C) Shopping in crowds
(D) Products only available at this sale

Question ❺ ⋯⋯⋯⋯⋯⋯⋯⋯⋯⋯⋯⋯⋯⋯⋯⋯⋯⋯ ❶ ❷ ❸ ❹ ❺

What does the man always do when he goes shopping?

(A) He buys very little.
(B) He doesn't fight with the crowds.
(C) He buys things he doesn't need.
(D) He only buys items he has planned to purchase.

答案與解析 ~answer

Answer 1 (C)
對話中的女性去了什麼類型的拍賣會呢？

(A) 二手店拍賣會
(B) 衣服的週年拍賣會
(C) 百貨公司的週年慶
(D) 小型店家的拍賣會

解析
答題關鍵在對話一開始，女性提到「百貨公司的週年慶」(department's annual sale)害她有點失心瘋，正確答案為(C)。注意其他選項也有sale(拍賣)這個單字，所以關鍵詞為department store，這才能看出拍賣的「類型」。

Answer 2 (B)
對話中的女性花了多少錢呢？

(A) 超過台幣兩萬元
(B) 不到台幣兩萬元
(C) 她沒有說花了多少。
(D) 台幣一千元

解析
在男性詢問女性花了多少錢時，她首先回答花了兩萬元；隨即說她的消費額有一千元的禮券可抵，所以「實際上」花的比兩萬元少(spent less than that)，因此選(B)。

Answer 3 (C)
男性為什麼不喜歡去逛週年慶呢？

(A) 他不需要那些便宜的好康。
(B) 他刷卡會花太多錢。
(C) 他不喜歡和其他人搶東西。
(D) 他不喜歡到百貨公司逛街。

解析
當女性問男性是否有買什麼東西時，他提到自己「不喜歡和一堆人搶東西的感覺」，fight over在此處並非真的爭奪，而是形容搶好康時的樣子，正確答案為(C)。

Answer 4 (A)
男性不去拍賣會逛逛會錯過什麼？

(A) 享受好的折扣優惠
(B) 買到好產品
(C) 體驗人擠人的購物現象
(D) 只在這個拍賣會才有的產品

解析
當男性提到自己不喜歡去人擠人的拍賣會時，女性回應這樣他就會「錯過很多好康」，good bargain指的是品質好、價格又低廉的產品，正是週年慶折扣時能搶到的好康，正確答案為(A)。

Answer 5 (D)
男性去購物時總是怎麼做？

(A) 他買很少東西。
(B) 不與大眾搶商品。
(C) 他會買自己不需要的物品。
(D) 他只買那些自己想好要買的商品。

解析
男子提到自己只有在需要時才去購物，而且總是「照他的購買清單採購」，不會亂買(stick to my shopping list)。此處的stick to與adhere(遵守)的意思相似，正確答案為(D)。

⊙慢速MP3 08-05　　⊙正常速MP3 08-06

Brenden: Look at all those shopping bags you are carrying!
布蘭登：　你手上的購物袋也太多了吧！

Laura:　I went a little crazy at **the department store's annual sale**.
蘿拉：　我在百貨公司的週年慶有點失心瘋。

Brenden: What did you buy?
布蘭登：　你買了些什麼？

Laura:　I bought blouses, skirts, jeans, scarves and some shoes.
蘿拉：　我買了上衣、裙子、牛仔褲、圍巾和幾雙鞋子。

Brenden: How much did you spend on those?
布蘭登：　你買那些花了多少錢啊？

Laura:　I spent NT$20,000 dollars. But I got **NT$1,000 dollars worth of vouchers back**, so I **actually spent less** than that.
蘿拉：　兩萬元，但我的消費額有一千元的禮券，所以實際上花的沒那麼多。

Brenden: Did you carry all that cash on you?
布蘭登：　你身上帶著那麼多現金？

Laura:　No. I used my card. Did you buy anything?
蘿拉：　不，我刷卡，那你有買什麼東西嗎？

Brenden: Well, I **don't like to fight over things with the crowd**.
布蘭登：　我不喜歡和一堆人搶東西的感覺。

Laura:　But you'll **miss out** on so many **good bargains**.
蘿拉：　但你這樣就會錯過很多好康耶！

Brenden: I only go shopping when I need something. And I always **stick to my shopping list**.
布蘭登：　我只有在需要時才去購物，而且我會依照我的購物清單採購。

短文聽力實戰

◉MP3 08-07(短文1)　◉MP3 08-08(短文2)

請仔細聆聽下面兩段短文，並分別回答Q1~Q2&Q3~Q5兩大題。

Question 1

What will make the girl's sister feel uncomfortable?

(A) If her style is different from others'.
(B) When she wears a T-shirt and jeans.
(C) When she buys clothes at a sale.
(D) If her whole style is not coordinated.

Question 2

Why doesn't the girl's sister let her choose the clothes she likes?

(A) Because she thinks the girl doesn't understand fashion.
(B) Because she wants to style the girl just like her.
(C) Because she doesn't want the girl to buy T-shirts.
(D) Because the girl wants to have a makeover.

Question 3

Why was the man so tired from the shopping trip?

(A) His girlfriend made him carry ten shopping bags.
(B) They walked round at least thirty shops.
(C) He had to wait for his girlfriend to try on many clothes.
(D) He didn't want to go shopping.

Question 4

Why is the man's girlfriend proud of the presents she bought?

(A) Because she spent less than NT$5,000.
(B) Because she spent more than NT$5,000.
(C) Because her bank savings account has over NT$5,000 in it.
(D) Because she saved more than NT$5,000.

Question 5

How much of a discount did they offer at the sale?

(A) A maximum of 70% for most items
(B) A minimum of 30% discount for most items
(C) Everything at only 30% of the original price
(D) Buy one, get one free

答案與解析 ~answer

Answer 1 (D)

女孩的姐姐會因為什麼事情而感到渾身不舒服？

(A) 當她的風格與其他人不同時。
(B) 當她穿著T恤與牛仔褲的時候。
(C) 當她在拍賣會上買衣服的時候。
(D) 當她的整體造型不協調時。

解析

文中提到女孩的姐姐非常認真看待打扮這件事，如果她從頭到腳有哪裡缺乏整體性的搭配，她就會渾身不舒服(uncomfortable)，正確答案為(D)。選項(A)(C)沒有被提到；而(B)是指說話者的穿著，而非她姐姐。

Answer 2 (A)

為什麼女孩的姐姐不讓她選自己喜歡的款式？

(A) 因為她覺得女孩不懂時尚。
(B) 因為她想把妹妹打扮得跟自己一樣。
(C) 因為她不希望女孩買T恤。
(D) 因為女孩希望能有個大改造。

解析

關鍵句在女孩提到姐姐不讓她選自己喜歡的款式，原因是姐姐覺得她「缺乏流行品味」(have no fashion sense)。選項(C)中，雖然女孩的姐姐不喜歡她穿樸素的T恤，但這並不直接牽涉本題，正確答案為(A)。

Answer 3 (C)

男性這一趟去購物為什麼會這麼累呢？

(A) 他女友讓他提十包購物袋。
(B) 他們起碼逛了三十家店。
(C) 他必須等他女友試穿很多衣服。
(D) 他不想去逛街。

解析

男性說他的「疲勞」(exhaustion)不是因為逛了大約三十家商店或要幫忙拿十幾個購物袋，而是因為要一直「等女朋友試穿不同的衣服」(try on all the different clothes)，正確答案為(C)。

Answer 4 (D)

男性的女友為什麼為她買的禮物感到開心？

(A) 因為花費不超過五千元。
(B) 因為她花的錢超過五千元。
(C) 因為她銀行存款超過五千元。
(D) 因為她省了至少五千元。

解析

男性的女朋友除了幫自己買衣服，還幫大部分的家人都先買了生日禮物。她認為預先買好這些禮物「至少幫她省了五千元」(a saving of over NT$5,000)，正確答案為(D)。

Answer 5 (B)

這次的拍賣會提供了多少折扣呢？

(A) 大多數商品最多打三折
(B) 大多數商品最少打七折
(C) 所有商品都打七折
(D) 買一送一

解析

男性在解釋女友預先買生日禮物至少幫她省了多少錢時，說她買的東西都「打了至少七折」(at least 30% off)，重點是「至少」有多少的折扣，所以正確答案為(B)。

中英文內容

短文 1

◎慢速MP3 08-09　　◎正常速MP3 08-10

My elder sister is a fashionista who knows most designer brands, the latest catwalk trends and all things fashion. She takes dressing up seriously and feels uncomfortable if she is not **styled coherently from head to toe**. Hence, she always rolls her eyes at me for just wearing a plain T-shirt and jeans. If we go shopping together, my sister makes it her responsibility to give me a complete makeover. She does not let me choose whatever I like because she thinks I **have no fashion sense**. I wish we could be more balanced when it comes to fashion and style.

　　我的姐姐是名時尚達人，她熟知大部分的設計師名牌、最新的伸展台流行趨勢，以及有關時尚的大小事。她很認真看待打扮這件事，如果她從頭到腳有哪裡缺乏整體性的打扮，她就會渾身不舒服，這也是為什麼我樸素T恤與牛仔褲的穿搭會讓她猛翻白眼。我們出門逛街的時候，我姐姐會把改造我的穿著視為她的責任，她不會讓我選我喜歡的款式，因為她覺得我缺乏流行品味。說到流行趨勢這回事，我還真希望我們兩個可以平衡一點。

短文 2

◎慢速MP3 08-11　　◎正常速MP3 08-12

It is tiring to go shopping with my girlfriend during a major sale. The sheer amount of walking around and fighting through the mad crowd is just unbelievable! My **exhaustion** didn't come from the physical exercise of going around to about thirty different stores and carrying about ten bags, but from **waiting for my girlfriend to try on all the different clothes**! She sure took full advantage of the sale. In addition to clothes, she also bought birthday presents for her family. She reckoned that she made **a saving of over NT$5,000** by purchasing them during the sale since the items were **at least 30% off** the original price. However, I'm not sure if she will still be so proud when she receives the credit card bill!

　　陪女朋友在大拍賣的時候去購物簡直累死人，光是走的路和爭先恐後的人潮就讓人不敢恭維！我的疲勞感並非來自於在三十幾家店穿梭來回或幫忙提十幾個購物袋，而是來自於要一直等我女朋友試穿各式各樣的衣服！她可真是充分把握這次打折的機會，不僅買了衣服，還幫家人買了生日禮物。她認為在這次的打折活動中買好禮物至少幫她省了五千元，因為買的商品都至少打七折。但我不確定等信用卡帳單寄來的時候，她還能不能這麼得意！

Unit 4 流行趨勢 The Fashion

📖 日常生活　🎤 娛樂活動　💬 意見交流　🏳 特殊場合

短對話聽力實戰

🎧 MP3 09-01

下面將播放五組短對話，請仔細聆聽，再依對話內容答題。

Question 1

Why is the woman excited about the fashion show?

(A) She can see the latest collection from the designer.

(B) She can see the model she likes in person.

(C) It is rare for her to attend a fashion show.

(D) She can talk to the model she likes.

Question 2

What is the man looking forward to?

(A) The prize draw for a shopping discount

(B) The prize draw for the after-party VIP pass

(C) The prize draw for some free clothes

(D) The ticket to attend the fashion show

Question 3

Why hasn't the woman written her report yet?

(A) She cannot focus on writing.

(B) She doesn't have enough to write about.

(C) She is still sorting out the information she has collected.

(D) She doesn't know what to write.

Question 4

What does the woman say the program is about?

(A) Fashion model wannabes competing for a modeling contract

(B) A competition for fashion design students

(C) A competition for amateurs to become fashion designers

(D) A competition for professional designers

Question 5

What advice does the woman give the man?

(A) Do not try to hit the target for sales

(B) Ask for a free T-shirt

(C) Do not count on reaching his sales target

(D) Do not believe what their manager promised him

答案與解析 ~answer

Answer 1 ◀)) (B)

女性為什麼對時裝秀感到如此興奮呢？

(A) 她能看到設計師的最新系列。

(B) 她能看到她喜愛的模特兒。

(C) 她很少參加時裝秀。

(D) 她能與喜愛的模特兒交談。

解析

女性一開始就說她很興奮，說「終於可以見到她喜愛的模特兒」(my favorite model)。男性後面雖然提到設計師的作品，但那是他原本以為女性開心的原因，因此正確答案為(B)。

Answer 2 ◀)) (A)

男性在期待的活動是什麼？

(A) 購物優惠的抽獎活動

(B) 秀後貴賓入場券的抽獎活動

(C) 免費衣服的抽獎活動

(D) 取得看時裝秀的票

解析

這對男女已經看完時裝秀，正在討論接下來的活動，所以請剔除(D)選項。男性最後說他很期待抽獎活動，因為贏得頭獎的話，他便能享有「最愛品牌全年八折的購物優惠」(關鍵字為discount)，正確答案為(A)。

Answer 3 ◀)) (C)

女性為何尚未寫她的報告呢？

(A) 她無法專心寫報告。

(B) 她沒有足夠的資訊寫報告。

(C) 她還在整理蒐集到的資料。

(D) 她不知道要寫什麼內容。

解析

女性在回答自己尚未完成報告後，說她「還在整理資料」(still processing all the information)，正確答案為(C)。這裡的process與sort out同義，皆為「整理」的意思。

Answer 4 ◀)) (C)

根據女性所說，該電視節目的內容是什麼？

(A) 想成為模特兒的人為了合約而彼此競爭

(B) 關於設計科學生們的競賽

(C) 讓業餘愛好者成為時尚設計師的比賽

(D) 給職業設計師參加的比賽

解析

女性說明節目是有關懷有「時尚設計師夢想的人」(wannabe fashion designers)彼此競爭，以爭取「成為專業設計師」，正確答案為(C)。amateur是「業餘愛好者」的意思。

Answer 5 ◀)) (D)

女性給了男性什麼建議呢？

(A) 不要達成預期營業額的目標

(B) 要求一件免費的T恤

(C) 不要依靠他所達成的營業額

(D) 不要相信他們經理的承諾

解析

當男性說他期待經理承諾給他的獎金時，女生回覆「如果是我，就不會抱希望」，並說明她的親身經驗，因此最佳答案為(D)。(此處的count on與believe同義；that則表示「經理的承諾」。)

⊙慢速MP3 09-02　　◎正常速MP3 09-03

💬短對話 ① *Conversation*

Erica: I'm so excited to see this fashion show. I can finally **see my favorite model**.
艾瑞卡：能參加這場時裝秀真令人興奮，我終於可以見到我最愛的模特兒了。
Dean: I thought you were here to see the latest collection from the designer.
狄恩： 我還以為你是來看這個設計師的新系列呢。

💬短對話 ② *Conversation*

Will: That was a brilliant fashion show! The collection was perfect.
威爾： 這場時裝秀實在太棒了！這季的系列設計很完美。
Lily: What's better is that we have a VIP pass to the after-party!
莉莉： 更好的是我們還有秀後派對的貴賓入場券！
Will: I'm looking forward to **the prize draw**. I hope I get the top prize, which is a 20% **discount** for my favorite brand for the whole year!
威爾： 我最期待的是抽獎活動。真希望能贏得頭獎，可以享有我最愛品牌全年八折的購物優惠呢！

💬短對話 ③ *Conversation*

Ned: Have you finished the report on the fashion trend analysis?
奈德： 妳時尚趨勢分析的報告完成了嗎？
Anna: Not yet. I'm **still processing all the information** from the catwalks I watched.
安娜： 還沒，我還在整理時裝秀的觀後資料呢。

💬短對話 ④ *Conversation*

Brian: What are you watching?
布萊恩：你在看什麼節目啊？
Gina: It is a program about **the wannabe fashion designers** competing against each other for **the chance to become a professional**.
吉娜： 一個讓懷有設計師夢想的人彼此競賽，以爭取成為專業設計師的節目。

💬短對話 ⑤ *Conversation*

Joey: I'm looking forward to that bonus the manager promised me for reaching the expected sales.
喬伊： 真期待經理上次承諾過的，達到預期營業額就要發的獎金。
Amy: I **wouldn't count on that**. Last time, I got a free T-shirt for the "bonus" he promised me.
愛咪： 我就不會抱希望，上次他也答應給我「獎金」，結果我只拿到免費T恤。

長 對 話 聽 力 實 戰

⊚ MP3 09-04

請仔細聆聽下面的長對話，再依對話內容選擇正確答案。

Question ❶

What does the man say he is going to do to the GPS?

(A) Install it in his car
(B) Remove it from his car
(C) Take it back to the shop
(D) Install updates on the GPS

Question ❷

Based on the dialogue, where did the GPS lead the man to?

(A) A field in a rural place
(B) A campsite field
(C) A country road
(D) The hotel he reserved

Question ❸

What did the man do after the car battery ran out of power?

(A) Ended the trip early and went home
(B) Asked for a passerby's help
(C) Asked for help from a roadside service company
(D) Tried to change the battery by himself

Question ❹

In the woman's opinion, what does the man's experience tell us?

(A) We should not trust technology.
(B) We should always rely on ourselves.
(C) We can do anything with technology.
(D) We depend on technology too much sometimes.

Question ❺

According to the man, what he will definitely do next time?

(A) Write his homework before he goes out
(B) Prepare for his route before the departure
(C) Use a new navigation system
(D) Ask people for directions

答案與解析 ～answer

Answer 1 (B)
對話中的男子說他會怎樣處理GPS呢？
(A) 在他車上安裝GPS
(B) 拆掉車上的GPS
(C) 把GPS退回商店
(D) 更新GPS的系統

> **解析**
> 對話一開始，男子就生氣地說他絕對要把他車上的GPS給「拆掉」(uninstall)，如果沒有聽清楚否定的字首un，也可以從後續的對談得知男子的GPS造成他的麻煩，因此不可能與(A)(D)的install有關，正確答案為(B)。

Answer 2 (A)
根據對話，男子的GPS最後引導他到哪裡？
(A) 鄉下地區的某個田野中
(B) 一個露營區
(C) 鄉間小路上
(D) 男子預約的旅館

> **解析**
> 男子提到GPS將他們導到一個「鳥不生蛋的田野中」(a field in the middle of nowhere)，正確答案為(A)。the middle of nowhere形容「鳥不生蛋；荒郊野外」，並非字面上在某處中央的意思。

Answer 3 (C)
在車輛的電池沒電後，男子做了什麼？
(A) 結束旅程，帶大家回家
(B) 請路邊的行人幫忙
(C) 請道路救援的公司幫忙
(D) 試著自己換電池

> **解析**
> 提到車子電池(battery)的問題時，男子說他「叫道路救援」(call the roadside service)，單從對話內容，我們無法得知他是否有結束假期、請路人幫忙，或是自己試著換電池，最佳答案為(C)。

Answer 4 (D)
就女性看來，男子的經驗給了我們什麼啟示呢？
(A) 我們不應該相信科技。
(B) 我們只能依靠自己的能力。
(C) 運用科技，什麼都能達成。
(D) 我們有時候太過依賴科技。

> **解析**
> 女性說我們有時「太過依賴科技」(over-rely on technology)，over加在動詞前有「過度」之意；對話最後，女性提到可以使用Google地圖，因此可剔除(A)(B)這種完全否定科技的選項，正確答案為(D)。

Answer 5 (B)
根據男子的應對，可得知他下次絕對會做的事為何？
(A) 出門前寫完他的作業
(B) 在出門前準備好路線的資訊
(C) 使用新的導航系統
(D) 詢問他人該怎麼走

> **解析**
> 聽完女性給的建議，男性回說這是好主意，他下次絕對會「做好功課」(do my homework)，這裡的做功課不同於一般的「寫作業」，帶有「準備」之意，正確答案為(B)。

 中英文內容

⊙ 慢速MP3 09-05　　◎ 正常速MP3 09-06

Bill: I'm definitely going to **uninstall** the GPS in my car.
比爾： 我絕對要把我車上的GPS拆了。

Tina: Why? What happened?
蒂娜： 為什麼？發生什麼事了嗎？

Bill: I took my family on a trip, and the GPS directed us to **a field in the middle of nowhere**.
比爾： 我開車帶全家人去旅遊，結果GPS把我們導到一個鳥不生蛋的田野中。

Tina: I hear that happens quite a lot, especially in rural or rugged areas.
蒂娜： 我聽説這好像滿常發生的，尤其是在鄉下或路線崎嶇的地方。

Bill: The worst part is, the car battery then died on us, so I had to **call a roadside service**. We waited at least for three hours before the guy found us!
比爾： 最糟的是，車子的電池沒電，所以我只能叫道路救援，結果至少等了三個小時，那個人才找到我們！

Tina: That does sound like a nightmare.
蒂娜： 那聽起來真像場噩夢。

Bill: I thought technology was meant to make life more convenient, not the opposite.
比爾： 我以為科技應該要讓生活更便利，而不是恰巧相反。

Tina: I guess your experience tells us we sometimes **over-rely on technology**.
蒂娜： 我覺得你的經驗説明我們有時候太過依賴科技了。

Bill: True. Maybe I should keep a map in the car from now on.
比爾： 沒錯，或許我從現在開始應該放一份地圖在車上。

Tina: You can **check Google Maps in advance** and print a hardcopy with you.
蒂娜： 你可以先查好Google地圖，再列印出來帶在身上。

Bill: That sounds great. I'll definitely **do my homework** in advance next time.
比爾： 聽起來是個好主意，我下次絕對會事先做好功課。

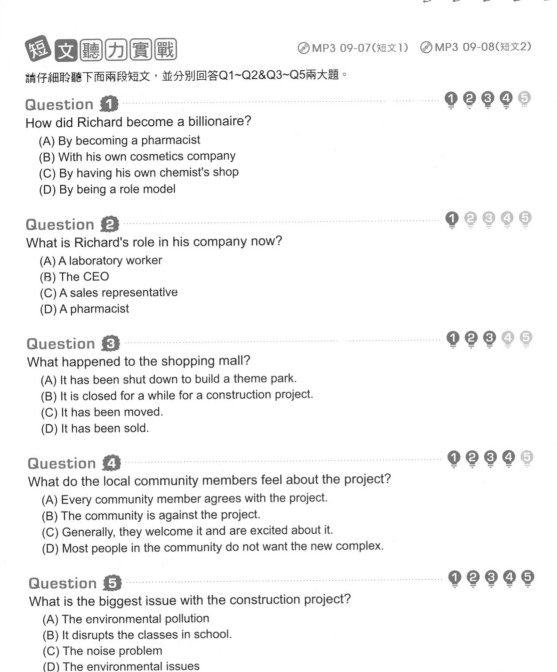

短文聽力實戰

MP3 09-07(短文1)　MP3 09-08(短文2)

請仔細聆聽下面兩段短文，並分別回答Q1~Q2&Q3~Q5兩大題。

Question 1

How did Richard become a billionaire?

(A) By becoming a pharmacist

(B) With his own cosmetics company

(C) By having his own chemist's shop

(D) By being a role model

Question 2

What is Richard's role in his company now?

(A) A laboratory worker

(B) The CEO

(C) A sales representative

(D) A pharmacist

Question 3

What happened to the shopping mall?

(A) It has been shut down to build a theme park.

(B) It is closed for a while for a construction project.

(C) It has been moved.

(D) It has been sold.

Question 4

What do the local community members feel about the project?

(A) Every community member agrees with the project.

(B) The community is against the project.

(C) Generally, they welcome it and are excited about it.

(D) Most people in the community do not want the new complex.

Question 5

What is the biggest issue with the construction project?

(A) The environmental pollution

(B) It disrupts the classes in school.

(C) The noise problem

(D) The environmental issues

答案與解析 ～answer

Answer 1 ◀)) (B)
理查是如何成為一位億萬富翁的呢？

(A) 成為一名藥劑師
(B) 創立他自己的化妝品公司
(C) 開設一間藥房
(D) 成為眾人學習的榜樣

解析
文章一開始就提到理查是個「有億萬身價、白手起家的事業家」，之後開始解釋他的歷程，注意選項(A)(C)都是經歷中的一部份，但説到財富的累積，就來自於他「一手創辦的化妝品公司」，正確答案為(B)。

Answer 2 ◀)) (B)
現在理查在公司的身分為何呢？

(A) 實驗室的工作人員
(B) 執行長
(C) 銷售員
(D) 藥劑師

解析
解題的線索在題目中，首先，題目使用現在式動詞is；問題最後也強調「現在」(now)，因此，雖然文章提到理查一開始要負責很多工作，包括(A)(C)，但現在他只需專心於「公司執行長」(CEO of his company)的角色，因此選(B)。

Answer 3 ◀)) (B)
購物中心發生了什麼事呢？

(A) 因為要蓋主題公園，所以被關閉。
(B) 正因一項開發計畫而暫停營業。
(C) 購物中心的地點遷到別處了。
(D) 購物中心被賣掉了。

解析
文中一開始就説明購物中心目前「暫停營業」(been temporarily closed)，這是為了配合一項「開發工程」(a construction project)，預計將它擴建轉型，正確答案為(B)。

Answer 4 ◀)) (C)
社區居民對這項開發計畫的態度為何？

(A) 每一位社區的居民都贊成這項計畫。
(B) 社區反對這項計畫。
(C) 整體而言，居民是歡迎且感到興奮的。
(D) 社區大部分的人都不想要新的綜合型設施。

解析
因為開發工程能帶動該市的經濟，所以這項計畫「基本上是受到社區住戶的熱烈歡迎」，正確答案為(C)。如果沒有聽到關鍵字overall(總的)，可以從學校對噪音的抱怨看出有部分居民不贊同，所以不能選(A)。

Answer 5 ◀)) (D)
工程計畫所帶來的問題中，「最嚴重」的為何？

(A) 環境汙染
(B) 打擾學校課程。
(C) 噪音問題
(D) 環境議題

解析
文中提到兩項問題，首先是鄰近學校抱怨工程的噪音，但又接著説「與環境問題比起來，這只是暫時性的小問題」，因此要選擇與「環境」有關的內容。其中(A)指汙染(水源、空氣…等)，但文章提到的是水土保持，最佳答案為(D)。

◎慢速MP3 09-09　　◎正常速MP3 09-10

Richard is a successful self-made billionaire entrepreneur. He started off as a pharmacist. He even owned a chemist's shop at one point, but **made his fortune** with **the cosmetics company he established later**. He had a humble beginning where he had to play multiple roles, including pitching sales as well as doing laboratory work. As his business is steady now, he only needs to **focus on the role as the CEO** of his company. His brand has many loyal customers all over the world. His success story has even been written about in some textbooks. Many people look up to him as their role model.

理查是個有億萬身價、白手起家的成功事業家。他一開始的工作是藥劑師，他有一段時間還開了間藥房，但他的財富主要來自於他之後一手創辦的化妝品公司。他在創業期間起步微小，一個人必須負責許多工作，包括推銷商品和實驗室的工作，現在他的公司發展穩定，所以他只需要專心於公司執行長的角色就好。他的品牌在世界各地都有許多忠實的消費者，他的創業故事甚至成為教科書的教材，許多人都將他視為學習的榜樣。

◎慢速MP3 09-11　　◎正常速MP3 09-12

The largest shopping mall in our city suburb has **been temporarily closed for a construction project**. The government planned to transform it into a super complex with the shopping center, hotels and a theme park in the same place. The project has been met with **overall enthusiasm in the community** because of its good economic prospects. However, since the construction began, some problems have become apparent. Schools nearby have complained that the noise of the construction disrupts their classes. This is **a small and temporary issue compared with the environmental issues**, though. There are reports saying that the excavation will lead to serious soil erosion in the area.

位於本市郊區最大的購物商場目前暫停營業，政府的開發工程計畫將此購物商場轉型成一個超大型的綜合設施，裡面包含購物中心、飯店和主題公園。因為預期這項計畫將能帶動本市的經濟，所以社區住戶都熱烈歡迎。但是，自從開始施工後，有些問題逐漸浮上檯面，鄰近學校抱怨工程的噪音妨礙上課，與環境問題相比，這還只是暫時性的小問題。根據報導指出，土地的開挖將造成嚴重的水土流失。

PART 2 流行與逛街

Unit 5 科技電子 Technology

日常生活　娛樂活動　意見交流　特殊場合

MP3 10-01

下面將播放五組短對話，請仔細聆聽，再依對話內容答題。

Question 1

What does the girl want to buy?

(A) The previous iPhone
(B) The iPhone which will be available soon
(C) The new iPad
(D) The latest laptop

Question 2

What disadvantage does the man say technology has?

(A) It is hard for him to check emails at work.
(B) People always force him to read emails.
(C) He can't switch off his computer and phone.
(D) He thinks about work even after office hours.

Question 3

What is the woman complaining about?

(A) She is not allowed to play on her phone.
(B) The man doesn't pay attention to his work.
(C) The man doesn't devote enough attention to her.
(D) The man should make technology a higher priority.

Question 4

Why does the woman say the man is like "a little boy at a toy shop"?

(A) Because he wants to buy a lot of things he sees.
(B) Because he puts his hands on everything.
(C) Because he wants to buy toys.
(D) Because he wants to take advantage of the deals.

Question 5

What does the boy say the girl shouldn't do?

(A) Stop him from playing games
(B) Generalize her image of game players
(C) Play video games with him
(D) Be devoted to video games

答案與解析 ~answer

Answer 1 (B)

對話中的女生想要購買什麼呢？

(A) 舊型的iPhone

(B) 將要上市的新iPhone

(C) 新的iPad

(D) 最新款的筆記型電腦

> **解析**
>
> 女生一開始就提到Apple宣布「最新的 iPhone」(latest iPhone)準備要開售了，而她「很想預購」(really want to preorder it)，正確答案為(B)。

Answer 2 (D)

就男子而言，科技的發展有什麼缺點呢？

(A) 他很難在工作的時候確認電子郵件。

(B) 人們會強迫他看信件內容。

(C) 他不能關電腦和手機。

(D) 他連下班時間都會想著工作。

> **解析**
>
> 男子說科技的「缺點」(downside)是，就算下班後也很難讓自己「關機休息」。這裡的switch off並非字面上「關掉某物開關」的意思，而是讓自己的腦袋休息(像電腦關機般)，正確答案為(D)。

Answer 3 (C)

女性在抱怨什麼呢？

(A) 她不能玩手機。

(B) 男子沒有專心工作。

(C) 男子沒有花足夠的時間注意她。

(D) 男子應該要更重視科技產品。

> **解析**
>
> 女性一開始就提議在約會時關機，可見她對手機不滿，之後又繼續解釋男子現在都「不注意聽她在說什麼」(don't pay enough attention to what I say)，因此正確答案為(C)。

Answer 4 (A)

為什麼女性會覺得男子像「到玩具店的小男孩」呢？

(A) 因為他看到很多東西都想買。

(B) 因為他看到產品就要碰一下。

(C) 因為他想要買玩具。

(D) 因為他想要善用展場的優惠。

> **解析**
>
> 關鍵片語get one's hands on sth.表示「某人得到某物」之意，其中everything 為誇大的形容，不一定代表所有東西，正確答案為(A)。

Answer 5 (B)

男生說女孩不應該怎麼樣？

(A) 阻止他玩遊戲

(B) 對遊戲玩家產生刻板印象

(C) 和他一起玩電動遊戲

(D) 把時間都貢獻給電動遊戲

> **解析**
>
> 當女孩形容男生們像群「呆頭呆腦的宅男」(geeks)時，男生說她不該對他們有這種「刻板印象」(stereotype)，正確答案為(B)。

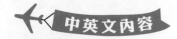

⊙慢速MP3 10-02　　⊙正常速MP3 10-03

短對話 ❶ *Conversation*

Lucy: Apple just announced the launch of **their latest iPhone. I really want to preorder it.**

露西： Apple剛剛宣布最新的iPhone準備要開售了，真想預購。

James: What?! I thought you just ordered the new iPad.

詹姆士：什麼？！我記得你不是才訂了新的iPad嗎？

短對話 ❷ *Conversation*

Rita: You are always on the phone. You need to draw the line somewhere and not let work get in the way of your private life.

芮塔： 你老是在看手機耶。你得有個限度，別讓工作干擾到你的私人生活。

Elmo: The downside of technology is that I **find it hard to switch off even after work.**

艾莫： 科技的一項缺點是，就算下班也很難讓自己關機休息。

短對話 ❸ *Conversation*

Linda: Don't you think we need to turn off our phones when we are on our date?

琳達： 你不覺得我們約會的時候應該關機嗎？

David: I don't think so. Why?

大衛： 我不認為需要，為什麼這麼説？

Linda: Because you **don't pay enough attention to what I say** anymore!

琳達： 因為你現在都不注意聽我在説什麼了！

短對話 ❹ *Conversation*

Alan: I love the computer expo. There are so many different technological products all in the same place.

亞倫： 我愛死電腦展了，在一個展場裡就有各式各樣的科技產品。

Carol: You are just like **a little boy at a toy shop**, wanting to **get your hands on everything** you see.

卡蘿： 你就像個到了玩具店的小男孩，看到什麼都想要。

短對話 ❺ *Conversation*

Fanny: Are you playing video games again? You guys are such **geeks!**

芬妮： 你們又在玩電動嗎？真是群呆頭呆腦的宅男耶！

Neil: You **shouldn't stereotype us.** We actually have a life outside of the game world!

尼爾： 你不該有這種刻板印象，我們的生活可不只有電動遊戲呢！

長對話聽力實戰

⊚MP3 10-04

請仔細聆聽下面的長對話，再依對話內容選擇正確答案。

Question 1
01 02 03 04 05

How did the girl get a smartphone?

(A) She won it in a competition.
(B) She asked her dad to buy her one.
(C) It's a reward for her good marks on her test.
(D) Her father gave it to her for her birthday.

Question 2
01 02 03 04 05

What does the boy think of smartphones as a reward?

(A) He thinks it's a bit too extravagant.
(B) He thinks it's a perfect reward.
(C) He thinks the reward is too small.
(D) He thinks it's a reward most kids want.

Question 3
01 02 03 04 05

How did the boy's mom respond to his request for a smartphone?

(A) She said she would think about it.
(B) She refused it straight away.
(C) She is still considering it.
(D) She said nothing.

Question 4
01 02 03 04 05

What could the consequence be if the boy gets a smartphone?

(A) He will skip classes.
(B) He will distract his friends.
(C) He will not perform well on his test.
(D) He will not focus on his homework.

Question 5
01 02 03 04 05

What does the girl suggest the boy do after hearing his mom's reaction?

(A) Ask his mom for a different present
(B) Tell his mom how good a smartphone is
(C) Force his mom to change her mind
(D) Tell his mom the same reason her dad mentioned

答案與解析 ~answer

Answer 1 ◀)) (C)
女孩是如何取得智慧型手機的呢？
- (A) 她從競賽中贏得的。
- (B) 她要求父親買給她的。
- (C) 是她考試表現良好的獎勵。
- (D) 她父親在她生日時送她的。

解析
女孩說明是因為自己「在期中考的表現很好」(did really well in my midterm exam)，所以父親才願意買智慧型手機給她，正確答案為(C)。注意女孩並沒有自己要求這個獎勵，所以不能選(B)。

Answer 2 ◀)) (A)
對於送智慧型手機當作獎勵，男孩是怎麼想的？
- (A) 他覺得那有點太奢侈了。
- (B) 他覺得那是個很棒的獎勵。
- (C) 他覺得那個獎勵太小了。
- (D) 他覺得那是大部分小孩都想要的獎勵。

解析
當女孩解釋她因為在期中考的表現很好，所以父親買智慧型手機給她，男孩的回應為a slightly excessive reward。excessive是「過多的」意思，表示男孩認為因為考試送手機太奢侈，所以選(A)。

Answer 3 ◀)) (B)
對於男孩想要智慧型手機的要求，他媽媽如何回應？
- (A) 她說會考慮看看。
- (B) 她立刻拒絕他的要求。
- (C) 她還在考慮這件事。
- (D) 她什麼話都沒說。

解析
根據對話內容，可得知男孩問過母親可否買智慧型手機給他，但she wouldn't even think about it，說她連考慮都不考慮，也就是直接拒絕要求之意，正確答案為(B)。

Answer 4 ◀)) (D)
買智慧型手機可能會給男孩帶來什麼影響？
- (A) 他會翹課。
- (B) 他會干擾到朋友。
- (C) 他在考試上的表現會變差。
- (D) 他不會專心做功課。

解析
男孩的母親之所以不買智慧型手機給他，是因為「他會分心，不好好做功課」，distract sb. from表示「讓某人分心」。注意必須選擇最貼近對話內容的選項(關鍵字：homework/distract)，正確答案為(D)。

Answer 5 ◀)) (D)
在聽到男孩母親的反應後，女孩給的建議為何？
- (A) 要求他母親送他不同的禮物
- (B) 告訴他母親智慧型手機有多好用
- (C) 強迫他母親改變心意
- (D) 將女孩父親提到的原因轉述給他母親聽

解析
女孩建議男孩「引述她爸說的話」(quote what my dad said)，看看他母親會不會改變心意，因此選(D)。注意雖然內容提到「看看他母親是否會改變心意」，但並沒有要男孩如(C)選項說的那般強迫他母親。

中英文內容

Lia: You won't believe it. My dad is buying me a smartphone!
莉亞：你不會相信的，我爸爸要送我智慧型手機！

Mark: How come? Didn't he say that a traditional phone is enough for you?
馬克：為什麼？他不是說傳統型電話就夠你用了嗎？

Lia: Well, I **did really well on my midterm exam**.
莉亞：我在期中考的表現很好。

Mark: Isn't that **a slightly excessive reward**? I mean, we have tests like that many times a year!
馬克：這個獎勵會不會有點太超過啊？我的意思是，類似的考試我們一年有好幾次耶！

Lia: He said if I have a smartphone, he can make video calls to me wherever I am. I guess he thinks it's a good way to check on my safety.
莉亞：他說如果我有智慧型手機，那不管我身在何處，他都可以跟我視訊，我猜他覺得這樣是個確認我是否平安的好方法。

Mark: I asked my mother for one, but she **wouldn't even think about it**.
馬克：我問我媽媽能不能買一台智慧型手機給我，但她根本不予考慮。

Lia: Why not?
莉亞：為什麼？

Mark: She said it'll **distract me from my homework**.
馬克：她說智慧型手機會讓我分心，不好好做功課。

Lia: Maybe you could **quote what my dad said**, and see if she will change her mind.
莉亞：也許你可以引述我爸的話，看你媽媽會不會改變心意。

Mark: But seriously, what she worries about is very likely to happen.
馬克：不過，說真的，她擔心的事非常有可能會發生。

短文聽力實戰

◎MP3 10-07(短文1)　◎MP3 10-08(短文2)

請仔細聆聽下面兩段短文，並分別回答Q1~Q2&Q3~Q5兩大題。

Question 1

What do some people find have greater value than digital things?

   (A) Traditional music

   (B) Digital books

   (C) Traditional devices and methods

   (D) Digital mixers

Question 2

Why do some DJs insist on using vinyl for mixing music?

   (A) They are easier to mix.

   (B) Digital music can't offer certain sound qualities that vinyl can.

   (C) Digital music is too cheap for them.

   (D) Digital music isn't traditional enough.

Question 3

How did the girl feel when she went to the computer expo?

   (A) She was not impressed.

   (B) She was amazed.

   (C) She was reluctant.

   (D) She was lost.

Question 4

Why didn't the girl want to go to the computer expo at first?

   (A) She didn't want to queue at a fair.

   (B) She didn't see anything she likes at the expo.

   (C) She had already bought her laptop.

   (D) She had already decided to make the purchase somewhere else.

Question 5

How did the girl get a cheaper laptop?

   (A) Trevor used his tips.

   (B) They went to another expo.

   (C) She negotiated a lot on price.

   (D) They went back to the department store's shop.

答案與解析 ～answer

Answer 1 (C)
和數位產品相比，有些人認為什麼具備更高的價值？

(A) 傳統音樂

(B) 電子書

(C) 傳統裝置與方法

(D) 數位混音器

解析
本題的關鍵句在文章後面，從despite(儘管)開始，可以推知後面將與前半部肯定數位生活的內容不同。本句提到「儘管數位裝置提供了便利性與優點，有些人還是認為「傳統媒材」(traditional mediums)較好，正確答案為(C)。

Answer 2 (B)
為什麼部分DJ會堅持用黑膠唱片來做混音呢？

(A) 黑膠唱片比較容易混音。

(B) 數位音樂無法提供像黑膠唱片那樣的音質。

(C) 數位音樂對那些DJ來說太便宜了。

(D) 數位音樂不夠傳統。

解析
文中最後舉例部分DJ堅持用黑膠唱片來做混音，其原因在黑膠唱片所具備的「溫暖音質」("warm" sound)無可取代，正確答案為提到音質(sound qualities)的(B)選項。

Answer 3 (B)
女孩對電腦展有什麼樣的感想呢？

(A) 她並沒有特別印象深刻。

(B) 她感到驚訝不已。

(C) 她感到很不情願。

(D) 她感到困惑不已。

解析
女孩提到會場的人山人海、秀場正妹，和充斥著電子產品的攤位讓她「驚嘆不已」(overwhelmed)，最接近的答案為選項(B)。注意選項(C)是女孩一開始(at first)的想法。

Answer 4 (D)
女孩一開始為什麼不想去電腦展呢？

(A) 她不想在展覽中排隊。

(B) 在電腦展中，她沒有看到喜歡的產品。

(C) 她在去之前已經買了筆記型電腦。

(D) 她打算在別的地方買筆記型電腦。

解析
女孩在At first,...的句子中，提到她一開始「不太情願」(reluctant)的原因，是因為她早就已經「鎖定」(have my eyes set on)要買的筆電，正確答案為(D)。注意(C)選項是指去展覽前就已經買好電腦，不符合文義。

Answer 5 (C)
女孩是如何取得更便宜的價格的呢？

(A) 崔維採用了他的訣竅。

(B) 他們去了別的展覽會。

(C) 她花了很多時間議價。

(D) 她們回去那間百貨公司的店家。

解析
文章最後，女孩說「經過激烈的殺價後」(after some hard bargaining)，她買到非常便宜的電腦，正確答案為(C)。bargain當動詞有「殺價；議價」之意，當名詞則特別指「便宜的好康」。

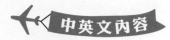中英文內容

短文 1

◉慢速MP3 10-09 ◉正常速MP3 10-10

We are in the midst of the digital era, where every part of our everyday life has been changed by technology. We seem to do everything digitally now. We use digital electronic devices, read digital books, take digital photos, and listen to digital music. Soon, the coming generation will not even know what vinyl records and tapes are. Despite the convenience and advantages of digital devices, some people find much greater value in **traditional mediums**. For instance, some DJs insist on using vinyl for mixing because they believe **vinyl's "warm" sound is irreplaceable**.

我們處於數位時代的洪流中，我們生活的每個細節都深受科技影響。現在，似乎所有事情都能數位化；我們使用數位電子產品、閱讀電子書、拍攝數位相片，也聽數位音樂。很快地，下個世代就不知道什麼是黑膠唱片和錄音帶了。儘管數位裝置提供了便利性與許多優點，有些人還是認為傳統媒材具備更高的價值。舉例來說，部分DJ堅信黑膠唱片溫暖的音質無可取代，所以堅持用它來做混音。

短文 2

◉慢速MP3 10-11 ◉正常速MP3 10-12

It was the first time I had gone to a computer expo. All the people, showgirls and different booths full of electronic products **overwhelmed me**. I was looking for a notebook, and my friend Trevor suggested I go to the expo to have a look. At first, I was reluctant because I had done my research and **already had my eyes set on** a notebook in a department store's shop. However, Trevor said I would be a fool not to shop around and compare prices in an expo. I must say he was right. He gave me a lot of good tips, and after **some hard bargaining** at the booths, I managed to get a model better than my original target for an even cheaper price, along with some free accessories!

這是我第一次去電腦展。會場的人山人海、秀場正妹，和充斥著電腦產品的攤位都讓我驚嘆不已。我打算買筆電，所以我的朋友崔維建議我去電腦展看看。一開始我不太情願，因為我早就做好功課，已經在百貨公司的店面鎖定我要買的筆電了。但是，崔維說我如果不去電腦展比價，就太不明智了。我必須承認他是對的。他給了我很多好建議，經過激烈的殺價後，我最後用更便宜的價格買到比我之前鎖定的筆電還要高階的型號，還拿到免費的周邊配件呢！

PART 3

運動與休閒

活動身體、娛樂放鬆，提升身心健康，
熱門話題不可少！

Unit 1 健身保養 Be Healthy

 日常生活 娛樂活動 意見交流 特殊場合

短對話聽力實戰

 MP3 11-01

下面將播放五組短對話，請仔細聆聽，再依對話內容答題。

Question 1

What's the advantage if the woman gets a gym membership?

(A) It will help her lose weight.

(B) It will help her get an instructor.

(C) It will encourage her to do more exercise.

(D) It will help her save money.

Question 2

What does the man want to offer the woman?

(A) A free lesson from an instructor

(B) An orientation on different lessons at the gym

(C) An aerobic dance lesson

(D) A mandatory session on how to use the facilities

Question 3

Why does the man enjoy the martial art lesson?

(A) He can use the steam room after working out.

(B) He learns useful techniques to protect himself.

(C) He gets to fight and exercise at the same time.

(D) He feels excited when fighting with others.

Question 4

What can the man get if he wins the kickboxing competition?

(A) A gym membership for half a year

(B) Some free instructional lessons for six months

(C) The prize money

(D) A formal title

Question 5

Why does the boy enjoy Wii so much?

(A) There are many different of sports games to play.

(B) The sports games make him exercise.

(C) His family doesn't get bored with it.

(D) It's boring to do real exercise.

答案與解析 ～answer

Answer 1 (C)
女性加入健身房會員後有什麼好處？
- (A) 能幫助她減重。
- (B) 能幫她找到一位專業教練。
- (C) 能鼓勵她持續做運動。
- (D) 能幫她省錢。

解析
女性一開始就提到自己不想花太多錢在健身房的會籍上，此時男子回覆健身房或許不便宜(剔除(D)選項)，但加入「能激勵她運動」(關鍵字為motivation)，正確答案為(C)。

Answer 2 (D)
男性想提供給女性什麼樣的服務呢？
- (A) 一堂免費的教練指導課程
- (B) 介紹健身房裡的多樣化課程
- (C) 一堂有氧舞蹈的課程
- (D) 介紹該如何使用設施

解析
女性提到自己不確定是否要上付費課程(I'm not sure...)，此時男教練回覆他先「講解設施該如何使用」(orientation 適應；熟悉情況)，關鍵字為facility(設施)，正確答案為(D)。

Answer 3 (B)
對話中的男性為什麼喜歡上武術課？
- (A) 他在運動完之後能使用蒸氣室。
- (B) 他會學到防身技巧。
- (C) 他在上課時能同時打架和運動。
- (D) 和人打架讓他感到很興奮。

解析
對話最後，男性提到他很喜歡武術課(enjoy it)，因為能學到「實用的防身技巧」(practical self-defense techniques)，關鍵字self-defense表示「自衛」，正確答案為(B)。

Answer 4 (A)
如果男性贏得自由搏擊比賽的話，他能得到什麼？
- (A) 半年的健身房會員資格
- (B) 六個月內的一些免費健身課程
- (C) 獎金
- (D) 一個正式的頭銜

解析
解題關鍵在對話最後，男性提到冠軍雖然沒有正式的贏家頭銜或獎金，但可以另外取得「六個月的健身房會員資格」(another six months of gym membership)，會員資格與(B)的免費課程並不相同，正確答案為(A)。

Answer 5 (A)
男孩為什麼那麼喜歡玩Wii呢？
- (A) 那上面有很多種類的運動遊戲可玩。
- (B) 玩運動遊戲可以運動。
- (C) 他的家人都還沒玩膩。
- (D) 真的去運動很無聊。

解析
當女孩問一直用Wii運動是否會無聊時，男孩的回覆是「它的運動遊戲種類很多」(The variety of sports games is massive)，符合選項(A)的敘述。注意選項(C)是(A)的結果，要弄清楚因果關係。

PART 3
運動與休閒

短對話 ❶ Conversation

Sally: I don't want to spend too much on a gym membership.

莎莉： 我不想花太多錢在健身房的會籍上。

Andy: It may not be cheap, but joining one will definitely **help with your motivation**.

安迪： 健身房或許是不便宜，但加入的話絕對能激勵你運動。

短對話 ❷ Conversation

Danny: Welcome to our gym. I'm the instructor here.

丹尼： 歡迎來到我們的健身房，我是這裡的教練。

Teresa: Hello, but **I'm not sure if I want to take any paid sessions** yet.

泰瑞莎：哈囉，但我還不確定我想要上付費的課程。

Danny: That's fine. I will just give you **an orientation** on the facilities.

丹尼： 沒關係，那我先講解這裡的設施該如何使用。

短對話 ❸ Conversation

Rick: I enjoy relaxing in a steam room after the martial art lesson.

瑞克： 我喜歡在上完武術課後進蒸氣室放鬆。

Anna: Martial art lesson? It sounds dangerous.

安娜： 武術課？聽起來好危險。

Rick: Not at all. It's an instructed lesson. I enjoy it because you learn some practical **self-defense techniques**.

瑞克： 完全不危險。有教練指導，我很喜歡，因為能學到實用的防身技巧。

短對話 ❹ Conversation

Mandy: You're already good enough for a kickboxing competition?

曼蒂： 你已經厲害到可以參加自由搏擊比賽啦？

Jeff: It's only an informal friendly game, no serious title or prize. However, the winner can get **another six months of gym membership**.

傑夫： 這只是非正式的友誼賽，沒有正式的頭銜或獎金。但贏家能另外得到六個月的健身房會員資格。

短對話 ❺ Conversation

Molly: Isn't it a bit boring to do exercise on Wii?

莫莉： 在Wii上運動不會無聊嗎？

Glenn: Not at all. The **variety** of sports games is **massive**. No one in my family has gotten bored with it yet.

葛蘭： 完全不會，它的運動遊戲種類很多，我家人都還沒玩膩呢。

長對話聽力實戰

請仔細聆聽下面的長對話,再依對話內容選擇正確答案。

Question ①

① ② ③ ④ ⑤

Why doesn't the man want to play tennis at first?

(A) He needs to stay in.
(B) He is feeling the heat inside.
(C) He's worried about getting heat stroke.
(D) He doesn't know how to play tennis.

Question ②

① ② ③ ④ ⑤

Where are the woman and her friend going to play tennis?

(A) On an indoor court
(B) On an outdoor court
(C) At the park
(D) On a school's court

Question ③

① ② ③ ④ ⑤

What does the man want to do after having his lunch?

(A) To take an afternoon nap
(B) To ask the woman out
(C) To go to bed early tonight
(D) To take some tennis lessons first

Question ④

① ② ③ ④ ⑤

What is the woman fed up with?

(A) The man is overweight.
(B) The man is "all talk and no action".
(C) The man doesn't want to play on an outdoor court.
(D) The man can't play tennis with her friend.

Question ⑤

① ② ③ ④ ⑤

What request does the man make after he agrees to go with the woman?

(A) To play a formal match with him
(B) To make tennis fun for him
(C) Don't be too easy on him
(D) Don't play against him too seriously

答案與解析 ~answer

Answer 1 (C)

男性為什麼一開始不想去打網球呢？

(A) 他必須待在家裡。

(B) 他感受到室內的熱氣。

(C) 他擔心外出會中暑。

(D) 他不知道怎麼打網球。

解析

面對女性的邀約，男性提到室外(outside)的熱度，因此可剔除選項(B)，接著提到他「寧願待在室內，也不想中暑」，使用rather than的句型，重點在than後面，可得知男性很在意中暑，答案選(C)。

Answer 2 (A)

女性和她朋友打算去哪裡打網球呢？

(A) 室內網球場

(B) 戶外網球場

(C) 公園內

(D) 學校的網球場

解析

女性提到她們要去「運動中心裡的網球場」(a court inside the sports center)，如果沒有聽清楚這句，後面女性也有提到「不須要擔心太陽的問題」，可以推測出是不用曬太陽的場地，因此選(A)。

Answer 3 (A)

男性在吃完午餐後想做什麼？

(A) 睡個午覺

(B) 邀女子出門

(C) 今天晚上早點睡

(D) 先去上幾堂網球課

解析

男性提到自己才剛吃完午餐，想要先去「小睡一下」(take a siesta)。關鍵字為siesta，原為西班牙文，指「午後小睡」，與一般晚間上床睡覺的意思不同，正確答案為(A)。

Answer 4 (B)

對話中的女性受夠了什麼事情？

(A) 男性的體重過重。

(B) 男性「光說不練」的個性。

(C) 男性不想在戶外球場打球。

(D) 男性無法和她朋友打網球。

解析

題目中的fed up為「受夠」之意。在對話中，女性提到自己受夠男子老是抱怨自己的身材，卻又不採取任何行動(complaining about your weight, but not taking any actions)，就是「光說不練」的意思，因此選(B)。

Answer 5 (D)

在男性決定要一起去打網球後，他要求了什麼？

(A) 來場正式的比賽

(B) 讓網球有趣一點

(C) 不要對他手下留情

(D) 和他對打別太認真

解析

對話最後，男性請女性「對他手下留情」，符合選項(D)的敘述。be easy on sb.就是對某人「手下留情」的意思。注意(C)因為有Don't的否定，意思為「不要手下留情」，因此不能選。

Kathy: I'm going to play tennis with my friend. Do you want to join us?
凱西：　我要和朋友去打網球，你想加入嗎？

Jason: No, thanks. Don't you feel the heat outside? I'd rather stay in than get **heat stroke**.
傑森：　不，謝了，你難道沒感受到室外的熱氣嗎？我寧可待在室內，也不想中暑。

Kathy: Actually, we're going to play on a court **inside the sports center**, so you don't need to worry about the sun.
凱西：　其實，我們打算去運動中心裡的網球場，所以你不用擔心太陽的問題。

Jason: But I've just had lunch. I will need a **siesta**.
傑森：　但是我才剛吃完午餐，我得先小睡一下。

Kathy: Don't be so lazy! I'm fed up with you complaining about your weight, but **not taking any actions**.
凱西：　別那麼懶！我受夠了你老是抱怨自己太胖，但又不採取行動。

Jason: Alright. I will go. Don't be so mad.
傑森：　好啦，我去，別那麼生氣。

Kathy: Now you're talking.
凱西：　這還差不多。

Jason: But please **go easy on me**. I'm an absolute beginner in tennis.
傑森：　但拜託對我手下留情，對於網球，我可是完全的門外漢。

Kathy: Don't you worry. My friend is a tennis coach. She can teach you.
凱西：　別擔心，我朋友是網球教練，她可以教你。

Jason: Brilliant! A young professional will teach me. Now I'm really motivated!
傑森：　太好了！一個年輕的專家要教我，現在我可是衝勁十足呢！

短文聽力實戰

MP3 11-07(短文1)　　MP3 11-08(短文2)

請仔細聆聽下面兩段短文，並分別回答Q1~Q2&Q3~Q5兩大題。

Question 1

What did the woman find out while visiting her friend's place last month?

- (A) Her friend gave her a morning call.
- (B) She realized she had to start exercising.
- (C) She started to go to the gym.
- (D) Her friend told her to lose weight.

Question 2

What did the woman's friend suggest she do?

- (A) Do a little exercise once in a while
- (B) Do a lot of exercise every day
- (C) Do a small amount of exercise frequently
- (D) Always exercise a lot after dinner

Question 3

Why did the man start to go to the gym less?

- (A) The gym was too expensive.
- (B) The gym couldn't retain his interest.
- (C) His friends often asked him to join hiking trips.
- (D) He didn't pay for the membership.

Question 4

What happened after the man's first hiking trip?

- (A) He found himself addicted to hiking.
- (B) He found the trip boring.
- (C) He started a career in hiking straight away.
- (D) He decided to take his friends on hiking trips.

Question 5

Why did the man decide to make a career out of hiking?

- (A) His friend invited him to be his partner.
- (B) He didn't want to go to the gym anymore.
- (C) He discovered he is good at it and passionate about it.
- (D) He earned a lot out of being a hiking tour guide.

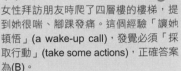

答案與解析 ～answer

Answer 1 🔊 (B)

女性上個月拜訪朋友的時候，意識到什麼事情？

(A) 她的朋友早上打電話叫她起床。

(B) 她必須開始運動了。

(C) 她開始上健身房。

(D) 她的朋友告誡她必須減肥。

> **解析**
>
> 女性拜訪朋友時爬了四層樓的樓梯，提到她很喘、腳踝發痛。這個經驗「讓她頓悟」(a wake-up call)，發覺必須「採取行動」(take some actions)，正確答案為(B)。

Answer 2 🔊 (C)

女性的朋友建議她怎麼做？

(A) 偶爾做少量運動

(B) 每天做大量運動

(C) 規律地做少量運動

(D) 總是在晚餐後做大量運動

> **解析**
>
> 解題的關鍵字為女性提到朋友的建議時所說的「少量定時」(little but regular)，意指少量但規律的運動型態。至於晚餐後去散步是女性自己的決定，和朋友的建議無關，正確答案為(C)。

Answer 3 🔊 (B)

男性為何越來越少去健身房了呢？

(A) 因為健身房太貴了。

(B) 因為健身房無法讓他保有興趣。

(C) 因為他朋友經常邀他去登山健行。

(D) 因為他沒有繳健身房的會費。

> **解析**
>
> 男性以前會去健身房，去的次數之所以快速減少，是因為「新鮮感很快就消失」，關鍵片語wear off表示「漸退；消失」，常和novelty(新鮮感)或是interest(興趣)等單字一起使用，正確答案為(B)。

Answer 4 🔊 (A)

參加了第一次的登山後，男性感到如何？

(A) 他發現自己愛上了登山活動。

(B) 他覺得那次的登山健行很無趣。

(C) 他立刻創辦他的登山事業。

(D) 他決定帶領朋友登山。

> **解析**
>
> 男性的第一個登山活動是由朋友邀請參加，要注意他在言談間給予的的肯定評價，所以選項(B)不正確；至於登山事業則是後來漸漸發展出來的，因此(C)選項有誤，(D)選項也不是他初次登山後就決定的事，最佳答案為(A)。

Answer 5 🔊 (C)

是什麼讓男性決定要創辦登山事業的呢？

(A) 他的朋友邀他成為事業合夥人。

(B) 他不想再去健身房了。

(C) 他發現自己擅長這件事，也對其充滿熱誠。

(D) 他做登山領隊賺很多錢。

> **解析**
>
> 在愛上登山活動後，男性說自己變的越來越「專業」(professional)，因此朋友開始請他帶團。接下來又提到他因為實在是「太享受登山」，才決定「讓它成為職業」(make a career out of it)，正確答案為(C)。

中英文內容

短文 1
　⊙慢速MP3 11-09　　◎正常速MP3 11-10

　　I never really took much notice of my weight problem until last month, when I had to walk up four flights of stairs to my friend's apartment. By the time I got to his place, I found myself panting and my ankles hurting a lot. This was **a wake-up call** for me, and I **realized** I had to **take some action**. Since I tend to finish work after eight at night, I thought I didn't have time to really do exercise. However, my friend told me if I did **a little but regular exercise**, it would help a lot. Therefore, instead of watching TV after dinner, I go for a 30-minute walk now. Through this new habit, my weight has dropped quite a lot during the past few weeks.

　　我一直都不覺得自己的體重是個問題，直到上個月，爬了四層樓的樓梯到朋友的公寓，我才意識到這個問題。抵達他家的時候，我發現自己喘得很厲害，腳踝也很痛。這個經驗讓我頓悟，發現自己非得採取行動才行。因為我幾乎都是晚上八點過後才下班，所以我覺得自己沒時間做什麼正式的運動，但我的朋友告訴我，如果我做少量定時的運動，對身體也很有幫助。所以，現在晚餐過後，我選擇不看電視，而是出去散步三十分鐘，藉由這樣的習慣改變，過去幾週內，我的體重已經掉了很多。

短文 2
　⊙慢速MP3 11-11　　◎正常速MP3 11-12

　　My career in hiking began unintentionally. I used to go to the gym and tried all kinds of equipment and activities offered. However, my gym visits soon got less and less frequent because **the novelty wore off** quickly. One day, my friend asked me to join a hiking trip. After I tried it, I found it much more interesting exploring nature than doing repetitive exercises in a gym. I found myself **hooked** after the first trip, and soon I was hiking around the country nearly every month. I became rather **professional** at it, so my friends started to ask me to take hikers on trips. Eventually, I decided to **make a career out of it since I enjoy it so much**.

　　我的登山事業是無意間發展出來的。我以前會去健身房運動，嘗試裡面各種不同的器材和課程，但隨著新鮮感的消失，我去健身房的次數很快就開始減少。有一天，我的朋友邀我參加登山活動，去了之後發現探索大自然比在健身房裡做重複性的運動有趣多了。第一次的登山結束後，我就愛上這項活動了，幾乎每個月都在全國各處登山。因為對登山變得越來越了解，所以朋友開始請我帶領隊友登山，因為實在很享受登山，所以我最後決定讓它成為我的職業。

Unit 2 水上活動 Play In Water

🖵 日常生活　🎤 娛樂活動　✏ 意見交流　🏳 特殊場合

短對話聽力實戰

◉ MP3 12-01

下面將播放五組短對話，請仔細聆聽，再依對話內容答題。

Question ❶

What kind of class is the woman taking?

(A) Water aerobics
(B) Swimming
(C) Normal aerobics
(D) She is not taking any classes.

Question ❷

What is the man's opinion of his training?

(A) It's a piece of cake for him.
(B) He needs to study more than he anticipated.
(C) It is much more difficult than he expected.
(D) He is not confident enough.

Question ❸

What does the man ask the woman to show him?

(A) Her warm-up routine
(B) Her weight loss exercise
(C) Her swimming technique
(D) Her daily routine

Question ❹

What is the current weather like in the conversation?

(A) Hot and raining hard
(B) It's raining a little.
(C) Hot, stuffy, but not raining
(D) It's hot and stuffy after the rain.

Question ❺

What does the girl mention is a shame?

(A) That Danny can't finish his dissertation.
(B) That Danny doesn't want to go on vacation.
(C) That Danny is writing his dissertation while on vacation.
(D) That Danny can't go on vacation with them.

答案與解析 ～answer

Answer 1 ◀⑴ (A)
對話中的女性在上什麼樣的課程？

(A) 水上有氧課
(B) 游泳課
(C) 普通有氧課
(D) 她沒有上任何課程。

解析

女性一開始就說她很喜歡上社區泳池的「水上有氧課」(the water aerobics class)，關鍵字為aerobics(有氧體操)，另外可以從後面的swimming pool得知與水上活動有關，正確答案為(A)。

Answer 2 ◀⑴ (B)
男性對訓練的內容有什麼樣的看法？

(A) 對他來說簡單的不得了。
(B) 他必須研讀的內容比預期的多。
(C) 比他預期中的還要困難。
(D) 他不夠有自信。

解析

解題關鍵在男性最後提到「需要唸的東西比他預期的還多」(the amount of study is more than I expected)，這與選項(C)所說「比他預期中的還要難」不同，正確答案應為(B)。

Answer 3 ◀⑴ (A)
對話中的男性叫女性教他什麼？

(A) 她固定的暖身操
(B) 她減肥的運動
(C) 她的游泳技巧
(D) 她每天固定的日程

解析

女性警告男性下水前必須「暖好身」(be warmed up)，接著提到自己有套固定的「簡單暖身操」(a simple routine)。這裡的routine指「一套固定的動作」，正確答案為(A)。

Answer 4 ◀⑴ (C)
根據對話內容，目前的天氣狀況怎麼樣？

(A) 很熱且正在下大雨
(B) 正在下毛毛雨。
(C) 很熱、很悶，但沒有下雨
(D) 下雨過後又熱又悶的天氣。

解析

男性一開始就在抱怨「悶熱的天氣」(stuffy weather)讓他感到煩躁，此時女性提到氣象預報，要男性等下雨，表示目前還沒有下雨，由此可知正確答案為(C)。

Answer 5 ◀⑴ (D)
對話中的女生覺得什麼事情很可惜？

(A) 丹尼無法順利完成論文內容。
(B) 丹尼不想去渡假。
(C) 丹尼在渡假的期間寫論文。
(D) 丹尼無法和大家一起去渡假。

解析

對話一開始就聽到關鍵句It's a shame that...，後面接的內容正是女生感到可惜之處，也就是丹尼無法和他們一起去渡假的事情，因為他必須趕論文。在此請勿選擇包含丹尼意願的選項(因為我們並不清楚他想不想去)，正確答案為(D)。

⊙慢速MP3 12-02　　◎正常速MP3 12-03

💬短對話 ❶ *Conversation*

Elle: I'm enjoying **the water aerobics class** at the community swimming pool.
艾兒： 我很喜歡上社區泳池的水上有氧課。
Mike: How's it going? I'm considering taking my daughter there.
麥克： 課程怎麼樣？我在考慮帶我的女兒去呢！

💬短對話 ❷ *Conversation*

Ethan: I'm training to become a lifeguard now.
伊森： 我現在正在接受成為救生員的訓練。
Gina: Is it difficult to become one?
吉娜： 要成為救生員很難嗎？
Ethan: The amount of study **is more than I expected**. I have to study lifeguarding and also emergency medical techniques.
伊森： 需要唸的東西比我預期的還多，我必須學習救生和緊急醫療的技巧。

💬短對話 ❸ *Conversation*

Mel: It's too hot! I can't wait to jump into the pool to swim.
梅爾： 實在太熱了！我等不及要跳進泳池裡游泳了。
Ruth: Make sure you **are warmed up**. I have a simple **routine** to prepare myself before I go into the pool.
露絲： 你一定要先暖好身，我下水之前都會做一套簡單的暖身操。
Mel: Cool! You can show me.
梅爾： 太好了！那你可以教我。

💬短對話 ❹ *Conversation*

Leo: The **stuffy** weather is annoying. I **sweat** before I even step out of the house.
里歐： 悶熱的天氣太惱人了，還沒踏出門，我就開始流汗了。
Jenny: Give it another hour or so. The forecast said it'll rain this afternoon.
珍妮： 再等一個小時左右吧，天氣預報說今天下午會下雨。
Leo: I hope so. It will be much cooler after it rains.
里歐： 我也希望，下完雨後就會涼爽多了。

💬短對話 ❺ *Conversation*

Vicky: It's a shame that Danny **can't go on the vacation with us**.
薇琪： 真可惜丹尼無法跟我們一起去渡假。
Darren: Yeah. He needs to finish his dissertation next month.
戴倫： 是啊，他下個月必須完成他的論文。

長對話聽力實戰

⊚MP3 12-04

請仔細聆聽下面的長對話，再依對話內容選擇正確答案。

Question 1

① ② ③ ④ ⑤

Based on the dialogue, what's the woman surprised about?

(A) Her friend didn't tell others they are playing beach volleyball.
(B) Other girls are wearing bikinis to play beach volleyball.
(C) She is the only girl playing beach volleyball today.
(D) They are playing sports on the beach.

Question 2

① ② ③ ④ ⑤

What does the woman find wrong with other girls' bikinis?

(A) They are wearing something not suitable for playing volleyball.
(B) They are wearing something not suitable for the beach.
(C) They are wearing something too small for them.
(D) What they are wearing is not practical for swimming.

Question 3

① ② ③ ④ ⑤

According to the man, what do most people do at the beach?

(A) To get a tan
(B) To sunbathe and flaunt their figures
(C) To play beach volleyball
(D) To get a nicer figure

Question 4

① ② ③ ④ ⑤

Why doesn't the woman need to attract guys' attention?

(A) Because she is not wearing a bikini.
(B) Because the man knows many guys like her.
(C) Because she already has a boyfriend.
(D) Because she is very attractive.

Question 5

① ② ③ ④ ⑤

Why does the woman think she should stop nagging?

(A) She is nagging the man's mother.
(B) The man's mother doesn't like her nagging.
(C) Her mom asked her to stop nagging.
(D) Her behavior is making her appear like a nagging mother.

答案與解析 ~answer

Answer 1 🔊 (B)
根據對話的內容，女性對什麼事情感到驚訝呢？

(A) 她的朋友沒有告訴其他人要打沙灘排球。

(B) 其他女孩穿比基尼來打沙灘排球。

(C) 她是唯一打沙灘排球的女生。

(D) 他們要在海灘上運動。

解析
女性一開始的My goodness(我的天啊)表示她對接下來的事情感到驚訝。她問男生是不是沒有通知其他人要打「沙灘排球」(beach volleyball)，因為其他女生都穿了「布料少到不行的比基尼」(tiny bikinis)，最接近的答案為(B)。

Answer 2 🔊 (A)
女性覺得其他女孩穿的比基尼有什麼問題？

(A) 她們穿的不適合打球。

(B) 她們的服裝不適合來海邊玩。

(C) 她們的衣服尺寸太小了。

(D) 她們的服裝不適合游泳。

解析
雖然男生有告知其他人要打海灘排球，但女性還是感到不可思議，因為她覺得其他女生穿的比基尼，根本不適合打球(not practical for playing volleyball)，正確答案為(A)。

Answer 3 🔊 (B)
根據男生的話，大部分的人來海邊要幹嘛呢？

(A) 享受日光浴

(B) 享受日光浴並炫耀身材

(C) 打沙灘排球

(D) 讓身材更好一點

解析
男生向女性解釋，大部分到海邊的人都是來「享受日光浴」(get a tan)和「炫耀身材」(show off their figures)的，與打球無關，最佳答案為(B)。注意和(A)相比，(B)的答案更完整，更符合談話內容。

Answer 4 🔊 (C)
女性為何不需要吸引男人的注意呢？

(A) 因為她沒有穿比基尼。

(B) 因為男生知道有很多男人喜歡她。

(C) 因為她已經有男朋友了。

(D) 因為她非常有魅力。

解析
當女性說她的穿著與其他人不同時，男生回應「她不需要吸引男人的注意」，因為她早就「死會了」，not available是「已婚或有男/女友」的口語用法，正確答案為(C)。

Answer 5 🔊 (D)
女性為何覺得自己不能再碎碎念下去了？

(A) 她叨念的對象是男生的母親。

(B) 男生的母親不喜歡她碎碎念。

(C) 女性的母親要求她停止叨念。

(D) 她這種行為很像愛碎碎念的老媽子。

解析
對話最後，女性說自己最好不要再碎碎念(nagging)，「聽起來活像個老媽子」(sound like a mom)。sound like是指「聽起來像」，所以跟任何人的母親都無關，正確答案為(D)。

⊙慢速MP3 12-05　　⊙正常速MP3 12-06

Janet: My goodness. Didn't you tell the girls we're **playing beach volleyball** today?
珍妮特：我的天啊，你沒有告訴其他女孩我們今天要打沙灘排球嗎？

Bruce: Sure I did.
布魯斯：當然有啊。

Janet: But look at the **tiny bikinis** they are wearing!
珍妮特：但是看看她們穿的比基尼，那布料也太少了！

Bruce: What's wrong with them?
布魯斯：那又有什麼不對？

Janet: They are **not practical for playing volleyball**, are they?
珍妮特：穿那樣不適合運動吧？

Bruce: Most people come to the beach to **get a tan** and **show off their figures**. Playing volleyball is just for fun.
布魯斯：大部分來海灘的人是來享受日光浴和炫耀身材的，打排球只是好玩。

Janet: Clearly, I'm the only one who's taking it seriously. I've got shorts and a T-shirt over my swimming suit.
珍妮特：看起來我是唯一想要認真運動的人，我還在泳裝外面穿了短褲和T恤。

Bruce: You don't need to attract guys' attention. You're **not available** anyway.
布魯斯：你又不須要吸引男人的注意，你都死會了。

Janet: Even if I was, I wouldn't expect to find my Mr. Right at the beach.
珍妮特：就算我還是單身，也不會期待在海邊找到我的夢中情人。

Bruce: You don't know that.
布魯斯：這你可不能斷言。

Janet: Anyway, I'd better stop nagging. I'm starting to **sound like a mom**.
珍妮特：算了，我最好不要再碎碎念了，聽起來活像個老媽子。

短文聽力實戰

MP3 12-07(短文1) MP3 12-08(短文2)

請仔細聆聽下面兩段短文，並分別回答Q1~Q2&Q3~Q5兩大題。

Question 1

Where is Niagara Falls situated?

(A) It's right between the States and Canada.
(B) It's in the United States.
(C) It is situated in Canada.
(D) It's in Ontario.

Question 2

What can honeymoon-goers receive when they visit Niagara Falls?

(A) An official honeymoon certificate
(B) The beautiful view
(C) A free boat tour
(D) A ticket to the wax museums

Question 3

What linguistic origins does The Taj Mahal come from?

(A) Persian
(B) Muslim
(C) Persian and Arabic
(D) Indian

Question 4

Where do The Taj Mahal visitors and tourists come from?

(A) Four corners of the country
(B) A small corner of the world
(C) Mainly from India
(D) All over the world

Question 5

Why did the emperor Shan Jahan order the Taj Mahal be built?

(A) To have the most beautiful architecture in the world
(B) In memory of his late wife
(C) To create a UNESCO World Heritage Site
(D) In memory of his wives

答案與解析 ~answer

Answer 1 ◀)) (A)
尼加拉瀑布的地理位置為何？
- (A) 它位於美國與加拿大的交界處。
- (B) 它位於美國境內。
- (C) 它位於加拿大境內。
- (D) 它位於加拿大的安大略省內。

解析
本文一開始就說尼加拉瀑布「位於美國和加拿大的交界處」(the border between the United States and Canada)，就內容而言，它既不在美國，也不屬於加拿大，正確答案為(A)。

Answer 2 ◀)) (A)
享受蜜月的夫妻造訪尼加拉瀑布時會拿到什麼？
- (A) 一張由官方發放的結婚證書
- (B) 美麗的景色
- (C) 免費搭船遊瀑布
- (D) 去蠟像館的門票

解析
解題關鍵在文章最後，提到尼加拉瀑布的旅遊局會發放「市長簽名的蜜月證書」(honeymoon certificates signed by the mayor)，因為有市長的簽名，所以具備官方性質，正確答案為(A)。

Answer 3 ◀)) (C)
泰姬瑪哈陵這個名稱的語言來源為何？
- (A) 波斯語
- (B) 伊斯蘭教
- (C) 波斯語和阿拉伯語
- (D) 印度語

解析
linguistic為「語言的」，origin則是「起源；由來」。本文一開始就說了泰姬瑪哈陵這個名稱的「語言來源」(originate from)為「波斯語和阿拉伯語」(Persian and Arabic)，正確答案為(C)。

Answer 4 ◀)) (D)
造訪泰姬瑪哈陵的遊客們都是從哪裡來的呢？
- (A) 國內各處的人們
- (B) 世界的某一處
- (C) 主要來自印度
- (D) 世界各地

解析
關鍵片語four corners of the earth代表「世界各個角落」，正確答案為(D)。注意選項(A)讓人混淆的地方在後面接的是「國內」(country)。

Answer 5 ◀)) (B)
沙賈汗皇帝為什麼下令建造泰姬瑪哈陵呢？
- (A) 為了擁有全世界最美的建築物
- (B) 為了紀念他過世的妻子
- (C) 為了成為聯合國教科文組織的世界遺產
- (D) 為了紀念他的妻子們

解析
沙賈汗因為他的愛妻逝世，傷心欲絕，才下令建造全世界最美的建築「來緬懷他的摯愛」(in the memory of his beloved)。全世界最美的建築是要求，而非原因，正確答案為(B)。

◉慢速MP3 12-09　◎正常速MP3 12-10

Niagara Falls is the collective name for three waterfalls located on the border **between the United States and Canada**. More specifically, it's between the province of Ontario and the state of New York. Countless tourists come here for the attraction this place offers, including wax museums and haunted houses. Of course, Niagara Falls will always be most popular. Due to its breathtaking view and huge popularity, Niagara Falls has earned its reputation as "The Honeymoon Capital of the World". Niagara Falls Tourism even gives out **honeymoon certificates** signed by the mayor.

尼加拉瀑布由三座瀑布組成，這些瀑布位於美國和加拿大的交界處，更詳細地說，是位於加拿大安大略省和美國紐約州的交界。無數的遊客會因此地的觀光景點而來，包括蠟像館和鬼屋。當然，最吸引人的景點還是尼加拉瀑布。由於瀑布的天然美景與響亮名聲，尼加拉瀑布贏得「世界蜜月首選」的美名，尼加拉瀑布的旅遊局甚至還會發放市長簽名的蜜月證書呢。

◉慢速MP3 12-11　◎正常速MP3 12-12

The Taj Mahal, with its name **originating from Persian and Arabic**, means "Crown of Palaces". It is one of the New Seven Wonders of the World and a UNESCO World Heritage Site. Every year, it attracts millions of tourists from **the four corners of the earth**. The Taj Mahal was voted as a New Wonder of the World for its grand and magnificent architecture, but many visitors are also drawn by the story of the eternal love behind it. The emperor Shah Jahan was so heartbroken because of the death of one of his wives -- Mumtaz Mahal. Therefore, he ordered the construction of the monument **in memory of his beloved**. It took 22 years and about 22,000 workers to construct this amazing architecture.

泰姬瑪哈陵的名稱源自波斯語和阿拉伯語，意思是「宮殿之王」。它是世界新七大奇景之一，同時被列為聯合國教科文組織的世界遺產。這個地方每年都吸引超過上百萬從世界各地來的遊客。泰姬瑪哈陵之所以被票選為新七大奇景之一，是因為它壯麗的建築，但也有很多遊客是被它背後至死不渝的愛情故事吸引而至。當時的皇帝沙賈汗因為他的愛妻蒙兀兒‧瑪哈的逝世傷心欲絕，因此下令建造紀念建築來緬懷他的摯愛，而這個令人驚豔的建築物共耗費了二十二年的時間和約兩萬兩千名工人才完成。

Unit 3 競技比賽 The Competition

 日常生活 娛樂活動 意見交流 特殊場合

短 對 話 聽 力 實 戰

⊙ MP3 13-01

下面將播放五組短對話，請仔細聆聽，再依對話內容答題。

Question 1

What kind of person can get the MVP award?

(A) The year's best performing player

(B) The main player of a team

(C) The retired player most people admire

(D) The first overall pick in the NBA

Question 2

How does the man feel when he uses the same product celebrities use?

(A) He feels he can also become famous.

(B) It makes him have the same lifestyle and success.

(C) He doesn't feel anything special.

(D) He feels he leads the same lifestyle and success.

Question 3

What is the man surprised about?

(A) That the woman got a scalped ticket.

(B) That the woman managed to buy a plane ticket to Brazil.

(C) That the woman managed to buy a World Cup ticket in Brazil.

(D) That the woman was interested in the World Cup.

Question 4

Why does the man prefer to attend a soccer game than watch it on TV?

(A) He enjoys the feeling of being with other fans at the game.

(B) He likes the heat while watching a game outside.

(C) He likes to buy beer at the game.

(D) He enjoys the luxury of beer and a sofa.

Question 5

Why are the boy and the girl lucky?

(A) They have paid an expensive price for the tickets.

(B) They have witnessed a great game.

(C) They have managed to get front row tickets.

(D) They have made it to the game.

答案與解析 ～answer

Answer 1 (A)

什麼樣的人能取得MVP的獎項？

(A) 整年裡表現最好的球員
(B) 隊伍裡的主力球員
(C) 大部分人景仰的退休球員
(D) NBA的選秀狀元

解析
男孩解釋MVP這個獎項會頒發給「每年表現最優秀的球員」(the best performing player of the year)，正確答案為(A)。關鍵字為perform，與「打球的表現」有關。

Answer 2 (D)

當男性使用與名人同款的產品時，感覺如何？

(A) 他感覺自己也會出名。
(B) 能讓他享有相同的生活方式與成功。
(C) 他沒什麼特別感覺。
(D) 他感覺自己擁有相似的生活方式與成就。

解析
男性提到和代言人用同款產品會讓人感覺「好像在分享他們的生活方式和成功」，正確答案為(D)。注意(B)選項並非男子的感覺，而是「實際上能讓他擁有相同的生活方式與成就」，所以不能選。

Answer 3 (C)

男性對什麼事感到驚訝？

(A) 女性買到黃牛票。
(B) 女性成功買到飛往巴西的機票。
(C) 女性成功買到在巴西舉辦的世足賽的門票。
(D) 女性竟然對世足賽有興趣。

解析
一聽到女性提到自己去巴西觀賞世足賽，男性立刻說他不敢相信她竟然「買到了票」(got a ticket)。這裡的票並非機票，而是世足賽的門票，因為他接下來還解釋球賽的熱門度導致出現黃牛票，正確答案為(C)。

Answer 4 (A)

和電視轉播相比，男性為何寧願去現場看球賽？

(A) 他喜歡和其他球迷一起看比賽的感覺。
(B) 他喜歡在室外看比賽的熱度。
(C) 他喜歡買啤酒在球場看比賽。
(D) 他享受坐在沙發喝啤酒的感覺。

解析
當女生問為什麼不在家一邊享受沙發和啤酒，一邊看著比賽，男性回答這樣的話就無法享受到「比賽的熱度和球迷的熱情」(the heat and passion)，正確答案選(A)。

Answer 5 (B)

對話中的男生和女生為什麼稱得上幸運呢？

(A) 他們付了錢買很貴的門票。
(B) 他們看了一場精采的球賽。
(C) 他們買到前排的座位。
(D) 他們趕上了比賽的時間。

解析
We are lucky to...後面的內容提到說話者們看到「競爭激烈、勢均力敵的球賽」，正確答案為(B)。雖然男生後面提到花的錢很值得，但這並非他們之所以「幸運」的原因，所以不能選(A)。

中英文內容

⊙慢速MP3 13-02　　⊙正常速MP3 13-03

💬短對話 ❶ *Conversation*

Mary: What does MVP mean? Is it a title of a basketball game?

瑪麗： MVP是什麼？是籃球比賽的名稱嗎？

Cody: It stands for Most Valuable Player. Only **the best performing player of the year** can get this.

寇迪： 這是「最有價值球員」的縮寫，整年當中表現最優秀的球員才能得到。

💬短對話 ❷ *Conversation*

Jenny: Does celebrity endorsement work for you?

珍妮： 名人代言這個行銷手法對你來說有用嗎？

Andy: Sure. By using the same product, I feel **I'm sharing their lifestyle and success**.

安迪： 當然有用，跟代言人用同款產品能讓我覺得在分享他們的生活方式和成功。

💬短對話 ❸ *Conversation*

Nelly: I went to Brazil to watch the FIFA World Cup this year!

奈莉： 我去了巴西觀看今年的世足賽！

Ryan: I can't believe you **got a ticket**! It was in such demand that there was a lot of ticket scalping.

萊恩： 我不敢相信你買到了票！球賽超熱門，有很多人在賣黃牛票呢。

💬短對話 ❹ *Conversation*

Chris: Let's go to a soccer match tonight.

克里斯：我們今晚去看場足球賽吧。

Kathy: Why don't we enjoy the game with the luxury of the sofa and beer at home?

凱西： 我們為什麼不在家看？還能坐在沙發上享用啤酒。

Chris: Because you won't **feel the heat and passion of being part of the crowd** by watching TV!

克里斯：因為看電視體會不到比賽的熱度與球迷的熱情啊！

💬短對話 ❺ *Conversation*

Anna: Wasn't that basketball game tense or what?

安娜： 剛剛那場籃球賽也太緊張刺激了，對吧？

Joey: Yeah. We were lucky to have watched such **a competitive and close game**. I think it was worth the price.

喬伊： 是啊，能看到競爭這麼激烈、勢均力敵的比賽，真夠幸運的，我覺得花的票錢很值得。

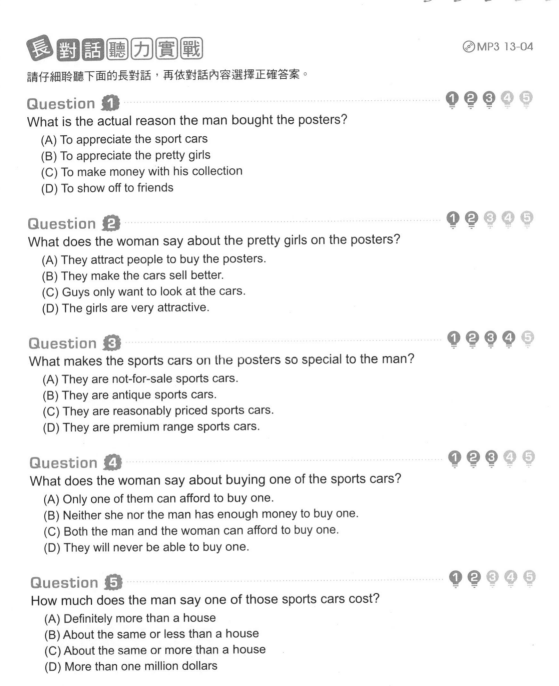

長對話聽力實戰

⊚ MP3 13-04

請仔細聆聽下面的長對話，再依對話內容選擇正確答案。

Question 1 ··· ① ② ③ ④ ⑤

What is the actual reason the man bought the posters?

(A) To appreciate the sport cars

(B) To appreciate the pretty girls

(C) To make money with his collection

(D) To show off to friends

Question 2 ··· ① ② ③ ④ ⑤

What does the woman say about the pretty girls on the posters?

(A) They attract people to buy the posters.

(B) They make the cars sell better.

(C) Guys only want to look at the cars.

(D) The girls are very attractive.

Question 3 ··· ① ② ③ ④ ⑤

What makes the sports cars on the posters so special to the man?

(A) They are not-for-sale sports cars.

(B) They are antique sports cars.

(C) They are reasonably priced sports cars.

(D) They are premium range sports cars.

Question 4 ··· ① ② ③ ④ ⑤

What does the woman say about buying one of the sports cars?

(A) Only one of them can afford to buy one.

(B) Neither she nor the man has enough money to buy one.

(C) Both the man and the woman can afford to buy one.

(D) They will never be able to buy one.

Question 5 ··· ① ② ③ ④ ⑤

How much does the man say one of those sports cars cost?

(A) Definitely more than a house

(B) About the same or less than a house

(C) About the same or more than a house

(D) More than one million dollars

答案與解析 ～answer

Answer 1 (A)
男子買那些海報的真正原因為何？

(A) 為了欣賞海報中的跑車
(B) 為了欣賞海報裡的美女
(C) 為了賣掉之後賺錢
(D) 為了向朋友炫耀

解析
對話一開始，男子就向女性解釋他買這些海報是為了「欣賞車輛，而不是美女」，請注意rather than的句型，以本句來說，前面所描述的內容比後面提到的事項更讓男子欣賞，正確答案為(A)。

Answer 2 (A)
針對海報上的美女，女性說了什麼？

(A) 那些美女能吸引人買海報。
(B) 那些美女能提高車輛的銷售。
(C) 男性只會看海報中的車輛。
(D) 那些美女很有魅力。

解析
聽到男子說他買海報是為了欣賞車輛時，女性驚訝地說她以為美女才是這些海報的「賣點」(selling point)，正確答案為(A)。注意(D)或許是真的，但女性並沒有特別提到海報的美女們多有魅力，所以不適合選。

Answer 3 (D)
對男子來說，海報上的跑車之所以特別的原因為何？

(A) 它們是不販售的跑車。
(B) 它們是古董跑車。
(C) 這些跑車的價格很合理。
(D) 它們是頂級的跑車。

解析
當女性問到海報中的跑車哪裡特別時，男子提到它們都是「最頂級的跑車」(top-of-the-range)，一般在街上是看不到的，正確答案為(D)，選項中的premium為「高價的；優質的」之意。

Answer 4 (B)
對於買海報中跑車的事，女性說了什麼？

(A) 兩個人當中只有一人負擔得起。
(B) 兩人都買不起那種跑車。
(C) 兩個人各買得起一台跑車。
(D) 他們兩人永遠都買不起那種跑車。

解析
當男子解釋這些跑車究竟有多「頂級」後，女性說「聽起來不像是你我買得起的車子」(It doesn't sound like a car you or I can afford)，can afford在此指「金錢上負擔得起」，正確答案為(B)。

Answer 5 (C)
男子提到那些跑車時，說一輛要花多少錢呢？

(A) 絕對比買一棟房子還貴
(B) 大約一棟房子的價格，或者更便宜
(C) 大約一棟房子的價格，或者更貴
(D) 超過一百萬的價格

解析
男子最後說這些車「隨便一台的價格都跟一棟房子差不多，甚至更貴！」(cost as much, or more than a house!)，正確答案為(C)。注意(A)選項對於比一棟房子的花費高這件事非常肯定(沒有提到花費差不多)，因此不能選。

Helen: You have quite a few posters of cars with hot girls.
海倫：　你蒐集了不少跑車和性感美女的海報嘛。

Melvin: Contrary to what you might believe, I collect these posters to **appreciate the cars rather than the girls**.
梅文：　和你想的可能恰恰相反，我蒐集這些海報是為了欣賞車，而不是美女。

Helen: Really? I thought the pretty girls are **the selling point** of these posters.
海倫：　真的嗎？我以為美女才是這些海報的賣點。

Melvin: Well, yes. They certainly make guys want to bring the poster home. But those amazing cars are actually most important.
梅文：　我不否認，她們的確能讓男性升起買海報回去的想法，但實際上，那些驚人的車輛才是重點。

Helen: So what's so special about the sports cars?
海倫：　所以那些跑車有什麼特別？

Melvin: They are all **top-of-the-range** sports cars. You don't often see them on the street.
梅文：　這可都是最頂級的跑車，一般街上看不太到。

Helen: How so?
海倫：　怎麼說？

Melvin: These models have either been featured in movies or are very rare models.
梅文：　這些車款要不就是在電影裡出現過，要嘛就是非常稀有的款式。

Helen: It **doesn't sound** like a car **you or I can afford**.
海倫：　聽起來不像你我買得起的車子。

Melvin: Certainly not. Each of the cars **cost as much, or more than a house**!
梅文：　肯定買不起。隨便一台的價格都和一棟房子一樣，甚至比房子更貴！

短文聽力實戰

MP3 13-07(短文1)　 MP3 13-08(短文2)

請仔細聆聽下面兩段短文，並分別回答Q1~Q2&Q3~Q5兩大題。

Question 1

What kind of opportunity would this dance audition bring to the girl?

(A) To break into a dance company
(B) To start a career in the professional dance industry
(C) To get to know people in the dance industry
(D) To lead a dance company

Question 2

What kind of preparation is the girl doing for the audition?

(A) Following an easy schedule
(B) Writing a schedule
(C) Taking classes and losing weight
(D) Following strict training and diet plans

Question 3

What sport would British people have in mind when they hear "football"?

(A) Soccer
(B) Rugby
(C) American football
(D) A championship game

Question 4

In which game do the players wear more protective gear?

(A) Soccer
(B) Rugby
(C) American football
(D) Both rugby and American football

Question 5

In addition to being strong, what must football players also be?

(A) Solid
(B) Active
(C) Able
(D) Agile

答案與解析 ～answer

Answer 1 (B)

這場舞蹈徵選能帶給女孩什麼樣的機會呢？

(A) 闖舞蹈公司空門的機會

(B) 於職業舞蹈界發跡的機會

(C) 認識舞蹈界人們的機會

(D) 帶領一家舞蹈公司的機會

解析

女孩説自己很緊張之後，進一步解釋 This is my opportunity to...，説這是她「進入職業舞蹈界」的機會。break into 在此指「進入」，若在片語後面加地點，則有「闖入」之意，選項(A)帶有「闖空門」的涵義，正確答案為(B)。

Answer 2 (D)

為了徵選，女孩會做什麼樣的準備呢？

(A) 實施輕鬆的日程表

(B) 寫一份日程表

(C) 上課與減肥

(D) 遵循嚴格的訓練和飲食計畫

解析

解題關鍵在文章最後，女孩提到自己擬好「嚴格的訓練時間表」(rigorous training schedule)以及「飲食計畫」(diet plan)。注意diet plan是指控制飲食，不能跟減肥畫上等號，正確答案為(D)。

Answer 3 (A)

聽到「football」時，英國人想到的運動是什麼？

(A) 足球

(B) 英式橄欖球

(C) 美式足球

(D) 職業級冠軍賽

解析

本文一開始就在解釋某些英國人之所以會對football一詞感到困惑的原因，文章用美國人的定義去解釋，所以要聽清楚後面的解釋在説「對英國人而言，他們所想的會是美國人所説的soccer」，也就是足球，因此選(A)。

Answer 4 (C)

哪一種比賽的球員會穿比較多的保護裝備呢？

(A) 足球

(B) 英式橄欖球

(C) 美式足球

(D) 英式橄欖球和美式足球

解析

文中指出「英式橄欖球」(rugby)與「美式足球」類似；但美式足球員會穿較多的保護裝備。重點在the American football players wear more protective gear這一句，正確答案為(C)。

Answer 5 (D)

除了強健的體魄外，美式足球員還必須具備何種素質？

(A) 結實的

(B) 主動的

(C) 有能力的

(D) 靈敏的

解析

本題所問的是「球員」所具備的特質。文中最後提到美式足球員必須同時具備驚人的體魄與「靈敏」(agility)於一身，選項(D)的agile(靈敏的)即為agility的形容詞，因此選(D)。

中英文內容

短文 1

⊙慢速MP3 13-09　　◎正常速MP3 13-10

I am nervous because I have an important dance audition in a few weeks. This is my opportunity to **break into the professional dance industry**. The audition is for a position as a dancer for a contemporary dance company that is going to tour around the world. The panel of judges at the audition consists of several leading dancers of the company and some renowned choreographers. I am determined to show them my ability and drive. I have made **a rigorous training schedule** as well as **a diet plan**. I must stick to them for the audition.

　　我幾週後就要去參加一場重要的舞蹈甄選，這讓我感到很緊張。這是我進入職業舞蹈界的機會。這次的舞蹈甄選是由一個即將展開世界巡迴展的現代舞蹈團，為了選出舞者而舉辦的。甄選的評審包括幾名舞團的首席舞者和幾位知名的編舞家。我已經下定決心，要好好向評審展現我的能力與雄心壯志。我已經擬好一份嚴格的訓練時間表以及飲食計畫，為了這場徵選，我必須要好好地按計畫實行。

短文 2

⊙慢速MP3 13-11　　◎正常速MP3 13-12

It is a little confusing to some British people when they hear Americans saying "football". For them, the word "football" means what the Americans call "**soccer**". In the UK, the game "rugby" is similar to American football. However, **the American football** players **wear more protective gear**. To American people, American football is their real pastime. They love it because it is a sport that combines athleticism, strategy, and spectacle. Football players must have incredible strength as well as **agility**. In addition to the sport itself, the professional championship, the Super Bowl, is also famous for the half-time shows.

　　對部分英國人來說，聽到「美式足球」(football)一詞時，他們會感到有些混淆。因為football對英國人來說等同於「足球」，這在美國則被稱為soccer。在英國，「橄欖球」(rugby)跟「美式足球」類似，但美式足球的球員會穿較多的保護裝備。對美國人來說，美式足球是他們真正的國民娛樂，他們熱愛美式足球，因為那結合了體育、策略與表演於一體。美式足球員必須同時擁有驚人的體魄與靈敏度。除了運動本身，美式足球的職業級冠軍賽--「超級盃」的中場表演也是赫赫有名的。

Unit 4 影視娛樂 TV & Movies

日常生活　　娛樂活動　　意見交流　　特殊場合

短 對 話 聽 力 實 戰

◎ MP3 14-01

下面將播放五組短對話，請仔細聆聽，再依對話內容答題。

Question 1

What is the woman most looking forward to about the Oscars?

(A) The nominated movies
(B) The award ceremony
(C) The red carpet entrance
(D) The fashion show

Question 2

How does the boy describe the girl?

(A) Someone who likes to listen to music
(B) Someone who likes to watch TV
(C) Someone who likes to receive their entertainment value
(D) Someone who likes to make remarks about other people

Question 3

What is the man asking the woman to help him with?

(A) To get his girlfriend to visit the station at 4 o'clock
(B) To get his girlfriend to listen to the radio at 4 o'clock
(C) To get his girlfriend to tune her guitar at 4 o'clock
(D) To surprise his girlfriend around 4 o'clock

Question 4

Why did the woman refuse to go to the cinema tonight?

(A) Their dinner is running late.
(B) She is working tonight.
(C) The movie is being shown too late for her.
(D) There are better times available in another cinema.

Question 5

Why does the man like to watch this kind of movie?

(A) They are distressing.
(B) The woman likes that kind of movie.
(C) He can forget them straight away.
(D) They help him relax.

答案與解析 ~answer

Answer 1 (C)
女性對奧斯卡頒獎典禮最期待的部分是什麼？
- (A) 被提名的電影
- (B) 頒獎典禮
- (C) 明星走紅毯
- (D) 時裝秀

解析
女性提到她期待奧斯卡頒獎典禮，當男性以為她喜歡看被提名的電影有哪些時，她補充說明對於明星「走紅毯」(walk down the red carpet)的部分感到「最興奮」(most excited)，所以本題選(C)。

Answer 2 (D)
對話中的男孩是如何評論女孩的呢？
- (A) 喜歡聽音樂的人
- (B) 喜歡看電視的人
- (C) 喜歡得到娛樂價值的人
- (D) 喜歡評論他人的人

解析
女孩興奮地告訴朋友葛萊美獎頒獎典禮上的情景，男孩因此形容她「真八卦」(so gossipy)，gossip當動詞用有說閒言閒語之意，與此最為接近的是選項(D)。

Answer 3 (B)
男性請女子幫他什麼忙？
- (A) 安排他女友在四點時參觀電視台
- (B) 讓他女友在四點時收聽廣播
- (C) 讓他女友在四點時調吉他的音
- (D) 在四點左右給他女友個驚喜

解析
男性一開始就提到自己要打電話進廣播節目，藉此向女朋友求婚，因此請女子確保他女朋友四點左右會「收聽節目」(tune in)，因此選(B)。注意(D)選項的解釋為「要女性朋友給女友一個驚喜」，並非此對話的重點。

Answer 4 (C)
女性為何拒絕今晚去看電影的提議呢？
- (A) 他們的晚餐要遲到了。
- (B) 她今天晚上要上班。
- (C) 電影的播映時間對她來說太晚了。
- (D) 在別家電影院有更好的播映時間。

解析
女性在拒絕男子的提議時，提到本地的電影院今晚「只有晚場」(only has a late night showing)，而她「明早還要上班」(have work in the morning)，因此最佳答案為(C)。

Answer 5 (D)
男性為什麼喜歡他們觀賞的這類電影呢？
- (A) 因為這類電影令人煩惱。
- (B) 因為女子喜歡這類電影。
- (C) 因為這類電影讓人看了就忘。
- (D) 因為這類電影能幫助他放鬆。

解析
不同於女子的評論，男性提到他還滿享受看這種讓人可以笑一笑的電影，可以「放鬆心情」(unwind 使心情輕鬆)，正確答案為(D)。

 中英文內容

短對話 1 *Conversation*

Emma: I'm looking forward to watching the Oscars tonight.
艾瑪：　我很期待今晚的奧斯卡頒獎典禮。

Jason: So you are into the nominated movies.
傑森：　所以你對提名的電影有興趣啊。

Emma: Actually, I'm **most excited** to watch **the stars walking down the red carpet**. It's like a fashion show.
艾瑪：　其實，我對明星走紅毯的部分最興奮，那簡直就是個時尚秀。

短對話 2 *Conversation*

Karen: Did you see the Grammy Awards? There was a cat fight between two singers!
凱倫：　你有看葛萊美獎頒獎典禮嗎？有兩個歌手打起來耶！

Leon: You are so **gossipy**.
里昂：　你還真八卦。

短對話 3 *Conversation*

Julius: I'm going to call into a radio program to propose to my girlfriend.
朱理斯：我要打電話進廣播，向女朋友求婚。

Alice: That is so romantic!
愛麗斯：這實在太浪漫了！

Julius: Please help me and try to **get her to tune in** around 4 o'clock.
朱理斯：拜託幫我一下，讓她在四點左右收聽節目。

短對話 4 *Conversation*

Jeff: Would you like to go and see "Into the Storm" tonight?
傑夫：　你今晚想去看《直闖暴風圈》嗎？

Belle: But the local cinema only has a late night showing. I **have work in the morning**. Sorry, probably not tonight.
貝兒：　但是本地的電影院只有晚場耶，我明早還要上班，不好意思，今晚可能就不去了。

短對話 5 *Conversation*

Cindy: To be honest, I found the film we just saw a bit boring.
辛蒂：　老實說，我覺得我們剛剛看的電影有點無聊耶。

Stewart: I quite enjoyed it. You can simply laugh and relax. It's good for **unwinding**.
史都華：我還滿享受的，邊看邊笑，放鬆一下，可以讓心情輕鬆。

長對話聽力實戰

◎MP3 14-04

請仔細聆聽下面的長對話，再依對話內容選擇正確答案。

Question ❶

Why doesn't the woman like the man's suggestion of watching DVDs?

(A) She doesn't like to watch movies.

(B) She has stayed in to watch DVDs on most weekends.

(C) She wants to go out on weekends.

(D) She always goes to the cinema on weekends.

Question ❷

Why didn't the man go see "Ninja Turtles" with his friend?

(A) He didn't want to spend too much money on movies.

(B) He didn't want to see that movie.

(C) He was busy, so he didn't have time for it.

(D) He didn't want to see it with his friend.

Question ❸

What difference does popcorn make to the atmosphere?

(A) A bit of difference

(B) No difference

(C) A huge difference

(D) A negative difference

Question ❹

Why doesn't the woman want to make it more atmospheric?

(A) Her boyfriend would stop watching the movie.

(B) Her boyfriend would keep talking.

(C) Her boyfriend could get lost.

(D) Her boyfriend would focus on the movie plot too much.

Question ❺

Why does the woman want her boyfriend to go out more often?

(A) Otherwise, her friends will leave her.

(B) Otherwise, he will become a recluse.

(C) Otherwise, they will never go to the cinema again.

(D) Otherwise, she has to make popcorn.

答案與解析 ~answer

Answer 1 ◄))（B）
女性為什麼不喜歡男性看DVD的提議？

(A) 她不喜歡看電影。
(B) 她大部分的週末都待在家裡看DVD。
(C) 她週末想要出門。
(D) 她週末都會去電影院。

解析
當男性要求租DVD回來看時，女性回應的Again?!表驚訝語氣，帶有「又看DVD？！」的意思，接著説他們的「最近的週末都在看DVD」(all we seem to do on weekends)，綜合這些資訊，可推測出正確答案為(B)。

Answer 2 ◄))（A）
男性為什麼沒有和朋友一起去看《忍者龜》呢？

(A) 他不想在電影院上花太多錢。
(B) 他不想看那部電影。
(C) 他很忙，所以沒時間去看電影。
(D) 他不想和朋友一起去看那部電影。

解析
當女性問為何男性回絕朋友看《忍者龜》的邀約時，他提到「如果每部想看的電影都去電影院看，那有多花錢」(the fortune I'll spend at the cinema if...)，可知男性顧慮的是花費，正確答案為(A)。

Answer 3 ◄))（C）
爆米花對氣氛的影響有多大呢？

(A) 一點點不同
(B) 沒有任何不同
(C) 完全不同
(D) 不好的變化

解析
當男性請女性準備爆米花和啤酒時，説爆米花makes a world of difference。a world of於此處的作用為「強調程度」，表示非常不同，正確答案為(C)。

Answer 4 ◄))（D）
女性為何不想要讓看電影的氣氛變得更好呢？

(A) 她男友會中斷電影。
(B) 她男友會一直講話。
(C) 她男友會迷路。
(D) 她男友會太沉迷於電影情節中。

解析
可從女性I don't know if...開頭的回覆看出女性的想法與男性不同，接下來她指出男性老是會「完全沉浸在劇情裡」。get lost單獨用指「迷路」，因此(C)選項不符合敘述，正確答案為(D)。

Answer 5 ◄))（B）
女性為什麼會希望男友多出去走走呢？

(A) 不然她的朋友都要離她而去了。
(B) 不然他會變成獨居隱士。
(C) 不然他們就不會再上電影院了。
(D) 不然她就必須準備爆米花。

解析
最後女性説他們應該多出去走走，以免男性變成「孤僻隱士」(hermit)，這裡考的是單字，同義的選項為(B)，recluse指「隱居者」。如果聽不懂單字，建議用刪去法解題。

| John: | Honey, I'm going to rent some DVDs to watch tonight. |
| 約翰： | 親愛的，我去租些DVD，我們晚上來看吧。 |

| Cindy: | Again?! That's **all we seem to do on weekends** now. |
| 辛蒂： | 又看DVD？！我們最近的週末好像都只有在看DVD耶。 |

| John: | There're just so many movies I really want to see, like the new "Ninja Turtles". |
| 約翰： | 因為有太多我想看的電影，像是新的《忍者龜》。 |

| Cindy: | I thought Cliff asked you to see it at the cinema, but you refused. |
| 辛蒂： | 我記得克里夫有找你去電影院看這部，但你回絕了。 |

| John: | Can you imagine **the fortune I'd spend** at the cinema if I went to see every single movie I wanted to watch? |
| 約翰： | 如果我每部電影都是去電影院看的話，你能想像那會多花錢嗎？ |

| Cindy: | I suppose you have a point. |
| 辛蒂： | 你說的也有道理。 |

| John: | So I get the DVDs. Can you make some popcorn and get some beer? Having popcorn makes **a world of difference** to the atmosphere. |
| 約翰： | 那我就去租DVD，你可以準備爆米花和啤酒嗎？爆米花會讓氣氛完全不同。 |

| Cindy: | I don't know if I want to make it more atmospheric. You seem to **get completely lost in the story** and ignore whatever I say. |
| 辛蒂： | 我不確定我想要讓氣氛更好。你會沉浸在劇情裡，不理我說的話。 |

| John: | Just like at the cinema, you're not meant to talk during the movie! |
| 約翰： | 就像在電影院，電影播放時不應該講話啊！ |

| Cindy: | I think we need to get out more often before you turn into a real **hermit**. |
| 辛蒂： | 我覺得我們應該多出去走走，以免你變成孤僻隱士。 |

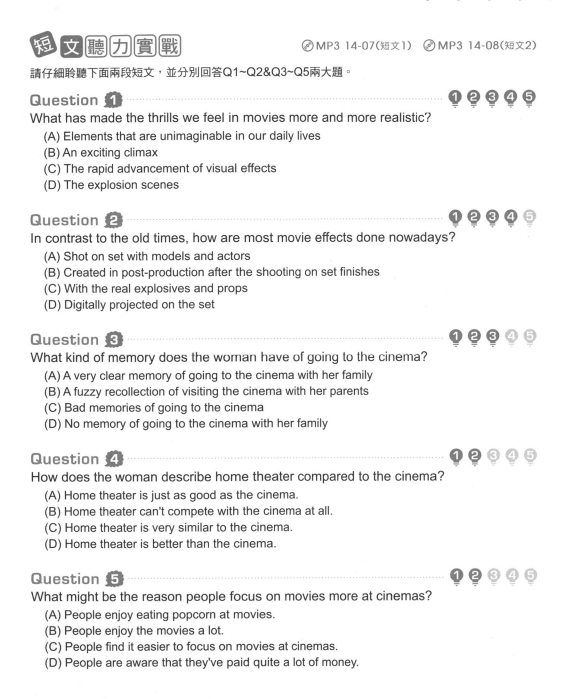

短文聽力實戰

MP3 14-07（短文1）　　MP3 14-08（短文2）

請仔細聆聽下面兩段短文，並分別回答Q1~Q2&Q3~Q5兩大題。

Question 1

What has made the thrills we feel in movies more and more realistic?

(A) Elements that are unimaginable in our daily lives
(B) An exciting climax
(C) The rapid advancement of visual effects
(D) The explosion scenes

Question 2

In contrast to the old times, how are most movie effects done nowadays?

(A) Shot on set with models and actors
(B) Created in post-production after the shooting on set finishes
(C) With the real explosives and props
(D) Digitally projected on the set

Question 3

What kind of memory does the woman have of going to the cinema?

(A) A very clear memory of going to the cinema with her family
(B) A fuzzy recollection of visiting the cinema with her parents
(C) Bad memories of going to the cinema
(D) No memory of going to the cinema with her family

Question 4

How does the woman describe home theater compared to the cinema?

(A) Home theater is just as good as the cinema.
(B) Home theater can't compete with the cinema at all.
(C) Home theater is very similar to the cinema.
(D) Home theater is better than the cinema.

Question 5

What might be the reason people focus on movies more at cinemas?

(A) People enjoy eating popcorn at movies.
(B) People enjoy the movies a lot.
(C) People find it easier to focus on movies at cinemas.
(D) People are aware that they've paid quite a lot of money.

答案與解析 ～answer

Answer 1 (C)
是什麼讓我們看電影時所感受到刺激感越來越真實？
- (A) 非現實生活中可想像的情節元素
- (B) 令人激動的高潮橋段
- (C) 視覺特效的進步
- (D) 爆破場景

解析
文中一開始就提到說我們很享受電影中令人激動的高潮橋段及非現實生活中可想像的情節元素，但這兩項特色並非使電影變得「更真實」的原因；接下來的 Thanks to...才點出原因為「視覺特效的進步」，正確答案為(C)。

Answer 2 (B)
和以前相比，現在大部分的電影效果都是怎麼做的呢？
- (A) 當場用模型和演員拍攝出來的
- (B) 在現場拍攝結束後，後製完成的
- (C) 用真實的爆破和道具完成的
- (D) 在拍攝現場數位投影出來的

解析
在提到幾十年前爆破場景的拍攝方式後，文中接著說現在我們大部分的特效都是「後製完成的」(digitally produced afterwards)，重點字為afterwards(事後)，所以選項中出現on set(現場)的選項(A)(D)都不能選，正確答案為(B)。

Answer 3 (A)
女性對去電影院這件事擁有什麼樣的回憶呢？
- (A) 和家人一起去電影院的清晰回憶
- (B) 隱約有和父母一起去電影院的模糊回憶
- (C) 去電影院的不好回憶
- (D) 完全沒有與家人一同去電影院的回憶

解析
女性說她和家人一起去電影院的「記憶依舊清晰」(a vivid memory)。vivid指「鮮明的；強烈的」，正確答案為(A)。

Answer 4 (B)
和電影院相比，女性覺得家庭劇院如何？
- (A) 家庭劇院和電影院一樣好。
- (B) 家庭劇院完全無法和電影院相比。
- (C) 家庭劇院和電影院很像。
- (D) 家庭劇院比電影院還好。

解析
雖然在文章中，女性有肯定家裡那台72吋電視螢幕的畫質，但後面立刻補充家庭劇院「完全無法跟電影院相比」(no match for the cinema)，正確答案為(B)。

Answer 5 (D)
什麼可能是人們在電影院更專注看電影的原因？
- (A) 觀眾喜歡邊看電影邊吃爆米花。
- (B) 觀眾非常享受電影本身。
- (C) 觀眾發現在電影院裡更容易專注於情節。
- (D) 觀眾意識到自己花了錢才能進來看電影。

解析
女性最後提到在電影院觀賞的觀眾比在家欣賞電影要專注許多，並推測或許是因為觀眾「意識到自己付了很多錢」，關鍵字為conscious，正確答案為(D)。注意就算其他選項「有可能」，還是必須以文中提到的內容為準。

⊙慢速MP3 14-09　　◎正常速MP3 14-10

We all enjoy movies with an exciting climax and elements that are rather unimaginable in reality. Thanks to **the rapid advancement of visual effects**, the thrills we experience in movies are becoming more and more realistic. A few decades ago, all the explosion scenes had to be done with real explosives with either full scale or miniature models. Now, though, the majority of the effects we see are **digitally produced afterwards** rather than created on set. As a result, we can enjoy realistic movie scenes that had been impossible before, such as a boy acting alongside a tiger in "Life of Pi". Who would have thought that the tiger they see in 85% of the movie is a computer-generated tiger!

　　我們很享受電影中令人激動的高潮橋段及非現實生活中可想像的情節元素。由於視覺特效的進步，我們感受到的刺激感越來越逼真。幾十年前，所有的爆破場景都是將真的火藥應用在實際大小或小型模型場景上，才得以製造出來，但現在，我們大部分看到的特效都是事後以數位方式製作，而非在拍攝現場拍攝的。也因此，我們得以觀賞以前無法想像到的逼真場景，例如讓一個男孩跟一隻老虎在《少年Pi的奇幻漂流》裡面對戲，有誰能想到在電影裡看到的那隻老虎，有85%都是電腦動畫做出來的呢！

⊙慢速MP3 14-11　　◎正常速MP3 14-12

Even though digital technology has evolved so much, the cinema still gives me a nostalgic feeling that keeps me coming back. I have **a vivid memory** of going to the cinema with my family and eating popcorn while watching movies. Even though I now have a 72-inch screen at home and I enjoy its quality very much, home theater is still **no match for the cinema**. The audience in a movie theater would gasp, laugh, or even scream together. And that kind of feeling simply can't be replaced by home theater. Not only that, I find people focus on the movies much more at cinemas than at home, perhaps because they **are conscious** that they **have paid quite a lot of money**.

　　就算數位科技日新月異，電影院還是帶給我一種很懷念的感覺，能讓我一再造訪。我和家人一起去電影院的記憶依舊清晰，記得我們邊吃爆米花邊看電影的情景。雖然我現在家裡有台72吋的電視螢幕，我也很享受它的畫質，但那還是完全無法跟電影院相比。電影院內的觀眾會一起因緊張而倒抽氣、一起大笑或尖叫，這是家庭劇院無法取代的感覺。不僅如此，我發現在電影院裡，大家看電影的專注程度比在家高得多，也許是因為意識到自己付了很多錢的關係吧。

Unit 5 人文藝術 Cultures & Art

📋 日常生活　🎵 娛樂活動　✏️ 意見交流　🏁 特殊場合

短對話聽力實戰

⊙ MP3 15-01

下面將播放五組短對話，請仔細聆聽，再依對話內容答題。

Question ❶

What good news does the girl announce?

(A) She has signed herself up to a record label.

(B) She has signed up for a recording lesson.

(C) A record label has made a deal with her.

(D) She has done a lot of recording in a studio.

Question ❷

Why it is difficult to tell if the producer like the man's music?

(A) The producer is inexperienced at judging music.

(B) The producer has bad taste.

(C) The producer didn't say anything.

(D) It depends on people's personal feelings.

Question ❸

Why isn't the man sure if he wants to go to the art exhibition?

(A) He's worried he won't understand the art.

(B) He's worried he won't like the art.

(C) He doesn't like modern art.

(D) Modern art is not sensible to him.

Question ❹

What does the man say a busker permit provides?

(A) The freedom for buskers to perform anywhere they like

(B) The freedom for buskers to perform in specific areas

(C) A designated area for each busker

(D) A permit to charge people for watching the performance

Question ❺

How does the man feel about his busker permit test?

(A) Relaxed

(B) Confident

(C) Nervous

(D) Encouraged

答案與解析 ~answer

Answer 1 ◀)) (C)
對話中的女孩宣布了什麼好消息？

(A) 她主動把自己簽給一家唱片公司。

(B) 她報名了一個錄音課程。

(C) 一家唱片公司和她協議簽約。

(D) 她在錄音室裡錄了很多首歌。

解析

對話一開始，女孩就宣布好消息，說她剛剛被一家「唱片公司簽下」(signed up by a record label)，這並非她單方就能決定的機會，所以答案非選項(A)，正確答案為(C)，表示由雙方協議而成。

Answer 2 ◀)) (D)
為什麼很難確定製作人是否喜歡男性的音樂作品？

(A) 製作人沒有判斷音樂好壞的經驗。

(B) 製作人的品味很差。

(C) 製作人什麼都沒有說。

(D) 喜不喜歡取決於個人的感覺。

解析

針對難以推測別人喜不喜歡男性的音樂作品，女性提到大家對音樂的愛好會「很主觀」(subjective)，和製作人怎樣無關，正確答案為(D)。

Answer 3 ◀)) (A)
男性為何對去看藝術展這件事感到猶豫呢？

(A) 他擔心自己看不懂現代藝術。

(B) 他擔心自己不會喜歡現代藝術。

(C) 他不喜歡現代藝術。

(D) 現代藝術對他來說不合邏輯。

解析

對於女性的邀約，對話中的男性遲疑的原因是因為他不確定自己看不看得懂這類藝術作品。make sense為「講得通；有意義」之意，正確答案為(A)。注意選項(D)的sensible(理性的)與make sense完全不同。

Answer 4 ◀)) (B)
根據男子所言，街頭藝人許可證有什麼好處？

(A) 讓街頭藝人自由選擇在他們想要的地方表演

(B) 讓街頭藝人在特定區域內自由表演

(C) 幫每一位街頭藝人規劃屬於自己的區域

(D) 能向觀賞表演的群眾收錢的許可

解析

男子提到街頭藝人許可證，後面解釋這樣就可以「在特別規劃的區域內表演」(an area especially designated for buskers)，正確答案為(B)。注意(C)雖然提到特別規劃的區域，但意思卻完全不同。

Answer 5 ◀)) (C)
面對街頭藝人許可證的資格考，男性心情如何？

(A) 很享受的

(B) 有自信的

(C) 緊張的

(D) 受到鼓勵的

解析

男性說他要去參加街頭藝人許可證的資格考，因而感到「很緊張」。have butterflies in one's stomach 是形容人們因為某件事情而感到七上八下的俚語，正確答案為(C)。

中英文內容

⊙慢速MP3 15-02　　◎正常速MP3 15-03

短對話 1 Conversation

Ivy: Good news! I've just **been signed up by** a record label.

艾薇： 好消息！我剛剛被一家唱片公司簽下來了。

Seth: That's amazing! I guess I won't be seeing you much from now on.

塞斯： 那真是太棒了！從現在開始，我想能和你碰面的機會應該很少吧。

短對話 2 Conversation

Larry: I went to present my demo to a producer today. I couldn't tell if he liked my work or not.

賴瑞： 我今天把我的試聽帶拿給一位製作人聽，但我看不出他喜不喜歡我的作品。

Cindy: It is difficult to say. Taste in music can be very **subjective**.

辛蒂： 這很難說，大家對音樂的愛好很主觀。

短對話 3 Conversation

Heather: Would you like to go to a modern art exhibition with me this weekend?

海瑟： 你這個週末願意跟我一起去看當代藝術展嗎？

Vince: I'm not sure if this kind of art **makes sense** to me.

文斯： 我不確定自己看不看得懂這類的藝術耶。

短對話 4 Conversation

Amy: I'm going to play guitar on the street to see if I can make some money by busking.

艾咪： 我要去街上演奏吉他，看能不能用街頭表演的方式賺錢。

Jack: Do you have a busker permit? It's better to have one so you can perform **in an area especially designated** for buskers.

傑克： 你有街頭藝人許可證嗎？最好有一張，這樣你就能在特別規劃區表演。

短對話 5 Conversation

Kyle: I'm going to my busker permit qualifying test. I've **got butterflies in my stomach**.

凱爾： 我要去參加街頭藝人許可證的資格考了，好緊張喔。

Julie: Just be confident in yourself and enjoy it.

茱莉： 只要對自己有信心，並享受過程就行了。

長對話聽力實戰

⊙MP3 15-04

請仔細聆聽下面的長對話，再依對話內容選擇正確答案。

Question 1

How is the communication between the woman and her boyfriend?

(A) Communication seems difficult for them.

(B) She thinks they like communicating.

(C) They don't talk much when going to an exhibition.

(D) They hate communicating with each other.

Question 2

According to the man, "what" doesn't come naturally?

(A) Reporting

(B) Consideration

(C) Good exhibitions

(D) Rapport

Question 3

Why won't the woman go to another exhibition with her boyfriend?

(A) They are not allowed to talk at exhibitions.

(B) They don't like the same kind of art.

(C) Her boyfriend doesn't chat to her about the exhibition.

(D) Her boyfriend finds it boring.

Question 4

How did the woman's date with her boyfriend go?

(A) Peaceful

(B) Boring

(C) Eventful

(D) Normal

Question 5

Why does the woman find it hard to communicate with her boyfriend?

(A) He doesn't like to talk to her.

(B) He doesn't see what the issue is.

(C) He doesn't want to communicate.

(D) He finds the woman annoying.

答案與解析 ~answer

Answer 1 (A)
女性和男友的溝通呈現怎麼樣的狀態呢？
- (A) 對他們來說，溝通似乎是件很困難的事。
- (B) 她覺得他們很喜愛溝通。
- (C) 他們去看展覽時都不太講話。
- (D) 他們討厭與彼此溝通。

解析
解題關鍵在When it comes to communication後面的內容(此為提出某議題的句型)，之後女性說溝通「對他們來說似乎很難」(we just seem to struggle)，但她並沒有說兩人討厭溝通或不講話，正確答案為(A)。

Answer 2 (D)
根據男性所言，「什麼」並非生來就有的呢？
- (A) 報告
- (B) 體貼
- (C) 好的展覽
- (D) 默契

解析
當女性訴苦說她與男友溝通不良時，男性說「默契當然不是生來就有的」(rapport doesn't come naturally)，正確答案為(D)。要注意rapport跟(A)選項的report的發音相似，容易搞混。

Answer 3 (C)
為什麼女性不想再和男友一起去看展覽了呢？
- (A) 他們在展場中不能說話。
- (B) 他們喜歡的藝術類型不同。
- (C) 她的男友不與她聊展覽的事情。
- (D) 她男友覺得看展覽很無趣。

解析
女性之所以不想再跟男朋友一起去看展覽，是因為男朋友都「不跟她討論和分享心得」(He wouldn't discuss and share his thoughts with me)，與此最接近的答案為(C)。

Answer 4 (B)
女性覺得和男友約會去看展覽怎麼樣呢？
- (A) 很平和
- (B) 很無趣
- (C) 很多變故
- (D) 很普通

解析
本題的關鍵在女性抱怨完男友不分享看展覽心得之後，男子安慰她說有些人就是喜歡默默地欣賞作品，此時她回答「但這樣約會就變得很乏味(dull)」，最接近原意的答案為(B)。

Answer 5 (B)
女性為什麼會覺得與男友溝通非常困難呢？
- (A) 他不喜歡跟她說話。
- (B) 他不覺得溝通是個問題。
- (C) 他不想要溝通。
- (D) 他覺得女友很煩。

解析
對話最後，女性提到溝通之所以變得非常困難(really hard)，是因為她男友「不覺得這是個問題」(doesn't see it as a problem)，因此選(B)。注意「不覺得是個問題」並不表示男友拒絕與她溝通，所以(A)(C)(D)都不適合。

Susan: My boyfriend and I seem to have much in common in terms of our passion for art.

蘇珊：　我男朋友和我對藝術的熱愛似乎有很多共通點。

Tony:　Sounds perfect.

東尼：　聽起來很好啊。

Susan: But when it comes to communication, we just seem to **struggle**.

蘇珊：　但是講到溝通，對我們來說似乎就很難了。

Tony:　Well, **rapport** doesn't come naturally. Communication certainly takes practice and adjustment over time.

東尼：　默契當然不是天生就有，溝通一定要經過長期的練習和調整的。

Susan: But he **won't discuss and share his thoughts** with me. I don't think I'll go to another exhibition with him.

蘇珊：　但他都不跟我討論和分享心得，我想我不會再跟他一起去看展覽了。

Tony:　Some people just like to appreciate work quietly.

東尼：　有些人就是喜歡默默地欣賞作品啊。

Susan: But that makes **our dates so dull**!

蘇珊：　但是這樣我們的約會就很乏味啊！

Tony:　Then you two need to talk about the communication problem.

東尼：　那你們就得好好聊一聊溝通問題了。

Susan: I find it really hard because **he doesn't see it as a problem**, but it's really bothering me.

蘇珊：　很難耶，因為他不覺得這是個問題，但是卻讓我很困擾。

Tony:　Just try it. I'm sure he'll listen to you.

東尼：　去試試看，我相信他會聽你說的。

短文聽力實戰

MP3 15-07(短文1)　　MP3 15-08(短文2)

請仔細聆聽下面兩段短文，並分別回答Q1~Q2&Q3~Q5兩大題。

Question 1

What is Andy Warhol most famous for?

(A) Promoting the pop-art movement
(B) The portrait of Marilyn Monroe
(C) Socializing with other pop-art artists
(D) Creating pop-art portraits of celebrities

Question 2

What did Warhol do in the 1960s?

(A) He started socializing with celebrities.
(B) He found a place to paint the portraits.
(C) He established his art studio.
(D) He set up a factory.

Question 3

What do most artists strive to create?

(A) Ideas and styles unique to them
(B) Ideas originating from other people's work
(C) Valuable artworks
(D) Unique artwork titles

Question 4

Most often, how are ideas born?

(A) They suddenly appear in our heads.
(B) People give them to us.
(C) They are created through large amounts of research.
(D) They are the conclusions made from a research project.

Question 5

What might happen when artists travel around?

(A) There's a chance they'll come to a crossroads.
(B) They might find inspiration from something they encounter.
(C) They might finish their next piece of artwork.
(D) They might meet people who will give them ideas.

答案與解析 ～answer

Answer 1 ◀)) (D)

安迪‧沃荷最出名的是什麼呢？

(A) 推動「普普藝術」

(B) 瑪麗蓮夢露的肖像

(C) 與其他普普藝術家交際

(D) 用普普藝術的風格幫名流畫肖像

解析 文中說安迪‧沃荷最知名的是「名流的肖像作品」(head shots of other celebrities)，正確答案為(D)。注意(A)有誤的地方在，文中只說沃荷可能是推動普普藝術的藝術家中，最為人所知的一個，但並不代表沃荷最出名的為此。

Answer 2 ◀)) (C)

沃荷在1960年代時做了什麼呢？

(A) 他開始與名流交際。

(B) 他找到一個地方畫肖像畫。

(C) 他成立了自己的藝術工作室。

(D) 他設立了一間工廠。

解析 安迪‧沃荷在1960年代時「成立」(founded)自己的藝術工作室，命名為"The Factory"(工廠)，正確答案為(C)。注意重點在藝術工作室(art studio)，「工廠」(Factory)只是工作室的名字。

Answer 3 ◀)) (A)

大部分藝術家致力於創造的是什麼呢？

(A) 原創的獨特概念與風格

(B) 從他人作品取得的想法

(C) 有價值的藝術品

(D) 獨特的作品名稱

解析 本文一開始就說大多的藝術家致力於創造「原創的獨特概念與風格」(original ideas and styles)，以自有的「獨特性」(uniqueness)出名，正確答案為(A)。關鍵的幾個字是strive to create，抓住關鍵字就能聽出答案。

Answer 4 ◀)) (C)

大多時候，靈感都是怎麼出現的呢？

(A) 突然就浮現在腦海中。

(B) 人們會提供靈感給我們。

(C) 經由大量的搜尋與研究。

(D) 從一份研究專題裡面得到。

解析 文中提到靈感不會憑空出現，反而需要「經由大量的搜尋與研究，才得以出現」(are born through a lot of research)，正確答案為(C)。選項(D)的a research project是偏學術的「研究專題」，意思不同。

Answer 5 ◀)) (B)

當藝術家們四處旅行時，可能會發生什麼事？

(A) 他們有可能會來到一個十字路口。

(B) 他們的所見所聞可能會成為作品的靈感來源。

(C) 他們也許會完成下一件藝術作品。

(D) 他們可能會遇到直接告訴他們想法的人。

解析 文中提到靈感有時須要經由搜尋與研究後才出現，接著That's why...的內容就說藝術家永遠不知道什麼時候會「偶然發現」(come across)某物，進而成為他們下個作品的「靈感來源」(inspiration)，正確答案為(B)。

中英文內容

短文 1

◎慢速MP3 15-09   ◎正常速MP3 15-10

Andy Warhol was a celebrity artist born in 1928 in Pittsburgh in the U.S.A. He is probably the most recognized artist from the "pop art" movement, which challenged traditional art by using popular culture as its subject. His particularly famous artworks are **head shots of other celebrities** such as Marilyn Monroe and Mao Ze Dong. In the 1960s, Warhol **founded his art studio "The Factory"**, in which many artists gathered to help him produce a large number of artworks, almost like how a factory produces products. He is also a controversial figure. Some criticized him for being "merely a business artist" because he spent a lot of time socializing with celebrities.

安迪‧沃荷於1928年出生於美國匹茲堡，是個明星藝術家。他可以算是最知名的「普普運動」藝術家，這種藝術以流行文化為主題，來挑戰傳統藝術。他最知名的作品是影星名人的大頭肖像，包括瑪麗蓮夢露和毛澤東等。沃荷在1960年代時成立了自己的藝術工作室「工廠」，許多藝術工作者聚集於此，協助沃荷創造大量的藝術作品，宛如一間製造商品的工廠。沃荷同時也是一位具爭議性的人物。有些人批評他是商業畫家，因為他花了很多時間與名流交際。

短文 2

◎慢速MP3 15-11   ◎正常速MP3 15-12

Most artists strive to create **original ideas and styles** so they can be known for their uniqueness. There is nothing wrong with using other people's work as a starting point to spark off some ideas. Most often, ideas don't just suddenly appear in your head. Instead, they are born through **a lot of research**. And that's why many artists spend a great deal of time traveling around and taking pictures. They never know when they might just **come across something** that will be the **inspiration for their next piece of artwork**. However, when they get an idea, it still takes a lot of trial and error to make the work their own.

大部分的藝術家致力於創造原創的獨特概念與風格，如此便能以自有的獨特性出名。為了激發創意，一開始用他人作品開頭是可以的。大多時候，靈感不會憑空浮現，反而需要經由大量的搜尋與研究，才得以出現，這也是為什麼許多藝術家花大量時間到處旅行和照相的原因，他們永遠不知道什麼時候會偶然發現某物，進而成為他們下個作品的靈感來源。不過，當他們有了初步的想法後，還是需要不斷摸索，才能創造出自己的作品。

PART

校園生活

課堂表現、課餘時間，校園必備的對話內容，
一聽就通！

學期開始 A New Semester

Unit 1

日常生活　娛樂活動　意見交流　特殊場合

MP3 16-01

下面將播放五組短對話，請仔細聆聽，再依對話內容答題。

Question 1

Who can attend the department's fresher's party?

(A) All students from the university

(B) Everyone

(C) Just students from the man's department

(D) The man's classmates and friends

Question 2

What's today's orientation about?

(A) The campus tour

(B) Life on campus

(C) Program registration

(D) The curriculum

Question 3

What kind of student is the girl?

(A) A part-time student

(B) A member of the international faculty

(C) An international exchange student

(D) A student going to Spain

Question 4

How much do students have to pay for the facilities?

(A) The same amount as other gyms

(B) Very little compared to other gyms

(C) Nothing at all

(D) Nearly the same amount as other gyms

Question 5

What is the main purpose of the library renovation?

(A) To get brand new hardware

(B) To upgrade all hardware

(C) To make everything in the library new

(D) To make its appearance look new

答案與解析 ～answer

Answer 1 ◀)) (A)
誰可以參加系上舉辦的迎新派對呢？

(A) 校內所有學生
(B) 每一個人
(C) 只有男生系上的學生
(D) 男生的同學與朋友

解析
聽到男生的邀約，女孩回答她非男生系上的學生(表示女孩認為自己不能參加)，此時男生表示他們的系主任「歡迎所有學生參加」，正確答案為(A)。注意(B)的「每一個人」可能擴及校外人士，所以不能選。

Answer 2 ◀)) (B)
今天新生導覽的內容為何？

(A) 有關校園導覽
(B) 有關校園生活
(C) 有關註冊課程
(D) 有關學校課程

解析
聽到對新生導覽內容的疑問後，女孩回答今天的講座要講解有關「校園生活」(campus life)的事情，並告訴學生如何報名「明天的」校園導覽，正確答案為(B)。

Answer 3 ◀)) (C)
對話中的女孩具備什麼樣的身分呢？

(A) 半工半讀的學生
(B) 國際教職員
(C) 國際交換學生
(D) 將要去西班牙的學生

解析
女孩一開始介紹自己「來自西班牙」(come from Spain)，和選項(D)的意思不同。接著說她這一年將會在這裡就學(on my exchange year)，正確答案為(C)。

Answer 4 ◀)) (B)
為了使用設備，學生需要付多少錢呢？

(A) 和外面健身房一樣的價格
(B) 和外面健身房相比，低到不行的價格
(C) 什麼都不用付
(D) 幾乎與外面健身房相同的價格

解析
當男生問到付費問題時，女生回答要付費，但是費用「跟外面的健身房相比，幾乎等於不用錢」，next to nothing表示「和免費差不多」，正確答案為(B)。

Answer 5 ◀)) (D)
圖書館翻修的主要目的是什麼？

(A) 購買新的硬體設備
(B) 升級所有硬體設施
(C) 更新圖書館內的所有物品
(D) 讓圖書館看起來煥然一新

解析
聽到圖書館翻修的消息，男生立刻問是否代表館內的物品都會更新，女孩回答會升級某些硬體設備，但「主要目的是讓圖書館看起來煥然一新」(a fresh new look)，抓緊main(主要的)這個關鍵字就能選出答案(D)。

⊙慢速MP3 16-02   ◉正常速MP3 16-03

💬 短對話 ❶ Conversation

Danny: Would you like to join our fresher's party?

丹尼: 你要參加我們的迎新派對嗎?

Kathy: But I'm not a student in your department.

凱西: 但我又不是你們系上的學生。

Danny: That's alright. Our Dean said **all students from the university** are welcome.

丹尼: 沒關係,系主任說歡迎本校所有學生參加。

💬 短對話 ❷ Conversation

Dana: What are they going to talk about at today's orientation?

黛娜: 今天的新生導覽會講什麼啊?

Faith: They'll give a general presentation on **campus life** and tell us how to register for tomorrow's campus tour.

菲絲: 他們會大概介紹校園生活,並教我們如何報名明天的校園導覽。

💬 短對話 ❸ Conversation

Tania: Hi, I **come from Spain**. And I'm on **my exchange year** here.

塔妮雅:嗨,我是來自西班牙的交換學生。

Craig: Nice to meet you. We might be classmates.

克雷格:很高興認識你,我們可能會變成同學呢。

💬 短對話 ❹ Conversation

Jeff: I love our fitness center! Do we have to pay to use the facilities on our campus?

傑夫: 我真喜歡我們的運動中心,使用學校的設施需要付費嗎?

Lori: Yes, we do. But it is **next to nothing** compared to other gyms.

蘿莉: 要付費,但是費用跟外面的健身房相比,幾乎和免費差不多。

💬 短對話 ❺ Conversation

Jenny: Our campus library is undergoing some renovation. It's quite exciting.

珍妮: 我們學校的圖書館準備要翻修,真令人期待。

Lincoln: So everything will be new then?

林肯: 所以到時候所有東西都會是全新的囉?

Jenny: They'll upgrade certain hardware, but it is **mainly** to give it **a fresh new look**.

珍妮: 會升級某些硬體設備,但翻修的主要目的是為了讓圖書館煥然一新。

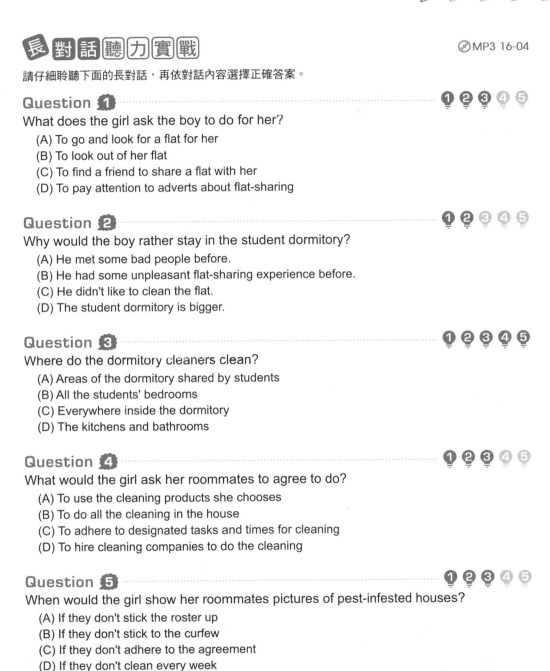

長 對 話 聽 力 實 戰

MP3 16-04

請仔細聆聽下面的長對話，再依對話內容選擇正確答案。

Question 1

What does the girl ask the boy to do for her?

(A) To go and look for a flat for her
(B) To look out of her flat
(C) To find a friend to share a flat with her
(D) To pay attention to adverts about flat-sharing

Question 2

Why would the boy rather stay in the student dormitory?

(A) He met some bad people before.
(B) He had some unpleasant flat-sharing experience before.
(C) He didn't like to clean the flat.
(D) The student dormitory is bigger.

Question 3

Where do the dormitory cleaners clean?

(A) Areas of the dormitory shared by students
(B) All the students' bedrooms
(C) Everywhere inside the dormitory
(D) The kitchens and bathrooms

Question 4

What would the girl ask her roommates to agree to do?

(A) To use the cleaning products she chooses
(B) To do all the cleaning in the house
(C) To adhere to designated tasks and times for cleaning
(D) To hire cleaning companies to do the cleaning

Question 5

When would the girl show her roommates pictures of pest-infested houses?

(A) If they don't stick the roster up
(B) If they don't stick to the curfew
(C) If they don't adhere to the agreement
(D) If they don't clean every week

答案與解析 ～answer

Answer 1 ◀ッ (D)

女孩請男孩幫忙她什麼事？

- (A) 幫她找公寓
- (B) 幫她看家
- (C) 介紹願意和她合租公寓的朋友給她
- (D) 幫她注意合租房子的廣告

解析

對話一開始，女孩就請男孩幫她「注意合租房子的廣告」(look out for some flat-sharing adverts)。look out for是「注意」的意思，跟一般look for「找某樣東西」不同，正確答案為(D)。

Answer 2 ◀ッ (B)

男孩為什麼寧願住學生宿舍呢？

- (A) 他以前遇過壞人。
- (B) 他以前和人合租，有過不愉快的經驗。
- (C) 他不喜歡清掃公寓。
- (D) 學生宿舍的空間比較大。

解析

男孩說他寧願住在宿舍，因為他有「和人合租的不好經驗」(some bad experience sharing a flat with others)，正確答案為(B)。

Answer 3 ◀ッ (A)

清潔人員會清理宿舍的什麼區域呢？

- (A) 宿舍裡學生共用的空間
- (B) 所有學生的房間
- (C) 宿舍裡的所有區域
- (D) 廚房與廁所

解析

男孩說至少在宿舍裡有清潔人員會來打掃「公共空間」(the communal area)，但沒有特別說公共空間包括哪些地方，因此最適合的答案為(A)。解題關鍵字為communal(公共的)。

Answer 4 ◀ッ (C)

女孩會要求她的室友同意做什麼？

- (A) 使用她選的清潔用品
- (B) 負責所有的清掃工作
- (C) 遵從安排好的清掃工作與時間
- (D) 請清潔公司來清理房子

解析

對話中的關鍵詞為女孩提到的「打掃工作執勤表」(a cleaning roster)，表示她會要求室友遵守個人的清掃時間，正確答案為(C)。

Answer 5 ◀ッ (C)

女孩何時會拿害蟲佔聚房子的照片給室友看呢？

- (A) 當她們不將工作執勤表貼出來時
- (B) 當她們沒有遵守宵禁時間時
- (C) 當她們沒有遵守協議時
- (D) 當她們沒有每個星期清掃時

解析

選項(C)中的agreement(協議)，其實就是女孩要求室友必須同意的「清理工作值勤表」，因此選(C)。注意選項(D)雖然也有室友沒打掃的意思在，但從對話中，我們無法判斷她們是否每星期打掃，因此不能選。

Carol: Can you **look out for some flat-sharing adverts** for me? I want to move out of the student dormitory.

卡蘿： 你可以幫我注意找人合租房子的廣告嗎？我想搬出學生宿舍。

Bert: I'd rather stay in the dormitory. I've had **some bad experience sharing a flat with others**.

伯特： 我寧願住宿舍，對於合租我有過很不好的經驗。

Carol: What happened?

卡蘿： 發生了什麼啊？

Bert: My roommates never cleaned. We had rats and cockroaches at one point!

伯特： 我的室友都不打掃，有段時間，公寓裡甚至有老鼠和蟑螂出沒呢！

Carol: That is disgusting!

卡蘿： 那也太噁心了！

Bert: That's why I live in the dormitory now. At least they have cleaners come cleaning **the communal area**.

伯特： 所以我現在才住宿舍，至少有清潔人員會來打掃公共空間。

Carol: Well, I always ask my roommates to agree to **follow a cleaning roster**.

卡蘿： 我都會先請室友同意遵照工作執勤表打掃。

Bert: What if they **don't stick to it**?

伯特： 那如果他們不按照分配表打掃呢？

Carol: When that happens, I will **show them pictures of pest-infested houses**.

卡蘿： 如果他們不遵守的話，我就會拿害蟲佔聚房子的照片給他們看。

Bert: Shock factor. That might work!

伯特： 用恐懼來制約，這招可能有效！

短 文 聽 力 實 戰

MP3 16-07(短文1)　MP3 16-08(短文2)

請仔細聆聽下面兩段短文，並分別回答Q1~Q2&Q3~Q5兩大題。

Question 1

What kind of meal did the students have at the party?

　(A) An all-you-can-eat buffet
　(B) A main dish served and a buffet
　(C) A three-course dinner
　(D) A cheap party buffet

Question 2

After the lavish party, which part did the boy find amazing?

　(A) He got a reception drink.
　(B) The party cost $300 dollars in total.
　(C) The food was so delicious.
　(D) The university had a large budget for the party.

Question 3

What did Ian ask the girl to do?

　(A) Be his ball date
　(B) Date him
　(C) Dance with him
　(D) Be his girlfriend

Question 4

According to the girl, what is Ian going to do?

　(A) He is going to buy a car for the ball.
　(B) He is going to take her to the ball.
　(C) He is going to be her boyfriend.
　(D) They are going to pick her dress together.

Question 5

Why is the girl considering taking a dance course?

　(A) So she won't fall over.
　(B) So she can dance with Ian.
　(C) So Ian will be happy.
　(D) So she won't tread on Ian's feet.

答案與解析 ~answer

Answer 1 (B)

學生們在派對上享用了什麼樣的餐點呢？

(A) 吃到飽的自助餐

(B) 一道主菜和自助餐

(C) 有三道菜的套餐

(D) 便宜的派對自助餐

> **解析**
> 講到餐點，文中提到服務生幫每人上了「龍蝦的主菜」(a main dish of lobster)，除此之外，他們還能去「自助餐區拿他們想吃的食物」(help ourselves to a buffet)，同時包含這兩種的選項(B)為最佳答案。

Answer 2 (D)

奢華的派對過後，男孩對什麼事感到相當驚訝？

(A) 他拿到迎賓酒。

(B) 派對總共才花了三百元。

(C) 食物非常美味。

(D) 學校有那麼多預算辦這場派對。

> **解析**
> 男孩提到 I am simply amazed...(後面接的就是讓他感到驚訝的部分)，即學校竟然有「那麼多預算(budget)」能舉辦這樣豪華的迎新派對，正確答案為(D)。

Answer 3 (A)

伊恩邀請女孩做什麼呢？

(A) 做他舞會的女伴

(B) 和他約會

(C) 和他跳舞

(D) 當他的女朋友

> **解析**
> 女孩一開始就提到伊恩邀請她當「大學年終舞會的女伴」(his date for the university's year-end ball)，這跟「當他女朋友」(be his girlfriend)或是跟他「約會」(to date)不同，正確答案為(A)。

Answer 4 (B)

根據女孩所述，伊恩將會做什麼呢？

(A) 他將為了舞會買車。

(B) 他將會接她一起去參加舞會。

(C) 他將會成為她的男朋友。

(D) 他們將一起去拿她舞會要穿的禮服。

> **解析**
> 女孩提到伊恩當天晚上要來「接她一起去參加舞會」(pick me up to go to the ball together)。此處的 pick sb. up to go somewhere 指「接送某人去某處」，正確答案為(B)。

Answer 5 (D)

女孩為什麼在考慮去上舞蹈課呢？

(A) 這樣她就不會跌倒。

(B) 這樣她就能與伊恩共舞。

(C) 這樣伊恩就會很高興。

(D) 這樣她就不會踩到伊恩的腳。

> **解析**
> 解題關鍵在文章最後，女孩在考慮是否該去上舞蹈課，以免當晚跳舞的時候「踩到伊恩的腳」(step on Ian's feet)，這與選項(D)的意思相同。

短文 1　　　　　　　⊙慢速MP3 16-09　　◎正常速MP3 16-10

We had the most amazing banquet food at our fresher's party last Saturday. On arrival, we were given a glass of sparkling wine as a reception drink. Once the party started, we were served **a main dish of lobster. In addition, we could help ourselves to a buffet** consisting of at least twenty dishes, including sushi and French onion soup. I am simply amazed at how the university has this kind of **budget** to hold such a lavish fresher's party, as we only paid $300 dollars per person! Of course, I'm not complaining about it. I hope they'll hold a party like this again soon.

　　我們上週六渡過了一個超棒的迎新盛宴。剛抵達時，我們每個人都先拿到一杯迎賓氣泡酒。當宴會開始後，服務生幫每人上了龍蝦的主菜，除此之外，我們還可以隨意地去自助餐區拿想吃的食物，那裡有超過二十道菜可以選擇，包括壽司和法式洋蔥湯。我實在很驚訝學校怎麼有那麼多的預算能舉辦這種豪華的迎新派對，我們每人才付了三百元呢！當然，我可不是在抱怨收費的事情，我希望他們很快就能再舉辦類似的宴會。

短文 2　　　　　　　⊙慢速MP3 16-11　　◎正常速MP3 16-12

I have just been asked by Ian **to be his date** for the university's year-end ball. Ian is the sweetest gentleman in my class. I'm so excited! I'm not just excited about the feast and wonderful party to come, but also the fact that Ian is going to **pick me up** to go to the ball together. It'll be like a formal date. Everyone from our class is going, and they're already talking about the wonderful food and program we are going to have on that day. But for now, all I can think about is what to wear for the ball. And I'm considering taking a dance course so that I **won't step on Ian's feet** when we dance!

　　剛剛伊恩來邀請我當他大學年終舞會的女伴。伊恩是我班上最貼心的紳士，我實在太開心了！我不僅為了即將來到的大餐和美好的派對而感到興奮，另外讓我感到飄飄然的原因是伊恩說他那天晚上會來接我一起去參加舞會，到時候就會像是正式的約會。班上所有的人都會去，大家都在討論那天的美食與節目，但是我現在滿腦子想的都是舞會要穿的衣服，而且我很認真在考慮要不要去上舞蹈課，以免跳舞的時候踩到伊恩的腳！

課業五四三 Schoolwork

📖 日常生活　🎤 娛樂活動　✏ 意見交流　📇 特殊場合

短對話聽力實戰

🎧 MP3 17-01

下面將播放五組短對話，請仔細聆聽，再依對話內容答題。

Question 1
What does the girl find difficult?

(A) Deciding on which subject to major in
(B) Deciding on which elective subjects to study
(C) Choosing which professor's course to take
(D) The marketing course

Question 2
Why didn't the boy go to the accounting lesson?

(A) He had to take notes for another class.
(B) He had to finish the accounting course's assignment.
(C) He had to finish another course's assignment.
(D) He had to go to another class instead.

Question 3
What does the boy suggest the girl do about the report?

(A) Ask for advice from other students
(B) Ask for advice from the professor
(C) Have a consultation with other students
(D) Write it by herself

Question 4
What does the girl find challenging about the team project?

(A) Working with others
(B) Writing reports
(C) Being a leader
(D) Coordinating tasks

Question 5
Why doesn't the girl's preparation for the midterm exam go well?

(A) She can't understand most of what she studied.
(B) She can't remember much of what she's studied.
(C) She can't study with the boy.
(D) The level of her study is very difficult.

答案與解析 ➤ ~answer

Answer 1 🔊 (B)

對話中的女孩覺得什麼很困難？

(A) 決定主修科目

(B) 決定選修課程

(C) 選擇上哪個教授的課

(D) 行銷課

解析

解題關鍵在elective(選修課程)這個字。注意選項(A)的major in為「主修」之意，所以不能選；選項(C)的內容與女孩的問題無關；選項(D)則是男生推薦的課程，正確答案為(B)。

Answer 2 🔊 (C)

男孩為什麼沒去上會計課？

(A) 他必須寫另外一堂課的筆記。

(B) 他必須完成會計課的作業。

(C) 他必須完成另一堂課的作業。

(D) 他必須去上另外一堂課。

解析

當女孩問男孩為何問抄筆記的事情時，男孩的回應正是本題的答案，他提到自己翹課來「完成另一堂課的作業」(finish another course's assignment)，正確答案為(C)。

Answer 3 🔊 (B)

關於做報告，男孩給了女孩什麼建議呢？

(A) 向其他學生尋求建議

(B) 詢求教授的建議

(C) 和其他同學商量

(D) 靠自己獨力完成

解析

男孩建議女孩應該「向教授尋求建議」，關鍵句為seek advice from (him)，正確答案為(B)。注意選項(D)指「獨力完成」，是男孩勸她別這麼做的內容。

Answer 4 🔊 (C)

針對小組計畫，女孩感到具挑戰的地方為何？

(A) 和其他人一起合作

(B) 寫報告

(C) 做領導者

(D) 協調工作任務

解析

女孩第一句話就提到小組計畫「考驗她的領導能力」(test my leadership skills)，關鍵字為leadership(領導力)，可由此選出正確答案(C)。

Answer 5 🔊 (B)

女孩的期中考準備為什麼不順利呢？

(A) 她不理解大部分的內容。

(B) 有很多唸的內容她都記不得。

(C) 她無法與男孩一起唸書。

(D) 她所準備的課業程度非常困難。

解析

對話一開始，女孩提到自己唸書都「一邊進，另一邊出」(go in from one end and come out of the other)，所以男孩才建議一起唸書，可以測驗彼此，正確答案為(B)。

⊙慢速MP3 17-02　　◎正常速MP3 17-03

短對話 1 Conversation

Jessie: **Choosing the electives** is really hard.

潔西：　選修課程真的很難選耶。

Mark: I recommend you take Professor Tang's course on marketing.

馬克：　我推薦你上唐教授的行銷課。

短對話 2 Conversation

Gary: Did you take notes in the accounting class today?

蓋瑞：　你今天的會計課有抄筆記嗎？

Mary: Yes. Why?

瑪麗：　有啊，為什麼這麼問？

Gary: I **skipped that class** to **finish another course's assignment**.

蓋瑞：　為了完成另一堂課的作業，我今天翹課了。

短對話 3 Conversation

Nina: I'm struggling with the report that Professor Lin assigned us.

妮娜：　林教授派的這份報告，我根本寫不出來。

Kent: I think you should **seek advice from him** rather than struggling over it by yourself.

肯特：　我覺得你應該向教授尋求建議，這比你獨自埋頭苦幹要好得多。

短對話 4 Conversation

Mandy: Our team project is really testing **my leadership skills**.

曼蒂：　我們的小組計畫真是考驗我的領導能力。

Peter: What happened?

彼得：　怎麼了嗎？

Mandy: One of my members didn't do much, so I had to find a way to handle this appropriately.

曼蒂：　我們其中一個組員不怎麼做事，所以我必須找到合適的方法來處理這件事。

短對話 5 Conversation

Jenny: My review of the midterm exam is not going well. Things seem to **go in from one end and come out of the other**.

珍妮：　我期中考的複習進行得不太順利，讀的東西似乎都一邊進，另一邊出。

Ross: Perhaps we could study together and test each other on the subjects.

羅斯：　或許我們能一起唸書，再測驗彼此各科的內容。

長對話聽力實戰

⊚MP3 17-04

請仔細聆聽下面的長對話，再依對話內容選擇正確答案。

Question 1

1 2 3 4 5

What does the girl's advisor think about her dissertation?

(A) She needs to track her progress better.

(B) She needs to rewrite a lot of her dissertation.

(C) Her dissertation is going in the right direction.

(D) She needs to change her topic.

Question 2

1 2 3 4 5

How did the boy's advisor react to his proposal at first?

(A) He was impartial and didn't give much feedback.

(B) He wasn't impressed by the proposal.

(C) He didn't give much feedback but seemed impressed.

(D) He asked the boy to rewrite his proposal.

Question 3

1 2 3 4 5

What did the boy's advisor say after reviewing his draft?

(A) He said the boy should change his topic.

(B) He said the boy could modify the topic.

(C) He said the boy is going in the right direction.

(D) He said the boy should rewrite his proposal.

Question 4

1 2 3 4 5

What does the girl suggest the boy tell his advisor?

(A) His idea on another topic

(B) The controversial content in his dissertation

(C) The deadline of his dissertation

(D) The difficulty of rewriting his dissertation

Question 5

1 2 3 4 5

What does the boy hope to achieve with his advisor?

(A) A compromise on the length of his dissertation

(B) A longer deadline

(C) A solution that is acceptable to both him and his advisor

(D) An agreement not to make any adjustments

答案與解析　～answer

Answer 1 （C）
女孩的指導教授對她論文的想法為何？
(A) 她必須更加小心掌控自己的進度。
(B) 她必須重寫論文中的很多內容。
(C) 她論文內容的方向很正確。
(D) 她必須改變論文主題。

解析
對話一開始，男孩先詢問女孩的論文進展，這時她提到指導教授在看完她的草稿後，覺得「她的方向正確」，on the right/wrong track指「想法或做法對/錯」，正確答案為(C)。

Answer 2 （A）
男孩的指導教授一開始對他的論文提案有何反應？
(A) 他的立場中立，沒有給什麼回饋。
(B) 男孩的提案並沒有讓他感到印象深刻。
(C) 他沒有給什麼回饋，但印象深刻。
(D) 他要求男孩重寫提案。

解析
解題關鍵在男孩提到指導教授看完論文大綱後「沒有特別覺得好或不好」(neutral 中立的)。接著提到教授「沒給什麼回饋意見」，正確答案為(A)。

Answer 3 （A）
男孩的指導教授看了他的論文初稿後，說了什麼？
(A) 他說男孩應該換題目。
(B) 他說男孩可以修改一下題目。
(C) 他說男孩寫的方向正確。
(D) 他說男孩應該重寫論文大綱。

解析
注意本題的重點在draft(草稿)這個字，而非談論proposal(論文大綱)。男孩在對話後半部提到教授看了論文初稿後，竟然要他「換題目」(change my topic)，因此答案選(A)。

Answer 4 （D）
女孩建議男孩告訴指導教授什麼事呢？
(A) 他想出的另一個主題
(B) 他論文裡面具爭議性的內容
(C) 他論文的最後繳交時間
(D) 重寫論文的困難之處

解析
聽到「換題目」的事之後，女孩建議應該與教授談論「這個階段重寫論文的可行性(feasibility)」，暗示重寫的困難度，因此，正確答案為(D)。

Answer 5 （C）
男孩希望能與指導教授達成什麼樣的結果呢？
(A) 對他論文長度的讓步
(B) 遲一點的繳交期限
(C) 他與教授都能接受的解決辦法
(D) 維持原狀，不做任何修改

解析
對話最後，男孩說他希望可以找到某種「雙方都能接受的折衷方式」(compromise that will work for both of us)，正確答案為(C)。注意男孩在對話中並沒有提到是什麼方式，所以過於具體的(A)(B)都不適合。

⊙慢速MP3 17-05   ◎正常速MP3 17-06

Adam: How are you getting on with your dissertation?
亞當： 你的畢業論文寫的如何？

Jill: It's on schedule. My advisor said I'm **on the right track** after he read my draft.
吉兒： 按時程表在進行，我的指導教授看完草稿後，說我寫的方向沒問題。

Adam: I'm not so lucky. My advisor was **neutral** about my proposal. He **didn't give me much feedback**.
亞當： 我就沒那麼幸運了。我的指導教授看我的論文大綱時，沒有特別覺得好或不好，也沒給什麼回饋。

Jill: Did he say you need to change anything?
吉兒： 那他有提到你哪裡該修正嗎？

Adam: No. He approved my proposal and said I could start writing it.
亞當： 沒有，他核准了我的提案，說我可以開始寫論文了。

Jill: So what's the problem?
吉兒： 那有什麼問題呢？

Adam: But when I showed him my draft today, he said I should **change my topic**!
亞當： 但當我今天給他看草稿時，他竟然說我應該換題目！

Jill: You should tell him about the **feasibility** of you rewriting your dissertation at this stage.
吉兒： 你應該向他解釋在這個階段重寫的可行性。

Adam: I will. I hope we can come to some sort of **compromise** that will **work for both of us**.
亞當： 我會跟他說的，希望能找到我們彼此都能接受的折衷方式。

短文聽力實戰

MP3 17-07(短文1)　MP3 17-08(短文2)

請仔細聆聽下面兩段短文，並分別回答Q1~Q2&Q3~Q5兩大題。

Question 1
1 2 3 4 5

What was new to the girl during her presentation last Wednesday?

(A) The presentation slides
(B) Public speaking
(C) The tough questions other students asked
(D) The Q&A after her presentation

Question 2
1 2 3 4 5

How does the girl want to improve her slides?

(A) To make them more detailed
(B) To make them more succinct and interesting
(C) To use simpler words in them
(D) To make the font bigger

Question 3
1 2 3 4 5

What does the boy say studying at university involves?

(A) Being proactive and doing things yourself
(B) Being reactive and doing things you are told to
(C) Doing a lot of research reports
(D) Completing endless assignments

Question 4
1 2 3 4 5

What do the university lecturers do?

(A) They ask students to memorize every word they say.
(B) They explain the details from the textbooks.
(C) They teach students the fundamentals.
(D) They expect students to write reports every week.

Question 5
1 2 3 4 5

Who set up the study group?

(A) The speaker
(B) The speaker's classmates
(C) The speaker's lecturer
(D) The university

答案與解析 ~answer

Answer 1 (D)
在上週三的簡報中，什麼對女孩是全新的經驗？

(A) 簡報的投影片
(B) 公開的演講
(C) 其他學生問的困難問題
(D) 簡報結束後的問答環節

> **解析**
> 女孩提到雖然她在學校有做過簡短的報告和演講，但是主要簡報結束後的「問答環節」(Q&A)對她來說是全新的經驗(new to me)，正確答案為(D)。注意(C)的重點在「問題」，而非問答環節。

Answer 2 (B)
女孩想要如何改善她的投影片呢？

(A) 使投影片內容更詳細
(B) 使投影片內容簡潔、有趣一點
(C) 在投影片中使用簡單一點的文字
(D) 把字體調大

> **解析**
> 文章最後的slide表示「投影片」，女孩提到自己得讓投影片「更簡潔、吸引人」，正確答案為(B)。關鍵字為concise(簡潔的)與engaging(吸引人的)，注意(C)的simple含有「將困難的用字遣字變簡單」，與簡潔無關。

Answer 3 (A)
根據男孩所說，大學生活涉及什麼呢？

(A) 主動完成事情的態度
(B) 被動執行別人的要求
(C) 做一大堆研究報告
(D) 完成無止盡的作業

> **解析**
> 本文一開始，男生就說大學生活要「自動自發」，關鍵片語為take one's initiative (採取主動的態度)。選項(B)的reactive意指「一個指令、一個動作」的被動反應，正確答案為(A)。

Answer 4 (C)
大學講師們的作法為何呢？

(A) 要學生記住他們所講的每一句話。
(B) 會解釋教科書上的細節。
(C) 教學生基本原則。
(D) 會期待學生每週寫報告。

> **解析**
> 男生說教授在課堂僅會「傳授概念」(deliver the principles)，如果沒有抓到關鍵字principle(原則)，也可以從前後文得知男生上大學之前有跑補習班，因此可剔除偏向補習班作法的(A)(B)(D)，正確答案選(C)。

Answer 5 (B)
男生提到的讀書會是誰創立的呢？

(A) 本文的說話者
(B) 本文說話者的同學
(C) 本文說話者的老師
(D) 本文說話者的大學

> **解析**
> 男生說他加入了「同學成立的讀書會」(the study group formed by my classmates)，說話者本身不一定是創立者之一，最佳答案為(B)。重點字為classmate(同學)以及be formed by(由…創立)。

 中英文內容

 短文 1 ⊙慢速MP3 17-09　◎正常速MP3 17-10

I made a presentation in front of a class of over one hundred students last Wednesday. It was rather scary! Even though I had done several short presentations and public speaking at school, **the Q&A after the main presentation** was **new to me**. I received some tough questions. Thankfully, I did okay in answering them. I learned a great deal this way because I gained different insights from other students. However, I still need to improve my presentation skills, such as appearing more confident in what I'm saying and making my presentation slides more **concise and engaging**.

　　我上週三在超過一百人的課堂上做了簡報，還真是令人害怕的經驗！雖然我在學校有做過簡短的報告和演講，但是簡報結束後的問答環節對我來說是全新的經驗。我被問到一些滿困難的問題，謝天謝地，我的回答還算令人滿意。這個經驗讓我學到很多，因為能從其他學生身上得到不同的啟發。不過，我還是需要改善自己的的簡報能力，舉例來說，我得對自己所說的內容更有自信，也得讓投影片更簡潔、更吸引人。

 短文 2 ⊙慢速MP3 17-11　◎正常速MP3 17-12

University is very much about **taking your own initiative**. It took me some time to adjust to such a different way of studying. Before, my life consisted of going to cram schools and trying to finish endless homework every day. Now, the lecturers only **deliver the principles**, and we are expected to do research and read about the topics. Furthermore, we often need to demonstrate our thoughts and arguments in our reports. It was a total disaster for me at first. Fortunately, I joined the study group **formed by my classmates**. Discussing the class with others is extremely useful.

　　大學生活是要自動自發的。剛升上大學的時候，我很不習慣，花了很長一段時間才適應這種完全不同的學習方式。大學之前，我的生活就是每天去補習班、寫著永無止境的作業。現在則完全不同，教授在講堂上只會傳授概念，我們必須自己花時間研究及閱讀相關的文章，除此之外，我們經常需要在報告裡表達自己的想法和論點。一開始的時候，我的表現簡直慘不忍睹，幸運的是，我加入了同學成立的讀書會，和同學討論想法對我的幫助非常大。

 Unit 3

課餘活動 After Classes

🖹日常生活　💡娛樂活動　✏意見交流　🏃特殊場合

短對話聽力實戰

 MP3 18-01

下面將播放五組短對話，請仔細聆聽，再依對話內容答題。

Question 1

Which student club is the girl joining?

- (A) The Dance Club
- (B) The Guitar Club
- (C) The Swimming and Dance Clubs
- (D) The Orchestra Club

Question 2

What is the Basketball Club giving raffle tickets in return for?

- (A) For sponsoring their club
- (B) For becoming one of their players
- (C) For watching their next match
- (D) For attending their orientation session

Question 3

Why does the girl think what the boy and his friends did was crazy?

- (A) Because they went to Kenting just for the seafood.
- (B) Because the view in Kenting is not worth the long journey.
- (C) Because they did a long journey on scooters.
- (D) Because all of them have scooters.

Question 4

What is the girl's main reason for tutoring?

- (A) To improve her teaching skills
- (B) To improve her knowledge of science
- (C) To make money
- (D) To start a career

Question 5

What does the girl warn the boy not to do?

- (A) Use other people's work
- (B) Disregard laws on utilizing other people's work
- (C) Give assignments to a private student
- (D) Rewrite assignment material

答案與解析 ~answer

Answer 1 (B)
女孩要加入哪個學生社團呢？

(A) 熱舞社
(B) 吉他社
(C) 游泳社和熱舞社
(D) 管樂社

> **解析**
> 雖然女孩說熱舞社和游泳社似乎很有趣，但是她後來提到自己已經「答應朋友要參加吉他社」(join her Guitar Society)，所以確定參加的是選項(B)。

Answer 2 (D)
籃球社提供的抽獎券是做了什麼的回報？

(A) 贊助他們社團
(B) 成為他們社團的球員
(C) 觀賞他們的下一場比賽
(D) 去參加他們的新生說明會

> **解析**
> 男孩說籃球社會給「報名參加社團說明會」的學生抽獎券(raffle ticket)，正確答案為(D)。原文中的sign up在此處有「報名參加」之意。

Answer 3 (C)
女生為什麼覺得男孩與朋友的舉動很瘋狂呢？

(A) 因為他們僅為了海鮮就跑去墾丁。
(B) 因為墾丁的景色不值得跑那麼遠。
(C) 因為他們騎機車騎了很久。
(D) 因為他們都有機車。

> **解析**
> 女孩說男孩說的高雄—墾丁騎車一日遊很瘋狂；她不敢相信他們「騎了那麼遠」(rode all that way)，正確答案為(C)。注意選項(A)裡的海鮮只是過程中享受的美食，並非男孩與朋友去的原因。

Answer 4 (A)
女孩做家教的主要原因為何？

(A) 改善她的家教技巧
(B) 改善她的科學知識
(C) 賺錢
(D) 創辦事業

> **解析**
> 雖然男孩一開始以為女孩是為了賺錢而開始工作，但女孩後來以Actually(實際上)帶出真正的原因，是為了「加強組織與教學的能力」(organize and deliver knowledge)，因此選(A)。

Answer 5 (B)
女生提醒男孩不要做出什麼行為？

(A) 使用其他人的作品
(B) 無視與使用他人著作有關的法律
(C) 把自己的作業指派給家教學生
(D) 重新編寫作業的內容

> **解析**
> 發現男孩在影印教授的作業為私用，女生提醒他「要小心，別侵犯智慧財產權」(infringe 違反；intellectual property rights 智慧財產權)，但沒有說男孩不能使用，正確答案為(B)。

⊙慢速MP3 18-02　　◎正常速MP3 18-03

💬短對話❶ *Conversation*

Sherry: There are so many stands at the fresher's fair. The Dance and Swimming Clubs both look interesting.

雪莉：　新生會上還真多社團攤位，熱舞社和游泳社看起來都很有趣。

Ron:　　I still recommend the Orchestra Club I'm in.

榮恩：　我還是推薦我參加的管樂社。

Sherry: Thanks, but I've already **promised** my friend to join **her Guitar Society**.

雪莉：　謝謝，但是我已經答應朋友要加入她的吉他社了。

💬短對話❷ *Conversation*

Carol:　Wow! They try so hard to attract freshmen to join their student clubs.

卡蘿：　哇！大家還真努力吸引新生加入社團。

Tim:　　The Basketball Club is even giving out raffle tickets to students **who sign up for their orientation session**.

提姆：　聽說籃球社甚至還給報名參加他們社團說明會的學生抽獎券呢。

💬短對話❸ *Conversation*

Jack:　My friends and I went on a one-day scooter trip from Kaohsiung to Kenting. We went sightseeing and had some great seafood.

傑克：　我跟朋友從高雄騎車到墾丁一日遊，既看了美景，也吃了美味的海鮮。

Sadie:　That's crazy! I can't believe you guys **rode all that way**.

莎蒂：　真瘋狂！不敢相信你們騎了那麼遠。

💬短對話❹ *Conversation*

Lucy:　I'm doing some private tutoring teaching chemistry.

露西：　我在做化學家教。

Dean:　You're already working for money!

狄恩：　你已經在工作賺錢啦！

Lucy:　Actually, it's more to help my ability to **organize and deliver knowledge**.

露西：　其實我做家教是為了加強我組織與教學的能力。

💬短對話❺ *Conversation*

Terry:　I'm photocopying my professor's assignment as homework for my private student.

泰瑞：　我在影印大學講師指派的作業給我家教的學生當功課。

Becky:　You must be careful **not to infringe intellectual property rights**.

貝琪：　你要小心，別侵犯智慧財產權。

長對話聽力實戰

MP3 18-04

請仔細聆聽下面的長對話,再依對話內容選擇正確答案。

Question 1

Why is the boy asking if the girl is free tonight?

(A) He wants her to go out with him.
(B) He wants her to write his report for him.
(C) He wants her to date his friend.
(D) He wants her to work at the bar for him.

Question 2

What did the boy ask the girl to do for him in class?

(A) To take notes for him
(B) To cover his shifts for him
(C) To go out with his friends
(D) To work at the bar for him

Question 3

What does the boy need to do tonight?

(A) Work his shift
(B) Study for a test
(C) Write his report
(D) Go out with his friends

Question 4

Why does the boy work so hard?

(A) He wants to earn money to buy a car.
(B) He wants to pay back his student loan and earn spending money.
(C) He wants to pay for his friends when they go out.
(D) He wants to pay his mortgage.

Question 5

What does the girl say the boy must do as a student?

(A) Not work at a bar
(B) Do more part-time jobs
(C) Think about what is most important
(D) Give priority to gaining work experience

答案與解析 ～answer

Answer 1 (D)

男孩為何詢問女孩今晚是否有空？

(A) 他想約女孩出門約會。

(B) 他希望女孩幫他寫報告。

(C) 她希望女孩和他朋友約會。

(D) 他希望女孩幫他值酒吧的班。

解析

男孩問女孩今晚是否有空，因為他今晚無法去打工，需要找人來「替他值酒吧的班」(cover my shift at the bar)，正確答案為(D)。shift指轉換，在工作上則特別指輪班制的值班時間。

Answer 2 (A)

男孩要求女孩在課堂上幫他什麼忙呢？

(A) 幫他抄筆記

(B) 幫他值班

(C) 和他朋友一起出去玩

(D) 為了他去酒吧值班

解析

解題關鍵有兩處，第一為題目中的in class(上課時)，所以聽答案的時候請專注於和上課有關的請託；第二就是對話中女孩提到的asked me to take notes，take notes指「抄筆記」，正確答案為(A)。

Answer 3 (C)

男孩今天晚上非做不可的事情是什麼？

(A) 值班

(B) 為考試復習

(C) 寫他的報告

(D) 和朋友一起出去玩

解析

男孩解釋說今晚他非得「完成報告」不可(need to finish my report)，正確答案為(C)。除此之外，沒有任何一個選項的內容符合題目當中的「必須性」。

Answer 4 (B)

男孩這麼努力工作的原因是什麼？

(A) 他想賺錢買車。

(B) 他想還清助學貸款和賺零用錢。

(C) 出去玩的時候，他想幫朋友付錢。

(D) 他想還清貸款。

解析

當女孩警告男孩過多的工作量會影響學業時，他提到想盡快「還清助學貸款」(pay back my student loan)，也想賺足夠的「零用錢」(pocket money)，正確答案為(B)。選項(D)雖然提到貸款，但沒有包含所有的原因。

Answer 5 (C)

女孩對男孩提到，身為學生，他必須做什麼？

(A) 別在酒吧工作

(B) 找更多兼職工作

(C) 搞清楚最重要的是什麼

(D) 優先著重在工作經驗上

解析

女孩勸男孩必須「把優先順序搞對」(get your priorities right)，從後面的「畢竟是學生」看得出來鼓勵打工的選項(B)不適合，最佳答案為(C)。

 中英文內容

⊙ 慢速MP3 18-05　　◎ 正常速MP3 18-06

Roy: Are you free tonight?
羅伊： 你今晚有空嗎？

Tessa: I think so. Why?
泰莎： 應該吧，為什麼這麼問？

Roy: I can't make the shift for my part time job tonight. I need to find someone to **cover my shift at the bar**.
羅伊： 我今晚沒辦法去打工，需要找人來頂替我在酒吧的排班。

Tessa: How many shifts are you doing? You always seem busy.
泰莎： 你有多少班啊？你看起來總是很忙。

Roy: I've got a shift nearly every night, and I'm getting tired and falling asleep in class.
羅伊： 我幾乎每天晚上都有班，還真是讓我感到越來越累，有時會在課堂上睡著。

Tessa: So that's why you asked me to **take notes** for you.
泰莎： 所以這就是為什麼你請我幫你抄筆記的原因。

Roy: Sorry about that. Anyway, I really **need to finish my report** tonight.
羅伊： 真的很抱歉，無論如何，今晚我非得完成報告不可。

Tessa: You won't learn well if you carry on like this.
泰莎： 這樣下去，你根本無法好好學習。

Roy: I know, but I want to **pay back my student loan** as soon as possible and have enough **pocket money** to go out with friends.
羅伊： 我知道，但我想盡快還清助學貸款，也想有足夠的零用錢和朋友出去玩。

Tessa: You must **get your priorities right**. After all, you are a student.
泰莎： 你必須搞清楚優先順序，你畢竟是學生。

Roy: Alright. I'll ask my boss to see if he can reduce my shifts.
羅伊： 好啦，我會問問老闆，看他能否減少我的排班。

短文聽力實戰

MP3 18-07（短文1）　MP3 18-08（短文2）

請仔細聆聽下面兩段短文，並分別回答Q1~Q2&Q3~Q5兩大題。

Question 1
Why did the boy go to Malaysia on his summer vacation?
- (A) He went on an exchange program.
- (B) He wanted to go traveling around Malaysia.
- (C) He wanted to improve his English.
- (D) His classmate from Malaysia invited him.

Question 2
What did the boy get from people on this trip?
- (A) A warm reception
- (B) Great gifts
- (C) English lessons
- (D) Souvenirs to take home

Question 3
Who arranged the exchange program?
- (A) The girl's department
- (B) The girl's tutor
- (C) The girl's English lecturer
- (D) Students who were in the same year as the girl

Question 4
What lessons did the girl attend in Sydney?
- (A) English language lessons
- (B) A variety of different lessons
- (C) Some English and Chinese lessons
- (D) Photography lessons

Question 5
What happened to the girl's English after the exchange program?
- (A) It progressively got worse.
- (B) It improved slightly.
- (C) It improved noticeably.
- (D) It dramatically worsened.

答案與解析 ~answer

Answer 1 (D)
男孩為什麼在放暑假的時候去馬來西亞？

- (A) 他因為交換學生的計畫而去。
- (B) 他想要到馬來西亞旅遊。
- (C) 他想要改進英文能力。
- (D) 他馬來西亞的同學邀請他去。

解析
文中一開始男孩提到班上某位來自馬來西亞的僑生，邀請了男孩今年夏天去拜訪他，解題關鍵字為invite，表示「邀請」，正確答案為(D)。

Answer 2 (A)
在旅程當中，男孩從人們那裡得到什麼？

- (A) 熱情的招待
- (B) 很棒的禮物
- (C) 上英文課程
- (D) 能帶回家的紀念品

解析
關鍵在男孩提到自己從遇到的每個人那裡得到(receive)熱情的款待(wonderful hospitality)，後面提到的美食則是熱情款待的例子。注意其他選項雖然有可能，但文中並沒有明確點出來，正確答案為(A)。

Answer 3 (A)
誰安排了交換學生計畫？

- (A) 女孩的系所
- (B) 女孩的導師
- (C) 女孩的英文講師
- (D) 與女孩同年級的學生們

解析
女孩說她參加了「系上安排的」暑期交換學生計畫，注意文中「(主詞) arrange sth. for sb.」的句型，我們要找的關鍵字為主詞(my department)，正確答案為(A)。老師只是被提及的參與者，並非安排的人。

Answer 4 (B)
女孩在雪梨的時候上了些什麼課程？

- (A) 英語的課程
- (B) 內容不同的各種課程
- (C) 一些英語課和中文課
- (D) 攝影課程

解析
解題關鍵在要搞清楚「用(某語言)授課」(lessons taught in...)與「課程內容」兩件事的差別。題目問的是課程內容，所以要找女孩提到的「多元化課程」(The subjects varied a lot)，正確答案為(B)。

Answer 5 (C)
在交換學生計畫結束後，女孩的英文怎麼樣了？

- (A) 逐漸退步。
- (B) 有些微的進步。
- (C) 有很明顯的改善。
- (D) 明顯地變退步了很多。

解析
文中的最後，女孩提到自己的英語在參加交換學生計畫後「突飛猛進」。dramatic為「戲劇化的」，進步用戲劇化來形容，表示其幅度令人驚訝，正確答案為(C)。

 中英文內容

短文 1

⊙慢速MP3 18-09　　◎正常速MP3 18-10

There's an overseas Chinese student from Malaysia in my class. **He invited me** to visit him this summer. So, I flew to Malaysia and stayed with his family in Kuala Lumpur for a week. I **received such wonderful hospitality** from everyone I met and enjoyed a wide range of delicious cuisine. I was surprised by the number of languages spoken in Malaysia and how well most people's English is. The experience has given me an even stronger motivation to improve my English, so I try to practice with my foreign friends now whenever I get the chance.

我們班上有一位來自馬來西亞的僑生。他邀請我今年夏天去拜訪他。因此，我就飛到馬來西亞，住在他位於吉隆坡的家，和他家人相處了一個星期。我遇到的每個人都很盛情款待我，我還品嚐到許多美味的佳餚。有一件事讓我感到驚訝，馬來西亞當地使用的語言非常多元，大多數人的英文程度也很好。這次的經驗讓我更有動力去提高自己的英文程度，所以我現在一有機會就會與我的外國朋友們練習英文。

短文 2

⊙慢速MP3 18-11　　◎正常速MP3 18-12

My first summer vacation at university was very eventful. I went on a summer exchange program that **my department arranged** for students. The tutor who accompanied the students on the program was Professor Lee, who teaches us English Literature. We spent the whole of July in Sydney, where we took classes taught in English every day. **The subjects varied a lot, ranging from different languages to photography**. I've heard the students from our sister university came to our school, too. They received lessons mainly in English but some in Chinese. After coming back from the exchange program, I noticed **a dramatic improvement** in my English.

我在大學渡過的第一個暑假可謂多采多姿。我參加了系上為學生安排的暑期交換學生計畫，陪同學生參加的導師是李教授，他是教我們英國文學的老師。我們整個七月份都待在雪梨，每天去上各種用英語授課的課，課程內容很多元，從各種語言課到攝影課都有。我聽說我們姊妹校的學生也有到我們學校，上課時主要以英語授課，但也有部分用中文教學。交換學生的計畫結束後，我發現自己的英文突飛猛進呢。

進修學習 Advanced Study

Unit 4

日常生活　娛樂活動　意見交流　特殊場合

短對話聽力實戰

◎ MP3 19-01

下面將播放五組短對話，請仔細聆聽，再依對話內容答題。

Question 1
Where is the girl going on her exchange program?
(A) America
(B) New York
(C) South Africa
(D) South America

Question 2
Why is the boy looking for a roommate?
(A) To find a new host family
(B) To share the host family's house
(C) To share accommodation during his exchange program
(D) To share accommodation after his exchange program

Question 3
What does the woman suggest the boy do?
(A) Try to use the self-service check-out system
(B) Try to use the self-service database search service
(C) Ask the database personnel to help him find a book
(D) Ask someone else to help him

Question 4
What is the girl asking the boy to do?
(A) To find out about a study abroad program for her
(B) To study abroad with her
(C) To attend a seminar with her
(D) To attend an English seminar with her

Question 5
What happens if the boy does not do well on the GMAT?
(A) He can't get into his first choice for university.
(B) He can't study abroad.
(C) He can't apply for a university.
(D) He will need to settle in another country.

答案與解析 ~answer

Answer 1 (C)

女孩所參加的交換學生計畫，要去的地方為何？

(A) 美國

(B) 紐約

(C) 南非

(D) 南美洲

解析

對話中容易被搞混的兩個關鍵字分別為 the States(美國)和South Africa(南非)。注意女孩的最後一句話，提到她交換學生的對象來自美國，但計畫「是要去南非」。take place指事情或計畫「發生」的地點，正確答案為(C)。

Answer 2 (D)

男孩為什麼在找合住的室友呢？

(A) 為了找新的寄宿家庭

(B) 為了找人與他合住在寄宿家庭的房子

(C) 為了交換學生計畫時合租房子

(D) 為了在交換學生計畫結束後合租房子

解析

男孩提到自己還要「再待一個月」(additional有「預定之外」的意思)，所以需要「另外找地方住」(accommodation 住處)，正確答案為(D)。

Answer 3 (B)

女性建議男孩怎麼做呢？

(A) 試著使用自助借書服務

(B) 試著使用自助式圖書資料庫搜索服務

(C) 請資料庫管理人員幫他找書

(D) 另外找人幫忙男孩

解析

館員建議男孩使用「自助式圖書資料庫搜索服務」(the self-service database search service)，正確答案為(B)。注意(A)與(C)分別出現self-service和database這兩個關鍵字，但都不是在講搜索服務。

Answer 4 (C)

女孩要求男孩做什麼呢？

(A) 為了她去了解出國留學的相關資訊

(B) 和她一起出國留學

(C) 和她一起去聽講座

(D) 和她去聽一個英文講座

解析

女孩對男孩說她要去聽「海外留學講座」(a study-abroad seminar)，問男孩要不要一起去。這是在邀請男孩去聽講座，並非和她一起留學，正確答案為(C)。

Answer 5 (A)

如果男孩的GMAT沒有考好，會怎麼樣呢？

(A) 他就上不了心目中第一志願的大學。

(B) 他就不能出國留學。

(C) 他就不能申請大學。

(D) 他就必須在另外一個國家定居。

解析

由對話前半部，可以聽出男孩的GMAT成績與申請學校有很大的關係。最後也提到如果沒有考好，就必須屈就於他的「第二或第三志願」，可看出考試影響他是否能進第一志願，正確答案為(A)。

中英文內容

⊙慢速MP3 19-02　　◎正常速MP3 19-03

短對話 1 Conversation

Ben: Are you going to the States for the student exchange program?

班： 你參加的交換學生計畫會去美國嗎？

Sara: My exchange partner is from the States, but the program is actually **taking place in South Africa**.

莎拉： 我的交換學生對象來自美國，但交換學生計畫要去的目的地是南非。

短對話 2 Conversation

Jason: Finding a suitable roommate is so hard.

傑森： 找到合適的室友真困難。

Lily: Aren't you staying with a host family on your student exchange program?

莉莉： 你當交換學生的期間不是住寄宿家庭嗎？

Jason: Yes, but I'm staying for **an additional month**, so I need **another accommodation**.

傑森： 是啊，但計畫結束後，我還要再待一個月，所以需要另外找地方住。

短對話 3 Conversation

Mike: Excuse me, could you help me look for a book?

麥克： 不好意思，請問你能不能幫我找一本書？

Librarian: May I suggest you use **the self-service database search service**?

館員： 我可以建議你使用自助式圖書資料庫搜索服務嗎？

短對話 4 Conversation

Tracy: I'm going to **a study-abroad seminar**. Do you want to come?

崔西： 我要去聽海外留學講座，你要不要一起來？

Vic: Study abroad? I haven't actually considered this option before.

維克： 出國留學嗎？我之前都沒怎麼考慮過這個選項。

短對話 5 Conversation

Adam: I must get a good mark on the GMAT to get into the university I've applied for.

亞當： 我必須在「管理學研究生入學資格考試」中取得好成績，才能上我申請的學校。

Betty: So getting a good mark is a requirement?

貝蒂： 所以取得好成績是他們要求的條件嗎？

Adam: Yes. If I don't, I'll have to **settle for my second or third choice** for university.

亞當： 沒錯，如果我沒有考好，就必須屈就於我的第二或第三志願了。

長對話聽力實戰

@MP3 19-04

請仔細聆聽下面的長對話，再依對話內容選擇正確答案。

Question 1

What has the man submitted to a top journal?

(A) His dissertation
(B) A research paper
(C) His assignment
(D) His homework

Question 2

When will the man's paper be published?

(A) Within the next month
(B) Next year
(C) This month
(D) In the next issue

Question 3

What has the man been invited to do?

(A) To present his paper to his professor
(B) To write more papers for a journal
(C) To work for the International Corporate Governance Institute
(D) To speak and present at a summit

Question 4

Why does the woman say the invitation from ICGI is rare?

(A) Because the man doesn't have much work experience.
(B) Because ICGI rarely holds summit seminars.
(C) Because ICGI only invites scholars.
(D) Because ICGI rarely invite speakers.

Question 5

Why is the man not sure if he can attend the event?

(A) He can't travel very far.
(B) He didn't reply to the invitation.
(C) He wants to prepare for the oral defense of his dissertation.
(D) He needs to prepare for the graduation ceremony.

答案與解析 ~answer

Answer 1 (B)

男性投給頂尖期刊的稿件是什麼呢？

- (A) 他的論文
- (B) 研究論文
- (C) 指派的作業
- (D) 回家功課

解析
對話一開始，男性就提到自己將最新的「研究論文」(research paper)投稿給一家頂尖期刊。這跟「畢業論文」(dissertation)不一樣，正確答案為(B)。

Answer 2 (D)

男性的研究論文何時會刊登呢？

- (A) 在下個月之內
- (B) 明年
- (C) 這個月
- (D) 在下一期的期刊

解析
當被問研究論文的刊登時間，男性提到它將在「下一期的期刊」(in the next issue)發表，進一步解釋「不是下個月發刊的那一期」，正確答案為(B)。issue在此處指「(報刊的)期號」。

Answer 3 (D)

男性被邀請去做什麼呢？

- (A) 在教授面前報告研究論文
- (B) 替期刊寫更多的研究論文
- (C) 在國際企業治理研究機構上班
- (D) 在高峰會上演講和報告

解析
男性提到國際企業治理研究機構也看過他的研究論文，並「邀請他去高峰會上做主題演講」，關鍵字為keynote speaker(主題演講的講者)，正確答案為(D)。

Answer 4 (A)

為什麼女性說從ICGI發來的邀請很罕見呢？

- (A) 因為男性並沒有太多工作經驗。
- (B) 因為ICGI很少辦高峰會講座。
- (C) 因為ICGI只邀請學者。
- (D) 因為ICGI很少會邀請講者。

解析
女性說男性得到邀請很罕見，因為國際企業治理研究機構通常只會邀請「擁有多年工作經驗的專業人士」(professionals who have many years of work experience)，暗示男性本身沒有很多工作經驗，正確答案為(A)。

Answer 5 (C)

男性為何無法確定自己是否能參加高峰會呢？

- (A) 他無法旅行至太遠的地方。
- (B) 他沒有回覆邀請。
- (C) 他想要準備論文答辯。
- (D) 他必須準備畢業典禮。

解析
男性最後說他不確定是否能參加高峰會，因為他得準備「論文答辯」(the oral defense)，正確答案為(C)。選項(D)雖然出現prepare for的關鍵片語，但請注意對話中沒有提到任何與「畢業」有關的話題。

⊙ 慢速MP3 19-05　　◎ 正常速MP3 19-06

Andy: I submitted **my latest research paper** to a top journal.
安迪： 我把我最新的研究論文投稿給一家名聲頂尖的期刊。

Lisa: Has it been published?
麗莎： 已經在期刊發表了嗎？

Andy: It will be featured **in the next issue**, not the one published next month.
安迪： 下一期的期刊將會發表，不是下個月發刊的那一期。

Lisa: Let me know when it comes out.
麗莎： 發刊時記得告訴我。

Andy: The International Corporate Governance Institute has also contacted me.
安迪： 國際企業治理研究機構也有跟我接洽。

Lisa: What for?
麗莎： 為什麼？

Andy: They also read my paper and **invited me** to be **the keynote speaker in their next summit**.
安迪： 他們也看過我的研究，邀我去他們下一個高峰會上做主題演講。

Lisa: That's rare! Normally, they only invite **professionals who have many years of work experience**.
麗莎： 這很稀奇耶！他們通常只會邀請擁有多年工作經驗的專業人士。

Andy: But I'm not sure if I can attend it or not. I need to prepare for **the oral defense of my dissertation**.
安迪： 但我不確定能不能參加，我得為論文答辯做準備。

Lisa: I believe the professor will definitely be more impressed by the keynote speaker experience.
麗莎： 主題演講的經驗絕對更能讓教授印象深刻。

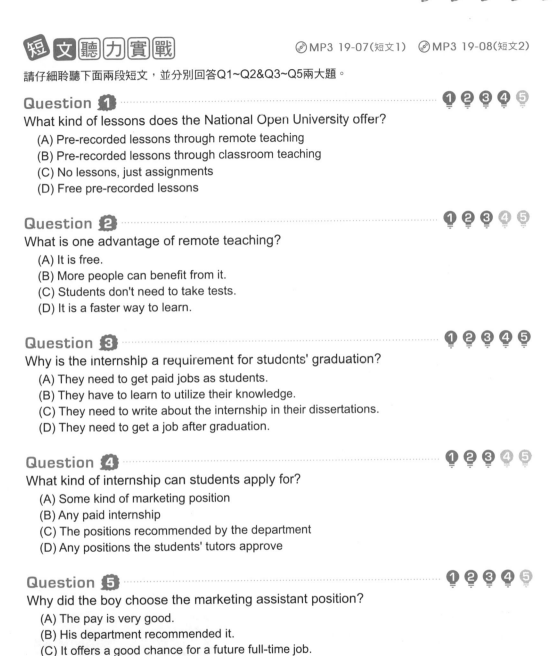

短文聽力實戰

MP3 19-07(短文1)　　MP3 19-08(短文2)

請仔細聆聽下面兩段短文，並分別回答Q1~Q2&Q3~Q5兩大題。

Question 1
What kind of lessons does the National Open University offer?

(A) Pre-recorded lessons through remote teaching
(B) Pre-recorded lessons through classroom teaching
(C) No lessons, just assignments
(D) Free pre-recorded lessons

Question 2
What is one advantage of remote teaching?

(A) It is free.
(B) More people can benefit from it.
(C) Students don't need to take tests.
(D) It is a faster way to learn.

Question 3
Why is the internship a requirement for students' graduation?

(A) They need to get paid jobs as students.
(B) They have to learn to utilize their knowledge.
(C) They need to write about the internship in their dissertations.
(D) They need to get a job after graduation.

Question 4
What kind of internship can students apply for?

(A) Some kind of marketing position
(B) Any paid internship
(C) The positions recommended by the department
(D) Any positions the students' tutors approve

Question 5
Why did the boy choose the marketing assistant position?

(A) The pay is very good.
(B) His department recommended it.
(C) It offers a good chance for a future full-time job.
(D) It was the only company that accepted his application.

答案與解析 ～answer

Answer 1 ◄)) (A)
國立空中大學提供什麼樣的課程呢？
- (A) 用遠程教學觀看預錄的課程
- (B) 在課堂上觀看預錄的課程
- (C) 沒有提供課程，只有作業
- (D) 免費的預錄課程

解析
題目明確地詢問「空中大學」所提供的課程，因此必須選明確以空中大學舉例的「遠程教學」，讓學生能在家裡觀看「預錄的課程」(pre-recorded lessons)，正確答案為(A)。

Answer 2 ◄)) (B)
遠程教學的優點是什麼呢？
- (A) 它完全免費。
- (B) 有更多人能因此受益。
- (C) 學生不用考試。
- (D) 這種方式的學習速度更快。

解析
本題的重點單字在題目與文中皆提到的 advantage(優點)。女性提到使用遠程教學的學生只需要定期與教授碰面，這種方式能「讓更多人享有受教育的機會」，正確答案為(B)。

Answer 3 ◄)) (B)
為什麼實習經驗會被列為學生的畢業門檻項目呢？
- (A) 學生必須賺錢。
- (B) 學生必須學著運用所學。
- (C) 學生必須把實習經驗寫進論文。
- (D) 學生必須在畢業後找到工作。

解析
文章一開始，男孩就提到系上重視「實際運用知識」(practically applying our knowledge)，因此實習才被列為畢業門檻的項目，正確答案為(B)。

Answer 4 ◄)) (D)
學生們能申請什麼樣的實習工作呢？
- (A) 與行銷有關的工作
- (B) 有薪資的實習工作
- (C) 系上推薦的工作
- (D) 學生導師同意的任何工作

解析
解題時要注意題目問的是「能申請」(can apply)。文中雖然提到系上會列出一些工作機會給學生，但這並非學生能申請的原因，可剔除選項(C)；真正的關鍵句在「只要導師同意，任何工作機會都能申請」，正確答案為(D)。

Answer 5 ◄)) (C)
男孩為什麼會選擇行銷助理的工作呢？
- (A) 這份工作的薪水很高。
- (B) 他的系所推薦這份工作。
- (C) 這份工作提供未來取得正職的機會。
- (D) 這是唯一接受他申請的公司。

解析
文章後半部，男孩有提到這份實習的薪水不是太好，可剔除選項(A)；接著說即便如此，他最大的考量是「未來能取得正職的機會」(full-time用來形容正職的工作或員工)，正確答案為(C)。

⊙慢速MP3 19-09　⊙正常速MP3 19-10

　　Speaking of education, traditional classroom teaching is no longer the sole way of delivering knowledge. Technology has created various different learning platforms. For instance, the National Open University in Taiwan uses **remote teaching** where students can watch **pre-recorded lessons** at home. **One advantage** of this learning method is that students only need to physically meet with their professors periodically. This makes education **available to more people**, including people on salary and students who live far from the university.

　　提到教育，傳統的課堂教學不再是傳遞知識的唯一方式了。科技創造出各種不同的學習平台。舉例來說，台灣的國立空中大學採用的遠程教學，讓學生可以在家裡看預錄的課程。這種學習方式的優點在於，學生只需要定期與教授碰面即可，這樣的形態能讓更多人享有受教育的機會，包括上班族以及住家離學校很遠的學生。

⊙慢速MP3 19-11　⊙正常速MP3 19-12

　　My department stresses the importance of **practically applying our knowledge**. Therefore, internship is required on the threshold of our graduation. The department has provided the students with a list of available internships. We can apply for **any jobs as long as our tutors approve them**. I've found a job as a marketing assistant at a financial services company. Even though the pay for the internship isn't fantastic, **the prospect of getting a full-time position** there is my biggest concern. I hope this will get me a head-start before I graduate.

　　我的系所強調實際運用知識的重要性，所以，實習經驗被列為我們的畢業門檻之一。系上會列出提供實習機會的公司給學生，只要導師同意，任何工作機會我們都能申請。我已經在一家金融服務公司找到行銷助理的職位，雖然實習的薪水不是太好，但未來很有機會在那裡取得正職，這是我最大的考量。希望這份實習經驗能讓我在畢業前就贏在起跑線上。

PART 4 校園生活

Unit 5 畢業歡送季 Graduation

📺 日常生活　🎭 娛樂活動　✏️ 意見交流　🎏 特殊場合

🎵 MP3 20-01

下面將播放五組短對話，請仔細聆聽，再依對話內容答題。

Question ❶

Where is the boy asking the girl to go with him?

(A) A job fair at the university
(B) A job interview the girl recommends
(C) A career fair the local government is holding
(D) The career center at the university

Question ❷

What does the boy suggest the girl try on her resume?

(A) Record a video as her resume
(B) Send her resume to more companies
(C) Go and talk to a potential employers in person
(D) Ask someone else to recommend her

Question ❸

Why are the speakers taking the TOEIC exam?

(A) Because they need it to graduate.
(B) Because it's an important criterion for employers.
(C) Because everyone else is taking the exam next month.
(D) Because somebody recommended that they take it.

Question ❹

Why is the girl so nervous?

(A) Because she can't dance.
(B) Because she hasn't got a dress yet.
(C) Because she doesn't know what to say to people.
(D) Because she needs to deliver a speech in front of people.

Question ❺

What does the boy think the girl will win?

(A) The raffle's top prize at the ball
(B) An award for being the best dancer
(C) An award for being the best dressed-person
(D) A small prize

186

答案與解析 ～answer

Answer 1 ◀ (C)
男孩邀請女孩和他一起去哪裡呢？

(A) 學校舉辦的就業博覽會

(B) 女孩推薦的面試機會

(C) 當地政府舉辦的就業博覽會

(D) 學校的就業指導中心

解析

解題關鍵在男孩提到的「本地就業指導中心舉辦的就業博覽會」；因為是當地的就業指導中心，因此可推斷是公家機構舉辦的，正確答案選(C)。注意A be held at B的用法，A表示舉辦的「活動」，B指主辦「機構」。

Answer 2 ◀ (A)
針對履歷，男孩給了女孩什麼樣的建議呢？

(A) 錄製影音履歷

(B) 寄履歷給更多家公司

(C) 直接找有可能雇用她的人談

(D) 請其他人推薦她

解析

針對如何讓自己的履歷脫穎而出，男孩建議「影音履歷」(a video resume)，這樣潛在雇主就可以看到女孩真人說話，正確答案為(A)。

Answer 3 ◀ (B)
對話中的男女為什麼要考多益？

(A) 因為考了多益才能畢業。

(B) 因為那對雇主來說是一項重要的標準。

(C) 因為其他人下個月都要考多益。

(D) 因為有人推薦他們去考多益。

解析

從對話中可以聽出男女兩人準備下個月考多益，原因在女孩說的「英語似乎是找到好工作的先決條件」(prerequisite 必要條件)，可視為雇主重視的條件，正確答案為(B)。

Answer 4 ◀ (D)
女孩為什麼會這麼緊張呢？

(A) 因為她不會跳舞。

(B) 因為她還沒找到合適的禮服。

(C) 因為她不知道該跟其他人說什麼。

(D) 因為她必須在大家面前演講。

解析

女孩一開始提到自己為了舞會而緊張，男孩為此感到奇怪，因為他認為已經上舞蹈課的女孩不應該會害怕跳舞，此時女孩才說自己緊張的是要「在大家面前演講」這件事，正確答案為(D)。

Answer 5 ◀ (C)
男孩覺得女孩會贏得什麼呢？

(A) 舞會抽獎券的最大獎

(B) 最佳舞者的獎項

(C) 最佳穿著的獎項

(D) 一份小獎品

解析

解題關鍵在男孩一開始看到女孩的穿著時，所提到的「最佳穿著獎」(the Best-Dressed Award)，後來提到的小獎品是每個參加者都能從抽獎活動中得到的，正確答案為(C)。

⊙慢速MP3 20-02　　◉正常速MP3 20-03

短對話 1 *Conversation*

Lisa: Graduation is around the corner! The next challenge is for us to find a job.

麗莎： 就快畢業了！下一個挑戰就是找工作。

Barry: Let's go to **the career fair being held at the local career center**.

巴瑞： 我們一起去本地就業指導中心舉辦的就業博覽會看看吧。

短對話 2 *Conversation*

Mary: Speaking of finding a job, I need to find a way to make my resume stand out.

瑪麗： 講到找工作，我得設法讓自己的履歷脫穎而出。

Todd: How about **a video resume**? Then they'll see you talk in person.

陶德： 影音履歷怎麼樣？這樣他們就能看到真人介紹履歷。

短對話 3 *Conversation*

Peter: I'm taking the TOEIC exam next month.

彼得： 我下個月要考多益。

Daisy: Me, too. English seems to be one of **the basic prerequisites for getting a good job** these days.

黛西： 我也是，現在，英語似乎是找到好工作的先決條件了。

短對話 4 *Conversation*

Amy: I'm so nervous about the graduation ball tomorrow.

愛咪： 明天的畢業舞會真令人緊張。

Chad: Why? I thought you've been taking some ballroom dancing lessons.

查德： 為什麼？你不是為了舞會，已經去上國標舞課了嗎？

Amy: I'm nervous about **giving a speech** in front of everyone.

愛咪： 我緊張的是要在大家面前演講啦。

短對話 5 *Conversation*

Leo: You look fantastic! I think you'll win **the Best-Dressed Award** at the ball tonight.

里歐： 你看起來美極了！我覺得你會贏得今晚舞會的「最佳穿著獎」。

Eve: I don't think that will happen.

伊芙： 我覺得不太可能。

Leo: No matter what, we'll all win a small prize from the raffle ticket.

里歐： 反正不管怎樣，我們今晚都會從抽獎活動中贏得一份小獎品。

長對話聽力實戰

MP3 20-04

請仔細聆聽下面的長對話，再依對話內容選擇正確答案。

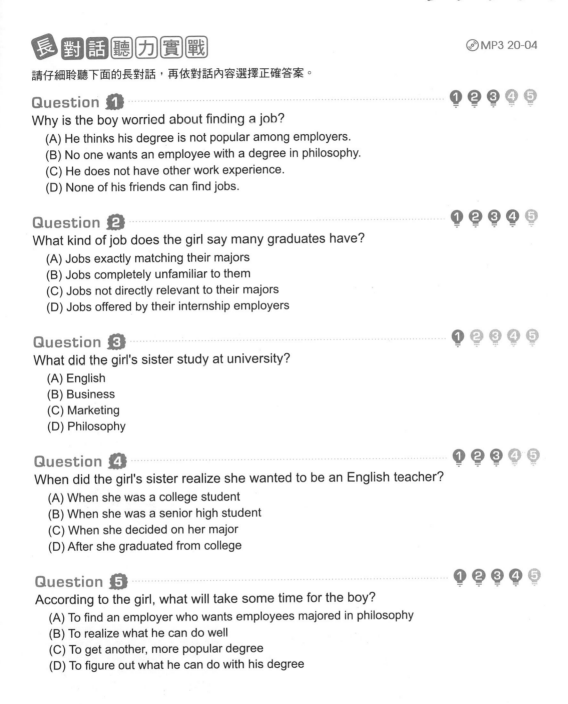

Question 1

Why is the boy worried about finding a job?

(A) He thinks his degree is not popular among employers.

(B) No one wants an employee with a degree in philosophy.

(C) He does not have other work experience.

(D) None of his friends can find jobs.

Question 2

What kind of job does the girl say many graduates have?

(A) Jobs exactly matching their majors

(B) Jobs completely unfamiliar to them

(C) Jobs not directly relevant to their majors

(D) Jobs offered by their internship employers

Question 3

What did the girl's sister study at university?

(A) English

(B) Business

(C) Marketing

(D) Philosophy

Question 4

When did the girl's sister realize she wanted to be an English teacher?

(A) When she was a college student

(B) When she was a senior high student

(C) When she decided on her major

(D) After she graduated from college

Question 5

According to the girl, what will take some time for the boy?

(A) To find an employer who wants employees majored in philosophy

(B) To realize what he can do well

(C) To get another, more popular degree

(D) To figure out what he can do with his degree

答案與解析 ~answer

Answer 1 ◀)) (A)
男孩為什麼會擔心找不到工作？

(A) 他覺得自己的哲學文憑雇主不會喜歡。

(B) 沒有人想要找唸哲學系的員工。

(C) 他沒有其他的工作經驗。

(D) 他所有的朋友都找不到工作。

解析

解題的重點有兩處，其一為男孩一開始說他擔心自己的文憑背景會找不到工作。關鍵字為degree(文憑)；第二個重點在他接著解釋哲學系並非「受歡迎的科系」(not a popular degree)，由此可推測正確答案為(A)。

Answer 2 ◀)) (C)
根據女孩所言，很多畢業生找到什麼樣的工作？

(A) 完全符合他們主修的工作

(B) 他們完全不熟悉的工作

(C) 不直接和他們的主修有關的工作

(D) 實習時的老闆所提供的工作

解析

注意題目中the girl say(女孩說的)與many graduates(很多畢業生)這兩處。同時符合這兩個條件的內容是女孩提到的「很多畢業生做的工作都跟文憑沒什麼直接關係」(not directly relevant to ...)，正確答案為(C)。

Answer 3 ◀)) (B)
女孩的姐姐大學時唸的科系是什麼？

(A) 英語

(B) 商科

(C) 行銷

(D) 哲學

解析

為了舉例解釋畢業生做的工作與文憑沒什麼直接關連，女孩提到她的姐姐，說她「主修商科」(major in business)，但現在卻在當老師，正確答案為(B)。

Answer 4 ◀)) (D)
女孩的姊姊什麼時候意識到自己想當英文老師的呢？

(A) 當她還是大學生時

(B) 當她還是高中生時

(C) 當她在決定主修科系時

(D) 在她從大學畢業之後

解析

當男孩問女孩的姐姐是否後悔大學沒唸英文系時，女孩回答「她後來才意識到自己想從事教學」。重點字afterwards為「後來」，可看出女孩姐姐大學或更之前時都沒有考慮過當老師，最佳答案為(D)。

Answer 5 ◀)) (B)
根據女孩所言，男孩需要花點時間才能如何呢？

(A) 找到想雇用哲學系員工的老闆

(B) 理解他擅長做什麼

(C) 另外取得受歡迎科系的文憑

(D) 找出他的哲學系文憑能做什麼

解析

對話最後，女孩安撫男孩說他會需要一些時間來「弄清楚他擅長做什麼」，就像女孩的姐姐那樣，畢業後才找到英文老師的出路，關鍵片語be good at表示「擅長」，正確答案為(B)。

⊙慢速MP3 20-05　　◎正常速MP3 20-06

| Kent:
肯特： | I'm worried about finding a job with my **educational background**.
真擔心我的文憑會找不到工作。 |

| Carrie:
卡莉： | Why?
為什麼呢？ |

| Kent:
肯特： | It's because of my major. Philosophy **isn't a popular degree** like business or engineering.
因為我主修的是哲學，不像商管系或工程系那樣受歡迎。 |

| Carrie:
卡莉： | Actually, many graduates end up in a job **not directly relevant** to their degrees.
事實上，很多畢業生做的工作都跟唸的科系沒什麼關係。 |

| Kent:
肯特： | Really?
真的嗎？ |

| Carrie:
卡莉： | Sure. For example, my sister **majored in business**, but now she's an English teacher.
對啊，拿我姐姐來說，她主修商科，但現在是英語老師。 |

| Kent:
肯特： | Did she regret not having studied English back in college?
那她會後悔在大學的時候沒有選擇英文系嗎？ |

| Carrie:
卡莉： | No. She didn't plan to be a teacher then. It's something she **realized afterwards**.
沒有，她那時候並不想當老師，她後來才意識到自己想成為老師。 |

| Kent:
肯特： | Alright. Perhaps I'm overthinking all this.
好吧，也許我想太多了。 |

| Carrie:
卡莉： | Don't worry. It'll take some time to **figure out what you're good at**.
別擔心，你會需要一些時間來弄清楚你擅長什麼。 |

短 文 聽 力 實 戰

⊙MP3 20-07(短文1)   ⊙MP3 20-08(短文2)

請仔細聆聽下面兩段短文，並分別回答Q1~Q2&Q3~Q5兩大題。

Question ① ① ② ③ ④ ⑤
What did the boy find most useful at the career fair?

(A) The recruitment information given out by the companies
(B) The companies' on-the-spot interviews
(C) The resume advice booth
(D) The interview opportunities provided by his university

Question ② ① ② ③ ④ ⑤
How did the boy get his on-the-spot interviews at the fair?

(A) By showing a video resume
(B) By following the adviser's suggestions on his resume
(C) By giving a presentation
(D) By giving his resume to all interviewers

Question ③ ① ② ③ ④ ⑤
What did the girl work as during her summer internship?

(A) A PR manager
(B) An assistant to a PR manager
(C) A PR agent
(D) A junior PR manager

Question ④ ① ② ③ ④ ⑤
Why did the company offer the girl the internship?

(A) Because she wrote to them.
(B) Because her professor strongly recommended her.
(C) Because her explanation was persuasive.
(D) Because they felt her background suited the position.

Question ⑤ ① ② ③ ④ ⑤
What chance may the girl have as soon as she graduates?

(A) To become a full-time intern
(B) To get better pay
(C) To work as a full-time PR manager's assistant
(D) To get a full-time job with the company

答案與解析 ～answer

Answer 1 🔊 (C)
男孩覺得博覽會上的什麼最有幫助？
- (A) 公司提供的招聘資訊
- (B) 當場的即時面試
- (C) 履歷諮詢攤位
- (D) 他大學提供的面試機會

解析
解題關鍵在題目中的most useful(特別有幫助)。所以必須找出男孩提到的某特定事項，即「履歷諮詢攤位」(the resume advice booth)，正確答案為(C)。

Answer 2 🔊 (B)
男孩是如何在博覽會上取得即時面試的機會呢？
- (A) 展示他的影音履歷
- (B) 根據顧問的建議修改他的履歷
- (C) 做了一份簡報
- (D) 把履歷給所有的面試者

解析
男孩提到自己之前就一直在投履歷，但是都沒有收到回覆，藉由「就業顧問給他的提示」(gave me some tips)，他當場「修改履歷」(edited my resume)，才有雇主感興趣，請他面試，正確答案為(B)。

Answer 3 🔊 (B)
女孩在暑期實習時，做的工作是什麼？
- (A) 一名公關經理
- (B) 公關經理的助理
- (C) 一名公關
- (D) 初階公關經理

解析
女孩一開始就提到自己的暑期實習，接著才說到那家公關公司找的「公關經理助理」本來是一份全職的職缺，正確答案為(B)。關鍵字為assistant(助理)。

Answer 4 🔊 (D)
那家公司為何願意給女孩這份實習工作？
- (A) 因為女孩寫信給公司。
- (B) 因為女孩的教授大力推薦她。
- (C) 因為女孩的解釋很有說服力。
- (D) 因為公司認為她的背景很適合這份工作。

解析
女孩提到自己很驚訝能成功取得這份實習工作，並進一步說明公司認為「她的背景非常適合」(my background very suitable)，正確答案為(D)。選項(A)的寫信給公司並非原因，只是女孩採取的行動而已。

Answer 5 🔊 (D)
女孩一畢業，可能取得什麼機會？
- (A) 成為全職的實習人員
- (B) 取得更好的薪水
- (C) 成為全職的公關經理助理
- (D) 在實習的那家公司取得正職工作

解析
本文最後，女孩的經理說，因為她在實習期間的表現優良，所以畢業之後，公司很可能願意雇用她「成為正職員工」(a full-time employee)，但並沒有說那份工作會與實習時的工作相同，正確答案為(D)。

中英文內容

短文 1

⊙慢速MP3 20-09　　◎正常速MP3 20-10

I went to a very large job fair held on my campus last weekend. I found it both interesting and useful. There were so many companies that had set up booths to give out recruitment information and do on-the-spot interviews. What I found **particularly beneficial** was **the resume advice booth**. I had been handing out my resume to several companies, but I hadn't gotten any replies in the past. After **the career adviser gave me some tips**, I **edited my resume** on the spot. And guess what? The employers who saw my new resume seemed much more interested. I was given several interviews straight away!

我上週末去了在我學校舉辦的大型就業博覽會，我覺得很有趣，也很有幫助。有很多企業在博覽會設立攤位，並提供招聘資訊和做即時的面試。對我來說，最有幫助的是履歷諮詢攤位。在這之前，我一直有在投履歷，但都沒有得到回覆。在就業顧問給了我一些提示後，我當場修改了履歷內容，你猜怎麼著？看到我新履歷的雇主變得更感興趣，我還因此被好幾個公司面試了呢！

短文 2

⊙慢速MP3 20-11　　◎正常速MP3 20-12

I just finished a great summer internship. It was with a PR agency in Taipei. The position of **PR manager's assistant** was a full-time opening. I wrote to the company and explained I was looking for an internship. Surprisingly, I managed to get the job as my internship because they **considered my background very suitable**. The company also made an exception in paying me a salary. They don't normally offer paid internships to students without work experience. According to my manager, they might hire me as **a full-time employee** as soon as I graduate because of my excellent performance in my internship.

我剛剛結束了一份很棒的暑期實習工作。我在一家台北的公關公司實習。「公關經理助理」其實是一份全職的職缺，我寫信給這家公司，向他們解釋我只能做短期實習，令人驚訝的是，我竟然成功得到這份實習工作，因為他們認為我的背景非常適合。這家公司還破例付我薪水，他們通常不會給毫無工作經驗的學生薪水。根據我經理的話，因為我實習期間的表現優良，所以我一畢業，他們有可能會願意雇用我，正式成為公司的一員。

5 PART

職場與工作

力爭上游、退休生活，
不聽不可的職場生存 must-know ！

Unit 1 應徵與指導
Recruitment

Unit 2 上班日常
My Daily Work

Unit 3 工作百百種
Various Jobs

Unit 4 職場閒談
Chatting Together

Unit 5 離職與退休
Get Retired

 應徵與指導 Recruitment

 日常生活　娛樂活動　意見交流　特殊場合

短 對 話 聽 力 實 戰

⊙ MP3 21-01

下面將播放五組短對話，請仔細聆聽，再依對話內容答題。

Question 1

According to the man, what will job banks do?

(A) They'll interview the woman.

(B) They'll let the woman know if there're suitable vacancies.

(C) They'll send her resume out to potential employers.

(D) They'll go through the job ads in the newspaper.

Question 2

Why hasn't the woman gotten any response?

(A) The employers don't like her resume.

(B) What she wrote in her resume is too plain.

(C) She used the template cover letter the job bank provides.

(D) She has not provided a cover letter with her application.

Question 3

What does the man appreciate about the woman?

(A) The way she shows her ambition and confidence

(B) The woman's leadership

(C) The fact that she was the chairman of the student society

(D) Her excellent work experience

Question 4

What is the woman surprised about?

(A) The man is practicing introducing himself.

(B) The man is murmuring to himself.

(C) The man isn't dressed appropriately for an interview.

(D) The man hasn't prepared a speech for the interview.

Question 5

Why does the woman ask the man to stop fiddling with his fingers?

(A) Otherwise, the interviewer will ask him to leave.

(B) Otherwise, he'll make himself more nervous.

(C) Otherwise, he'll have to explain why he's nervous.

(D) Otherwise, he'll leave a bad impression.

答案與解析 ～answer

Answer 1 (B)
根據男性所言，人力銀行會做什麼呢？
- (A) 他們會面試對話中的女子。
- (B) 有適當的職缺時，他們會通知女子。
- (C) 他們會把女子的履歷寄給可能錄用她的雇主。
- (D) 他們會看完報紙上的徵人廣告。

> **解析**
> 女子抱怨從報紙裡找工作很花時間，男性因而建議她上網到人力銀行註冊，這樣只要有符合女子「設定條件」(match the criteria)的職缺時，系統就會「發電子郵件通知」(notify)，正確答案為(B)。

Answer 2 (C)
女性為什麼尚未收到任何回覆呢？
- (A) 雇主們不喜歡她的履歷。
- (B) 她履歷中的內容太平淡無奇。
- (C) 她使用人力銀行提供的標準求職信。
- (D) 她應徵工作時沒有附上求職信。

> **解析**
> 解題時必須以對話中提到的原因為準。男性提醒女性寄履歷時不要用「人力銀行提供的標準求職信」。女性的回應表示她用了標準求職信，正確答案為(C)。

Answer 3 (A)
男性欣賞女子的哪個部分呢？
- (A) 她展現企圖心與自信的方式
- (B) 女子的領導能力
- (C) 她曾擔任學生會會長的經驗
- (D) 她優秀的工作經驗

> **解析**
> 本題重點必須放在男面試官的回應，所以女子提到的學生會長與領導能力並非主要原因。答案在最後一句，面試官欣賞女子替自己辯護的「方式」，因為「展現了企圖心和自信心」(ambition and confidence)，正確答案為(A)。

Answer 4 (C)
讓女性感到訝異的事情是什麼呢？
- (A) 男性在練習自我介紹。
- (B) 男性在喃喃自語。
- (C) 男性的穿著不適合面試。
- (D) 男性沒有準備面試用的演講內容。

> **解析**
> 題目問的是讓女性「訝異」(surprised)的事情，所以普通的疑問不適用，可剔除(B)。聽到男性在練習自我介紹後，女性以What?!開頭表示她的驚訝，後面提到a nice shirt(襯衫)，可知與服裝有關，正確答案為(C)。

Answer 5 (D)
女性為什麼要求男性停止轉手指的動作？
- (A) 不然面試官會請他離開。
- (B) 不然他可能會變得更緊張。
- (C) 不然他就必須解釋緊張的原因。
- (D) 不然他會給人不好的印象。

> **解析**
> 本題的答案在第一句，女性認為轉手指的動作會給面試官「留下不好的印象」(won't leave a good impression)，正確答案為(D)。注意選項(B)的意思是男性「會變得更緊張」，不符合文義。

⊙慢速MP3 21-02　　⊙正常速MP3 21-03

短對話 ❶ *Conversation*

Vicky: It's taking me forever to go through all the job ads in the newspapers!

薇琪： 要看完報紙裡的工作分類廣告好花時間喔！

Quinn: Why don't you sign up with some job banks? They'll email to **notify you of vacancies that match the criteria** you set.

昆恩： 你為什麼不在網路人力銀行註冊？有符合你要求的職缺時，他們就會通知你。

短對話 ❷ *Conversation*

Fanny: I've applied for many jobs through a job bank.

芬妮： 我已經透過人力銀行應徵了很多工作。

Seth: Make sure you don't use **the standard template** they provide for **cover letter**.

賽斯： 確認你寄履歷時不是用網站提供的標準求職信。

Fanny: Oh! That might be the reason why I haven't had any replies yet.

芬妮： 喔！那可能是我到目前為止沒收到任何回覆的原因。

短對話 ❸ *Conversation*

Interviewer: I see you're a fresh graduate without work experience.

面試官： 所以，你是應屆畢業生，沒有任何工作經驗。

Sophie: I was the chairman of the student society. That can prove my leadership.

蘇菲： 我曾任學生會會長，那能證明我的領導能力。

Interviewer: I like how you defended for yourself. It demonstrates your **ambition and confidence**.

面試官： 我欣賞你替自己辯護的方式，展現了企圖心和自信心。

短對話 ❹ *Conversation*

Emily: Why are you murmuring to yourself?

愛蜜莉： 你為什麼要喃喃自語啊？

Michael: I'm going for an interview, and I'm practicing introducing myself.

麥可： 我要去面試，所以在練習自我介紹的內容。

Emily: What?! **Shouldn't you at least wear a nice shirt**?

愛蜜莉： 什麼？！那你至少該穿件襯衫吧？

短對話 ❺ *Conversation*

Susie: Stop fiddling with your fingers. It **won't leave a good impression** on the interviewer.

蘇西： 別再轉手指了，這樣會給面試官留下不好的印象。

Peter: That's what I do when I'm nervous.

彼得： 這是我緊張時的習慣動作啊。

長對話聽力實戰

MP3 21-04

請仔細聆聽下面的長對話，再依對話內容選擇正確答案。

Question 1

When will the new colleague receive her orientation training?

- (A) Next week
- (B) Whenever is convenient for her
- (C) This Friday
- (D) Within the first week of work

Question 2

What is the man going to tell the new colleague about?

- (A) IT systems
- (B) HR policies
- (C) General policies
- (D) Facility policies

Question 3

When is the man going to teach the new colleague about their database?

- (A) This Friday
- (B) On her first day
- (C) Next month
- (D) We are not told.

Question 4

What will the man have to make sure after the orientation training?

- (A) The new staff is given a test.
- (B) The new staff repeats everything they said.
- (C) The new staff signs a declaration form.
- (D) The new staff signs a contract.

Question 5

Why does signing the declaration form become mandatory?

- (A) Because it's the basic requirement.
- (B) Because somebody lied about being informed of certain policies.
- (C) Because somebody asked for it.
- (D) Because new colleagues need it as proof.

答案與解析 ～answer

Answer 1 ◀)) (C)
新同事將會於何時接受到職培訓呢？

(A) 下週
(B) 新同事方便的時間
(C) 本週五
(D) 上班的第一個星期內

解析
對話一開始女性就提到新同事，說對方「這個星期五」(this Friday)會進公司參加「到職培訓」(the orientation training)，正確答案為(C)。

Answer 2 ◀)) (A)
男性將告訴新同事關於什麼的事項呢？

(A) 資訊系統
(B) 人資方面的政策
(C) 一般性政策
(D) 與設備相關的政策

解析
解題關鍵在女性提到新同事會參加到職培訓後，請男性教她「公司資訊系統」(IT systems)方面的細節，後面也提到電子郵件與網路政策，能包含這些例子的只有選項(A)。

Answer 3 ◀)) (D)
男性何時會教新同事資料庫的事情？

(A) 本週五
(B) 她第一天上班的時候
(C) 下個月
(D) 不知道

解析
當男性問是否該跟新同事講解有關公司的數據庫時，女性回答「到職培訓時也許先不用講」(not in the initial orientation)，但沒有特別說何時，因此正確答案為(D)。

Answer 4 ◀)) (C)
到職培訓結束後，男性必須確認什麼事情？

(A) 新同事接受考試。
(B) 新同事複誦他們說的事項。
(C) 新同事簽署聲明書。
(D) 新同事簽署合約。

解析
對話後半部，女性要求男性確保(make sure)新同事簽署「聲明書」(declaration form)，確認他們有替她上過到職培訓，正確答案為(C)。注意選項(D)簽署的是合約(contract)，與聲明書的性質不同。

Answer 5 ◀)) (B)
簽署聲明書為什麼會變成強制性質的呢？

(A) 因為這是基本要求。
(B) 因為有人說過謊，說沒講解到部分政策。
(C) 因為有人這麼要求。
(D) 因為新同事需要簽署書作證明。

解析
當男性訝異現在還必須簽署聲明書時，女性解釋之前有人撒謊，說「到職培訓時，公司人員沒有講解到部分政策」，關鍵字為lie(說謊)，正確答案為(B)。

中英文內容

⊙慢速MP3 21-05　　◎正常速MP3 21-06

Elaine: Our new colleague will come in **this Friday** to start with **the orientation training**. I'd like you to give her an orientation on **IT systems.**
伊蓮：　我們的新同事本週五會進公司參加到職培訓，我想請你教她公司資訊系統方面的細節。

George:Sure. Can we quickly draft a list of specific things I need to tell her?
喬治：　沒問題，能大致列一下我必須告訴她的具體事項有哪些嗎？

Elaine: The basics are email and Internet policies. File-naming conventions are also essential.
伊蓮：　基本的包括電子郵件和網路的使用政策，檔案命名規則也必須教她。

George:OK. What about our database? Should I go through that?
喬治：　好，那數據庫呢？要跟她講解這個嗎？

Elaine: Perhaps **not in the initial orientation**. It'll be too much for her.
伊蓮：　到職培訓的時候也許先不用，不然對她來說會有太多的資訊要消化。

George:No problem.
喬治：　沒問題。

Elaine: Could you also make sure she signs **a declaration form** to confirm she has received orientation?
伊蓮：　可以請你確保她簽署了聲明書嗎？確認我們有給她上過到職培訓的內容。

George:We need to do that now?
喬治：　我們現在得做到那種程度嗎？

Elaine: Yes. We had **a guy lying that he didn't receive orientation** on certain policies before. So the declaration form is mandatory now.
伊蓮：　沒錯，因為之前有人撒謊，說他參加到職培訓時，我們沒講解部分政策，所以現在聲明書都是強制性質的。

短文聽力實戰

MP3 21-07(短文1)　　MP3 21-08(短文2)

請仔細聆聽下面兩段短文，並分別回答Q1~Q2&Q3~Q5兩大題。

Question 1

What has the man just joined?

(A) A recruitment fair taking place at his college

(B) A new study program

(C) A graduate training program at his college

(D) A training program for new employees

Question 2

What is the man most excited about?

(A) Receiving free hotel accommodation and food

(B) Receiving the salary offered straight away

(C) Receiving training in Singapore

(D) Receiving more money than most other graduates do

Question 3

Whose pressure would be highest when looking for a job?

(A) People without a degree in a popular subject

(B) People without a degree in philosophy

(C) People with a degree in business or marketing

(D) People who graduate from a double degree program

Question 4

Why did the girl choose to study philosophy?

(A) She really liked the campus environment.

(B) She enjoyed the courses she chose this semester.

(C) She enjoyed the lessons before becoming a college student.

(D) Her father persuaded her to study philosophy.

Question 5

What does the girl's father say is not a sign of failure?

(A) Having a degree in philosophy

(B) Having a job related to her degree

(C) Changing her job if she thinks it is not right for her

(D) Not working in a philosophy-related job position

答案與解析 ～answer

Answer 1 (D)

男性參加了什麼呢？

(A) 在大學舉辦的應徵會

(B) 一個新的研究計畫

(C) 在他大學舉辦的畢業生培訓計畫

(D) 替新員工舉辦的培訓計畫

> **解析**
> 男性提到自己被公司選入參加「新進員工的培訓計畫」，接下來進一步解釋計畫「專門用來培訓應屆畢業生」(newly recruited graduates)，正確答案為(D)。注意(C)錯誤的地方在「並非在男性的學校舉辦」。

Answer 2 (B)

最讓男性感到興奮的事情是什麼？

(A) 享受免費的住宿和食物

(B) 馬上就能領到薪水

(C) 在新加坡受訓

(D) 比其他畢業生領到更多錢

> **解析**
> 男性在最後提到自己之所以會如此興奮的原因並非因為他們所有的基本生活開銷都由公司支付，而是因為他「馬上會領到薪資」。句型not because...but...所強調的重點在but後面，正確答案為(B)。

Answer 3 (A)

下面哪一種人在找工作時的壓力最大？

(A) 沒有受歡迎科系文憑的人

(B) 非哲學系畢業的人

(C) 商學系或行銷科系畢業的人

(D) 雙主修畢業的人

> **解析**
> 女孩一開始就提到進入職場可能令人感到畏縮，尤其當你「沒有如商業或行銷這類的熱門學位背景時」，正確答案為(A)。

Answer 4 (C)

女孩為什麼會選擇唸哲學系呢？

(A) 她很喜歡學校的環境。

(B) 她很喜歡這學期修的課程。

(C) 她很喜歡上大學前上過的課。

(D) 她的父親說服她唸哲學系。

> **解析**
> 解題關鍵在女孩提到自己高中時曾經聽過為「有可能成為校內學生而舉辦的試聽課」(taster session)，正確答案為(C)。如果沒有聽出關鍵的試聽課，也能從後句的when I was in senior high推測出是她上大學前所聽的課。

Answer 5 (C)

女孩的父親認為「什麼」不代表失敗？

(A) 畢業於哲學系

(B) 找到與她主修有關連的工作

(C) 感到工作不適合她而換工作

(D) 沒有找到與哲學相關的工作

> **解析**
> 女孩最後提到父親很支持她，表示「如果工作不適合她，也不代表失敗」。does not work for sb.表示「某事不適合某人」或「某人無法繼續某事而中斷」，在此指女孩找到工作後，做不下去而放棄，正確答案為(C)。

中英文內容

短文 1

⊙慢速MP3 21-09　　⊘正常速MP3 21-10

I feel so lucky to have been selected for the graduate training program at my company. It is designed to train **newly recruited graduates** regardless of their backgrounds. Although I applied for the program, I didn't expect to get into it. I guess my part-time work experience paid off and impressed the interviewers. Starting from next week, I will be going on a month-long training program in Singapore. I'm excited not because all the basic living costs are paid for, but because I will start **receiving a full salary straight away**.

能被公司選定參加新進員工的培訓計畫實在太幸運了。這個計畫專門用來培訓應屆畢業生，不論這些新員工的學歷背景為何。雖然我有申請，但並沒有想到會被選進去，也許是我的打工經驗讓面試官們感到印象深刻吧。從下週開始，我就要參加在新加坡舉行、為期一個月的培訓課程，我感到非常興奮，這可不是因為我們所有的基本生活開銷都由公司支付，而是因為我馬上就能拿到全額的薪資了。

短文 2

⊙慢速MP3 21-11　　⊘正常速MP3 21-12

Stepping out of school and going into the working world could be very daunting. The pressure is even higher when you **do not have a degree in a popular subject** like business or marketing. I chose to major in philosophy because I truly enjoyed **the taster session offered to prospective students** when I was in senior high. Now though, I am worried that I will not be able to find a suitable job. Fortunately, my father is very supportive and encouraging. He reassured me that most people do not have a job related to their degrees. And if **a job does not work for me**, it is not a sign of failure.

走出校園並踏入職場能讓人感到畏縮，尤其是當你沒有如商業或行銷這類的熱門學位背景時，壓力就會更大。我選擇哲學系的原因是因為我高中的時候，去聽了為有可能成為校內學生而舉辦的試聽課，聽完之後很喜歡，所以決定唸哲學。但現在，我很擔心自己找不到合適的工作。幸運的是，我的父親很支持和鼓勵我，他安慰我說，大多數人的工作與大學唸的主修都沒什麼關係，如果最後發現工作不適合我，也不代表失敗。

Unit 2 上班日常 My Daily Work

日常生活　娛樂活動　意見交流　特殊場合

 短對話聽力實戰

◎MP3 22-01

下面將播放五組短對話，請仔細聆聽，再依對話內容答題。

Question 1

Why does the woman bring in cake for her colleagues?

(A) She wants to celebrate her birthday.
(B) She had some cake left from her son's birthday party.
(C) She had some cake left from her birthday party.
(D) She wants her colleagues to celebrate her promotion.

Question 2

Why is the woman unhappy about Joe's promotion?

(A) Because he doesn't perform as well as the others.
(B) Because he is new to the team.
(C) Because he doesn't hang out with the right people.
(D) Because he will not make a good manager.

Question 3

What will the woman do to finish the sales report?

(A) Ask help from the man
(B) Have one very strong coffee
(C) Stay at work for a few hours
(D) Stay awake all night to finish it

Question 4

Why does the man dislike Mr. Lin?

(A) Mr. Lin made him remake his coffee.
(B) Mr. Lin is bad at his job.
(C) Mr. Lin never likes the coffee he makes.
(D) He thinks Mr. Lin deliberately complains about him.

Question 5

Why is the woman nervous?

(A) She is going to make a presentation at the meeting.
(B) The meeting is related to the bonus they might get.
(C) Her department hasn't performed well this quarter.
(D) Her manager is reviewing her performance.

答案與解析 ～answer

Answer 1 ◀)) (B)

女性為什麼會帶蛋糕來給她的同事吃呢？

(A) 她想要慶祝自己的生日。

(B) 她兒子的生日派對有剩下的蛋糕。

(C) 她的生日派對有剩下的蛋糕。

(D) 她希望同事一起慶祝她的升遷。

解析

聽到女性帶蛋糕請大家吃，男性問她是否得到升遷，但這個原因被女性否定，並說明蛋糕是「她兒子生日派對所剩下的」。關鍵字leftover指「吃剩的飯菜」，正確答案為(B)。

Answer 2 ◀)) (A)

為什麼女性對喬的升遷感到不滿？

(A) 因為他的表現沒有其他人好。

(B) 因為他在團隊中還是個新人。

(C) 因為他沒有和對的人混在一起。

(D) 因為他無法成為一名好經理。

解析

男性一提到喬的升遷，女性就說他們的表現「一直都比喬好」，關鍵字為perform，在此指「工作上的表現」，正確答案為(A)。

Answer 3 ◀)) (D)

為了完成銷售報告，女性必須怎麼做？

(A) 拜託男子幫忙

(B) 泡一杯濃烈的咖啡

(C) 加班幾個小時

(D) 整晚不睡覺，熬夜完成

解析

解題關鍵句在女性回答的have to stay up all night(必須熬夜一整晚)，後面接「為了完成銷售報告」，點出了因果關係，正確答案為(D)。至於選項(B)提到的咖啡，只是為了達到熬夜目的而採取的手段而已。

Answer 4 ◀)) (D)

男性為什麼不喜歡林經理？

(A) 林經理要求他重泡咖啡。

(B) 林經理的工作績效很差。

(C) 林經理從來沒喜歡過他泡的咖啡。

(D) 他覺得林經理故意針對他抱怨。

解析

本題重點在男性一開始提到的「存心和他過不去」，關鍵片語為pick on sb.(故意挑某人毛病；和某人過不去)，正確答案為(D)。

Answer 5 ◀)) (B)

女性為什麼感到緊張？

(A) 她要在會議上報告。

(B) 會議能左右他們是否能得到獎金。

(C) 她部門這一季的表現不佳。

(D) 她的經理正在審核她的工作績效。

解析

當男性問女性說為何不需要報告還緊張時，女性提到檢討會「涉及」(concern)部門是否能得到「優渥的獎金」(a good bonus)，正確答案為(B)。注意句型whether...or not意指「是否」，表示無法確定的事項。

 中英文內容

短對話 ① Conversation

Jill: I've brought in some cake. Please help yourselves.
吉兒： 我帶了一些蛋糕，請享用吧，不用客氣。
Lance: Wow! Have you been promoted?
蘭斯： 哇！你升遷了嗎？
Jill: That's not been confirmed yet. These are **the leftovers from my son's birthday party**.
吉兒： 這倒還沒確定，這些是我兒子生日派對剩下的蛋糕。

短對話 ② Conversation

Hans: Have you heard about Joe's promotion?
漢斯： 你聽說喬升遷了嗎？
Bella: What?! But we've all been **performing better than he has**. This is unfair!
貝拉： 什麼？！但我們一直都表現得比他好，這太不公平了！

短對話 ③ Conversation

Jay: Are you making strong coffee? But it's nearly going home time.
杰： 你在泡特濃咖啡嗎？都快下班了耶。
Penny: I'll probably have to **stay up all night** to finish this sales report.
佩妮： 為了完成這份銷售報告，我可能必須整晚熬夜才行。

短對話 ④ Conversation

Paul: I hate Mr. Lin. I think **he picks on me**.
保羅： 我討厭林經理，感覺他存心和我過不去。
Emma: Trust me. Making his coffee three times is nothing.
艾瑪： 相信我，幫他重泡三次咖啡根本沒什麼。

短對話 ⑤ Conversation

Winnie: I'm nervous about the performance review meeting tomorrow.
維妮： 明天的績效檢討會真令我緊張。
Billy: Why? You don't need to present.
比利： 為什麼？你又不用報告。
Winnie: It concerns whether our department will **get a good bonus or not**. That's why.
維妮： 它涉及我們部門是否能得到優渥的獎金，這就是我緊張的原因。

長對話聽力實戰

@MP3 22-04

請仔細聆聽下面的長對話，再依對話內容選擇正確答案。

Question 1

Based on the dialogue, what is bothering the man?

(A) He has to do shift work.
(B) He has to work on weekdays.
(C) His colleagues are not very nice.
(D) He must attend his family events.

Question 2

Why is it hard for the man to find someone to cover his shift?

(A) He can't find anyone suitable.
(B) His shifts are long.
(C) His colleagues don't want to cover for him.
(D) Most of his colleagues don't want to work on weekends.

Question 3

Why can't the man's family plan the events around his schedule?

(A) They only want to meet on weekends.
(B) Their work schedules are conflicting.
(C) They don't like the man's work schedule.
(D) They also do shift work.

Question 4

Whose responsibility is it to find one cover for the man's shift?

(A) It's the man's own responsibility.
(B) It's the manager's responsibility.
(C) It's his colleagues' responsibility.
(D) Nobody needs to be responsible for it.

Question 5

In the end, what solution does the woman offer to the man?

(A) She finds someone to cover the man's shift.
(B) She attends the family events for the man.
(C) She offers to work part-time at the man's company.
(D) She talks to the man's manager about his shifts.

答案與解析 ~answer

Answer 1 (A)
根據對話內容，什麼讓男性感到困擾呢？
- (A) 他的工作須要排班。
- (B) 他週一到週五必須上班。
- (C) 他的同事人不是很好。
- (D) 他一定得參加家庭聚會。

解析
男性在對話一開始就說他討厭「工作需要排班」(work shifts)，後面也提到排班影響到他能否參加家庭聚會，正確答案為(A)。必須注意(D)的must(一定要)語氣過於強烈，對話中男性並沒有說他非得出席家庭聚會不可。

Answer 2 (D)
為什麼男性很難找到代班的人選？
- (A) 他找不到合適的人。
- (B) 他值班的工作時間都很長。
- (C) 他的同事不想幫他代班。
- (D) 大部分的同事都不想在週末上班。

解析
當女性問男性是否找不到合適的人選時，男性提到一般人都「希望週末休息」(wants weekends off)，這才導致很難找到人代班，正確答案為(D)。

Answer 3 (B)
男性的家人為什麼不能依他的班表安排聚會呢？
- (A) 他們只想在週末聚會。
- (B) 他們與男性的工作時間相衝突。
- (C) 他們不喜歡男性的值班時間。
- (D) 他們的工作也採取排班制。

解析
當女性建議男性請他家人依他的班表安排聚會時，男性解釋他大部分的週末都必須上班，但其他人大多都是「朝九晚五的上班族」(regular nine-to-five jobs)，代表他們的時間有衝突，正確答案為(B)。

Answer 4 (A)
幫男性找人代班是誰的責任呢？
- (A) 男性他自己的責任。
- (B) 是經理的的責任。
- (C) 是男性同事的責任。
- (D) 沒有人必須為此負責。

解析
男性提到雖然經理會幫忙找人代班，但這其實是「他們自己的責任」(our responsibility)，因此除了說話的男性以外，不能選其他人，正確答案為(A)。

Answer 5 (C)
對話最後，女性提供了什麼解決方案給男性？
- (A) 她去找人替男性代班。
- (B) 她替男性參加家庭聚會。
- (C) 她願意在男性的公司兼職。
- (D) 她去找男性的經理談值班表的時間。

解析
對話最後，女性提到她需要額外的收入，問男性是否能在他的公司兼職，這樣一來，如果男性需要找人代班，她就能幫忙，正確答案為(C)。選項(A)指的是女性另外找人幫忙，所以不適合。

⊙慢速MP3 22-05　　◎正常速MP3 22-06

Kevin: I hate having to **work shifts** for my job.
凱文：　我討厭我的工作需要排班。

Laura: What's wrong?
蘿拉：　怎麼了？

Kevin: Every time there's an important family event, I have to find someone to cover my shift.
凱文：　每當有重要的家庭活動，我就得找人代班。

Laura: Is it difficult to find somebody suitable?
蘿拉：　很難找到合適的人嗎？

Kevin: Generally, everyone wants **weekends off**. And my family tends to **gather on weekends**.
凱文：　一般來說，每個人都希望週末休息，但我的家人傾向在週末聚會。

Laura: Why don't you plan events around your shift schedule sometimes?
蘿拉：　那你們何不偶爾依你的班表安排活動呢？

Kevin: It's hard to do so. I need to work on most weekends, whereas most of my family members have **regular nine-to-five jobs**.
凱文：　很難，我週末幾乎都得工作，而我家人大多是朝九晚五的上班族。

Laura: So your manager won't help you find someone?
蘿拉：　你的經理不會幫你找代班的人嗎？

Kevin: She will, but it's **our responsibility** to find a person.
凱文：　會是會，但找人代班其實是我們自己的責任。

Laura: I need some extra income. Do you think I can **get a part-time job** at your company? If you need someone to cover your shifts, my time is quite flexible.
蘿拉：　我需要額外的收入，你覺得我能在你的公司取得兼職嗎？如果你需要找人代班，我的時間還滿有彈性的。

短文聽力實戰

MP3 22-07(短文1)　　MP3 22-08(短文2)

請仔細聆聽下面兩段短文，並分別回答Q1~Q2&Q3~Q5兩大題。

Question 1

How often does the man need to travel for his job?

(A) Sometimes

(B) Everyday

(C) Very frequently

(D) He rarely needs to travel.

Question 2

Why can the man make a good living from his job?

(A) He makes good investments with his bonuses.

(B) His manager has given him a promotion.

(C) His basic salary is very good.

(D) He receives a lot of bonuses from his sales.

Question 3

Why did the woman just stay at home for her holidays before?

(A) She didn't have enough money to go out.

(B) She thought it was the best way to relax.

(C) She didn't have enough time to go away on holidays.

(D) She enjoyed sitting at home doing nothing.

Question 4

What did the woman actually do when she stayed at home?

(A) She watched TV all the time.

(B) She just relaxed.

(C) She would play video games all day long.

(D) She would still do company work.

Question 5

How does the woman feel after she recharges her batteries?

(A) She feels aches and pains.

(B) She is full of energy and drive for work.

(C) She feels tired and stressed.

(D) She feels sad to finish her holiday.

答案與解析 ~answer

Answer 1 ◄)) (C)
男性為工作而旅行的頻率如何？

(A) 有時候需要
(B) 每天都會去
(C) 經常旅行
(D) 他幾乎不需要旅行。

解析
男性提到自己必須拜訪潛在客戶群後，進一步說明這代表他「經常得走訪全國上下」，關鍵字為quite extensively(相當廣泛地)，此處形容「很多時間用在走訪上」，正確答案為(C)。

Answer 2 ◄)) (D)
男性如何從工作中賺取相當不錯的所得呢？

(A) 他將獎金投注在好的投資上。
(B) 他的經理替他升遷。
(C) 他的基本薪資相當優渥。
(D) 他的銷售表現替他贏得許多獎金。

解析
男性提到自己的基本薪資很普通，所以不會選(C)；之所以能賺取高所得是因為他「賺取銷售獎金」。make a very good living表示自己賺的很多，後面的through my sales bonus則是解題關鍵，through(藉由)表手段，正確答案為(D)。

Answer 3 ◄)) (B)
女性之前休假時為什麼只會待在家裡呢？

(A) 她沒有足夠的錢出門。
(B) 她認為那是休息的最佳方式。
(C) 她沒有外出渡假的時間。
(D) 她喜歡呆坐在家裡，什麼也不做。

解析
女性提到她以前休假，就是呆坐在家裡，什麼也不做。這是因為「她以為這是休息的最佳方式」(the best way to get some rest)，正確答案為(B)。注意女性並沒有說她是否享受這樣的方式，所以不宜選(D)。

Answer 4 ◄)) (D)
當女性休假待在家時，她實際做了些什麼？

(A) 她看一整天的電視。
(B) 她單純就在放鬆。
(C) 她整天都在玩電動。
(D) 她還是會處理公事。

解析
題目的重點在actually(實際上)，所以必須找出女性實際做的事。雖然她提到自己放假會呆坐在家裡，什麼也不做，但這只是一種形容方式，後面接著說她反而會「確認電子郵件，處理工作」，正確答案為(D)。

Answer 5 ◄)) (B)
在女性充了電之後，她有什麼感覺？

(A) 她感到痠痛與疼痛。
(B) 她充滿工作需要的精力和動力。
(C) 她感到疲倦、壓力大。
(D) 她對假期的結束感到難過。

解析
本題中的recharge one's batteries 是用電子產品充電時的待機狀態形容「(人)休息」，因此要回答的是女性提到的「精力充沛地帶著幹勁」(be energized and motivated)，正確答案為(B)。

I like my job. It is not office-based since I need to visit our potential clients. This means I travel up and down the country **quite extensively**. I also go on several business trips abroad when necessary. My job is very interesting and dynamic because it is not nine-to-five. I really enjoy the interaction with people. That's why I chose to be a salesman. My base salary is fairly average. However, because of my excellent performance, I **make a very good living** through **my sales bonuses**.

　　我喜歡自己的工作。它不是坐在辦公室的工作，因為我須要拜訪潛在客戶群。這意味著我經常得走訪全國上下，需要的時候，我也曾到國外出差過幾次。因為我的工作並非朝九晚五的固定型態，所以非常有趣，不會一成不變。我真的很喜歡與人互動的感覺，這是我之所以成為銷售員的原因。我的基本薪資很普通，但因為我的業績優良，所以能賺取銷售獎金，所得相當高呢。

A few years ago, I started to go on annual holiday and take some time for myself. Before then, if I had holiday to use up, I would just take a couple of days off, sitting at home and doing nothing. I thought this was **the best way to get some rest**, but I found myself constantly **checking work emails** and **dealing with some cases**. And before I knew it, my holiday had passed. Now, I have learnt to switch off from work during my holiday so I can really recharge my batteries and be **energized and motivated** when I go back to work. This year, I'm going to Bali. The first thing I will definitely do is get a good massage.

　　幾年前，我開始渡假，撥一些時間給自己。在此之前，如果我有年假要用掉，我就只會休幾天假，呆坐在家裡，什麼也不做。我以為這是休息的最佳方式，但我發現自己會不定時的確認電子郵件，處理工作，然後一晃眼，我的假期就過了。現在，我學會在放假時把工作拋諸腦後，這樣我才真的能充電，精力充沛地帶著幹勁回到工作崗位。今年我準備去峇里島渡假，抵達之後，我絕對要做的第一件事，就是好好地享受按摩。

Unit 3 工作百百種 Various Jobs

📱 日常生活　👤 娛樂活動　✏ 意見交流　🏳 特殊場合

短 對話 聽力 實戰

🎧 MP3 23-01

下面將播放五組短對話，請仔細聆聽，再依對話內容答題。

Question ❶ ··· ❶❷❸❹❺

Why has the man been going home late?

(A) The woman asks him to come home later.
(B) He is told to do overtime in order to settle into the job.
(C) He wants to stay at work to get used to the job.
(D) His job requires him to stay behind in the office.

Question ❷ ··· ❶❷❸❹❺

Why does the man ask the woman not to envy his salary?

(A) His payment isn't that good as she thought.
(B) His job is too complex for most people.
(C) He is on call even after work.
(D) He has to stay late at the office every day.

Question ❸ ··· ❶❷❸❹❺

What does the man ask the woman to write on the customs form?

(A) The way to send the parcel
(B) The parcel's worth and its purpose
(C) Every single item in the parcel and their values
(D) The weight and value of the parcel

Question ❹ ··· ❶❷❸❹❺

According to the woman, when should the man receive his order?

(A) By the coming Thursday
(B) By the coming Wednesday
(C) Last Friday
(D) By the coming Friday

Question ❺ ··· ❶❷❸❹❺

What is the man's suggestion to the woman's problem?

(A) He'll check the system and issue a new invoice.
(B) He'll check the overcharged amount.
(C) He'll return the overcharged amount of money.
(D) He'll deduct the overcharged amount from the next invoice.

答案與解析 ～answer

Answer 1 (C)
男性最近為何常常很晚才回家？

(A) 女性要求他晚點回家。
(B) 有人要求他留下來加班，以適應工作。
(C) 他想要留下來，以適應工作。
(D) 他的工作性質讓他必須留下來加班。

> **解析**
> 在回答女性的疑問時，男性提到加班算是「自願性的」(voluntary)，由此可剔除隱含「不得不；被要求」的(A)(B)(D)。如果沒有聽懂的話，由後句可得知他希望盡快「適應工作」(settle into the job)，正確答案為(C)。

Answer 2 (C)
男性為什麼要女性別羨慕他的薪水？

(A) 他的薪水沒有女性想的那麼好。
(B) 他的工作對大多數人來說太複雜。
(C) 他下班後也必須隨時待命。
(D) 他每天都必須留在公司加班。

> **解析**
> 男性提到高薪的代價。他必須「隨時待命」(be on call at all time)，就算是下班後也不例外(off duty 下班後)，正確答案為(C)。

Answer 3 (B)
男性請女性在報關表上填寫什麼內容？

(A) 寄送包裹的方式
(B) 包裹的價值以及用途
(C) 包裹裡的每一項物品及其價值
(D) 包裹的重量與價值

> **解析**
> 職員請女性填寫報關表，說她必須清楚標明物品的「價值」(value)，說明是否含有「商業性質」(commercial nature)，具備商業性質的物品表示其與商業用途有關，正確答案為(B)。

Answer 4 (A)
根據女性的話，男子何時應該就會收到貨品？

(A) 接下來的星期四
(B) 接下來的星期三
(C) 上個星期五
(D) 接下來的星期五

> **解析**
> 女性查詢系統後，告訴男性貨物將於「本週三出貨」(dispatch 遞送)，「週四應該就會送達」幾個關鍵字為 delivered by Thursday，介係詞by形容時間的話有「在…之前」之意，正確答案為(A)。

Answer 5 (D)
針對女性的問題，男性提供了什麼建議？

(A) 他將確認系統並開立新發票。
(B) 他將確認超收的金額。
(C) 他將退回超收的金額。
(D) 他將從下一張發票抵扣差額。

> **解析**
> 針對女性提出的超收問題，男性提到他們會從「下一張發票抵扣差額」(deduct the difference)，此處的difference表示「差額」，即「被多收的金額」，正確答案為(D)。

⊙慢速MP3 23-02　　◎正常速MP3 23-03

短對話 ❶ *Conversation*

Gina: You've been coming home late a lot. Do you have to do a lot of overtime?

吉娜： 你最近經常很晚才回家，你常需要加班嗎？

Ernie: It's more **voluntary**. I don't have to stay behind, but I want to **settle into the job** as quickly as I can.

爾尼： 這算是自願性的，我不用留下來加班，但是我希望能盡快適應工作。

短對話 ❷ *Conversation*

Merry: I envy your salary package.

梅莉： 真羨慕你的薪水啊。

Jack: Please don't. There's a price for it. I have to **be on call at all times**, even when I'm **off duty**.

傑克： 千萬別羨慕，這可是有代價的。就算是下班後，我也必須隨時待命呢。

短對話 ❸ *Conversation*

Helen: Hi, I'd like to send this parcel to the States.

海倫： 您好，我想寄這個包裹到美國。

Clerk: Sure. Please fill out this customs form. You must clearly indicate **the value of it** and whether it is **of commercial nature**.

職員： 沒問題，請填寫這張報關表，您必須清楚標明包裹的價值，並說明它是否為具備商業性質的物品。

短對話 ❹ *Conversation*

Vernon: Hello, I'd like to have a delivery update on the stock we ordered last Friday.

弗農： 你好，我想查詢我們上週五訂單的遞送狀態。

Fay: No problem. The system says your goods will be dispatched this Wednesday and should **be delivered to you by Thursday**.

菲： 沒問題，系統說貨物將於本週三出貨，週四應該就會送達。

短對話 ❺ *Conversation*

Vicky: Hello, I'm calling because we seem to have been overcharged on the materials we ordered last week.

維琪： 你好，我打來是要說我們上週訂購的原料似乎被多收錢了。

Danny: We're terribly sorry! If it's okay with you, we'll **deduct the difference from your next invoice**.

丹尼： 實在很抱歉！如果你們願意的話，我們會從你們的下一張發票抵扣這次多收的差額。

長對話聽力實戰

請仔細聆聽下面的長對話，再依對話內容選擇正確答案。

Question 1

What kind of grant is the man applying for?

(A) A grant to help students studying digital art
(B) A grant to help entrepreneurs start up their businesses
(C) A grant to help businesses in all industries
(D) A grant to help businesses expand

Question 2

What is the man preparing for the grant application?

(A) He's revising his business proposal for submission.
(B) He's writing his business proposal.
(C) He's submitting his business proposal.
(D) He is preparing for the presentation to the panelists.

Question 3

How many companies will be selected?

(A) 10
(B) The information was not mentioned.
(C) 15
(D) Between 10 and 15

Question 4

When will the man receive an answer regarding the grant?

(A) On the last day of next month
(B) By the end of this month
(C) In two months
(D) Next week

Question 5

What is the man going to do if he doesn't get the grant?

(A) Apply for a low-interest loan from a bank
(B) Borrow some money from his friends
(C) Accept the money his father offered to give him
(D) Apply for the grant again next year

答案與解析 ~answer

Answer 1 (B)

男性申請的是什麼類型的補助呢？

(A) 學生就讀數位藝術的補助

(B) 企業家創業的補助

(C) 對所有企業的補助

(D) 幫助企業擴張的補助

> **解析**
> 男性提到政府目前積極鼓勵「數位產業的創業」，關鍵字在start-up(創業)，由此可知正確答案為(B)。注意選項(C)雖然提到企業，但補助只針對「數位產業」，所以不宜選。

Answer 2 (D)

為了補助申請，男性正在準備什麼呢？

(A) 他正在修改創業提案，以提交出去。

(B) 他正在寫創業的提案。

(C) 他正提交他的創業提案。

(D) 他正準備著要在補助會委員前做的簡報。

> **解析**
> 解題關鍵在女性詢問「申請進行得如何」之後，男性說他已經交出提案，所以(A)(B)(C)都不可能，用刪除法可知正確答案為(D)。之後男性也提到他正在準備要對補助會委員做的「簡報」(presentation)。

Answer 3 (B)

會有幾間公司被選上呢？

(A) 十間公司

(B) 無法得知

(C) 十五間公司

(D) 介於十到十五間

> **解析**
> 本題出現的陷阱為選項(D)。針對數量，男性回答It's not specified(沒有特別規定)，只是「聽說」一般介於10到15家之間(usually between 10 and 15)，但這不代表「一定是」這個數字，最佳答案為(B)。

Answer 4 (B)

男性何時會收到補助審核的結果呢？

(A) 下個月的最後一天

(B) 這個月的月底之前

(C) 兩個月後

(D) 下個禮拜

> **解析**
> 女性問到公布審核結果的時間，男性回答「這個月的月底前」(by the end of this month)應該就會確定，正確答案為(B)。

Answer 5 (A)

如果男性沒有取得補助的話，他打算怎麼做呢？

(A) 向銀行申請低息貸款

(B) 向朋友借錢

(C) 接受他爸爸要給他的錢

(D) 明年再申請補助

> **解析**
> 雖然男性的爸爸願意出錢幫他，但他說自己應該會去申請「銀行的低息貸款」，重點在but I think I'll...，連接詞but表轉折語氣，暗示他不打算拿爸爸的錢，正確答案為(A)。

中英文內容

⊙慢速MP3 23-05　　◉正常速MP3 23-06

Kelly: What are you working on?
凱莉：　你在忙什麼啊？

Simon: The government is encouraging **business start-ups in the digital industry**. I'm trying to **get the grant** they provide.
賽門：　政府目前正積極鼓勵數位產業的創業，我在嘗試拿到政府提供的補助。

Kelly: How's the application going?
凱莉：　申請進行得怎樣了呢？

Simon: I've already submitted the proposal. Now I'm preparing **the presentation** I need to deliver to the panelists next week.
賽門：　我已經交提案了，正在準備我下星期要對補助會委員做的簡報。

Kelly: How many companies will they choose?
凱莉：　他們會選幾家企業啊？

Simon: **It hasn't been specified**, but I've heard it's usually between 10 and 15.
賽門：　沒有特別規定，但我聽到一般會有10到15家。

Kelly: And when will you get an answer?
凱莉：　那結果什麼時候會出來呢？

Simon: Well, they say the decision should be made **by the end of this month**.
賽門：　聽說本月底前應該就能知道結果了。

Kelly: By the way, what if you don't get the grant?
凱莉：　順便問一下，那如果沒有拿到補助的話，你打算怎麼辦？

Simon: My dad offered to give me some money, but I think I'll apply for **a low-interest loan from the banks**.
賽門：　我爸爸願意幫我出一些錢，但我應該會申請銀行的低息貸款吧。

短 文 聽 力 實 戰 　　◎MP3 23-07(短文1)　◎MP3 23-08(短文2)

請仔細聆聽下面兩段短文，並分別回答Q1~Q2&Q3~Q5兩大題。

Question 1
What do people see an anchorperson do while they watch TV?
- (A) Read news scripts prepared by other people
- (B) Read news scripts prepared by themselves
- (C) Research news stories
- (D) Write a script as soon as possible

Question 2
Why people's high expectation to anchorpeople could be hard for them?
- (A) It forces them to behave themselves.
- (B) They need to wear make-up all the time.
- (C) They expect themselves to look immaculate all the time.
- (D) The public expects them to be immaculate like they are on TV.

Question 3
What is hard for people to imagine when they watch a movie?
- (A) How animators can have all their ideas
- (B) How the animation is done
- (C) How much money the movies make
- (D) How much time and effort it takes

Question 4
Why does the man work flexible hours?
- (A) Because he doesn't like to work 9 to 5.
- (B) Because ideas sometimes happen after standard office hours.
- (C) Because ideas appear whenever he needs them.
- (D) Because it allows him to take better care of his family.

Question 5
What part of the job really motivates the man?
- (A) A potentially good income
- (B) The fact that his job is not typical
- (C) The chance to improve his skills
- (D) People's positive comments to his work

答案與解析 ~answer

Answer 1 (A)

人們在看電視主播播報時，看到的是什麼？

(A) 主播唸他人準備好的新聞稿

(B) 主播唸他們自己準備的新聞稿

(C) 主播針對新聞找資料

(D) 主播盡快完成新聞稿

解析
注意本題問的是「新聞播報的期間」，按文中所提到的內容，主播必須「唸幫他們寫好的新聞稿」(read off scripts that are prepared for them)，正確答案為(A)。

Answer 2 (D)

人們對主播的高度期望對他們來說為何會是困擾？

(A) 這種期望逼迫他們注意自己的行為。

(B) 他們無論何時都必須化妝。

(C) 他們要求自己無論何時看起來都很完美。

(D) 大眾期許他們和電視上的模樣一樣完美。

解析
本文最後，女性提到因為主播在電視上的「完美模樣」(the immaculate look)，會導致大眾對他們的外觀有「很高的期望」(high expectation)，正確答案為(D)。選項(B)(C)雖然也有可能，但並非最佳答案。

Answer 3 (D)

當人們在觀賞電影時，很難想像什麼事情？

(A) 動畫師如何想到這些點子

(B) 動畫是如何完成的

(C) 電影賺了多少錢

(D) 電影花費了多少時間與精力完成

解析
男性一開始就提到人們看電影時，可能很難想像短短兩小時的作品需要投入「多少的時間和精力」(the amount of hours and work)，正確答案為(D)。

Answer 4 (B)

男性為什麼選擇工作時間很彈性的職業？

(A) 因為他不喜歡朝九晚五的工作型態。

(B) 因為靈感有時會在普通上班時間結束後出現。

(C) 因為只要他需要，靈感就會浮現。

(D) 因為這能讓他更有時間照顧家人。

解析
男性提到工作時間之所以很彈性，是因為這種方式才能搭配他的創作靈感，並解釋創意「不一定在一般工作時間的時候浮現」，正確答案為(B)。注意選項(A)不符合是因為男性有提到自己其實很習慣朝九晚五的型態。

Answer 5 (B)

男性工作的哪一部分帶給他動力呢？

(A) 有可能取得的高薪收入

(B) 他無法預期的工作型態

(C) 改善自己技術的機會

(D) 人們對他作品的肯定評價

解析
男性提到動畫師沒有所謂「典型的一天」(a typical day)，暗示他的工作變化性很大，所以讓他充滿樂趣和動力(motivating 有動力的)，正確答案為(B)。

PART 5
職場與工作

中英文內容

短文 1　　　　　🔘慢速MP3 23-09　　🔘正常速MP3 23-10

Some people have the false impression that becoming a journalist is a rather glamorous job. What they see are the anchormen and anchorwomen who **read off scripts that are prepared for them**. However, news doesn't come out of the blue. In reality, journalists' working hours might be longer than you can imagine. They need to research the news and revise the scripts if necessary. If an incident happens as the anchorperson is reporting, they must act on the spot and form a script very quickly. Being an anchorperson isn't easy, either. Because of **the immaculate look** required for TV, people usually have **high expectations of how they should look**!

有些人會對新聞工作者有錯誤的印象，以為那是相當光鮮亮麗的工作。他們眼裡看到的，是拿著別人準備好的新聞稿，照著唸的男主播與女主播。然而，新聞可不會憑空出現。實際上，記者的工作時數可能長到你無法想像，他們必須針對新聞找資料，有需要的時候也得修改新聞稿。主播在播報新聞的當下，如果有事件發生，記者就必須當場反應，迅速寫好新聞稿。當主播也不容易，受到平日電視上完美模樣的影響，所以大眾會對他們的外觀有很高的期望！

短文 2　　　　　🔘慢速MP3 23-11　　🔘正常速MP3 23-12

When people go to the cinema and watch a movie, it's probably hard for them to imagine **the amount of hours and work** put into something that lasts only two hours. Typically, an animation film can take from two to three years to complete, and sometimes even longer. As an animator, I have the freedom of working flexible hours in order to take advantage of my creativity. Even though I'm more of a 9-to-5 person, **ideas don't always come during standard office hours**. Therefore, animators **do not have "a typical day"**, which makes it really fun and **motivating for me**. As for the salary, it can range quite a lot depending on your skills and more importantly, your ideas.

當人們去電影院看電影時，可能很難想像短短兩小時的作品中究竟投入了多少的時間和精力。一般而言，一部動畫電影要完成，需耗時兩到三年，有時甚至更久。身為一名動畫家，我的工作時間很有彈性，這種工作方式才能配合我的創作靈感。儘管我是個滿習慣朝九晚五的人，但創意可不一定會在一般的工作時間來臨。因此，動畫師沒有所謂「典型的一天」，這讓我的工作充滿樂趣和動力。至於薪資，落差就很大了，這要看你的技術，更重要的是取決於你的創意。

職場閒談 Chatting Together

□ 日常生活　💡 娛樂活動　✎ 意見交流　▶ 特殊場合

🎧 短 對 話 聽 力 實 戰

◎ MP3 24-01

下面將播放五組短對話，請仔細聆聽，再依對話內容答題。

Question 1

Who does the man ask the woman not to invite?

(A) The marketing team
(B) The new girl in the accounting department
(C) Their supervisor
(D) The accounting department's new manager

Question 2

Why is the woman upset?

(A) A colleague who doesn't deserve promotion got promoted.
(B) Her manager told her she nearly got promoted.
(C) The lazy colleague told everybody about her promotion.
(D) Her salary is not as good as the woman who got promoted.

Question 3

What doesn't the woman understand?

(A) Why the manager asks her to run errands for the PA.
(B) Why the manager's PA doesn't run errands for him.
(C) Why the manager likes her but not his PA.
(D) Why she is always asked to run the errands for the manager.

Question 4

What did the CEO tell the employees do not be affected by?

(A) Team rapport
(B) Sales performance
(C) Office politics
(D) Irony

Question 5

Why is the man looking for a new job?

(A) He wants better opportunities for promotion.
(B) He wants better money for his current position.
(C) His colleagues also quit.
(D) He has little chance of getting a raise.

答案與解析 ▶ ~answer

Answer 1 (B)
男性要求女性別邀請誰呢？

(A) 行銷團隊

(B) 會計部新來的女孩

(C) 他們的主管

(D) 會計部的新任經理

> **解析**
> 男性特別反問可不可以不邀請「會計部新來的女孩」(the new girl from accounting)。leave out指「將某人或某物省略」，正確答案為(B)。

Answer 2 (A)
女性為了什麼而感到沮喪呢？

(A) 一名不應得到升遷的同事被升遷。

(B) 她的經理說她差一點就能升遷了。

(C) 那名懶惰的同事告訴大家自己升遷的事。

(D) 她的薪水不如那名升遷的同事。

> **解析**
> 本題的關鍵字在promotion(升遷)。女性原本以為「她會得到升遷」(get the promotion)，但卻選了另外的同事吉娜，女性說吉娜是她認識的人當中「最懶惰的」，表示她不認為吉娜應得到升遷，正確答案為(A)。

Answer 3 (D)
女性無法了解的事情是什麼？

(A) 經理叫她幫他的私人助理跑腿。

(B) 經理的私人助理不幫他跑腿。

(C) 經理不喜歡私人助理，反而喜歡她。

(D) 她老是被經理要求替他跑腿。

> **解析**
> 關鍵片語為run errands for(幫某人跑腿)。女性說她不明白為什麼有私人助理的經理還老是「要她跑腿」。跑腿的人是說話的女性，提出要求的是經理，正確答案為(D)。

Answer 4 (C)
執行長要求員工不要被「什麼」影響？

(A) 團隊默契

(B) 銷售表現

(C) 辦公室政治

(D) 諷刺

> **解析**
> 女性一開始就提到執行長對員工的要求，要他們不被「辦公室政治」(office politics)影響到團隊的默契和表現，接著男性則說他覺得這很諷刺，但男性的感覺與本題無關，正確答案為(C)。

Answer 5 (A)
男性為什麼在找新工作？

(A) 他想要取得更好的升遷機會。

(B) 他希望目前的職位能有更好的薪水。

(C) 他的同事也辭職了。

(D) 他加薪的機會很小。

> **解析**
> 當女性說男性公司的福利很好時，他解釋自己找工作的原因與福利無關，而是因為「晉升機會不大」；除非高層有人辭職，否則就難以升遷，升遷就是工作上所得到的機會，正確答案為(A)。

 中英文內容

⊙慢速MP3 24-02　　◎正常速MP3 24-03

短對話 1 *Conversation*

Emma: Shall we ask everyone to go for some drinks after work?

艾瑪： 我們要不要邀大家下班後去喝幾杯？

Frank: Can we leave the new girl from accounting out? I don't like the way she criticizes the marketing team.

法蘭克：能不邀會計部新來的那個女孩嗎？我不喜歡她批評行銷部的團隊。

短對話 2 *Conversation*

Gavin: What's the matter? Why are you crying?

蓋文： 怎麼了？你為什麼在哭？

Stacy: I thought I'd get the promotion, but Gina got it. She's the laziest person I know!

史黛西：我以為我會得到升遷，但居然是吉娜，她是我認識的人當中最懶惰的一個！

短對話 3 *Conversation*

Ginny: I don't understand why Mr. Lee always asks me to run errands for him when he has a PA.

金妮： 我不懂，李經理明明有私人助理，為什麼還老是要我幫他跑腿？

Sam: I think it's his way of hinting he likes you.

山姆： 我認為這是他暗示他喜歡你的方式。

Ginny: Really? I'd rather he didn't like me then!

金妮： 真的嗎？那我寧願他不喜歡我呢！

短對話 4 *Conversation*

Debby: The CEO asked us not to let office politics affect our team's rapport and performance.

黛比： 執行長說我們不應該讓辦公室政治影響到團隊的默契和表現。

John: I find that very ironic. The man he trusts most is the person creating it!

約翰： 這真諷刺，他最信任的部屬不就是那個製造分裂的人嗎？！

短對話 5 *Conversation*

Becky: Why are you looking for a new job? I thought your benefits were good.

貝琪： 你為什麼要找新工作？你公司的福利很好耶。

Kevin: It's not that. The career prospects in my company aren't good. We have little chance of being promoted unless people above quit.

凱文： 不是福利好不好的問題。我公司內部的晉升機會不大，除非更高層有人辭職，不然我們很難得到升遷。

長對話聽力實戰

⊚MP3 24-04

請仔細聆聽下面的長對話，再依對話內容選擇正確答案。

Question 1

❶❷❸❹❺

According to the man, what is hard to do?

(A) Draw a line at work

(B) Determine what amount of work is too much

(C) Tell his manager that he is giving the employees too much work

(D) Finish the amount of work in one day

Question 2

❶❷❸❹❺

What does the man's manager ask him to do?

(A) More and more work tasks

(B) Too much work to do in one day

(C) Ask other people to work more

(D) Take on some of other colleagues' workload

Question 3

❶❷❸❹❺

How does the man's manager give him pressure?

(A) By giving him very strict orders

(B) By shouting at the man

(C) In an indirect way

(D) By asking other people to check on the man's progress

Question 4

❶❷❸❹❺

Why is the man unsure about quitting his job?

(A) He's worried that he might not get a good salary in a new job.

(B) He's worried he'll experience the same problem again.

(C) He's worried his short service at this job won't look good.

(D) He wants to receive the year-end bonus before quitting.

Question 5

❶❷❸❹❺

What does the woman suggest the man do?

(A) Ask her colleagues if they have the same problem

(B) Tell his concerns to the HR department

(C) Talk to his manager in a confident voice

(D) Express how he feels to his manager in an email

答案與解析 ～answer

Answer 1 ◀))（**B**）

根據男性所言，什麼很難做到？

(A) 上班時畫一條線

(B) 判定多少工作量算太多

(C) 告訴經理他給員工的工作太多

(D) 在一天內完成所有工作

解析

男性一開始就說「工作量太大的定義很難界定。關鍵片語draw the line意指「界定」，不是選項(A)說的實際畫一條線。正確答案為(B)。

Answer 2 ◀))（**A**）

男性的經理對他的要求是什麼呢？

(A) 交給他越來越多的工作

(B) 一天之內要完成太多工作

(C) 要求其他人做更多工作

(D) 負擔部分同事的工作量

解析

當女性詢問男性，經理給他的工作是否太多時，他給予肯定的回答，並接著說經理「不斷交給他更多工作」，關鍵字為more work(越來越多工作)，正確答案為(A)。

Answer 3 ◀))（**C**）

男性的經理以什麼方式給他壓力呢？

(A) 給他嚴苛的命令

(B) 大聲責罵他

(C) 用間接的方式

(D) 叫別人來確認男性的進度

解析

男性提到經理老是說不急，但每隔半小時就來確認他的進度。聽到這些話的女性說這名經理以「間接」(indirect way)的方式施壓，正確答案為(C)。選項(D)錯誤的地方在，經理是自己來確認進度的。

Answer 4 ◀))（**C**）

為什麼男性會對辭職感到猶豫？

(A) 他擔心其他工作的薪水不高。

(B) 他擔心會碰到同樣的問題。

(C) 他擔心不長的在職時間不好看。

(D) 他想要在離職前拿到年度獎金。

解析

男性雖然在考慮辭職，但想到自己才做了一年多，「履歷上會不好看」(won't look good on the resume)，正確答案為(C)。

Answer 5 ◀))（**D**）

女性建議男性怎麼做呢？

(A) 詢問同事是否也有相同的困擾

(B) 將他的憂慮告訴人資部

(C) 用自信的態度和經理談

(D) 寄電子郵件給經理，表達其感受

解析

女性建議男性「寫一封禮貌的電子郵件給經理」(voice your concern...by writing him a polite email)。voice在此處為動詞，表示「表達；發聲」，通常與opinion/concern等字搭配使用，正確答案為(D)。

◉ 慢速MP3 24-05　　◉ 正常速MP3 24-06

Peter: It's really hard to **draw the line** at **how much work is too heavy of a workload**.
彼得：　工作量太大的定義實在很難界定。

Mary: What happened? Did your manager ask you to do too much work?
瑪麗：　怎麼了嗎？難道你的經理要求你做的工作太多了？

Peter: Yes. He **keeps handing me more work**. He always says it's not urgent, but he'll come to check me every half an hour.
彼得：　沒錯，他不斷交給我更多的工作，口頭上說不急，但每隔半小時就來確認我的進度。

Mary: I see, so he gives you pressure in **an indirect way**.
瑪麗：　我懂了，他以一種間接的方式施壓。

Peter: Also, he gives orders tentatively and changes his mind all the time.
彼得：　而且他在下達指令時很猶豫不決，一直改變心意。

Mary: I thought my mother was bad, but your manager sounds more difficult.
瑪麗：　我以為我媽在這方面已經夠糟了，你的經理聽起來更嚴重。

Peter: I'm thinking of quitting, but I've only been here **a little over a year**. It **won't look good on the resume**.
彼得：　我在考慮辭職，但我才來了一年多，履歷上會不好看。

Mary: Can you **voice your concern** to him by writing him **a polite email**?
瑪麗：　你可以寫一封禮貌的電子郵件給他，藉以表達你介意的事嗎？

Peter: I don't know how to put it in words. What if he simply fires me?
彼得：　我不知道怎麼把我的問題文字化，如果他因此把我給炒魷魚呢？

Mary: Just be frank and say that it's affecting your performance.
瑪麗：　就坦白說，告訴他這已經影響到你的工作表現了。

Peter: I guess I have to take some action; otherwise, I might go mad.
彼得：　我是該採取一些行動，否則我早晚會發瘋。

短文聽力實戰 　　　MP3 24-07(短文1)　　MP3 24-08(短文2)

請仔細聆聽下面兩段短文，並分別回答Q1~Q2&Q3~Q5兩大題。

Question 1

What does the man say is childish and unconstructive?

(A) Underpaying hardworking employees
(B) Intentionally undermining other people
(C) Taking other people's stuff at work
(D) Unintentionally criticizing other people

Question 2

Regarding the new guy's behavior, what does the man hope?

(A) The new guy decides to quit.
(B) The manager decides to fire the new guy.
(C) The manager's judgment won't be affected.
(D) He can get a promotion faster than the new guy.

Question 3

What does the woman think is not a good idea?

(A) Work professionalism
(B) Teamwork
(C) Office romances
(D) Romantic relationships in general

Question 4

What happened after the ex-colleague started dating her manager?

(A) Her pay improved for the same position.
(B) She became the manager's PA.
(C) She was determined not to do any work.
(D) Her work performance got worse and worse.

Question 5

Why did the woman's ex-colleague get fired?

(A) She often took time off without formal permission.
(B) She often took time off without telling the manager.
(C) She took time off together with the manager.
(D) She went on holiday without finishing her work.

答案與解析 ～answer

Answer 1 ◀ѕ) (B)
根據男性所說，什麼事幼稚又毫無建設性呢？

(A) 付給努力工作的員工低薪
(B) 刻意貶低他人
(C) 拿走辦公室內其他人的物品
(D) 無意地批評他人

解析
男性提到「故意矮化他人」(deliberate undermining)的做法既幼稚又沒建設性，接著舉了新同事的例子，說新同事只會批評他的工作，吹噓自己能做得更好。選項(D)說的是無意的批評，但新同事總帶著惡意，正確答案為(B)。

Answer 2 ◀ѕ) (C)
關於新同事的言行舉止，男性有何希望呢？

(A) 新同事決定辭職。
(B) 經理決定炒新同事魷魚。
(C) 經理的判斷不會受到影響。
(D) 他能比新同事快得到升遷。

解析
男性最後提到，希望經理「看透新同事在搞什麼」，不會因此覺得他是個差勁的員工。此處的see pass sth./sb.意指「看透某事或某人的意圖」，正確答案為(C)。

Answer 3 ◀ѕ) (C)
女性認為什麼不是個好主意？

(A) 工作的敬業精神
(B) 團隊合作
(C) 辦公室戀情
(D) 戀愛

解析
女性一開始就點出自己認為「辦公室戀情」(office romance)絕對不是個好主意，正確答案為(C)。注意選項(D)的戀愛範圍較廣，但女性並沒有說戀愛不好，強調的是「辦公室」戀情。

Answer 4 ◀ѕ) (D)
前同事與她的經理開始交往後，出現了什麼情況？

(A) 她沒有升職，但薪水越來越高。
(B) 她成為經理的私人助理。
(C) 她決定什麼工作都不做。
(D) 她的工作表現越來越差。

解析

前同事開始與經理約會後，她的「工作表現就開始走下坡」。關鍵字deteriorate指「惡化；退化」。注意選項(C)，即便前同事的工作表現變差，但並沒有提到前同事是否完全不做事，正確答案為(D)。

Answer 5 ◀ѕ) (A)
女性的前同事為什麼會被炒魷魚？

(A) 她經常沒有正式請假就曠職。
(B) 她經常沒有告知經理就請假。
(C) 她與經理一同請假。
(D) 她沒完成工作就去渡假。

解析

女性最後提到前同事後來被發現經常沒有「正式批准」(formal approval)就曠職，而且「只通知經理」(notify)。並沒有提到前同事是否與經理一起請假，正確答案為(A)。

中英文內容

I believe healthy competition at work can bring more motivation and improvement. In contrast, **deliberate undermining** is childish and unconstructive. This new guy in my department is clearly ambitious. It is not a bad thing to be so. The problem is, he doesn't show it by working hard but by criticizing my work and boasting how he could have done better. I've had enough. I really hope my manager can **see past** what he's doing and **doesn't think I'm a bad worker**. Otherwise, I might quit soon.

我相信工作上的良性競爭能帶來動力與進步；另一方面，故意矮化他人就顯得幼稚又沒建設性。我們部門新來的員工顯然很有企圖心，這並不是一件壞事。問題是，他的企圖心並沒有用在工作上，反而只會批評我的工作表現，並吹噓他能做得更好。我已經受夠了，希望經理能看透他在搞什麼，而不會覺得我是差勁的員工，否則我大概很快就會辭職了。

I think **office romances** are never a good idea because work should be strictly about professionalism and teamwork. However, one of our ex-colleagues dated her manager. Soon, her work performance started to **deteriorate**, but the manager turned a blind eye. This affected team morale because others felt it was unfair that they had to work harder than the girl. Thank God the situation didn't last too long since the girl was later caught being **frequently absent without formal approval**. She only notified the manager, so both of them were fired in the end.

我認為辦公室戀情絕對不是個好主意，因為工作應該只涉及敬業精神和團隊合作。我們有一位前同事之前和她的經理約會，很快地，她的工作表現開始走下坡，但是經理卻視而不見。這件事影響了團隊的士氣，因為其他同事們覺得自己必須比女孩做更多，這點很不公平。謝天謝地，這個情況並沒有持續太久，因為這個女孩後來被抓到她經常沒有經過正式批准就曠職，她只通知了經理而已，最後她和經理兩個人都被炒魷魚了。

Unit 5 離職與退休 Get Retired

日常生活　娛樂活動　意見交流　特殊場合

◎ MP3 25-01

下面將播放五組短對話，請仔細聆聽，再依對話內容答題。

Question 1

Why is the woman studying fashion design?

(A) To further her career in fashion merchandizing
(B) To make a career change to fashion design
(C) To start a career in fashion merchandizing
(D) To get a job in the fashion industry

Question 2

Why does the woman want to set up her own business?

(A) She can make more money being her own boss.
(B) She doesn't like her boss.
(C) She wants to work at home.
(D) She wants a more flexible working schedule.

Question 3

Why is the man late for work?

(A) He went on a strike at the metro station.
(B) His train was delayed due to the metro staff's strike.
(C) His train was delayed due to an attack.
(D) The trains were cancelled due to the metro staff's strike.

Question 4

What do the man and woman have to do?

(A) Express their opinions on employee benefits by taking the survey
(B) Take other people's opinions on employee benefits seriously
(C) Gather others' opinions on employee benefits
(D) Hand in the completed survey back to the office

Question 5

Why is the woman so sad to see her colleague leave?

(A) She doesn't like to write emails and send texts.
(B) Other people in the office don't talk to her very much.
(C) She doesn't like other people in the office.
(D) She can't tell secrets to other people in the office.

答案與解析 ～answer

Answer 1 ◀)) (B)
女性為什麼要去唸服裝設計的課程？

(A) 讓自己服裝銷售的事業更進一步

(B) 轉換職場跑道至服裝設計

(C) 開創服裝銷售的事業

(D) 在服裝業工作

解析
女性一開始提到課程的事，並於最後說明她想要轉換工作跑道的決心，希望從銷售轉到設計，正確答案為(B)。注意選項(D)表示「原本沒有在服裝業工作」，但女性原本做服裝銷售，本來就是服裝業的一員。

Answer 2 ◀)) (D)
女性為什麼想創立自己的事業？

(A) 因為當老闆能賺更多錢。

(B) 因為她不喜歡她的老闆。

(C) 因為她想要在家裡工作。

(D) 因為她希望擁有更彈性的上班時間。

解析
雖然男性提到自己當老闆賺的比較多，但題目問的是女性創業的原因，所以重點必須放在女性身上。她提到「上班時間比較有彈性」很吸引他，所以正確答案為(D)。

Answer 3 ◀)) (B)
男性上班為什麼會遲到？

(A) 他參加地鐵站的罷工行動。

(B) 他的火車因為地鐵人員的罷工而誤點。

(C) 他的火車因為攻擊事件而誤點。

(D) 所有的火車都因為地鐵人員的罷工而取消。

解析
男性說今天上午許多「地鐵人員罷工」(go on strike)，結果「所有的列車都誤點」。關鍵片語為go on strike(罷工)。他本人並沒有參與罷工，列車也沒有被取消，正確答案為(B)。

Answer 4 ◀)) (A)
男性與女性必須做什麼呢？

(A) 透過調查表表達對員工福利的意見

(B) 認真考慮其他人對員工福利的意見

(C) 蒐集其他人對員工福利的意見

(D) 將填寫完畢的調查表繳回辦公室

解析
男性提到「員工福利調查表」(employee benefits survey)，說他們必須回答調查表上的問題，女性又補充說她希望上面會認真看待他們的「意見」(opinions)，可知透過調查表，他們能表達自己的想法，正確答案為(A)。

Answer 5 ◀)) (D)
對於同事將離開的事，女性為何這麼難過呢？

(A) 她不喜歡寫電子郵件或傳簡訊。

(B) 其他同事很少和她聊天。

(C) 她不喜歡辦公室裡的其他人。

(D) 她無法向其他同事吐露心事。

解析
女性提到雪莉將離開，並解釋對方是她在公司裡「唯一真的可以傾訴心事的對象」，關鍵片語為confide in，表「向…吐露秘密」。正確答案為(D)。請注意女性沒有說她不喜歡其他人或很少與人交流，所以(B)(C)皆不宜選。

中英文內容　　　　　　　⊙慢速MP3 25-02　　⊙正常速MP3 25-03

短對話 1 *Conversation*

Amy: I've just enrolled myself in a fashion design course.

艾咪： 我剛剛註冊了一個服裝設計的課程。

Mike: Do you want to take up fashion design as a serious hobby?

麥克： 你想要認真經營服裝設計這個興趣嗎？

Amy: Actually, I want to **change my career path** from fashion merchandizing.

艾咪： 其實我是想要從服裝銷售這行轉換跑道。

短對話 2 *Conversation*

Taylor: I guess you will make more money being your own boss.

泰勒： 我猜你自己當老闆應該會賺的比較多。

Jenny: That we don't know yet. But my schedule will certainly be **more flexible**, and that's **the most appealing part** to me.

珍妮： 還不知道呢。但上班時間會比較有彈性，這是最吸引我的一點。

短對話 3 *Conversation*

Ted: Sorry, I'm late. Many metro staff **went on strike** this morning. **All the trains were delayed**.

泰德： 對不起，我遲到了。今天早上有很多地鐵人員罷工，所有的列車都誤點了。

Sandy: I know. Thank God I came to work earlier than usual.

仙蒂： 我知道，好險我比平常要早來上班。

短對話 4 *Conversation*

Hank: Here's **an employee benefits survey**. You have to answer all the questions.

漢克： 這是一份員工福利調查表，你必須回答所有的問題。

Tina: I hope they will take **our opinions** seriously and not just do this for show!

蒂娜： 希望他們會認真看待我們的意見，而不僅是在做秀！

短對話 5 *Conversation*

Cindy: My colleague Sherry is leaving next week. I'm so sad. She's the only colleague I can really **confide in**.

辛蒂： 我的同事雪莉下週要離職，我好難過，她是我唯一能傾訴心事的同事。

Vincent: I'm sure you can still keep in touch by emails and messages.

文森： 你還是可以透過電子郵件和簡訊來跟她保持聯絡啊。

長對話聽力實戰

MP3 25-04

請仔細聆聽下面的長對話，再依對話內容選擇正確答案。

Question ①
❶❷❸❹❺

What kind of courses is the woman looking at?

(A) Full-time training courses
(B) Part-time training courses
(C) Training courses for her current job
(D) Courses for a graduate student

Question ②
❶❷❸❹❺

Why is the woman looking for the courses?

(A) Her manager asked her to take more training courses.
(B) It's a plan to get a pay raise at work.
(C) It's a plan to get a promotion at work.
(D) It's a plan in case she has to go on unpaid holiday.

Question ③
❶❷❸❹❺

Does the woman think she will get fired?

(A) She doesn't think so since the company will pull through.
(B) She thinks it's very likely to happen.
(C) She finds it hard to tell if the company will fire employees or not.
(D) She is sure that she'll be fired.

Question ④
❶❷❸❹❺

According to the man, what might be a good idea?

(A) Go on furlough now
(B) Wait until the company makes a decision
(C) Take a training course anyway
(D) Look for another job

Question ⑤
❶❷❸❹❺

What does the woman need to do if she is on furlough?

(A) Take some time to relax
(B) Use her time well and look for other job opportunities
(C) Send her resume to different companies
(D) Take a course on time utilization and opportunity seeking

答案與解析 ～answer

Answer 1 (B)
女性在找什麼樣的課程？

(A) 全職的職訓課程

(B) 兼職的職訓課程

(C) 對她目前工作有幫助的職訓課程

(D) 研究生的課程

解析
男性一開始就問女性為何要看「職訓課程」(the training courses)，但要回答本題，還必須聽女性的回應，她提到這些課程是兼職性質，正確答案為(B)。注意關鍵字part-time(兼職的)表示女性上班也能參與的課程。

Answer 2 (D)
女性為什麼在查看這些課程呢？

(A) 她的經理要求她多上職訓課程。

(B) 為了取得加薪。

(C) 為了在工作上得到升遷。

(D) 以防她被放無薪假。

解析
最快速的解題關鍵在女性提到職訓課程「並非為了現在的工作」(not for my current job)，可直接由刪除法得到正確答案(D)。對話後面女性也有提到，如果被放無薪假，她得善用時間。

Answer 3 (C)
女性覺得自己會被炒魷魚嗎？

(A) 不會，因為公司會撐過去的。

(B) 她覺得很有可能。

(C) 她覺得很難說。

(D) 她很確定自己會被炒魷魚。

解析
當男性提到公司裁員的話題時，女性回答「目前很難說」。hard to say通常用來表示說話者的「不確定感」，正確答案為(C)。注意選項(A)雖然曾經發生過，但女性最後補上「你永遠都不知道會發生什麼」。

Answer 4 (C)
根據男性所言，「什麼」可能是個好主意？

(A) 現在就放無薪假

(B) 等公司做決定

(C) 無論如何都去上職訓課程

(D) 另外找一份新工作

解析
聽到女性的解釋後，男性提到「上職訓課程或許是個好主意」(take part in this training course)，正確答案為(C)。

Answer 5 (B)
如果女性放無薪假的話，她必須怎麼做？

(A) 抓緊時間好好休息

(B) 善用時間並尋找其他工作機會

(C) 寄履歷給不同的公司

(D) 上一門有關「善用時間與找尋機會」的課

解析
女性最後提到如果她開始放無薪假的話，她就得「好好利用時間，找尋其他機會」。utilize為「善用」之意，常與時間、資源等字合用，正確答案為(B)。

Larry: Why are you looking at **the training courses**? Are you thinking of studying on top of doing your job?

賴瑞： 你為什麼要看職訓課程？在考慮工作之餘去進修嗎？

Anna: The courses I'm looking at are **part-time**, but it's not for my current job.

安娜： 我在看的是兼職的職訓課程，但這不是為了我現在的工作。

Larry: Are you thinking of quitting to join another company?

賴瑞： 你想辭掉現在的工作，加入另一家公司嗎？

Anna: Well, this is **more like an insurance plan** for me.

安娜： 這比較像是我的保險計畫。

Larry: What do you mean?

賴瑞： 什麼意思？

Anna: My company has started to implement **a furlough plan**, which worries me that I might be next.

安娜： 我的公司已開始放無薪假，我很擔心自己會是下一個放無薪假的人。

Larry: So you are afraid that they might start firing people.

賴瑞： 所以你害怕他們開始裁員。

Anna: It is **hard to say** now. We had the same situation before, and we pulled through. But you just don't know.

安娜： 目前很難說，我們之前也遇過相同的情況，那時也撐過來了，但你永遠不知道會發生什麼事。

Larry: **Taking part in this training course** might be a good idea.

賴瑞： 上職訓課程也許是個好主意。

Anna: I agree. If they put me on furlough, I need to **utilize my time and seek for other opportunities**.

安娜： 同意，如果我放無薪假，勢必得好好利用時間，尋找其他機會。

短文聽力實戰

◎MP3 25-07(短文1)   ◎MP3 25-08(短文2)

請仔細聆聽下面兩段短文，並分別回答Q1~Q2&Q3~Q5兩大題。

Question 1

Why doesn't the woman like the receptionist?

(A) She heard the receptionist saying bad things about others.
(B) The receptionist gossips too much.
(C) The receptionist says bad things about her behind her back.
(D) The receptionist isn't polite to others.

Question 2

What kind of people does the woman prefer to hang out with?

(A) Overly polite people
(B) Overly pretentious people
(C) More genuine people
(D) People who never bad-mouth others

Question 3

What had always been the man's motto?

(A) Work hard, play harder
(B) Work hard, play hard
(C) Work hard when you need money
(D) Work hard and retire early

Question 4

What did the man attend yesterday?

(A) A retirement planning seminar organized by his company
(B) A retirement planning seminar he found online
(C) A retirement planning seminar he presented at
(D) A retirement planning seminar he registered for

Question 5

What has the consultant made the man realize?

(A) The importance of delaying your retirement until later
(B) That he should not worry about his retirement
(C) The importance of starting planning his retirement early
(D) The importance of earning money

答案與解析 ~answer

Answer 1 ◀)) (A)
女性為何不喜歡坐櫃台的那位接待員？

(A) 她曾經聽到接待員講人壞話。

(B) 那名接待員太愛講八卦。

(C) 那名接待員在她背後講她的壞話。

(D) 那名接待員對人沒有禮貌。

解析

女性提到她有一次「無意中聽到」(overheard)那名接待員「惡意批評」(bad-mouth)一個先前當面稱讚的人，作風很雙面，所以她不喜歡，正確答案為(A)。注意選項(B)中的gossip只是在講人很愛傳播消息，沒有惡意批評的意思。

Answer 2 ◀)) (C)
女性寧願和什麼樣的人來往呢？

(A) 過於有禮貌的人

(B) 過於做作的人

(C) 較為真誠的人

(D) 從來不惡意批評他人的人

解析

女性說她不喜歡像該名櫃台人員這樣的雙面人；她寧願和個性「較真誠」(more genuine)的人來往。這並不表示絕對不能講別人的壞話，正確答案為 (C)。

Answer 3 ◀)) (B)
一直以來，男性的座右銘是什麼？

(A) 努力工作，但要更努力享樂

(B) 努力工作，並努力玩樂

(C) 需要錢的時候努力工作

(D) 努力工作，早點退休

解析

男性提到自己的「座右銘」(motto)一直以來都是「努力工作、盡力玩樂」(work hard and play hard)，兩者同等重要，正確答案為(B)。選項(A)使用了比較級，表示「玩樂更加重要」，這並非答案。

Answer 4 ◀)) (A)
男性昨天參加了什麼活動？

(A) 由公司安排的退休規劃講座

(B) 他上網查到的退休規劃講座

(C) 他上台演講的退休規劃講座

(D) 他之前註冊的退休規劃講座

解析

選項當中全都提到a retirement planning seminar，所以聽的時候可以把這幾個字當作線索，仔細聽講座的「性質」即可(關鍵字為seminar)。文章中提到公司邀請了一名退休規劃顧問(my company invited)，因此答案選(A)。

Answer 5 ◀)) (C)
那名顧問讓男性理解了什麼事？

(A) 晚點再安排退休計畫的重要性

(B) 他不須要擔心自己的退休

(C) 及早規劃退休的重要性

(D) 賺錢的重要性

解析

男性提到顧問讓他意識到「提前規劃退休」(an advanced retirement plan)有多重要，關鍵字在advanced(提前的)，由此可剔除(A)選項，正確答案為(C)。

短文 1　　　　　　　　　⊙慢速MP3 25-09　　◎正常速MP3 25-10

　　Some people are not what they seem at all! I have one colleague who is a perfect example of this. This woman, who works at reception, always addresses people in the most polite manner and asks how they are. However, **I once overheard her bad-mouthing someone** she had just praised directly. I **don't like two-faced people** like her. Instead, I prefer to hang out with those who are more genuine. Politeness is important, but being **overly pretentious** is just unnecessary. I really hope this woman doesn't say bad things about me behind my back!

　　有些人骨子裡和他表面上的樣子完全不同！我有個同事就是這類人的典型例子。這位女同事坐櫃檯，待人永遠都極度有禮，會向大家問好。但我有一次無意間聽到她帶著惡意在批評她先前當面稱讚的人。我不喜歡像她這樣的雙面人，我反而寧願和個性真誠的人來往。禮貌固然重要，但過於做作就沒有必要，真希望這個女同事不會背著我講我的壞話！

短文 2　　　　　　　　　⊙慢速MP3 25-11　　◎正常速MP3 25-12

　　Like most people, I focus on my daily job to earn the money to pay my bills and going out with friends. My **motto** had always been to **work hard and play hard**. However, I realize that's not enough. Yesterday, my company invited a **retirement planning consultant** to our office. She delivered a seminar and let me become her Facebook friend. She also said that I can talk to her online if I have further questions. Through her speech, I realized the importance of **an advanced retirement plan**. It's the way to sustain a certain lifestyle when I retire.

　　像大多數人一樣，我專注於日常工作，賺錢以支付帳單以及跟朋友出去玩。一直以來，我的座右銘都是「努力工作、盡力玩樂」，但是，我發覺這樣還不夠。昨天，公司邀請了一位退休規劃的顧問來，她替員工上了堂講座，並讓我成為她的臉書朋友，她也說如果我有進一步的問題，可以在線上問她。聽完她的演說，我意識到了提前規劃退休的重要性，有了事前規劃，才能讓我在退休後維持特定的生活方式。

6 PART

旅遊與文化

行前準備、文化交流，休閒時刻的對談，
這樣聽真簡單！

Unit 1 準備旅程
Get Ready

Unit 2 搭乘飛機
On The Plane

Unit 3 住宿相關
Accommodations

Unit 4 異國風情
Exotic Cultures

Unit 5 文化交流
The Cultures

Unit
1

準備旅程 Get Ready

日常生活　娛樂活動　意見交流　特殊場合

短 對 話 聽 力 實 戰

MP3 26-01

下面將播放五組短對話，請仔細聆聽，再依對話內容答題。

Question 1

Where does the woman want to go on holiday?

(A) Hokkaido

(B) Okinawa

(C) Tokyo

(D) Somewhere not in Japan

Question 2

What does the travel agent suggest the woman do?

(A) Consider waiting for a place on the group tours

(B) Consider a flight and hotel package deal

(C) Get booked into a hotel first

(D) Take whatever available deal that comes first

Question 3

What doesn't the man want to do for his holiday?

(A) Stay at a place where tourists go

(B) Have spa treatment

(C) Get away from city chaos

(D) See popular tourist sites like most tourists do

Question 4

Why does the woman ask the man to buy the 1-day travel pass?

(A) You can use a 1-day travel pass for the whole week.

(B) It's cheaper than purchasing multiple singles.

(C) They can only buy 1-day travel passes.

(D) They are going to two different places today.

Question 5

Why does the man want to book his train ticket now?

(A) The woman recommends he do so.

(B) It's more convenient than buying the ticket in Japan.

(C) He can get a special discount as a student.

(D) He can get a special discount as an overseas tourist.

答案與解析 ～answer

Answer 1 🔊 (C)
女性想去哪裡渡假呢？

(A) 北海道
(B) 沖繩
(C) 東京
(D) 日本以外的地方

解析

女性提到自己去過東京，「很想再去一次」(really want to go back)，但她先生卻想嘗試不同的地方。不過，本題問的是「女性想去的地方」，因此正確答案選(C)。

Answer 2 🔊 (B)
旅行社員工推薦女性什麼呢？

(A) 考慮旅行團的候補名單
(B) 考慮機票加酒店的優惠行程
(C) 先預訂酒店
(D) 不管有什麼行程都接受

解析

旅行社員工向女性解釋全包式的旅行團都已經額滿，但提供「機票加酒店的行程」，package deal前面的酒店與機票表示囊括的費用，正確答案為(B)。

Answer 3 🔊 (D)
男性渡假的時候不想做什麼？

(A) 像一般觀光客一樣待在某個地點
(B) 享受SPA按摩
(C) 逃離城市的喧囂
(D) 像大多數觀光客般參觀熱門景點

解析

當旅行社員工推薦峇里島行程，男生說不想要「典型的景點觀光方式」，typical為「典型的」意思，在此用來形容「參加旅行團最常見的安排」，即「參觀各處景點，走馬看花」，因此正確答案為(D)。

Answer 4 🔊 (B)
女性為什麼要男性買一日票呢？

(A) 一整個星期都能用一日票。
(B) 買一日票會比買好幾張單程票要便宜。
(C) 他們只能購買一日票。
(D) 他們今天要去兩個不同的地方。

解析

聽到女性的提醒，男性想到「一日票會比買幾張單程票來的便宜」，比較級cheaper...than...帶有「比…便宜」之意，如果沒有聽清楚「價格」這項重點，也可由比較級的概念找出正確答案為(B)。

Answer 5 🔊 (D)
男性為什麼現在就要訂購列車車票？

(A) 女性推薦他這麼做。
(B) 這樣比在日本當地購票方便。
(C) 他能因學生身分取得優惠折扣。
(D) 國外觀光客能取得優惠折扣。

解析

針對女性的疑問，男性最後提到「海外訂購的外國遊客能取得優惠折扣」，重點在international tourist(外國遊客)，正確答案為(D)。

⊙慢速MP3 26-02 　　⊙正常速MP3 26-03

短對話 1 Conversation

Chris: Where are you going for your holiday? Tokyo or Okinawa?

克里斯：你打算去哪裡渡假？東京還是沖繩？

Rena: I've **been to Tokyo** once. **I really want to go back**, but my husband wants to try somewhere different this time.

芮娜： 我去過一次東京，很想再去一次，但我先生這次想去不同的地方。

短對話 2 Conversation

Mrs.Baker: I'm looking for a tour group going to Indonesia. What tours do you have?

貝克太太： 我想找印尼的旅遊團，你們有什麼選擇？

Travel agent: The all-inclusive tours are fully booked now. There are **some flight and hotel package deals**. Would you like to consider those?

旅行社員工： 全包式的旅行團目前都已額滿，有一些機票加酒店的優惠行程，您覺得如何？

短對話 3 Conversation

Travel agent: Can I recommend our Bali Island tour for this Easter?

旅行社員工： 我可以推薦我們復活節期間推出的峇里島行程嗎？

Benjamin: I don't want to do the **typical sightseeing at tourist sites**.

班傑明： 我不想要那種典型的景點觀光行程。

短對話 4 Conversation

Brian: I'll go and buy the underground tickets for us.

布萊恩：我去買地鐵車票。

Debby: Make sure you get the 1-day travel pass.

黛比： 要記得買一日票喔。

Brian: Oh, right. It'll be **cheaper** to have a day pass **than buying several single tickets**.

布萊恩：對喔，買一日票會比買幾張單程票來的便宜。

短對話 5 Conversation

John: I need to book the train ticket before I fly to Japan.

約翰： 出發到日本前，我必須先訂好列車車票。

Kate: Why don't you buy it there? It's more convenient.

凱特： 為什麼不到那邊再買？這樣比較方便。

John: But you **get a special international tourist discount** by purchasing it overseas.

約翰： 但是，海外訂購的遊客能取得優惠折扣。

長對話聽力實戰

◎ MP3 26-04

請仔細聆聽下面的長對話，再依對話內容選擇正確答案。

Question ①

When is the boy going on his trip to Tibet?

(A) During his spring break
(B) During the winter vacation
(C) At Christmas
(D) After he graduates

Question ②

What has the boy planned to do?

(A) Go on a golf trip with his father
(B) Travel around Taiwan
(C) Travel around Tibet
(D) Stay at home and do nothing

Question ③

When will the boy's friend join him?

(A) While he is in Tibet
(B) When he flies to Tibet
(C) On his return flight
(D) Back at home

Question ④

How long is the boy's trip in Tibet?

(A) Three days
(B) One week
(C) The whole of his spring break
(D) Ten days

Question ⑤

What does the boy say he's done a lot of research on?

(A) Places to go in Taipei
(B) Tourist sites to visit
(C) Safety for female travelers
(D) Safety for people traveling on their own

答案與解析 ～answer

Answer 1 (A)
男孩的西藏之旅是什麼時候？

(A) 春假期間
(B) 寒假期間
(C) 聖誕節的時候
(D) 他畢業之後

> **解析**
> 當女孩問男孩「春假」(Spring break)有沒有計畫時，男孩回說有，這就可以得出正確答案為(A)。注意選項(B)的內容是男孩計畫西藏之旅的時間，而並非旅行的日子。

Answer 2 (C)
男孩計劃要做什麼呢？

(A) 和父親一起去高爾夫之旅
(B) 在臺灣各處旅遊
(C) 在西藏各處旅遊
(D) 待在家裡，什麼也不做

> **解析**
> 解題的重點首先在題目，要看出問的是「男孩的計畫」。男孩的爸爸想帶他去打高爾夫，但「他規劃的行程是去西藏」，重點在what I have in mind這個句型後面帶出的內容，正確答案為(C)。

Answer 3 (C)
男孩的朋友什麼時候會與他會合？

(A) 當男孩在西藏的時候
(B) 男孩飛往西藏的飛機上
(C) 男孩回程的飛機上
(D) 回到家之後

> **解析**
> 男孩自己也提到，當他回來時，會在台北停留，屆時會有朋友和他搭同一班飛機回來，重點在join me on the flight back home這一句，正確答案為(C)。

Answer 4 (D)
男孩在西藏的旅行總共有幾天？

(A) 三天
(B) 一個星期
(C) 整個春假
(D) 十天

> **解析**
> 男孩首先提到會「在首都待三天」(for three days)，在那之後的「一整個星期」(for a whole week)會在不同的地方，兩種行程都是在西藏完成的，所以必須將天數加起來，正確答案為(D)。

Answer 5 (D)
男孩在什麼上面做了很多研究？

(A) 臺北能去的地方
(B) 要去的觀光景點
(C) 女性遊客的安全注意事項
(D) 獨自旅行者的安全注意事項

> **解析**
> 對話最後，女孩提醒男孩要小心安全。此時男孩提到自己花了很多時間研究了有關「單獨旅行的安全資訊」(lone traveler safety)，正確答案為(D)。注意選項(C)僅強調「女性」，但男孩並沒有提到性別差異。

中英文內容

⊙ 慢速MP3 26-05　　⊘ 正常速MP3 26-06

Jessie: Have you got any plans for your **spring break**?
潔西：　你春假有沒有什麼計畫？

Alvin: Sure. I **planned** it already **during the winter vacation**.
亞文：　當然，我在寒假期間已經規劃好行程了。

Jessie: Where are you going?
潔西：　你要去哪裡？

Alvin: My dad was planning a day golfing trip, but what I have in mind is **a trip to Tibet**.
亞文：　我爸爸想帶我去高爾夫一日遊，但我心裡的打算是去西藏。

Jessie: Wow! It's not the type of trip I normally hear about!
潔西：　哇！這可不是我一般會聽到的行程呢！

Alvin: When I fly back, I will have a stopover in Taipei. A friend will **join me on the flight back home then**.
亞文：　我回來時，會在台北停留，有個朋友那時會和我搭同一班飛機回來。

Jessie: So how many days are you staying in Tibet?
潔西：　所以你在西藏會待幾天？

Alvin: I'll stay in the capital for **three days**. After that, I'll be trekking in various places **for a whole week**.
亞文：　我會在首都待三天，在那之後的一整個星期，我會在不同的地方徒步旅行。

Jessie: I'm sure you'll have a great time exploring Tibet; stay safe.
潔西：　我相信你的西藏之旅會很棒，要小心安全喔。

Alvin: I will. I've done a lot of research on **lone traveler safety**.
亞文：　我會的，我花了很多時間研究有關單獨旅行的安全資訊。

短文聽力實戰

MP3 26-07(短文1)   MP3 26-08(短文2)

請仔細聆聽下面兩段短文，並分別回答Q1~Q2&Q3~Q5兩大題。

Question 1

Why didn't the woman enjoy her last trip?

(A) The package was too expensive.

(B) She didn't find anything interesting to buy.

(C) They didn't go to any popular tourist sites.

(D) She didn't enjoy going to a lot of souvenir shops.

Question 2

What makes staying at hostels more attractive to the woman?

(A) The cost would be cheaper than staying in hotels.

(B) Hostels offer great food to all tourists.

(C) Tourists there have interesting stories to share.

(D) She doesn't need to go to the souvenir shops anymore.

Question 3

What does the man say many people suffer from nowadays?

(A) Illnesses contracted at work

(B) Stress-related illnesses

(C) Long-term illnesses like depression

(D) Hereditary illnesses

Question 4

What are more and more companies doing about staff benefits?

(A) Paying their employees a salary when they take some days off

(B) Making staff travel mandatory for employees

(C) Using trips as a prize for those who improve their performance

(D) Including staff travel as part of employee benefits

Question 5

What can staff travel do apart from relieving stress?

(A) Help employees work more efficiently

(B) Help employees establish better relationships with each other

(C) Help employees get better benefits

(D) Help employees purchase bonds

答案與解析 ～answer

Answer 1 (D)

女性為何不喜歡她上一次的旅遊呢？

(A) 行程太貴了。

(B) 她沒有看到有趣的東西可買。

(C) 他們沒有去參觀熱門景點。

(D) 她不喜歡去紀念品店的行程。

解析

針對自己上一次參加旅行團的經驗，女性提到他們「在紀念品商店的購物行程很多」，但因為她不想買東西，所以只能坐在那邊乾等，表示這種行程很無聊，正確答案為(D)。

Answer 2 (C)

什麼因素讓女性覺得住青年旅館很吸引她？

(A) 住宿的費用比飯店便宜。

(B) 青年旅館會提供遊客美味的食物。

(C) 住在那裡的遊客會分享有趣的故事。

(D) 女性不用再去紀念品店。

解析

女性提到自己很享受與青年旅館的其他住客交流，聽他們講有趣的故事，正確答案為(D)。其他選項如(A)(B)，因為沒有被提及，所以無法得知相關資訊。

Answer 3 (B)

根據男性的話，現在很多人都深受什麼所苦呢？

(A) 在工作場所被傳染感冒

(B) 與壓力有關的疾病

(C) 像憂鬱症那種的長期性疾病

(D) 遺傳性疾病

解析

男性提到很多人「受到與壓力有關的疾病所苦」，關鍵字為stress-related(與壓力有關的)，正確答案為(B)。注意選項(C)中的depression(憂鬱症)雖然有被提到，但只是被拿來舉例而已。

Answer 4 (D)

針對員工福利，越來越多公司採取什麼作法？

(A) 在員工休假時，支付他們薪水

(B) 將員工旅遊列為員工非做不可的事項

(C) 讓工作表現有進步的員工參加員工旅遊

(D) 將員工旅遊列為福利的一部分

解析

男性提到有越來越多的公司「將員工旅遊列為公司福利的一部分」重點句型在include sth. as part of，表示「某事物被包括在…裡面」，正確答案為(D)。

Answer 5 (B)

除了舒緩壓力之外，員工旅遊還有什麼作用？

(A) 幫助員工提升績效

(B) 幫助員工彼此建立更好的關係

(C) 幫助員工取得更好的福利

(D) 幫助員工購買債券

解析

男性說員工旅遊不僅可以幫助員工緩解壓力，還能「增進員工彼此的關係」。這裡的bond指的是「員工間的關係」，正確答案為(B)。選項(D)中的bond意指「債券」，並非文章的原意。

I enjoy the freedom of traveling alone. It's because of my last trip. I joined a tour group then. We had a lot of shopping stops in souvenir stores. I **didn't want to buy anything**, so all I could do was **sit and wait**. That's why I now prefer traveling alone. I don't book hotels in advance because I want to have the freedom to stay in one city longer. Hostels are usually my first choice because I **enjoy meeting other travelers** and **hearing their interesting stories**. More importantly, they will recommend what's worthwhile doing, seeing, and eating.

我喜歡獨自旅行，會這樣與我上次的旅行經驗有關。我那時候參加了旅行團，好多個行程都是去紀念品店購物。我什麼都不想買，結果就只能乾坐在那邊等其他人，所以我現在都寧願獨自去旅行。我不會事先預訂飯店，因為我希望能自由決定在一個城市的停留時間。青年旅館通常是我的首選，因為我非常享受和其他的住客交流，聽他們講有趣的故事，更重要的是，他們還會推薦值得做的活動、該看的景點、以及一定要品嚐的美食給我。

Work-life balance is now gaining more attention because there're more and more people suffering from **stress-related illnesses**, including panic attacks and depression. People are often given too much work and too little time to do it, which ends up causing a lot of problems. To solve this, more and more companies now **include staff travel as part of their benefits package**. Traveling not only helps employees relieve stress, but it also **helps people bond**. Working hard is important, but having a good quality of life can actually facilitate success at work.

工作與生活間的平衡近來成為大家關注的議題，因為有越來越多人受到與壓力有關的疾病所苦，包括了恐慌症和憂鬱症等等。人們通常都被交付太多工作，卻沒有足夠的時間完成，因此造成了許多問題。為了解決這個問題，現在有越來越多的公司將員工旅遊列入公司福利的一部分。旅遊不僅能幫助員工緩解壓力，還能增進員工彼此的關係。認真工作固然重要，但良好的生活品質能促進你在工作上的成效。

Unit 2 搭乘飛機 On The Plane

日常生活　娛樂活動　意見交流　特殊場合

短對話聽力實戰

◎ MP3 27-01

下面將播放五組短對話，請仔細聆聽，再依對話內容答題。

Question 1
1 2 3 4 5

What will the stewardess do for the man?

(A) Help him put his bag under the seat
(B) Put his bag in another passenger's compartment
(C) Go and find another compartment to put his bag in
(D) Check if the man's put something too big in the bag

Question 2
1 2 3 4 5

What does the steward ask the woman to do?

(A) Wait until they serve the meal to ask for wine
(B) Wait until the meal is finished to ask for wine
(C) Ask another flight attendant for wine
(D) Have a different drink with the meal

Question 3
1 2 3 4 5

What is the woman going to do?

(A) Give the man's jacket back
(B) Ask for a jacket
(C) Ask for an extra blanket
(D) Ask for a cup of hot tea

Question 4
1 2 3 4 5

How does the woman want to pay for her shopping?

(A) Part by cash, part by card
(B) By writing a check
(C) By using her credit card
(D) By cash when she lands

Question 5
1 2 3 4 5

What is the woman worrying about?

(A) She has lost her baggage.
(B) She thinks she might have lost her baggage.
(C) She's been told her baggage is at the lost-and-found counter.
(D) The lost-and-found counter doesn't have her baggage.

答案與解析 ～answer

Answer 1 ◄)) (C)

空服員將會為男性做什麼呢？

- (A) 幫忙他將袋子放在座位底下
- (B) 將他的袋子放在別人的置物箱
- (C) 另外找置物箱放他的袋子
- (D) 確認男性是否在袋子裡裝進太大的物品

解析
男性詢問空姐是否能將袋子放在腳邊，得到自己袋子太大不能這麼做的回應。空姐提到會「另外找置物箱放他的袋子」，重點單字為 another compartment，正確答案為(C)。

Answer 2 ◄)) (A)

空服員請女性做什麼呢？

- (A) 等他們供餐時再點酒
- (B) 等用餐結束後再點酒
- (C) 向其他空服員點酒
- (D) 點其他飲料來配餐點

解析
女性一開始向空服員點了一杯白酒，空服員提到「很快就會開始供應餐點，並一起供應飲料」，問女性是否介意等多幾分鐘，要注意供餐僅為解釋，希望女性等待才是空服員的要求，正確答案為(A)。

Answer 3 ◄)) (D)

女性準備要做什麼？

- (A) 將男性的外套還給他
- (B) 要求給她一件外套
- (C) 要求另外再給她一條毯子
- (D) 要求給她一杯熱茶

解析
聽到女性會冷，男性請她先穿上他的外套，並打算再幫她要一條毯子，注意這些全是男性要做的事。女性自己要做的則是等空姐過來時「要一杯熱茶」(ask for a cup of hot tea)，正確答案為(D)。

Answer 4 ◄)) (C)

女性打算如何購買產品呢？

- (A) 部分付現，部分刷卡
- (B) 寫支票
- (C) 刷信用卡
- (D) 飛機降落後再付現

解析
當空服員問女性她要如何付款時，女性回答要「刷信用卡付款」(by credit card)，正確答案為(C)。因為對話中沒有提到任何與「現金」(cash)有關的單字，所以其他選項都可剔除。

Answer 5 ◄)) (B)

女性正在擔心什麼事情？

- (A) 她的行李不見了。
- (B) 她覺得自己的行李有可能不見了。
- (C) 有人告訴她，她的行李在失物招領處。
- (D) 失物招領處沒有她的行李。

解析
女性一開始就提到大多數乘客都拿了自己的行李，但「她還沒看到自己的」(I still can't see mine)，表示她擔心行李不見，但這並不表示行李已經確定弄丟，正確答案為(B)。

⊙慢速MP3 27-02　　⊙正常速MP3 27-03

短對話 1　Conversation

Benjamin:　Excuse me. Can I put my bag by my feet?
班傑明：　　不好意思，我可以把袋子放在腳邊嗎？
Stewardess:It's too large to be put under the seat. Let me **find another compartment** for your bag.
空姐：　　　您的袋子太大，不能放在坐位下方，我會另外替您找置物箱放置。

短對話 2　Conversation

Rebecca: May I get a glass of white wine?
芮貝卡：　可以給我一杯白酒嗎？
Steward: We'll be serving the meal and **drinks with it shortly**. Would you mind **waiting a couple of minutes**?
空少：　　我們很快就會開始供餐，並一起供應飲料，您介意多等幾分鐘嗎？

短對話 3　Conversation

Sophie: The air conditioning onboard is very strong.
蘇菲：　機艙裡面的空調好強。
Jeff:　Put on my jacket, and I'll ask for an extra blanket for you.
傑夫：　穿上我的外套，我會再幫你要一條毯子。
Sophie: I'll also **ask for a cup of hot tea** when the flight attendant comes round.
蘇菲：　等空姐過來時，我也會請她給我杯熱茶。

短對話 4　Conversation

Linda:　I want to buy these duty-free items, please.
琳達：　我想買這些免稅商品，謝謝。
Steward: Sure. How would you like to pay?
空少：　　沒問題，請問您想要怎麼付款呢？
Linda:　**By credit card.** Thank you.
琳達：　我要刷信用卡，謝謝。

短對話 5　Conversation

Ellie:　Most passengers have claimed their baggage, but **I still can't see mine.**
艾莉：　大部分的乘客都拿了行李，但我還沒看到我的。
Andrew: I'm sure it'll turn up soon. **If it is lost**, we can go to the lost-and-found counter then.
安德魯：肯定很快就會看到。如果真的不見了，我們可以去失物招領處詢問。

長對話聽力實戰

MP3 27-04

請仔細聆聽下面的長對話，再依對話內容選擇正確答案。

Question 1

What is the main purpose of the man's trip?

(A) To attend a tour group
(B) To attend his friend's wedding
(C) To attend a friend's birthday party
(D) To join his friend's backpack trip

Question 2

How long will the man stay in the country?

(A) No more than a week
(B) Till next Monday
(C) More than ten days
(D) Ten days or fewer

Question 3

What proof does the officer ask the man to offer?

(A) Where the wedding is being held
(B) Where he will visit in the country
(C) Where he will stay while he's in the country
(D) How long he is staying for

Question 4

What does the man say his friend has sent him?

(A) An invitation letter with the plane ticket inside
(B) An invitation letter with popular tourist sites
(C) An invitation letter with the wedding venue's address
(D) An invitation letter stating the friend's address

Question 5

What does the officer ask the man to do later?

(A) To make a declaration if he possesses anything on the list
(B) To make a declaration if he possesses any alcohol
(C) To write a report if he has anything described on the list
(D) To send them the proof of his accommodation

答案與解析 ~answer

Answer 1 (B)
男性旅遊的最主要目的為何？

(A) 參加旅行團
(B) 參加朋友的婚禮
(C) 參加朋友的生日派對
(D) 加入朋友的背包客旅行

> **解析**
> 男性提到自己「要來參加朋友的婚禮」(for a friend's wedding)，雖然他也說會造訪幾個不同的地方，但請注意內文中的also指「也會」，表示這並非主要原因，正確答案為(B)。

Answer 2 (D)
男性在該國會待幾天呢？

(A) 不超過一個星期
(B) 待到下週一為止
(C) 十天以上
(D) 不超過十天

> **解析**
> 男性提到下週一或下週三是他在解釋回程航班可能會改變，與他待的天數無直接關係。要仔細聽的是接下來的 definitely no more than ten days，正確答案為(D)。

Answer 3 (C)
官員要求男性出示「什麼」的相關證明？

(A) 婚禮舉行的場所
(B) 他在該國會參觀的地方
(C) 他停留期間會住的地方
(D) 他會待多久

> **解析**
> 題目問的是相關證明，所以必須回答對話中明確點出proof這個字的內容。當男性說他會住在朋友家時，海關人員問他是否有「相關的資料可供證明」(proof of that)，正確答案為(C)。

Answer 4 (D)
男性說朋友寄給他什麼東西？

(A) 附機票的邀請函
(B) 介紹熱門景點的邀請函
(C) 寫著婚禮舉行地點的邀請函
(D) 寫著朋友地址的邀請函

> **解析**
> 海關人員請男性出示住宿方面的相關證明時，男性拿出朋友寄的「邀請函」，並解釋上面印有「他住的地方」(where I'll be staying)，正確答案為(D)。

Answer 5 (A)
官員要求男性晚點做什麼？

(A) 擁有清單上的物品就要申報
(B) 有帶酒的話要申報
(C) 寫一份他是否有清單上物品的報告
(D) 給他們一份關於住處的相關證明

> **解析**
> 對話最後，海關人員提醒男性，如果他有「列表中描述的任何物品」(items described on the list)，晚點一定要申報，正確答案為(A)。注意(B)(C)分別只講對了一半，所以都不可以選。

中英文內容

⊙慢速MP3 27-05　　⊘正常速MP3 27-06

Customs Officer: What is the purpose of your trip?
海關人員： 您這次旅行的目的是什麼呢？

Lawrence: I'm here for **a friend's wedding**. And I'll also visit a few different places.
勞倫斯： 我來參加朋友的婚禮，也會造訪幾個不同的地方。

Customs Officer: How long will you stay?
海關人員： 請問您會待多久呢？

Lawrence: My return flight is on next Monday, but I might change it to next Wednesday. Anyway, it will definitely be **no more than ten days**.
勞倫斯： 我回程的航班是在下週一，但是我可能會改到下週三，無論如何，我確定待的時間不會超過十天。

Customs Officer: How about your **accommodation**?
海關人員： 那您的住宿呢？

Lawrence: I'll be staying at my friend's place.
勞倫斯： 我會住在朋友家。

Customs Officer: Do you have **any proof of that**?
海關人員： 您是否有任何相關的資料可供證明？

Lawrence: Here, my friend has sent me **an invitation letter. The address on it is where I'll be staying**.
勞倫斯： 請看這個，我朋友寄了張邀請函，上面的住址就是我會住的地方。

Customs Officer: OK. If you have any **items described on the list** here, make sure you **declare them later**.
海關人員： 好的，如果您帶有此列表中描述的任何物品，等一下請務必申報。

短文聽力實戰

⊘ MP3 27-07(短文1)　⊘ MP3 27-08(短文2)

請仔細聆聽下面兩段短文，並分別回答Q1~Q2&Q3~Q5兩大題。

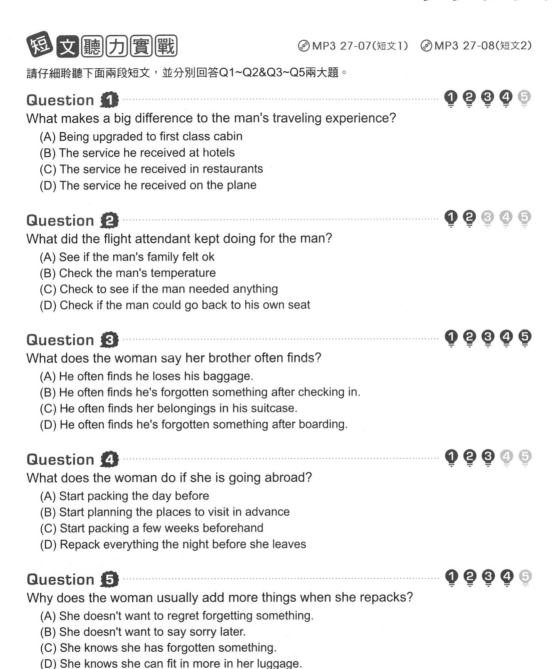

Question 1

What makes a big difference to the man's traveling experience?

(A) Being upgraded to first class cabin
(B) The service he received at hotels
(C) The service he received in restaurants
(D) The service he received on the plane

Question 2

What did the flight attendant kept doing for the man?

(A) See if the man's family felt ok
(B) Check the man's temperature
(C) Check to see if the man needed anything
(D) Check if the man could go back to his own seat

Question 3

What does the woman say her brother often finds?

(A) He often finds he loses his baggage.
(B) He often finds he's forgotten something after checking in.
(C) He often finds her belongings in his suitcase.
(D) He often finds he's forgotten something after boarding.

Question 4

What does the woman do if she is going abroad?

(A) Start packing the day before
(B) Start planning the places to visit in advance
(C) Start packing a few weeks beforehand
(D) Repack everything the night before she leaves

Question 5

Why does the woman usually add more things when she repacks?

(A) She doesn't want to regret forgetting something.
(B) She doesn't want to say sorry later.
(C) She knows she has forgotten something.
(D) She knows she can fit in more in her luggage.

答案與解析 ～answer

Answer 1 ◀)) (D)
什麼讓男性對旅行的經驗有了完全不同的感受呢？

 (A) 被升等到頭等艙
 (B) 飯店的服務品質
 (C) 餐廳的服務品質
 (D) 飛機上的服務品質

解析
男性提到這次的飛行經驗讓他真正感受到「機上的服務」(the service onboard) 能產生很大的影響。要注意的是選項(A)的升等雖然也有發生，但文章所強調的是空服員整體的服務，所以要選包含了所有服務的(D)。

Answer 2 ◀)) (C)
空服員為了男性，一直做什麼事呢？

 (A) 查看男性的家人是否還好
 (B) 確認男性的體溫
 (C) 確認男性是否需要任何物品
 (D) 確認男性是否能回到自己的座位

解析
解題關鍵在題目中的keep doing，表示空服員有「重複做某件事」。對話中的線索在空服員每隔一小時就來「確認男子需要的東西都有備齊」，正確答案為(C)。

Answer 3 ◀)) (B)
女性說她弟弟經常怎麼樣？

 (A) 發現自己的行李不見了。
 (B) 辦理好登機手續後發現忘了帶東西。
 (C) 在他的行李箱內發現姊姊的物品。
 (D) 登機後發現自己忘了帶東西。

解析
女性說她弟弟老是在最後打包，所以經常會在「辦好登機手續後發現自己忘記帶東西」。注意check in只是在櫃台辦理登機手續(包含確認護照、機票、托運行李等)，但選項(D)的board指的是登機，所以正確答案選(B)。

Answer 4 ◀)) (C)
如果女性要出國，她會做什麼呢？

 (A) 前一天開始打包行李
 (B) 事先規劃要去參觀的地方
 (C) 幾週前就開始打包
 (D) 在出發前一天重新打包行李

解析
女性提到自己如果要出國，至少會「提前幾個星期開始打包」(a couple of weeks in advance)，正確答案為(C)。注意(D)在文中是「有時候」(sometimes)會做的事，並非她計劃出國時的常態。

Answer 5 ◀)) (A)
女性重新打包時，為何通常會增加行李的物品？

 (A) 她不想為了忘記帶東西而後悔。
 (B) 她不想之後道歉。
 (C) 她知道自己忘了些什麼。
 (D) 她知道行李可以裝更多東西。

解析
女性提到自己有時會重新打包，然後通常會再增加一些行李，因為她「寧願小心點也不要後悔」(it's better to be safe than sorry)，正確答案為(A)。注意這句的sorry表示「後悔」，而非平常使用的「道歉」之意。

⊙慢速MP3 27-09　　◎正常速MP3 27-10

I just got back from my trip to Hong Kong with the family. The flight experience this time really made me realize how much **the service onboard** makes a big difference. On our way to Hong Kong, I felt nausea and headache. The flight attendant upgraded me and my family to first class cabin to allow me to lie down. And she kept **checking on me** every hour to **make sure I had everything I needed**. I'm really grateful of the great service and attitude from the flight attendant. I will definitely email the airline to express my gratefulness.

　　我剛和家人從香港渡假回來。這次的飛行經驗讓我感受到機上的服務真能產生很大的影響。飛往香港的途中，我感到噁心和頭痛，空姐把我和我的家人升級到頭等艙，以便讓我可以躺下，她每隔一小時就來關心我的狀態，確認我需要的東西都有備齊。我真的很感激這位空姐的優良服務和態度，我絕對會發封電子郵件給航空公司，表達我的感謝之情。

⊙慢速MP3 27-11　　◎正常速MP3 27-12

I can never understand why people leave packing to the last minute. My younger brother does that, and he often finds he has **forgotten something after he checks in**. On the contrary, I always start my packing **at least a couple of weeks in advance** when I'm going abroad. Sometimes, I would spend the night before repacking, and usually add more things to my luggage because I think **it is better to be safe than sorry**. My brother thinks I stress too much over packing, but I like to be organized. Otherwise, I might not be able to enjoy my vacation.

　　我永遠無法理解為什麼有人可以將打包行李這件事留到最後做。我弟弟就會這樣做，而且經常會在辦好登機手續後才發現自己有東西忘了。我則相反，如果我要出國，至少會提前幾個星期開始打包。有時候，我會在出發的前一晚重新打包，通常都會再增加一些要放到行李內的東西，我寧願小心點也不想之後後悔。我弟弟認為我在行李打包上花太多心思，但我喜歡做事有條理的感覺，否則，我也許無法好好享受假期。

Unit 3 住宿相關 Accommodations

📖 日常生活　🎤 娛樂活動　✏️ 意見交流　🐟 特殊場合

◎ MP3 28-01

下面將播放五組短對話，請仔細聆聽，再依對話內容答題。

Question 1

When can the man check in?

(A) At 2 o'clock
(B) In two hours
(C) Between now and 2 o'clock
(D) Anytime he wants

Question 2

What does the man ask the woman to do?

(A) Pay for two nights by cash
(B) Withdraw cash from an ATM
(C) Pay for her extra night of stay by cash
(D) Pay for one night by credit card

Question 3

What does the man ask the woman to do with her laundry?

(A) Put it in the designated bag
(B) Leave her dirty clothes as they are
(C) Leave her dirty clothes in the wardrobe
(D) Use the self-service washing machines

Question 4

How much is it to use the computer and Wi-Fi at the hotel?

(A) It's all free.
(B) $200 for Wi-Fi
(C) $200 for the computer and Wi-Fi for one day
(D) Nothing for Wi-Fi, and $200 per hour for the computer

Question 5

How much is the woman's total bill?

(A) $5,460
(B) $5,260
(C) $5,200
(D) $5,140

答案與解析 ～answer

Answer 1 ◀》(B)
男性何時可以辦理入住的手續？

(A) 兩點的時候

(B) 兩個小時後

(C) 現在到兩點間

(D) 什麼時候都可以

解析
男性想辦理入住，櫃檯人員說「兩個小時後才接受辦理入住」(not available for another two hours)，但我們並不知道是幾點。這裡的available意指「可得的」，正確答案為(B)。

Answer 2 ◀》(C)
男性要求女性怎麼做呢？

(A) 兩個晚上的費用付現

(B) 從自動提款機中提領現金

(C) 用現金支付她要延長住宿的天數

(D) 刷信用卡支付一個晚上的住宿費用

解析
女性想延長住宿天數一天，櫃檯人員提到如果要延長的話，只接受現金，表示女性需要用現金支付，正確答案為(C)。至於是否要去提款則非對話的重點。

Answer 3 ◀》(A)
男性要求女性怎樣處理她的髒衣物呢？

(A) 放進指定的袋子裡

(B) 就照原樣放著即可

(C) 將髒衣物放進衣櫥

(D) 使用自助式洗衣機

解析
女性詢問是否有自助式洗衣機，但住房服務員並沒有正面回答這個問題，所以可剔除(D)。男性只請她將要洗的衣服放進「衣櫥裡的洗衣袋」(the laundry bag in your wardrobe)，清潔人員就會去處理，正確答案為(A)。

Answer 4 ◀》(D)
在飯店使用電腦和無線網路要多少錢？

(A) 全都是免費使用

(B) 無線網路要花兩百元

(C) 使用兩者一整天要花兩百元

(D) 無線網路免費，電腦一小時兩百元。

解析
櫃檯人員解釋商務中心的收費方式，提到「使用無線網路免費」(complementary 補充的，在此表示無線網路可免費使用)，但使用電腦要以小時計費，正確答案為(D)。

Answer 5 ◀》(C)
女性帳單的總數為多少呢？

(A) 5,460元

(B) 5,260元

(C) 5,200元

(D) 5,140元

解析
解題的重點在對話中5,200元後出現的which includes，表示這個價格已經包含後面敘述的物品，因此不用另外計算果汁的費用，直接回答5,200元即可，正確答案為(C)。

261

中英文內容　　　　　⊙慢速MP3 28-02　　⊙正常速MP3 28-03

短對話 1 *Conversation*

George: Hello, I've made a reservation. I'd like to check in.

喬治：　你好，我預訂了房間，要辦理入住。

Receptionist: Checking in is **not available for another two hours**. But we can keep your luggage behind the counter.

櫃檯服務人員：兩個小時後才接受辦理入住，但我們可以先將您的行李寄放在櫃檯後面。

短對話 2 *Conversation*

Annie: Excuse me. I'd like to extend my stay for one more night.

安妮：　不好意思，我想延長停留時間，多待一個晚上。

Receptionist: No problem. But you paid for your room by card before. We only **accept cash for extension of stay**.

櫃檯服務人員：當然可以。但您之前已經用信用卡支付了住宿費用，如果要延長住宿天數，我們只接受現金。

短對話 3 *Conversation*

Anna: Do you have any self-service washing machines here?

安娜：　你們有自助式洗衣機嗎？

Staff: You can just **put them into the laundry bag in your wardrobe**. Our room service staff will deal with it.

服務員：您只需要將要髒衣服放進衣櫥裡面的洗衣袋即可，清潔人員會負責處理。

短對話 4 *Conversation*

Sam: Do you have a business center with computers and internet?

山姆：　你們有商務中心提供電腦和網路嗎？

Receptionist: Yes. It is **complementary to use the Wi-Fi**, but computers are charged by **an hourly rate at $200**.

櫃檯服務人員：有的，無線網路可免費使用，但電腦每小時計價200元。

短對話 5 *Conversation*

Joanne: This is my key. I'd like to check out.

瓊安：　這是我的鑰匙，我要退房。

Receptionist: Your bill is **$5,200, which includes** the $60 juice you had.

櫃檯服務人員：您的帳單為5,200元，金額包含您拿的60元果汁。

長對話聽力實戰

請仔細聆聽下面的長對話，再依對話內容選擇正確答案。

Question 1

What is the man asking the woman about?

(A) Her opinion on the lake-view room
(B) The type of room to stay in
(C) The breakfast she prefers
(D) The budget they have for the room

Question 2

How much does the lake-view room cost?

(A) $3,000
(B) $2,500
(C) $3,500
(D) $5,000

Question 3

What does the man say is special about the lake-view room?

(A) You can have breakfast in the restaurant beside the lake.
(B) You can have an all-you-can-eat breakfast.
(C) You can have breakfast on the balcony overlooking the lake.
(D) The breakfast would be complementary.

Question 4

Why the man is considering leaving their luggage in the storage room?

(A) The hotel will be responsible for their belongings.
(B) They want to have breakfast first.
(C) All luggage must be put in the storage room.
(D) They can't check in until 2 p.m.

Question 5

What does the hotel recommend the woman and man do?

(A) Carry their valuable items on them
(B) Lock their valuables in the storage room
(C) Check their valuables afterwards
(D) Take all the luggage with them

答案與解析 ～answer

Answer 1 ◀》(B)
男性詢問女性什麼問題呢？
- (A) 她對湖景房的看法
- (B) 想要住哪一種房間
- (C) 她喜歡的早餐
- (D) 他們住宿的預算

解析
對話一開始，男性就問應該「住湖景房還是山景房」(the lake-view room or mountain-view room)，選項(A)僅提到湖景房；選項(C)不符合對話中提到早餐的內容；選項(D)提到預算，但女性僅詢問了房價差距，正確答案為(B)。

Answer 2 ◀》(C)
湖景房的房價是多少？
- (A) 三千元
- (B) 兩千五百元
- (C) 三千五百元
- (D) 五千元

解析
男性提到「山景房3,000元，另外一種(即湖景房)則多500元」(for an extra $500)，extra在此指另外還要多的價格，因此湖景房的價格為3,000元加上500元，正確答案為(C)。

Answer 3 ◀》(C)
男性提到湖景房有什麼特別的呢？
- (A) 可以在湖邊的餐廳享用早餐。
- (B) 早餐可以吃到飽。
- (C) 可以在能俯瞰湖泊的陽台上吃早餐。
- (D) 會附免費的早餐。

解析
當女性問是否值得付額外的錢住湖景房時，男性提到他們可以在「能俯瞰湖泊的陽台上享用早餐」，正確答案為(C)。注意早餐本身並非對話重點，回答時必須注意「在湖景房用早餐」這一點。

Answer 4 ◀》(D)
男性為何在考慮將行李放在儲藏室呢？
- (A) 飯店會負責他們的財物。
- (B) 他們想先去吃早餐。
- (C) 所有的行李都必須放在儲藏室。
- (D) 他們下午兩點前都無法入住。

解析
男性提到下午兩點後才能辦理手續，但是行李可以寄放在儲藏室。助動詞can表示「可以這麼做，但不強制」，與(C)的意思不同，正確答案為(D)。

Answer 5 ◀》(A)
飯店建議男性和女性怎麼做呢？
- (A) 隨身攜帶貴重物品
- (B) 把貴重物品放在儲藏室
- (C) 之後確認貴重物品
- (D) 隨身攜帶所有的行李

解析
男性提到儲藏室會上鎖，但飯店人員建議他們「隨身攜帶貴重物品」(keep valuables on ourselves)，此處的valuable是指可數的貴重物品，正確答案為(A)。

中英文內容

⊙ 慢速MP3 28-05　　◎ 正常速MP3 28-06

Kyle:　Shall we stay in **the lake-view room or mountain-view room?**
凱爾：　我們應該住湖景房還是山景房？

Fiona:　What's the price difference?
費奧娜：價格差多少？

Kyle:　A mountain-view room is $3,000, and the other is **an extra $500**.
凱爾：　山景房三千元，另外一種則多五百元。

Fiona:　Do you think it's worth paying extra for the lake view?
費奧娜：額外多付錢住湖景房，你覺得值得嗎？

Kyle:　I think it's worth it. We can **enjoy our breakfast on the balcony overlooking the lake**.
凱爾：　我認為值得，我們可以在能俯瞰湖泊的陽台上享受早餐。

Fiona:　Is breakfast included in the rate?
費奧娜：費用有含早餐嗎？

Kyle:　Yes. It's included **regardless of the type of room**.
凱爾：　有，無論哪種房型都有附早餐。

Fiona:　Let's go for it and check in then.
費奧娜：那就決定了，我們辦理入住吧。

Kyle:　We **can't check in until 2 p.m.**, but we can leave our luggage in the storage room.
凱爾：　下午兩點才能辦理入住，我們可以把行李寄放於儲藏室。

Fiona:　Will they be responsible for the safety of our belongings?
費奧娜：他們會負責我們的財物安全嗎？

Kyle:　They say the storage room is kept locked. However, we are recommended to **keep valuables on ourselves**.
凱爾：　他們說儲藏室會上鎖，但建議我們隨身攜帶貴重物品。

短文聽力實戰

⊚ MP3 28-07(短文1)　⊚ MP3 28-08(短文2)

請仔細聆聽下面兩段短文，並分別回答Q1~Q2&Q3~Q5兩大題。

Question ❶

What are people's expectations of hotels often like?

    (A) Not very high
    (B) Higher than average
    (C) Average
    (D) Very high

Question ❷

Why are the facilities and decoration also important?

    (A) So that the guests will feel the price is worth it.
    (B) So that the hotel will get a higher rating.
    (C) So that the rooms and food will cost more.
    (D) So that the service will become better.

Question ❸

When did the woman and her boyfriend go on holiday to Boracay?

    (A) Two years ago
    (B) Last year
    (C) This year
    (D) She doesn't say.

Question ❹

How does the woman describe all the services and facilities there?

    (A) As they expected
    (B) Impossible to use
    (C) Perfect
    (D) Not what they expected

Question ❺

What was the extra cost the woman and her boyfriend had to pay?

    (A) Tips for the staff
    (B) Evening meals
    (C) Massages
    (D) Souvenirs

答案與解析 ~answer

Answer 1 (D)
人們對飯店的期望通常如何？

(A) 不是很高
(B) 比普通的期望高
(C) 普通高
(D) 非常高

> **解析**
> 本文的答案出現在男性一開始提到人們對飯店的期望通常會「非常高」(extremely high)。關鍵字為extremely，指「非常；極端」，所以答題時要選盡可能高的期望值，正確答案為(D)。

Answer 2 (A)
飯店的設施和裝修為什麼也很重要呢？

(A) 因為客人會覺得物有所值。
(B) 因為飯店的評價等級會變高。
(C) 因為房間和食物的收費會變高。
(D) 因為服務會變得更好。

> **解析**
> 男性在提到飯店品質時，首先說到服務(service)，接著又補充「設施和裝修也必須有一定的水準」(be of certain standards)，才能讓客人「有值回票價的感覺」，正確答案為(A)。

Answer 3 (B)
女性與她男友是何時到長灘島渡假的呢？

(A) 兩年前
(B) 去年
(C) 今年
(D) 她沒有說

> **解析**
> 解題關鍵在女性提到的Last year, after two years of saving,...。逗號中間的「存了兩年的錢」只是補充說明，刪除也不影響整句話的重點，所以要看去長灘島的時間，就在句首的「去年」(Last year)，正確答案為(B)。

Answer 4 (C)
女性如何形容當地的服務與設施？

(A) 和他們預期的一樣
(B) 完全無法使用
(C) 無可挑剔的完美
(D) 沒有達到他們的預期

> **解析**
> 女性提到從設施到服務都「無可挑剔」，關鍵字為impeccable(無缺點的)。注意女性並沒有提到自己的預期，所以不能選(A)(D)；而整篇聽下來可確定女性滿意這次的旅程，因此要選給予肯定的(C)。

Answer 5 (A)
女性與她男友必須支付的額外花費是什麼？

(A) 給服務人員的小費
(B) 晚餐費用
(C) 按摩的費用
(D) 買紀念品的費用

> **解析**
> 提到價格，就必須注意女性提到所有的服務和伙食都包括在他們付的價格裡面(were all included)，他們唯一需要額外支付的就只有「給服務人員的小費」(tip for the staff)，關鍵字為tip(小費)，正確答案為(A)。

 中英文內容

⊙慢速MP3 28-09　　◉正常速MP3 28-10

The hotel industry is very competitive. People's expectations towards hotels are often **extremely high** because many of them go for their vacation and expect everything to be perfect. The success of a hotel mainly lies in its service. Of course, the facilities and decoration must also be of certain standards to make guests feel they are not just paying for a roof over their heads and have **gotten their money's worth**. Most hotels have regular accreditation and assessment to obtain ratings that people can use as criteria while choosing their accommodation. Keeping customers satisfied and remaining competitive in the industry is an endless job.

飯店產業的競爭很激烈。人們對飯店的期望通常會非常高，因為很多人是去渡假，所以期望一切都完美無缺。一家飯店的成功主要取決於飯店服務，當然，設施和裝修也必須有一定的水準，才不會讓客人覺得他們付的錢只得到了可暫時棲身的遮蔽處，而能有值回票價的感覺。多數飯店會有定期的審核和評估，以得到評價等級，提供人們選擇住所時參考。為了讓客戶滿意，並在產業中維持競爭力，飯店需要不斷地努力奮鬥。

⊙慢速MP3 28-11　　◉正常速MP3 28-12

My boyfriend and I had heard about so many great trips to Boracay. **Last year**, after two years of saving, we finally went on a holiday to Boracay. We stayed in a private villa by the beach. Everything there, from facilities to service, was **impeccable**. The services and food were all included in the price we paid for the package, so the only extra money we had to spend was on **tips for the staff**. We enjoyed massages and fresh seafood every day. It really was a holiday in paradise. I'd love to go back again someday.

我男友和我聽說過很多有關長灘島的美好旅行。在存了兩年的錢之後，我們去年終於前往長灘島渡假。我們住在海灘邊的獨棟別墅，那裡的一切(從設施到服務)都無可挑剔。所有的服務和伙食都包括在我們付的價格裡面，唯一需要額外支付的就只有給服務人員的小費。我們每天都享受按摩和新鮮的海鮮，那真像在天堂渡假，真希望哪一天有機會再去那裡。

異國風情 Exotic Cultures

日常生活　　娛樂活動　　意見交流　　特殊場合

短對話聽力實戰

◎ MP3 29-01

下面將播放五組短對話，請仔細聆聽，再依對話內容答題。

Question ❶ ·································· ❶❷❸❹❺

What might the London Underground be for the first time?

(A) The Underground can be scary.

(B) The Underground can be expensive.

(C) The routes can be slightly complex.

(D) It is particularly convenient.

Question ❷ ·································· ❶❷❸❹❺

Why doesn't the woman like the man's idea?

(A) She doesn't want to do snowboarding on her honeymoon.

(B) She finds it too cold in Hokkaido.

(C) She doesn't like snowboarding.

(D) She has a better idea for their honeymoon.

Question ❸ ·································· ❶❷❸❹❺

Why is the man studying the cultures of Southeast Asia?

(A) A local tour guide asked him to do so.

(B) He finds the cultures there offending.

(C) He doesn't want to miss certain places to visit.

(D) He doesn't want to unintentionally upset local people.

Question ❹ ·································· ❶❷❸❹❺

What is the man's expectation of the tour guide?

(A) To be able to take them to better markets

(B) To know the local history well

(C) To take them to go shopping more

(D) To be able to tell them where to find bargains

Question ❺ ·································· ❶❷❸❹❺

What is the girl's request of the tour guide?

(A) Don't take her to the popular tourist sites

(B) Take her to the local markets

(C) Take her to places he doesn't know

(D) Show her some unique places

答案與解析 ～answer

Answer 1 ◀)) (C)

對初次造訪的人來說，倫敦地鐵可能怎麼樣？

(A) 地鐵可能讓人感到可怕。

(B) 地鐵可能太貴了。

(C) 地鐵路線可能有點複雜。

(D) 地鐵特別方便。

> **解析**
> 男性提到搭倫敦的地鐵非常方便，但題目問的是「對初次造訪的人來說」(for the first time)，所以重點必須放在後面提到的「地鐵線可能會有點複雜」，關鍵字為complicated(複雜的)，正確答案為(C)。

Answer 2 ◀)) (A)

女性為什麼不喜歡男性的想法？

(A) 她不想在渡蜜月的時候玩滑雪板。

(B) 她覺得去北海道太冷了。

(C) 她不喜歡玩滑雪板。

(D) 針對蜜月之旅，她有更好的主意。

> **解析**
> 女性回答時說她「不認為渡蜜月時玩極限運動是個好主意」，這不代表她不想去北海道或是討厭玩滑雪板，所以不能選(B)或(C)，正確答案為(A)。

Answer 3 ◀)) (D)

男性為什麼在研究東南亞的文化呢？

(A) 一位當地導遊要求他這麼做。

(B) 他發現東南亞的文化會引起問題。

(C) 他不想錯過某些能參觀的地方。

(D) 他不想在無意中冒犯當地人。

> **解析**
> 男性提到自己閱讀書籍的原因是為了防範他們在東南亞旅遊時「不小心做出冒犯人的事」，關鍵字為accidentally(不小心)和offend(冒犯)，正確答案為(D)。

Answer 4 ◀)) (B)

男性對導遊的期待是什麼？

(A) 能帶他們去更好的市場

(B) 通曉當地歷史

(C) 多帶他去購物

(D) 能告訴他們哪裡買得到便宜好貨

> **解析**
> 男性的不滿來自於他「期待導遊會了解當地歷史」，have good knowledge of 表示「對…的知識相當充足」，但導遊卻回答不了他的任何問題，正確答案為(B)。

Answer 5 ◀)) (D)

女孩對導遊要求了什麼事情呢？

(A) 不要帶她去參觀熱門景點

(B) 帶她到當地的市場

(C) 帶她到導遊都不知道的地方

(D) 帶她參觀一些特別的地方

> **解析**
> 女孩的要求是請導遊「帶他們去大部分遊客不知道的好地方」(most tourists don't know)，正確答案為(D)。注意In addition to為「除了…之外」的意思，所以女孩並沒有排斥去著名景點，選項(A)不適合。

短對話 ❶ Conversation

Lauren: What's the Underground in London like?

蘿倫：　倫敦的地鐵怎麼樣？

Steve: It's super convenient, but there are **so many different lines**. It's **a bit complicated** for the first time.

史蒂夫：他們的地鐵超方便，但地鐵線分很多條，第一次搭會有點複雜。

短對話 ❷ Conversation

Andy:　How about we go snowboarding in Hokkaido for our honeymoon?

安迪：　我們渡蜜月的時候去北海道玩滑雪板如何？

Ellie:　I'm not sure **doing an extreme sport** is a good idea for honeymoon.

艾莉：　我不認為渡蜜月時玩極限運動是個好主意。

短對話 ❸ Conversation

Jenny:　What's that big book on the "Cultures of Southeast Asia" for?

珍妮：　你拿那本超厚的《東南亞文化》是有什麼打算嗎？

Steve: In case we **accidentally offend people there** when we go traveling.

史帝夫：以防我們去旅行的時候不小心冒犯了當地人啊。

短對話 ❹ Conversation

Leanne:Don't you like this trip? You look upset.

黎安：　你不喜歡這趟旅行嗎？你看起來很不高興耶。

Philip:　I was expecting the guide to have **good knowledge of the local history**, but he can't answer any of my questions.

菲利浦：我期待導遊會很了解當地的歷史，但他回答不了我的任何問題。

短對話 ❺ Conversation

Bill:　Hi, I am your guide for today. I'm Bill.

比爾：　嗨，我是你們今天的導遊，我叫比爾。

Lilly:　Hi, Bill. In addition to the famous sites, can you take us to **some great places most tourists don't know**?

莉莉：　嗨，比爾，除了著名景點，你能帶我們去大部分遊客不知道的好地方嗎？

長對話聽力實戰

◎MP3 29-04

請仔細聆聽下面的長對話，再依對話內容選擇正確答案。

Question 1

Why is it difficult for the girl to plan a family trip?

(A) They like different types of shops.
(B) They enjoy and pursue different activities.
(C) Their preferences for food are different.
(D) They want to join different tour groups.

Question 2

What do the girl's parents enjoy?

(A) Visiting parks and enjoying nature
(B) Doing shopping
(C) Visiting museums
(D) Going to galleries

Question 3

What is the girl's first impression of a busy capital like London?

(A) It's good for a family like hers.
(B) It's good for people with little kids.
(C) It's good for people who like shopping, like her sister.
(D) It's good for her sister, who enjoys a busy lifestyle.

Question 4

What does the girl say she can do when her sister goes shopping?

(A) She can wait for her sister in the mall.
(B) She can go on a picnic with her parents.
(C) She can go visit the museums and galleries.
(D) She can shop with her sister.

Question 5

What can the girl and her family do in Hyde Park?

(A) Go on a walking tour, go cycling, and have a picnic
(B) Take a bus tour, go cycling, and have a picnic
(C) Go riding and have a picnic
(D) Go swimming and cycling and have a picnic

答案與解析 ~answer

Answer 1 ◀)) (B)

對女孩來說，規劃家族旅遊為什麼很困難？

(A) 他們喜歡的商店類型都不同。

(B) 他們喜歡和追求的活動各有不同。

(C) 他們對食物的喜好不同。

(D) 他們想加入的旅行團不同。

> **解析**
> 女孩一開始就提到她家人的「需求都不一樣」(look for different things)，這裡的束西指的是喜歡的活動，因為女孩接下來解釋了大家喜歡活動類型，look for指「追求」，正確答案為(B)。

Answer 2 ◀)) (A)

女孩的父母喜歡做什麼呢？

(A) 造訪公園，享受大自然

(B) 逛街血拚

(C) 參觀博物館

(D) 去藝廊

> **解析**
> 女孩解釋大家喜歡做的活動類型時，提到她的父母喜歡「公園和大自然」(parks and nature)，正確答案為(A)。注意選項(B)為女孩妹妹喜歡的活動，(C)(D)則是男性稍後提到的活動。

Answer 3 ◀)) (C)

對倫敦這樣的繁忙首都，女孩的第一印象為何？

(A) 對她家人是個好選擇。

(B) 對有小孩的人來說是好選擇。

(C) 像她妹妹那樣愛逛街的人會喜歡。

(D) 喜歡忙碌生活的妹妹會喜歡。

> **解析**
> 當男性提議去倫敦時，女孩對倫敦的印象是繁忙的首都，並說「對她妹妹來說會很棒」(great for my sister)，正確答案為(C)。

Answer 4 ◀)) (C)

女孩的妹妹去逛街時，她能做什麼？

(A) 她可以在購物中心等妹妹。

(B) 她可以和父母去野餐。

(C) 她可以去參觀博物館和畫廊。

(D) 她可以和妹妹一起去逛街。

> **解析**
> 當男性解釋倫敦不只能逛街，還有許多博物館和畫廊可參觀時，女孩開心地說自己「不必在妹妹購物時乾等」(don't have to wait for my sister)，表示去博物館能讓她打發時間，正確答案為(C)。

Answer 5 ◀)) (A)

女孩與家人在海德公園裡可以做什麼？

(A) 參加步行導覽、騎腳踏車和野餐

(B) 參加公車遊覽、騎腳踏車和野餐

(C) 騎腳踏車和野餐

(D) 游泳、騎腳踏車和野餐

> **解析**
> 當選項內都包含騎腳踏車(cycling)和野餐(picnic)這兩個單字時，可以只把聽的重點放在第三項，以集中注意力。男性提到海德公園時，說可以「參加步行導覽、騎自行車與野餐」，關鍵在join walking tours，正確答案為(A)。

⊙慢速MP3 29-05　　◎正常速MP3 29-06

Hannah: It's hard to plan a holiday for my family. We all **look for different things**.
漢娜：　　要規劃家族旅遊真難，我家人的需求都不同。

Hardy:　What do you mean by that?
哈帝：　什麼意思？

Hannah: Well, I'm more of a culture person; my sister **loves fashion and shopping**, and my parents enjoy **parks and nature**.
漢娜：　　嗯，我喜歡有文化的地方；我妹妹則熱愛時尚和購物；而我父母喜歡公園和大自然。

Hardy:　How about London?
哈帝：　倫敦怎麼樣？

Hannah: A busy capital? It'll be **great for my sister** but not for the rest of us.
漢娜：　　繁忙的首都嗎？對我妹妹來說會很棒，但不適合我們其他人。

Hardy:　There is a lot more to London than fashion. There are various **museums and galleries** you can visit.
哈帝：　倫敦除了時尚還有很多東西可看，有各式各樣的博物館和畫廊可以參觀。

Hannah: Fantastic! Then I **don't have to wait for my sister in the malls** while she's shopping.
漢娜：　　好極了！這樣我就不必在我妹妹購物時在購物中心乾等她了。

Hardy:　There're also many large parks and squares, such as Hyde Park. You can join **walking tours, go cycling, and have a picnic** in the park.
哈帝：　那裡也有許多大型的公園和廣場，例如海德公園。你在公園可以參加步行導覽、騎自行車，也可以野餐。

Hannah: I love the idea of a picnic. My parents will definitely enjoy it, too.
漢娜：　　我喜歡野餐這個主意，我父母肯定也會喜歡的。

Hardy:　Looks like I've found a solution for you.
哈帝：　看來我幫你的找到解決方案了呢。

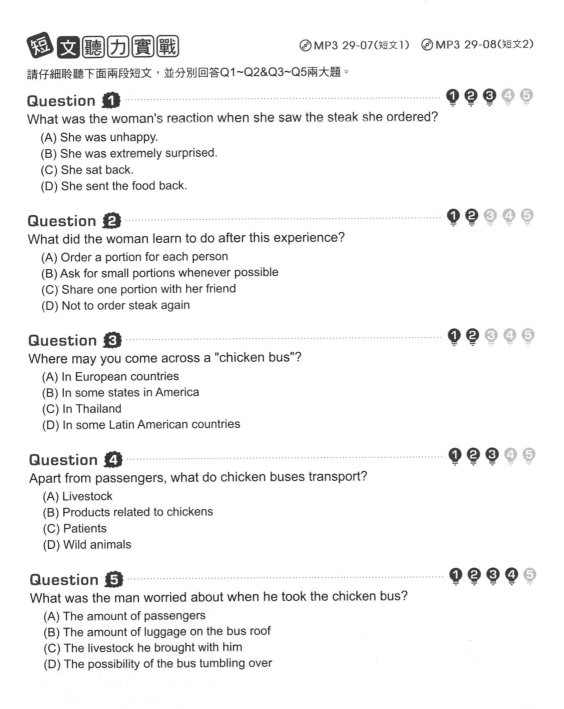

短文聽力實戰

MP3 29-07（短文1）　　MP3 29-08（短文2）

請仔細聆聽下面兩段短文，並分別回答Q1~Q2&Q3~Q5兩大題。

Question 1

What was the woman's reaction when she saw the steak she ordered?

(A) She was unhappy.

(B) She was extremely surprised.

(C) She sat back.

(D) She sent the food back.

Question 2

What did the woman learn to do after this experience?

(A) Order a portion for each person

(B) Ask for small portions whenever possible

(C) Share one portion with her friend

(D) Not to order steak again

Question 3

Where may you come across a "chicken bus"?

(A) In European countries

(B) In some states in America

(C) In Thailand

(D) In some Latin American countries

Question 4

Apart from passengers, what do chicken buses transport?

(A) Livestock

(B) Products related to chickens

(C) Patients

(D) Wild animals

Question 5

What was the man worried about when he took the chicken bus?

(A) The amount of passengers

(B) The amount of luggage on the bus roof

(C) The livestock he brought with him

(D) The possibility of the bus tumbling over

答案與解析 ～answer

Answer 1 ◀》(B)
看到自己點的牛排時，女性的反應為何？

(A) 她不高興。
(B) 她大吃一驚。
(C) 她放鬆地坐。
(D) 她將餐點退回廚房。

解析

解題關鍵在女性看到牛排後的內容，她提到my jaw dropped(下巴都掉下來了)，表示她非常吃驚，正確答案為(B)。這裡還有一個關鍵片語be taken aback，指「吃驚；出乎意料」。

Answer 2 ◀》(C)
這次經驗之後，女性學到要怎麼做？

(A) 每人各點一份餐點
(B) 可能的話點小份一點
(C) 和朋友合點一份
(D) 不要再點牛排

解析

女性從牛排館的經驗學到教訓，接下來的行程她們都「盡量合點，共享一份餐點」(order and share one portion)，正確答案為(C)。

Answer 3 ◀》(D)
你可能在哪裡見到「野雞公車」呢？

(A) 在歐洲國家
(B) 在美國的幾個州
(C) 在泰國
(D) 在拉丁美洲的部分國家

解析

男性提到旅行的交通工具並不侷限於我們熟知的幾個，舉例時提到在許多「拉丁美洲國家」(Latin American countries)會看到「野雞公車」，所以本題答案並非單一國家，而是(D)。

Answer 4 ◀》(A)
除了乘客之外，野雞公車還運送什麼？

(A) 家畜
(B) 與雞有關的製品
(C) 病人
(D) 野生動物

解析

男性提到野雞公車時，說這種公車不僅用來載客，也運送「家畜」(livestock)，正確答案為(A)。注意選項(B)指的是與雞有關的製品，但野雞公車載的是動物本身。

Answer 5 ◀》(D)
男性搭乘野雞公車的時候在擔心什麼？

(A) 乘客的數量
(B) 公車車頂上的行李數量
(C) 他帶著的家畜
(D) 公車翻過去的可能性

解析

男性在最後提到自己很驚訝他們有辦法把「那麼多的行李和牲畜塞到公車車頂上」，但是他擔心(worry)的並非此項事實，而是因為車頂太重而翻車的可能性。關鍵片語tumble over為「翻過去」之意，正確答案為(D)。

⊙慢速MP3 29-09　◎正常速MP3 29-10

I must have put on a lot of weight during my two-week stay in America. I had heard that things tend to be super-sized there, but I was still **taken aback** by the food portion sizes when I saw them with my own eyes. My friend and I went to a steak house on our first night. **My jaw dropped** when the food came because they were literally the biggest steaks I had ever seen. We ordered different plates, but one portion was actually enough for us. Because of this experience, we tried to **order and share one portion** for the rest of our trip.

我在美國逗留的兩個星期的內一定胖了很多。我有聽說那邊東西的尺寸往往很大，但當我親眼見識到食物份量後，還是大吃了一驚。我和朋友在那裡的第一個晚上去了一家牛排館。食物送來的時候，我驚訝得下巴都要掉下來了，因為那是我看過最大的牛排。我們兩人各點了一份，但其實一份的份量就足夠我們吃了。那天晚上之後的行程裡，我們都盡量合點一份餐點共享。

⊙慢速MP3 29-11　◎正常速MP3 29-12

Cars, trains and planes aren't the only way to get around a country. There are some really unique modes of transportation around the world. For instance, in many **Latin American countries**, you will come across "chicken buses". These vehicles are used not only for passengers but also for **livestock**. And that's how they got the name. There're often two men in the operation of the bus. One is the driver, and the other helps passengers with their luggage. When I got on one in Panama, I was surprised by the amount of luggage and livestock they managed to fit on the roof of the bus. At one point, I was rather worried **the bus would tumble over** because of the heavy weight on the roof.

汽車、火車和飛機並不是在一個國家內旅行的唯一方式。世界上有一些非常獨特的交通工具。舉例來說，在許多拉丁美洲國家，你會看到「野雞公車」。這種公車不僅用來載客，同時也用來運送家畜，因而得名。野雞公車通常由兩人負責運作，一名是司機，另一名則幫忙乘客放行李。我在巴拿馬搭野雞公車時感到很驚訝，因為他們竟然能把那麼多的行李和牲畜塞到車頂上，因為車頂的重量，我有一度還真擔心車子會翻過去呢。

Unit 5 文化交流 The Cultures
日常生活　娛樂活動　意見交流　特殊場合

短 對 話 聽 力 實 戰

◎ MP3 30-01

下面將播放五組短對話，請仔細聆聽，再依對話內容答題。

Question 1 .... ❶❷❸❹❺

What's the woman's suggestion on what the man should do with his client?

　(A) Have some authentic American food and drinks
　(B) Play golf for a day and drink in a bar in the evening
　(C) Have an aboriginal meal in a city restaurant
　(D) Take a day trip to an aboriginal tribe

Question 2 ....

Why does the man still prefer to live in the city?

　(A) He'll appreciate the countryside more when he visits there.
　(B) He doesn't appreciate the quietness of the countryside.
　(C) He doesn't think it's interesting to live there.
　(D) He enjoys the busy and stressful city life.

Question 3 ....

Why didn't the speakers find Greece as enjoyable as they imagined?

　(A) They couldn't visit all the shops in the town.
　(B) They didn't enjoy the stress-free lifestyle.
　(C) They got bored because the shops shut too early.
　(D) They got bored because the selection of shops was poor.

Question 4 ....

How does the girl find the customs of the Ghost Festival?

　(A) Slightly boring
　(B) Very strange
　(C) Very interesting
　(D) She doesn't understand them.

Question 5 ....

Why is the boy going to Tainan?

　(A) To take his mid-term in the morning
　(B) To worship Confucius and to wish for good luck for his exam
　(C) To prepare for his mid-term in Tainan
　(D) To worship Confucius with his family

答案與解析 ~answer

Answer 1 ◀》(D)

針對男性的客戶，女性提出什麼建議？

(A) 品嚐道地美國風味的食物與飲料

(B) 找一天打高爾夫球，晚上再去酒吧

(C) 在城市中的餐廳品嚐原住民餐點

(D) 參加原住民部落一日遊

> **解析**
> 女性一開始就建議男性帶客戶參加「原住民部落一日遊」，說這樣的行程比較特別。重點字為aboriginal tribe(原住民的部落)，正確答案為(D)。

Answer 2 ◀》(A)

男性為何還是寧願住在大城市呢？

(A) 他去鄉下玩時才能更欣賞那裡的氣氛。

(B) 他不喜歡鄉下獨特的寧靜。

(C) 他不覺得住在鄉下會有趣。

(D) 他比較喜歡忙碌又具壓力的城市生活。

> **解析**
> 聽到女性對鄉下的讚美，男性也跟著附和，所以不宜選對鄉下帶有負面評論的(B)(C)。接著男性又提到他寧願住在城市，這樣當他來到鄉下時才會「更加珍惜欣賞這裡的安寧」，正確答案為(A)。

Answer 3 ◀》(C)

希臘之旅為何沒有說話者原本想像的好玩呢？

(A) 他們無法逛完鎮上的所有店家。

(B) 他們不喜歡毫無壓力的生活型態。

(C) 店家太早關店，所以很無聊。

(D) 店家的選擇不多，所以很無聊。

> **解析**
> 男性一開始就提到對希臘之旅的失望，接著女性提到的原因才是解題關鍵。她說「大多數的店家中午過後就關門，沒什麼事好做」，由此可知很早關門這件事讓他們感到無聊，正確答案為(C)。

Answer 4 ◀》(C)

女孩覺得中元節的習俗如何？

(A) 有點無趣

(B) 非常奇怪

(C) 很有趣

(D) 她無法理解。

> **解析**
> 對話中的女孩答應幫男孩燒紙錢的同時，說她覺得這「好有趣」(fascinating)，中國習俗待鬼幾乎與待人一樣，正確答案為(C)。

Answer 5 ◀》(B)

男孩為什麼要前往臺南？

(A) 為了早上去考期中考

(B) 為了去孔廟祈求考試順利

(C) 為了在臺南準備期中考

(D) 為了和家人一起去孔廟祭拜

> **解析**
> 從女孩一開始的話可得知男孩的期中考即將來臨，接下來男孩提到That's why...，表示期中考與回臺南有聯繫。後面接著解釋他要去孔廟「拜孔夫子求好運」。worship為「祭拜」之意，正確答案為(B)。

⊙慢速MP3 30-02   ⊙正常速MP3 30-03

短對話 ❶ Conversation

Sheila: How about taking your client to **an aboriginal tribe for a day trip**? It would be a special experience for him.

希拉： 要不要帶你客戶參加原住民部落一日遊？那會很特別。

Ted: Nice. If he doesn't like it, I can always take him to a bar in the evening.

泰德： 不錯耶。如果他不喜歡，我晚上還是可以帶他去酒吧。

短對話 ❷ Conversation

Elaine: The quietness of the countryside is so nice.

伊蓮： 鄉下的寧靜真是美好。

Mike: It is, but I'd rather live in the city so I can **appreciate the tranquility more**.

麥克： 的確，但我還是寧願住在城市裡，這樣我才會更珍惜、欣賞這裡的安寧。

短對話 ❸ Conversation

Bob: Our trip to Greece wasn't as enjoyable as I'd imagined.

鮑伯： 我們的希臘之旅沒有想像中的好玩。

Kate: Yeah, most of **the stores are shut after noon**. There **wasn't much to do**.

凱特： 是啊，大部分商店中午過後就關門，根本沒什麼事好做。

短對話 ❹ Conversation

David: Can you help me burn the paper money for the Ghost Festival?

大衛： 可以請你幫我燒這些中元節用的紙錢嗎？

Lisa: Sure. I find it **fascinating** how you treat the ghosts almost like people.

麗莎： 當然。這真有趣，你們待鬼幾乎與待人一樣。

短對話 ❺ Conversation

Lily: Why are you going to Tainan? Isn't your mid-term next week?

莉莉： 你為什麼要去臺南？下週不就期中考了嗎？

Tom: That's why I'm going to the Confucius Temple to **worship for good luck**.

湯姆： 正因為如此，所以我才要去孔廟拜拜求好運啊。

長 對 話 聽 力 實 戰

🎧 MP3 30-04

請仔細聆聽下面的長對話，再依對話內容選擇正確答案。

Question ❶

⚡⚡⚡⚡⚡

Which wedding will come first?

(A) The wedding in England
(B) They didn't mention it.
(C) The wedding in Taiwan
(D) The wedding held overseas

Question ❷

⚡⚡⚡⚡⚡

Why is the couple holding weddings in Taiwan and England?

(A) Their friends don't want to attend a wedding overseas.
(B) Some of their guest can't afford the cost of flying overseas.
(C) It is a tradition for foreigners to hold two weddings.
(D) Their parents want them to have two weddings.

Question ❸

⚡⚡⚡⚡⚡

What isn't mentioned as being part of the English tradition?

(A) Something blue
(B) Brand-new stuff
(C) Something borrowed from others
(D) Money to put in the woman's shoe

Question ❹

⚡⚡⚡⚡⚡

Why is it important to follow certain wedding traditions in Taiwan?

(A) Because the woman insists on doing so.
(B) Otherwise, the woman's parents will be angry.
(C) Because families have equal significance in a wedding.
(D) Otherwise, there could be bad luck.

Question ❺

⚡⚡⚡⚡⚡

What will the man help the woman prepare?

(A) The presents for their guest on wedding day
(B) The presents for the man's parents
(C) The gifts for the senior members in the woman's family
(D) The gifts for friends attending their wedding

答案與解析 ～answer

Answer 1 (C)

哪一場婚禮會先舉辦呢？

- (A) 英國的那場婚禮
- (B) 他們沒有討論到這件事。
- (C) 在臺灣的那場婚禮
- (D) 在海外舉辦的婚禮

解析

本題的答案在一開始，女性提到她不敢相信他們要在臺灣辦一場婚禮，接著再到英國辦一場。關鍵字為then(然後；接著)，表示順序，正確答案為(C)。

Answer 2 (B)

對話中的新人為什麼要在臺灣與英國各辦一場婚禮？

- (A) 他們的朋友不想到海外參加婚禮。
- (B) 有些客人負擔不了飛往國外的花費。
- (C) 辦兩場婚禮對外國人來說是習俗。
- (D) 父母希望他們辦兩場婚禮。

解析

女性一開始就提到他們會在不同的國家舉辦婚禮，此時男性回應「既然不是每個人都能負擔出國的費用」，在兩國各辦一場婚禮可能是最好的辦法。關鍵在 can afford 這個用法，正確答案為(B)。

Answer 3 (D)

講到英國習俗時，「沒有」被提到的是什麼？

- (A) 藍色的東西
- (B) 全新的物品
- (C) 向他人借的東西
- (D) 放在女性鞋裡的錢

解析

這題考的是男性提到英國習俗時所舉的例子，從對話中可以聽出都是敘述具備「某項特質」的物品，並沒有指定明確的東西，所以(D)會是本題的答案。

Answer 4 (C)

為什麼遵循部分臺灣的婚禮傳統也很重要？

- (A) 因為女性很堅持。
- (B) 不然女性的父母會生氣。
- (C) 因為家族在婚禮中的角色也很重要。
- (D) 不然可能會有厄運。

解析

在講完英國習俗的例子之後，女性提到「婚禮不只關於新人，也涉及家族」，所以臺灣習俗也很重要，重點在 as much as 的句型(涉及兩物的比較)，可知前後兩者同等重要，正確答案為(C)。

Answer 5 (C)

男性會幫忙女性準備什麼？

- (A) 婚禮當天送給賓客的禮物
- (B) 給男方家長的禮物
- (C) 給女方家族長輩的禮物
- (D) 給出席婚禮朋友的禮物

解析

女性最後提到他們還必須準備「給長輩的禮物」，關鍵字在 senior members(長輩)，正確答案為(C)。注意選項(B)的父母雖然也是長輩，但對話中女性有特別強調 my family，所以特別指女方。

中英文內容

⊙慢速MP3 30-05　　◎正常速MP3 30-06

Ellie: I can't believe we are holding **a wedding in Taiwan**, and **then** a wedding in England.

艾莉：　不敢相信我們要分別在臺灣和英國各辦一次婚禮。

Andrew: Since not everyone **can afford to fly abroad**, that would be the best solution.

安德魯：　既然不是所有人都能負擔出國的費用，這是最好的方法。

Ellie: We need to consider both Taiwanese and English wedding traditions.

艾莉：　我們得同時考慮到臺灣和英國的婚禮傳統。

Andrew: Don't forget the English tradition of **"something old, something new, something borrowed and something blue"**.

安德魯：　別忘了英國習俗要有「舊的東西、新的東西、借來的東西和藍色的東西」。

Ellie: I'm handing that task over to my bridesmaids.

艾莉：　我打算把這個交給伴娘處理。

Andrew: Yeah. Letting others help you is a good idea.

安德魯：　讓其他人幫忙的確是個好主意。

Ellie: And since the wedding **is about the families as much as about the couple**, certain Taiwanese traditions are important, too.

艾莉：　因為婚禮不只關於新人，也涉及家族，所以部分臺灣習俗也很重要。

Andrew: So what else do we need to prepare?

安德魯：　所以我們還需要準備什麼呢？

Ellie: We need **the gifts for the senior members of my family**.

艾莉：　我們還需要準備給我家這邊長輩的禮物。

Andrew: I can help with that. I'll go and pick out the presents tomorrow.

安德魯：　這我可以幫忙，我明天就去選禮物。

短文聽力實戰

MP3 30-07(短文1)　　MP3 30-08(短文2)

請仔細聆聽下面兩段短文，並分別回答Q1~Q2&Q3~Q5兩大題。

Question 1

Who did the man go to Disney World with?

(A) His kids

(B) His brother and some friends

(C) His brother and the brother's kids

(D) His younger brothers

Question 2

What was the unpleasant experience the man had at Disney World?

(A) His brother's kid was sick after a ride.

(B) He went to the toilet and embarrassed himself.

(C) He didn't have enough to eat for lunch.

(D) A thrill ride made him sick.

Question 3

When did the woman become addicted to traveling?

(A) After her first backpacking experience in Asia

(B) Before she went to Asia

(C) After she was able to speak different languages

(D) When she had delicious cuisines in Asia

Question 4

What happened after the woman started working full-time?

(A) She can only visit certain places during her trips.

(B) She can't backpack anymore.

(C) She can't travel overseas anymore.

(D) Each of her trips cannot be for a long period of time.

Question 5

What is the woman's goal?

(A) Go on an around-the-world backpacking trip

(B) Visit all the countries in the world in her lifetime

(C) Visit all the countries in Asia in her lifetime

(D) Go back to Asia for another backpacking trip

答案與解析 ～answer

Answer 1 ◀)) (C)
男性和誰一起去迪士尼樂園呢？

(A) 他的孩子
(B) 他的哥哥和朋友
(C) 他的哥哥與其孩子
(D) 他的弟弟們

解析
男性提到自己去年夏天去了迪士尼樂園，加入了他哥哥的家族旅遊，所以本題重點必須圍繞在哥哥與哥哥的家人身上，最佳答案為(C)。

Answer 2 ◀)) (D)
男性在迪士尼樂園的不愉快回憶是什麼？

(A) 他哥哥的小孩在乘坐遊樂設施後感到不適。
(B) 他跑去廁所，並出了糗。
(C) 他中午沒有吃飽。
(D) 刺激的遊樂設施害他感到不適。

解析
男性提到唯一讓他感到不快的嘔吐事件。說他在乘坐了「刺激的遊樂設施」(a thrill ride)後，把午餐全吐了出來，差點就在大庭廣眾下出糗。關鍵片語為throw up(嘔吐)，正確答案為(D)。

Answer 3 ◀)) (A)
女性何時愛上旅行的呢？

(A) 在她初次到亞洲展開背包客之旅後
(B) 在她去亞洲之前
(C) 在她能說不同的語言之後
(D) 當她在亞洲品嚐到美食的時候

解析
女性一開始就提到「自從她初次在亞洲展開背包旅行後」，便愛上了旅行，重點單字為一開始的ever since，表示「從…之後」。後面雖然有提到會講不同語言的事，但那並非她愛上旅遊的契機，所以選(A)。

Answer 4 ◀)) (D)
女性有了全職的工作後，發生了什麼變化呢？

(A) 她旅遊時只能造訪特定的地點。
(B) 她不能再展開背包客的旅程了。
(C) 她無法再出國旅遊。
(D) 她每次旅行的時間不能安排得太久。

解析
女性提到自己「現在有全職的工作」，Although所帶出的子句與逗號後面的內容有反差，可以推知女性想表達她「依然會去旅遊」，可剔除(B)(C)。接著提到她無法「旅行太久」，正確答案為(D)。

Answer 5 ◀)) (B)
女性的目標是什麼？

(A) 展開環遊世界的背包客之旅
(B) 在她有生之年造訪全世界的國家
(C) 在她有生之前造訪亞洲所有國家
(D) 再度去亞洲展開背包客之旅

解析
女性最後提到自己的目標為「有生之年走訪世界各地」，關鍵在visit all the countries around the world。這並不表示要如選項(A)那樣，以背包客的方式環遊世界，正確答案為(B)。

中英文內容

短文 1

⊙慢速MP3 30-09　　◎正常速MP3 30-10

I discovered my inner child again when I visited Disney World in Florida last summer. I **joined my brother on his family trip with his kids**, and we had such a great time. Disney World is fun for people of all ages, where your childhood dreams seem to come true. With all the interesting equipment and characters, it was truly a wonderland to me. The only unpleasant experience I had there was **a thrill ride** I went on, which made me **throw up my lunch** afterwards. Fortunately, I didn't have too much to eat and found a toilet in time, or I would definitely have been embarrassed in public!

　　去年夏天，我去了佛羅里達州的迪士尼樂園，並找回我的童真。我加入我哥哥與他孩子的家族旅遊，玩得超級盡興。迪士尼是個老少咸宜的地方，能讓你感覺到童年的夢想成真。看著那些有趣的設施和角色，對我來說簡直就是仙境。唯一讓我感到不快的經驗是我乘坐了一個刺激的遊樂設施，結束後把我的午餐全吐了。幸運的是，我中餐吃的不多，並及時找到廁所，不然我肯定會在大庭廣眾之下出糗！

短文 2

⊙慢速MP3 30-11　　◎正常速MP3 30-12

Ever **since my first backpacking experience in Asia**, I have become rather addicted to traveling. That trip really broadened my horizons. Compared to the past, I now enjoy all kinds of cuisines from around the world. I also appreciate different cultures and am even able to speak several languages. Although I'm now in a full-time job and can't travel for **an extensive period at one time**, I take at least one trip overseas every year. My goal is to **visit all the countries around the world** in my lifetime. I know it's hard, but isn't dreaming the start of achieving something?

　　自從我初次在亞洲展開背包旅行後，我就愛上旅遊了，那次的旅程拓寬了我的視野。和以前相比，我現在喜歡嘗試來自世界各地的美食，能欣賞不同的文化，甚至會講幾種不同的語言。雖然我現在有全職的工作，沒辦法一次旅行太久，但我每年至少都會出國一次。我的目標是在有生之年走訪全世界的國家，我當然知道這很困難，但想要達成某些事，一開始不就是從夢想起步的嗎？

PART

人際互動

人際關係、百變情緒，提升好感度，
就從聽懂這一句開始！

 認識與邀約
Make Friends

 戀情款款
Love Affairs

 構築家庭
Get Married

 喜怒哀樂
The Emotions

 閒話家常
The Daily Life

認識與邀約 Make Friends

Unit **1**

■日常生活　🦄娛樂活動　✏意見交流　🏳特殊場合

MP3 31-01

下面將播放五組短對話，請仔細聆聽，再依對話內容答題。

Question **1**

Why is the boy inviting the girl to play basketball with them?

(A) He needs her to cheer for them.
(B) He needs her to play for him.
(C) She wants to practice basketball.
(D) He needs one more player for the game.

Question **2**

How often do the golf club members gather to play?

(A) Every two weeks
(B) Every month
(C) Whenever they want
(D) By the end of every month

Question **3**

Why doesn't the man want to join a book club?

(A) He is already a member of another book club.
(B) He finds it strange to meet in a group when he can read alone.
(C) He doesn't find it interesting to share thoughts with others.
(D) He always has a different view from other members.

Question **4**

What does the man have to do for the movie night?

(A) Fill in a registration form
(B) Bring a food dish to the movie night
(C) Provide the movie for the members
(D) Nothing at all

Question **5**

Why doesn't the woman enjoy a foot massage?

(A) She doesn't like the tickly sensation.
(B) It is too painful for her.
(C) She has never tried it before and is afraid of it.
(D) Someone told her it's not comfortable.

答案與解析 ➤ ~answer

Answer 1 (D)
男孩為何邀請女孩和他們一起打籃球？

(A) 男孩需要有人幫他們加油。

(B) 男孩需要她代替他打球。

(C) 女孩想要練習籃球。

(D) 比賽人數還缺一人。

> **解析**
> 男孩一開始就提到他們要打三對三的鬥牛，但「缺1個人」(short by one person)，因此詢問女生是否有意願加入，short在此有「缺少」的意思。選項(B)的play for him是「代替他打球」，意思不同，正確答案為(D)。

Answer 2 (A)
高爾夫球社團的成員們多久會聚在一起打球？

(A) 兩週一次

(B) 每個月一次

(C) 想要的時候就會

(D) 每個月的月底之前

> **解析**
> 男性提到今天是他們高爾夫球社團「每兩週一次的聚會」(biweekly gathering)，關鍵字為biweekly(每兩週的)，表示頻率。請注意字首bi-開頭的單字都具備「雙；兩個」的意思，正確答案為(A)。

Answer 3 (B)
男性為何不想加入讀書會？

(A) 他已經是其他讀書會的成員。

(B) 能自己閱讀卻要和大家一起的感覺很怪。

(C) 他不覺得和人分享想法有趣。

(D) 他和其他成員的意見總是不同。

> **解析**
> 面對女性的邀約，男性提到自己「無法理解」(don't understand)明明自己能閱讀卻要加入社團的情況，正確答案為(B)。

Answer 4 (B)
男性必須為了「電影之夜」做什麼？

(A) 填寫申請表

(B) 為電影之夜帶一道菜去

(C) 替成員準備要觀賞的電影

(D) 什麼都不用做

> **解析**
> 解題關鍵在女性的回應。當男性詢問是否要填寫申請表時，女性提到不用那麼正式，只需要「帶一道菜來」(bring a dish)即可。dish在日常生活中常用來指「一道菜」，正確答案為(B)。

Answer 5 (A)
女性為什麼不享受足部按摩的感覺呢？

(A) 她不喜歡那種搔癢的感覺。

(B) 那對她來說太痛了。

(C) 她從來沒試過，所以害怕。

(D) 有人告訴她那並不舒服。

> **解析**
> 句型too much for sb.通常表示對某人來說「太超過」，所以某人不喜歡或不願意做某事。以本題來說，女性提到按摩對她來說「太癢」(tickles too much)，關鍵字為tickle(搔癢)，正確答案為(A)。

PART 7
人際互動

⊙慢速MP3 31-02   ⊙正常速MP3 31-03

💬 短對話 ❶ *Conversation*

Dean: We are **short by one person** for the 3-on-3 basketball game. Would you like to join us?

狄恩： 我們的三對三鬥牛缺一個人，你想加入嗎？

Nicole: It's been a while since I played basketball, but I'd love to.

妮可： 我不打籃球已經好一陣子了，但我很樂意加入你們。

💬 短對話 ❷ *Conversation*

Warren: Today is our golf club's **biweekly gathering**. We always have a match and a meal afterwards.

華倫： 今天是我們高爾夫球社團每兩週一次的聚會。我們總會先打場比賽再吃飯。

Helen: Sounds fun. I usually only meet with friends about once a month.

海倫： 聽起來很好玩，我一個月大概只會跟朋友碰面一次而已。

💬 短對話 ❸ *Conversation*

Paula: I'm recruiting new members for our book club.

寶拉： 我在找新成員加入我們的讀書會。

Scott: I don't understand why I would want to **join a club when I can read on my own**?

史考特：明明自己就能看書，為什麼還會想要加入讀書會啊？

Paula: Because it's interesting to know other people's different views.

寶拉： 因為能聽到大家不同的觀點很有趣啊。

💬 短對話 ❹ *Conversation*

Janet: It's our club's movie night tonight. Do you want to come?

珍妮特：今晚是我們社團的「電影之夜」喔，你要來嗎？

Dave: Is there a registration procedure of some kind?

戴夫： 是不是要做什麼登記加入的手續啊？

Janet: It's not that formal. **Bringing a dish** for the night is all you have to do.

珍妮特：不用那麼正式，只要帶一道菜來就好。

💬 短對話 ❺ *Conversation*

Tom: Would you like to enjoy a nice foot massage?

湯姆： 你想享受一下很棒的足部按摩嗎？

Anna: No, thanks; it **tickles too much for me to enjoy it**.

安娜： 不，謝了，那對我來說太癢，一點都不享受。

長對話聽力實戰

◎MP3 31-04

請仔細聆聽下面的長對話，再依對話內容選擇正確答案。

Question ❶
Why is the man taking the woman to a night market?
- (A) Because she likes the foods at the night market.
- (B) Because she's been to a night market before and loves it.
- (C) Because he thinks the experience will be different for her.
- (D) Because he doesn't know where else to take her to.

Question ❷
What should the speakers do while trying food at the night market?
- (A) Buy half a portion of everything
- (B) Share the portions of food if possible
- (C) Eat at least one portion of every dish
- (D) Try every single dish at the night market

Question ❸
What does the man suggest the woman do while going shopping?
- (A) Compare all the different styles
- (B) Compare prices and bargain with the vendors
- (C) Compare the quality of the materials
- (D) Ask for at least 50% off of the original price

Question ❹
Why is the woman not sure about going to a KTV?
- (A) She only wants to go to a night market.
- (B) She thinks she is not a good singer.
- (C) She can only sing if she is on her own.
- (D) She doesn't like to sing in public.

Question ❺
How does the man persuade the woman to go to a KTV?
- (A) By explaining they have a private room to sing in
- (B) By guaranteeing that people there will like her singing
- (C) By lying to her that there will only be him and her
- (D) By reassuring her their friends will also go to the KTV

答案與解析 ～answer

Answer 1 ◀ঞ (C)
男性為什麼要帶女性去逛夜市呢？

(A) 因為她很喜歡夜市的食物。

(B) 因為她之前去過，很愛夜市。

(C) 因為他覺得這個經驗對她而言會很不同。

(D) 因為他不知道還有什麼地方可去。

解析

男性一開頭就說要帶女性去逛夜市，並推測她絕對「沒有體驗過」(never experienced anything like that)。因此，隱含女性去過夜市的選項如(A)或(B)都必須剔除。另外一個解題關鍵字為 experience，強調經驗，所以選(C)。

Answer 2 ◀ঞ (B)
在夜市品嚐食物時，他們應該怎麼做呢？

(A) 每樣食物只買半份

(B) 盡量共享一份餐點

(C) 每道小吃都至少吃一份

(D) 吃遍夜市的每一個小吃攤

解析

解題關鍵在There's just one thing後面，男性提到「要盡量共享」(share 分享)，食物，否則很快就飽了，正確答案為(B)。注意之後男性提到的建議是有關買衣服的比價與殺價，與品嚐食物無關。

Answer 3 ◀ঞ (B)
男性給女性的購物建議是什麼？

(A) 比較所有不同的風格

(B) 比較價格並向攤販殺價

(C) 比較物品材質的品質

(D) 至少向攤販殺到五折價

解析

當女性詢問其他建議時，男性提到夜市有許多賣衣服的攤販，但要記得「比價和殺價」(compare prices and haggle)。這不代表要如選項(D)那樣殺到五折，最佳答案為(B)。

Answer 4 ◀ঞ (D)
女性為什麼不想去KTV呢？

(A) 她只想去逛夜市。

(B) 她覺得自己唱得不好聽。

(C) 只有她自己一個人時，她才敢唱。

(D) 她不喜歡在大眾面前唱歌。

解析

一聽到去KTV，女性就說她「不喜歡在大庭廣眾下唱歌」(sing in front of people)，注意這並不代表她像選項(C)那樣，只有獨自一人時才能唱歌，正確答案為(D)。

Answer 5 ◀ঞ (A)
男性如何說服女性去KTV的呢？

(A) 解釋他們會在私人包廂裡唱歌

(B) 向她保證那裡的人都會喜歡她唱歌

(C) 騙她那裡只會有他們兩個人

(D) 向她保證他們的朋友也會去KTV

解析

男性有解釋女性「不用在大眾面前唱歌」，可以剔除選項(B)；但真正的解題關鍵還是在「私人包廂」(a private booth)，private(私人的)形容包廂的性質，與去的人數無關，正確答案為(A)。

James: I must take you to a night market. I think **you've never experienced anything like that**.

詹姆士：我一定要帶妳去逛夜市，妳絕對沒有體驗過。

Nina: Great! I've heard the snacks at the night market can be very tasty.

妮娜：　太棒了！我聽説夜市會有超美味的小吃。

James: There's just one thing. We should **share portions of the snacks whenever it's possible**. Otherwise, we'll be full really soon.

詹姆士：有件事先跟你説好，我們最好盡量共享食物，否則很快就飽了。

Nina: OK. Are there any tips I should know?

妮娜：　知道了，還有其他的建議嗎？

James: There will also be many stalls for shopping. Just remember to **compare prices and haggle**.

詹姆士：也有許多賣衣服之類的攤販，記得要比價和殺價。

Nina: I think I'll be good at that.

妮娜：　這個我應該能做得很好。

James: After the night market, we can go to a KTV for singing.

詹姆士：逛完夜市後，我們還可以去KTV唱歌。

Nina: That I'm not too sure about. I don't like to **sing in front of people**.

妮娜：　這我就不太確定了，我不喜歡在大庭廣眾下唱歌。

James: Don't worry. We pay for **a private booth** for that. You don't have to sing in public.

詹姆士：別擔心，那是私人包廂，你不會在大眾面前唱歌的。

短文聽力實戰

MP3 31-07(短文1)　MP3 31-08(短文2)

請仔細聆聽下面兩段短文，並分別回答Q1~Q2&Q3~Q5兩大題。

Question ①
How does the woman describe the guy she is dating?

    (A) He fits well into her social circle.

    (B) He has the qualities she looks for in an ideal partner.

    (C) His appearance is the type she likes.

    (D) His salary meets her standards.

Question ②
What does the woman hope after the meal next week?

    (A) She can make sure he doesn't have any bad habits.

    (B) She can determine if she wants to be his girlfriend.

    (C) She can go to a concert with him on the weekend.

    (D) She can find out if their hobbies are well matched.

Question ③
What did Nancy invite the boy to do?

    (A) Spend some money to do Christmas shopping

    (B) Spend Christmas at the dormitory with others

    (C) Go to her home to celebrate Christmas with her family

    (D) Spend Easter holiday with her family

Question ④
What did Nancy's family members do with gifts?

    (A) They went shopping together to buy each other gifts.

    (B) They wrapped up gifts for others before Christmas.

    (C) They opened their gifts after Christmas.

    (D) They sat together and opened their gifts.

Question ⑤
How did Nancy reassure the man not to feel embarrassed?

    (A) By saying that nobody in her family expected him to buy gifts.

    (B) By saying that her relatives wouldn't accept his gifts.

    (C) By saying that he could buy presents after Christmas.

    (D) By saying that they didn't expect the man to join them.

答案與解析 ～answer

Answer 1 (B)
女性如何形容她最近的約會對象？

(A) 他很能融入她的社交圈。
(B) 他具備她理想對象的條件。
(C) 他的外貌是她喜歡的那一型。
(D) 他的薪水符合她所設的標準。

解析
文章一開始，女性提到自己對交往對象的概念，接著提到最近認識的這位男性「符合她的標準」(fits my criteria)，綜合前面的內容，她所謂的標準是能明白她的專業和欣賞她在工作上的努力，正確答案為(B)。

Answer 2 (D)
在下週一起去吃飯後，女性希望怎麼樣呢？

(A) 她能確定他沒有不良嗜好。
(B) 她能決定要不要成為他的女朋友。
(C) 週末能一起去欣賞音樂會。
(D) 她能確認兩人的嗜好合拍。

解析
女性最後提到她邀男性一起去吃飯，並希望兩人「在興趣方面也很契合」，關鍵字為compatible(能共處的)，在此表示興趣上的合拍，正確答案為(D)。

Answer 3 (C)
南西邀請男孩做什麼？

(A) 花錢去做聖誕節的採購
(B) 在宿舍和其他人共度聖誕節
(C) 去她家和她家人共度聖誕節
(D) 與她家人共度復活節假期

解析
男孩提到他的美國朋友南西「邀請他與她的家人共度聖誕節」，spend...with...意指「與某人共度某段時間」，正確答案為(C)。文章後面提到男孩去南西家的細節，所以他不可能是待在宿舍過節的。

Answer 4 (D)
關於禮物，南西的家人是怎麼處理的呢？

(A) 他們一起去逛街，買禮物。
(B) 他們在聖誕節之前包裝禮物。
(C) 他們在聖誕節之後打開禮物。
(D) 他們坐在一起，打開禮物。

解析
男孩提到南西的家人都會準備彼此的禮物，並「在爐火前拆禮物」(got each other gifts...unwrapped them in front of each other)。關鍵字為unwrap(拆開)，注意選項(B)說的是「包裝」(wrap)，正確答案為(D)。

Answer 5 (A)
南西是如何叫男孩放寬心，不用感到不好意思呢？

(A) 她的家人不會預期他去買禮物。
(B) 她的親戚不會收他的禮物。
(C) 他可以在聖誕節過後買禮物。
(D) 她的家人沒有預期他會跟他們一起過節。

解析
男孩提到南西「叫他放心」(reassure 使放心)，說「沒人對他有這方面的期待」。be expected of sb.表示「對某人有什麼期待或要求」，本題指的就是準備禮物一事，正確答案為(A)。

中英文內容

短文 1

⊙慢速MP3 31-09　　◎正常速MP3 31-10

For me, it is important to date someone who understands my profession and appreciates the effort I spend on work. I find it difficult if my boyfriend is disinterested in my job and complains too much about my working hours. I think this guy I'm dating **fits my criteria**. We work in the same building, but we've only seen each other a few times. Last week, he asked me to go out for a drink with him after work. He works in finance, and I work as a business lawyer, so we have a good understanding of each other's job and busy schedule. I invited him out for a meal next week. Hopefully, I will discover we **are compatible in terms of our hobbies**, too.

對我來說，交往的對象能明白我的專業和欣賞我在工作上的努力是非常重要的一點。如果我的男友對我的工作毫無興趣，或總是在抱怨我工作的時間過長，那這段關係就很難維持。我覺得我最近開始約會的這位男性滿符合我的標準。我們在同一棟大樓上班，但我們只見過對方幾次。上週他邀請我下班後和他去喝一杯。他在金融界上班，而我是商業律師，所以我們對於彼此的工作和忙碌的行程都很能理解。我邀請他下週出去吃飯，希望我們在興趣方面也很契合。

短文 2

⊙慢速MP3 31-11　　◎正常速MP3 31-12

It was my first winter vacation abroad, and I wasn't sure what to do when most students were going home for Christmas. Then, my American friend Nancy invited me to **spend Christmas with her family**. Before then, all I knew of Christmas were the trees and Santa. However, Nancy explained to me that the main purpose of Christmas is to commemorate the birth of Jesus. We ate and drank a lot, and all the family members got each other gifts. They **unwrapped the gifts in front of each other** in front of a fire. I felt a little embarrassed that I didn't prepare any gifts for them, but Nancy reassured me it **wasn't expected of me**. And they were very happy to have me around.

這是我在國外遇到的第一個寒假，所以當大多數學生都準備回家過聖誕節的時候，我完全不知道要做什麼。接著，我的美國朋友南西邀請我與她的家人共度聖誕節。在這之前，我對聖誕節的認知就只有樹和聖誕老人，不過，南西向我解釋說，聖誕節其實是為了紀念耶穌的誕生。我們一起享用了美食和飲料，所有的家族成員都有準備彼此的禮物，大家在爐火前拆開送給彼此的禮物。我有點不好意思，因為我沒準備禮物給他們，但南西叫我放心，說沒人對我有這方面的期待，他們很高興我能與他們共度佳節。

戀情款款 Love Affairs

短對話聽力實戰

MP3 32-01

下面將播放五組短對話，請仔細聆聽，再依對話內容答題。

Question 1 .... ❶ ❷ ❸ ❹ ❺

What does the man say he enjoys doing with his girlfriend?

(A) Playing video games
(B) Sitting together and doing nothing
(C) Doing Exercise
(D) Cooking

Question 2 .... ❶ ❷ ❸ ❹ ❺

What doesn't the woman know how to do?

(A) How to decide where to go on a date
(B) How to ask the man's sister to introduce her
(C) How to get to know their new colleague
(D) How to talk to their new colleague about his job

Question 3 .... ❶ ❷ ❸ ❹ ❺

What does the man say about Tim and the woman?

(A) Tim crashed into the woman on the way to work.
(B) A lot of people are asking about Tim and the woman.
(C) Tim and the woman are secretly dating.
(D) Tim is a secret admirer of the woman.

Question 4 .... ❶ ❷ ❸ ❹ ❺

What did the woman do to her boyfriend?

(A) She ended their relationship.
(B) She broke his belongings.
(C) She cheated on him.
(D) She broke into tears in front of him.

Question 5 .... ❶ ❷ ❸ ❹ ❺

What does the woman find awkward?

(A) To go on a date with a stranger
(B) To have an arranged marriage
(C) To date someone she knows
(D) To be introduced to a guy by her friend

答案與解析 ~answer

Answer 1 (D)
男性提到自己很喜歡跟女友一起做什麼事？
- (A) 打電動
- (B) 坐在一起，什麼都不做
- (C) 做運動
- (D) 下廚做菜

> **解析**
> 選項(A)的電動是女生抱怨她男友自己喜歡做的事，而對話中男性則建議她說服男友享受兩人一起做事的感覺，接著舉例說他每星期「和女朋友一同下廚」(cooking)，正確答案為(D)。

Answer 2 (C)
女性不知道該怎麼做的事情是什麼？
- (A) 該邀新同事去哪裡約會
- (B) 如何請男性的妹妹介紹她
- (C) 如何認識他們的新同事
- (D) 該怎麼和新同事講他的工作

> **解析**
> 女性「很喜歡」新同事，卻不知道「該如何接近他」(how to approach him)。注意此處的approach(接近)指的是抽象的「認識對方」，並非單純的靠近說話，正確答案為(C)。

Answer 3 (D)
根據男子所說，提姆和女性之間發生了什麼事？
- (A) 提姆在上班途中撞到女性。
- (B) 有很多人都在問提姆和女性的事。
- (C) 提姆和女性正偷在交往。
- (D) 提姆私下暗戀這名女性。

> **解析**
> 解題關鍵為have a crush on sb.，表示「喜歡、暗戀某人」，介係詞on後面接著是「被暗戀者」，正確答案為(D)。注意選項(A)的crash為「碰撞；衝撞」之意。

Answer 4 (A)
女性對男友做了什麼？
- (A) 她結束了彼此的關係。
- (B) 她打破男友的物品。
- (C) 她對男友不貞。
- (D) 她在男友面前哭了。

> **解析**
> 解題關鍵在女性一開始提到的「與男友分手了」(broke up with my boyfriend)。break up with sb.代表「與某人分手」，此為慣用片語，正確答案為(A)。

Answer 5 (A)
女性覺得什麼事情很彆扭？
- (A) 和陌生人約會
- (B) 去參加相親
- (C) 和她認識的人約會
- (D) 朋友介紹男性給她認識

> **解析**
> 女性覺得「和不認識的人約會很彆扭」(someone I've never met before)。在此要特別注意她後面接著形容像「相親」，但這只是比喻，並非真的去相親，正確答案為(A)。

⊙慢速MP3 32-02　　◎正常速MP3 32-03

短對話 1 *Conversation*

Sarah: My boyfriend spends most of his spare time playing video games. It's so annoying.

莎拉： 我男朋友大部分空閒時間都在打電動，真的很惱人。

James: You need to persuade him to enjoy doing something together. I **do cooking with my girlfriend** once a week. It's really nice.

詹姆士：你得說服他一起做點什麼，像我每個星期會和女友一起下廚一次，感覺非常好。

短對話 2 *Conversation*

Doris: I really fancy our new colleague, but I don't know how to **approach him**.

朵莉絲：我好喜歡我們的新同事，但我不知道該如何認識他。

William: I know his sister. Maybe I can introduce you to him.

威廉： 我認識他的妹妹，也許我能介紹你跟他認識。

短對話 3 *Conversation*

Bill: I think Tim **has a crush on you**.

比爾： 我覺得提姆在暗戀妳。

Ellie: How could you tell?

艾莉： 你怎麼知道？

Bill: He's been asking others a lot about you. I'm surprised you don't know!

比爾： 他一直在打聽關於你的事，我很驚訝你居然不知道！

短對話 4 *Conversation*

Tina: I **broke up with** my boyfriend last night.

蒂娜： 我昨晚跟我男朋友分手了。

Jim: How come? Didn't he just propose to you last month?

吉姆： 怎麼會這樣呢？他上個月不是才向你求婚嗎？

Tina: I caught him cheating on me!

蒂娜： 我抓到他對我不貞！

短對話 5 *Conversation*

Kate: I find it awkward to **go on a date with someone I've never met before**. I mean, it's not like we're doing arranged marriages these days.

凱特： 我覺得和沒見過面的人約會很彆扭，我是說，這又不是在相親。

Gavin: You never know, the guy might just happen to be your Mr. Right.

蓋文： 很難說，這個男的可能就是你的如意郎君呢。

長對話聽力實戰

@MP3 32-04

請仔細聆聽下面的長對話，再依對話內容選擇正確答案。

Question 1
What does the woman show to the man?
- (A) Fresh flowers
- (B) A sports car
- (C) A diamond ring
- (D) A pair of earrings

Question 2
How does the woman describe her boyfriend?
- (A) He makes a lot of effort to make her happy.
- (B) He is always saying how much he loves her.
- (C) He gives her whatever she wants.
- (D) He always buys the most expensive things for her.

Question 3
According to the woman, what is every girl's dream?
- (A) To have a billionaire boyfriend
- (B) To be spoiled like she has been
- (C) To be able to buy a sports car
- (D) To be sent a lot of jewelry

Question 4
What's the man's attitude towards the woman's romance?
- (A) It's very romantic, so he would support her.
- (B) The jewelry is expensive. She should reject the gifts.
- (C) The freshness may be gone. She should think about it more.
- (D) Their relationship is stable. She should get married.

Question 5
What does the woman say the man is jealous of?
- (A) He doesn't do things like sending flowers.
- (B) He is not as handsome as the woman's boyfriend.
- (C) He hasn't received those things before.
- (D) He doesn't have the money to buy what the woman received.

答案與解析 ～answer

Answer 1 (C)
女性把什麼東西拿給男性看？

(A) 新鮮的花
(B) 一輛跑車
(C) 一顆鑽戒
(D) 一對耳環

解析
本題的答案在對話一開始，女性把男友送她的東西拿給男性看，此時男性吃驚地說是顆「鑽戒」(a diamond ring)。注意對話中的鮮花與珠寶並非對話當下拿給男性看的物品，正確答案為(C)。

Answer 2 (A)
女性如何形容她的男友？

(A) 為了讓她開心，男友花很多心思。
(B) 他總是在向她訴衷情。
(C) 不管她想要什麼，男友都會送她。
(D) 他總是買最昂貴的物品給她。

解析
當男性反問女性怎麼知道男友是真命天子時，她回答「花很多心思讓她開心」，正確答案為(A)。在此請注意後面描述的禮物，是男友主動送的，可剔除(C)，而且也不一定「總是」最昂貴，因此(D)也不適合。

Answer 3 (B)
根據女性所言，所有女孩都會有什麼夢想呢？

(A) 擁有一個有上億家產的男友
(B) 像她一樣被寵愛
(C) 能夠買一輛跑車
(D) 有人送很多珠寶給她

解析
解題關鍵在女性提到的「被寵愛」(be pampered)。以她的例子來說是收到如飾品這樣的禮物，但她沒有實際說所謂的寵愛一定要怎樣，正確答案為(B)。

Answer 4 (C)
男性對女性的愛情的反應為何？

(A) 太浪漫了，他會支持她。
(B) 珠寶很貴，她應該拒絕收下。
(C) 新鮮感可能消失，她應該多想想。
(D) 兩人關係很穩定，她應該結婚。

解析
對話中雖然沒有直接提到男性的想法，但他有問女性，如果「新鮮感消失了」(novelty goes away)該怎麼辦，這代表男性對這種愛情關係的擔憂，正面支持的選項如(A)(D)都應該剔除，正確答案為(C)。

Answer 5 (D)
根據女性所言，男性在忌妒什麼事呢？

(A) 他不做送花這類的事。
(B) 他不像女性的男友般英俊。
(C) 他從來沒有收過那些東西。
(D) 他沒有能力買女性收到的禮物。

解析
女性聽到男性的反應很消極，問他該不會是因為「買不起這些東西」(can't afford the things)而忌妒，正確答案為(D)。只要聽到關鍵字afford，就能選出是與金錢支出有關的選項。

⊙慢速MP3 32-05　　◎正常速MP3 32-06

Betty: My boyfriend just gave me this!
貝蒂：　我男友剛給了我這個！

Simon: **A diamond ring**?! I thought you haven't been dating for that long?
賽門：　鑽戒？！你們不是交往才沒多久嗎？

Betty: A little over two months. I think I've found the one.
貝蒂：　兩個多月囉，我覺得我已經找到真命天子了。

Simon: How do you know?
賽門：　你又知道他是了？

Betty: He puts so **much effort into making me pleased**, like sending flowers and giving me jewelry as gifts.
貝蒂：　他花很多心思讓我開心，像是送花給我和送珠寶當禮物等等。

Simon: Are you sure that's not his money doing the work?
賽門：　你確定這是花心思，而不是用錢取悅你嗎？

Betty: Of course he needs money to do these things. I'm sure it's every girl's dream to **be pampered** like this.
貝蒂：　他做這些事當然會需要錢，我敢肯定每個女孩都希望能像這樣被寵愛。

Simon: Perhaps. But what if the **novelty goes away**?
賽門：　也許吧，但如果新鮮感消失了怎麼辦？

Betty: I thought you'd be happy for me. Are you being jealous because you **can't afford** the things?
貝蒂：　我還以為你會為我感到高興。你該不會是因為買不起這些才這麼說吧？

Simon: At least I spend my time with my girlfriend and share her feelings when she needs me.
賽門：　至少我會花時間陪我女友，並在她需要的時候分享她的喜怒哀樂。

302

短文聽力實戰

MP3 32-07（短文1）　　MP3 32-08（短文2）

請仔細聆聽下面兩段短文，並分別回答Q1~Q2&Q3~Q5兩大題。

Question ①

How did the man used to feel if he didn't buy his wife expensive gifts?

(A) He felt angry with himself.

(B) He felt guilty in some way.

(C) He would feel embarrassed.

(D) He felt that she didn't like the gifts.

Question ②

Why did the man's wife like the handmade cards?

(A) The cards were very well-crafted.

(B) The cards made her feel they were for someone special.

(C) She liked to do things by herself.

(D) She thought they were different from the man's taste.

Question ③

What might happen if one person is particularly jealous in a relationship?

(A) It makes for a stronger relationship.

(B) The couple might break up with each other.

(C) They will spend the time being together if possible.

(D) It will create a relationship full of pressure.

Question ④

What had gradually changed in Eddie's ex-girlfriend?

(A) She became very bossy in front of Ed's friends.

(B) She became ill-tempered when talking to Eddie.

(C) She became very obsessive with Eddie's total attention.

(D) She became very demanding of Eddie.

Question ⑤

Why did Eddie's friends start to stay away from him?

(A) They didn't want to make the couple fight.

(B) They knew his ex-girlfriend very well.

(C) His ex-girlfriend asked them to do so.

(D) They thought Eddie had changed because of his ex-girlfriend.

答案與解析 ～answer

Answer 1 (B)
如果沒有買昂貴的禮物給老婆，男性會感到如何？
(A) 他會生自己的氣。
(B) 他會感到有些愧疚。
(C) 他會覺得很丟臉。
(D) 他感覺老婆不怎麼喜歡禮物。

解析
男性一開始提到自己以前(used to)認為禮物的價格能表示心意，所以，如果買給老婆的東西不夠昂貴，他會感到有點「內疚」(a little guilty)，關鍵字為guilty，正確答案為(B)。

Answer 2 (B)
男性的老婆為什麼喜歡那些手作卡片呢？
(A) 那些卡片的作工很精緻。
(B) 她能感受到卡片是為了特別的人而做的。
(C) 她喜歡自己動手做東西。
(D) 她覺得那些卡片和男性的品味很不同。

解析
從One day開始的內容，是男性提到改變自己送禮想法的轉捩點，老婆喜歡作工不特別精緻的卡片，是因為能感受到那是「為了特別的人而做的」(mean a lot to sb. 對某人很有意義)，正確答案為(B)。

Answer 3 (D)
戀愛關係裡若有一方的忌妒心特別重，會怎麼樣呢？
(A) 關係會更穩定。
(B) 情侶可能會分手。
(C) 可能的話會多待在一起。
(D) 會帶給彼此很大的壓力。

解析
本文一開始，提到一段關係中若有一方忌妒心特別重，就會對兩人的關係帶來很大的壓力(create a lot of tension)。tension在此表示會帶來關係緊張的結果，最接近的答案為(D)。注意(B)僅為文中的舉例。

Answer 4 (C)
艾迪的前女友後來慢慢變得如何呢？
(A) 她在艾迪朋友面前很愛指使人。
(B) 她一和艾迪說話就變得暴躁。
(C) 她要求艾迪將注意力都放在她身上。
(D) 她對艾迪的要求變很多。

解析
文中提到艾迪前女友的佔有欲變得越來越強(more and more possessive)，選項(C)中的obsessive表示「著迷的；過份關心的」，整句表示「佔據艾迪所有注意力」，正確答案為(C)。

Answer 5 (A)
為什麼艾迪的朋友會開始遠離他呢？
(A) 他們不想害那對情侶吵架。
(B) 他們非常了解艾迪的前女友。
(C) 他的前女友要求他們這樣做。
(D) 他們覺得艾迪為了前女友而改變了。

解析
文中提到有些朋友甚至漸漸疏遠艾迪(stay away from him)，因為他們不想「成為艾迪與女友爭吵的原因」(become the cause of their arguments)，在此要選具備因果關係的選項(A)。(原因：朋友/結果：吵架)

⊙慢速MP3 32-09　　◎正常速MP3 32-10

I used to think the price of gifts could express my love for someone to some extent. Therefore, I would get **a little guilty** if I got my wife something not expensive enough. One day, when we were out shopping. I noticed her eyes brightened up when she saw some handmade cards. Those cards were not particularly well-crafted, so I asked what attracted her to them so much. She then told me that she could feel **the effort** spent on the cards. They must have **meant a lot to someone really special**. Until then, I didn't realize what meant more to her. Now, I try to make her a card or cook for her on special occasions, and she has been very happy with these gifts.

　　我曾經以為，禮物的價格某種程度上能表達我對某人的愛。所以，如果我買給我老婆的禮物不夠昂貴，我就會感到有點愧疚。有一天，我們出門逛街時，我注意到她因為一些手工卡片而眼神發亮。那些卡片的作工並不特別精美，所以我問她到底喜歡那些卡片的什麼地方，她接著告訴我，她能感覺到在卡片上花的心思，這些卡片對某些特別的人來說肯定很有意義，那個時候，我才理解對她而言更重要的是什麼。現在，每遇到特殊的日子，我都會盡量做一張手作卡片送她，或是親自為她下廚，她對這些禮物非常滿意和感動。

⊙慢速MP3 32-11　　◎正常速MP3 32-12

Love is most ideal when the two parties love each other equally and trust each other. If one person is particularly jealous, it can **create a lot of tension** in the relationship. Take my best friend Eddie and his ex-girlfriend for example. When they started dating, everything seemed perfect. However, his ex-girlfriend gradually became more and more **possessive**. Some of our friends even started to stay away from him as they didn't want to **become the cause of their arguments**. After two years of dating, Eddie decided to break up with her because she was too suspicious about everything. Fortunately, he met a great girl at work and started a new relationship.

　　愛情最為理想的狀態是雙方相愛的程度差不多，且互相信任。如果有一方的忌妒心特別重，就會對兩人的關係帶來很大的壓力。拿我最好的朋友艾迪和他前女朋友為例，他們一開始交往時，一切都顯得如此完美，但漸漸地，他前女友的佔有慾變得越來越強。我們甚至有些朋友漸漸疏離艾迪，因為他們不想成為他和女友吵架的導火線。在交往了兩年之後，因為她對什麼事情都疑神疑鬼，所以艾迪決定與她分手，幸運的是，在那之後，他在職場遇到一個好女孩並開始交往。

 Unit 3

構築家庭 Get Married

📷 日常生活　🎤 娛樂活動　✏️ 意見交流　🚩 特殊場合

 短對話聽力實戰

🎧 MP3 33-01

下面將播放五組短對話，請仔細聆聽，再依對話內容答題。

Question 1

How is the man planning to propose to his girlfriend?

(A) Take her to a theater and propose

(B) Take her to a nice restaurant to propose

(C) Watch a romantic movie and propose

(D) Hide the ring in her dinner

Question 2

What was the girl's reaction to how her parents met?

(A) She smiled.

(B) She cried out loud.

(C) She laughed so hard that tears fell.

(D) She found it truly unbelievable.

Question 3

What is the woman's dad going to do next month?

(A) Marry someone young enough to be the woman's sibling

(B) Marry a woman whose husband died many years ago

(C) Enter into a new marriage after the woman's mother died

(D) Get divorced and remarry another woman

Question 4

What is the woman asking the man to do?

(A) Join her birthday party this weekend

(B) Attend her wedding this weekend

(C) Celebrate the woman and her fiancé's engagement

(D) Celebrate the couple moving in their new house

Question 5

Why is the man so angry?

(A) He thinks his wife is seeing someone behind his back.

(B) His wife is cheating on him.

(C) He doesn't have the time to talk to his wife.

(D) A private detective told him his wife is cheating on him.

答案與解析 ~answer

Answer 1 (A)
男性準備如何和女友求婚呢？

(A) 帶她到電影院再求婚

(B) 帶她上好餐廳求婚

(C) 觀賞浪漫的電影再求婚

(D) 把婚戒藏在她的晚餐裡

解析

男性說他要「包下電影院」(hire out 包場)，「播放一段他自己做的影片後求婚」(propose after a special video I made)，最接近的答案為(A)。注意(C)錯誤的地方在男性並沒有打算看電影。

Answer 2 (C)
在聽完父母的相識過程後，女孩的反應為何？

(A) 她微笑。

(B) 她大聲哭了出來。

(C) 她笑到流淚。

(D) 她覺得過程不可思議。

解析

本題必須先聽完全部對話後再答題，因為女孩首先提到自己「聽到哭」(it made me cry)，男生因此以為很感人，接著女孩才說自己是「笑到流淚」(so funny that I laughed myself to tears)，正確答案為(C)。

Answer 3 (C)
女性的父親下個月要做什麼？

(A) 和年紀足以和女性做姊妹的女人結婚

(B) 和一名丈夫死了很多年的女性結婚

(C) 在女性的母親死後，開始另一段婚姻

(D) 離婚再與另一名女性結婚

解析

解題關鍵字為一開始的「再婚」(remarry)與「守寡」(being widowed)；接著要搞清楚being widowed所形容的對象為主詞的「我爸爸」(my dad)，因此選(C)。

Answer 4 (D)
女性要求男性做什麼呢？

(A) 這個週末參加她的生日派對

(B) 這個週末參加她的婚禮

(C) 慶祝女性與未婚夫的訂婚

(D) 慶祝這對情侶搬新家

解析

女性一開始提到這個週末要辦「喬遷派對」(a housewarming party)，所以詢問男性要不要參加，關鍵字為housewarming，正確答案為(D)。

Answer 5 (A)
男性為什麼如此火冒三丈？

(A) 他認為他妻子背著他外遇。

(B) 他的妻子外遇。

(C) 他沒有時間和妻子聊聊。

(D) 私家偵探告訴他，他的妻子外遇。

解析

解題時請務必聽清楚話題中「外遇」(cheat on sb.)的性質。最重要的關鍵在男性一開始提的「有人告訴我」(Somebody told me)，表示此為未經證實的諸傳，正確答案為(A)。注意選項(B)表示外遇是已證實的事實。

⊙慢速MP3 33-02　　◎正常速MP3 33-03

💬短對話 1　*Conversation*

Benny: I'm planning a surprise proposal. I'm going to **hire out** a theater and propose after **a special video I made**.

班尼：　我在計畫求婚驚喜。我準備包下電影院，先播放自製影片，再求婚。

Phoebe: That sounds so romantic!

菲比：　這聽起來超浪漫！

💬短對話 2　*Conversation*

Ruth:　Last night, my mom told us how she and my father met, and it made me cry.

露絲：　昨晚我媽媽告訴我們，她和我爸爸相識的故事，聽得我都哭了。

Vic:　　I bet it was romantic and moving.

維克：　我相信那一定既浪漫又感人。

Ruth:　In fact, it was so funny that I **laughed myself to tears**!

露絲：　事實上，過程超好笑，我笑到流淚！

💬短對話 3　*Conversation*

Debbie: My dad is **remarrying** next month after **being widowed** for over ten years.

黛比：　我爸爸在守寡了十多年後，將於下個月再婚。

Sean:　You must be happy for him.

西恩：　你肯定很替他感到高興。

Debbie: I am, but my step-siblings are young enough to be my children!

黛比：　的確，但我的繼弟妹都小到足以當我的孩子耶！

💬短對話 4　*Conversation*

Sarah:　My fiancé and I are holding **a housewarming party** this weekend. Please **come if you can**.

莎拉：　我的未婚夫和我這個週末要辦喬遷派對，如果你有空的話，請來參加。

Mark:　Congratulations! I guess I'll have to call you Mrs. Smith.

馬克：　恭喜！我猜我得叫妳史密斯太太了。

💬短對話 5　*Conversation*

Dean:　I'm calling a private detective agency. **Somebody told me** my wife's **cheating on me**!

狄恩：　我要打電話給徵信社，有人告訴我，我妻子讓我戴綠帽！

Martha: Calm down. Have you talked to her about your relationship?

瑪莎：　先冷靜一點，你有沒有跟她聊過你們的關係？

長對話聽力實戰

◎MP3 33-04

請仔細聆聽下面的長對話，再依對話內容選擇正確答案。

Question ❶
What does the woman want to talk about?
- (A) Deciding on some basic rules
- (B) Decorating the ground floor of their house
- (C) Establishing their daily routines
- (D) What she feels unhappy about in their relationship

Question ❷
Why does the woman think the discussion is necessary?
- (A) So that they can both go out and work.
- (B) So that the woman would feel happier.
- (C) So that they wouldn't annoy each other.
- (D) So that they can enjoy doing housework together.

Question ❸
What housework does the woman ask the man to do?
- (A) Shopping and cooking
- (B) A thorough clean of their house
- (C) Doing laundry and taking care of the kids
- (D) Washing dishes and tidying up

Question ❹
How can the couple avoid the situation of not being able to find things?
- (A) The woman does the tidying up by herself.
- (B) The man puts certain things in the same place.
- (C) They do the tidying up together.
- (D) They decide where to store things in advance.

Question ❺
What does the man suggest they should hire a cleaner for?
- (A) To do thorough cleaning around the house sometimes
- (B) To do a thorough cleaning for them on a regular basis
- (C) To do all the washing up and tidying for them
- (D) To cook for them when the wife feels lazy

答案與解析 ～answer

Answer 1 ◀))(A)
女性想要談什麼事呢？
- (A) 講好一些基本規則
- (B) 裝飾他們家的一樓
- (C) 決定他們每天要做的例行事項
- (D) 她對這段關係不滿的地方

解析
女性想和她的老公談談，講好一些「基本規則」(ground rules)，此處的ground表示「基本的」，重點在後面的「規則」(rules)，正確答案為(A)。

Answer 2 ◀))(C)
女性為什麼覺得這段討論很必要？
- (A) 這樣他們就都能出門工作。
- (B) 這樣女性就會感覺比較開心。
- (C) 這樣他們就不會惹惱對方。
- (D) 這樣他們就能享受一起做家務的感覺。

解析
提到討論的原因，女性說並非為了單一事件而生氣，而是希望能「減少」惹惱彼此的機會(minimize the chance)，關鍵字為「被惹惱」(being annoyed)，正確答案為(C)。

Answer 3 ◀))(D)
女性要求男性做的家務是什麼？
- (A) 購物和煮飯
- (B) 給家裡大掃除
- (C) 洗衣服和照顧小孩
- (D) 洗碗和收拾東西

解析
女性的先生很乾脆地答應幫忙，此時女性提到的兩件家事為「洗碗」(wash up)與「收拾整理」(tidy up)，正確答案為(D)。注意選項(C)的do laundry特別指「洗衣服」，與此處的wash不同。

Answer 4 ◀))(D)
為了防止找不到東西的窘況，這對夫妻能怎麼做？
- (A) 女性自己來收拾東西。
- (B) 男性把部分東西放在同一處。
- (C) 他們一起收拾東西。
- (D) 他們事先決定要把東西放在哪裡。

解析
片語go through依著使用情境會產生不同的意思，此處為「討論」之意，利用刪除法可以剔除不包含「討論」動作的選項，選出正確答案(D)。

Answer 5 ◀))(A)
男性建議要雇用清潔人員做什麼？
- (A) 偶爾來幫他們進行大掃除
- (B) 定期來幫他們進行大掃除
- (C) 替他們洗碗和收拾東西
- (D) 當妻子不想下廚的時候來煮飯

解析
此處要注意單字cleaner(清潔人員)，才能聽出要對方做的事情為「大掃除」(do thorough cleaning)。除此之外，還必須把握every now and then的意思等同於sometimes(有時候)，由此選出答案(A)。

⊙慢速MP3 33-05　　◎正常速MP3 33-06

Rebecca: Honey, I want to talk to you and establish some **ground rules**.
蕾貝卡：　親愛的，我想和你談談，講好一些基本規則。

Vincent: If something upset you, you could just tell me.
文森：　　如果有什麼事惹你不開心，你可以直接和我說。

Rebecca: It's not that I'm unhappy about you or anything. I just want to **minimize the chance of either of us being annoyed**.
蕾貝卡：　我並沒有對你或什麼不滿，只是想要減少彼此生氣的機率。

Vincent: That's fine. What do you want me to do?
文森：　　這沒問題，你要我做什麼？

Rebecca: I think it would be better if we shared the housework. Can you help with the **washing up** and **tidying up**?
蕾貝卡：　我覺得分擔家務會比較好，你能幫忙洗碗和收拾嗎？

Vincent: But you might not find things if I tidy up.
文森：　　但如果我負責收拾的話，你可能會找不到東西吧。

Rebecca: We can go through **where things are supposed to go** beforehand.
蕾貝卡：　我們可以事先溝通好什麼東西該收去哪裡。

Vincent: But if I feel lazy, can we just go out to eat? Also, we could hire a cleaner to **do thorough cleaning every now and then**.
文森：　　不過，如果我不想洗碗的話，可以出去吃嗎？另外，我們其實可以偶爾雇用清潔人員來大掃除。

Rebecca: Are you actually going to do any work or not?!
蕾貝卡：　你到底有沒有要做事啊？！

Vincent: Of course I am. Don't be mad.
文森：　　我當然有，別生氣了。

短文聽力實戰

MP3 33-07(短文1)　　MP3 33-08(短文2)

請仔細聆聽下面兩段短文，並分別回答Q1~Q2&Q3~Q5兩大題。

Question ❶

According to the woman, what doesn't she really like?

(A) Going to a fancy restaurant for romantic meals

(B) Being proposed to in a dramatic way in public

(C) Receiving a ring when being proposed to

(D) Saying no to her lover's proposal

Question ❷

Why do some girls feel pressured while facing such a special proposal?

(A) They feel uncomfortable refusing it in front of others.

(B) They get pressure from other people.

(C) They will compare with other friends' proposals.

(D) They will try to share their lovers' feeling.

Question ❸

What might spoil people's children?

(A) Caring too much about what their children want

(B) Showing their love simply through money and material

(C) Buying them presents for their birthdays

(D) Arguing with their children's teachers

Question ❹

What does the man want his son to do when he becomes an adult?

(A) To take the man's business

(B) To work part-time

(C) To be responsible for himself

(D) To move out of the family home

Question ❺

What might be the cause of the man's son quitting the job so quickly?

(A) The fact his son doesn't need money

(B) The man's attitude towards his son's job

(C) The pressure from the boss

(D) The way the man used to show his love

答案與解析 ~answer

Answer 1 (B)

根據女性所說,她不怎麼喜歡什麼事?

(A) 去精緻的餐廳,在浪漫的氣氛下享用餐點
(B) 在大庭廣眾下以戲劇化的方式被求婚
(C) 在被求婚的時候拿到戒指
(D) 拒絕她情人的求婚

> **解析**
> 女性一開始描述了一些女生喜歡的求婚方式,接著提到自己「不熱衷」這種像在做秀的求婚。關鍵片語keen on表示一個人的喜好;關鍵字showy與選項(B)的dramatic(戲劇化的)最接近,因此選(B)。

Answer 2 (A)

面對特別的求婚時,為什麼有些女孩的壓力會很大?

(A) 在大眾面前拒絕讓人感到不自在。
(B) 其他人會給她們壓力。
(C) 她們會拿自己的求婚與其他朋友比較。
(D) 她們想要顧及情人的感受。

> **解析**
> 女性說完自己不怎麼喜歡過於誇張的求婚之後,以Besides開頭,點出其他女生可能有的問題在「想拒絕時怎麼辦」(what if...)?肯定會因此覺得「壓力很大」,正確答案為(A)。

Answer 3 (B)

什麼可能會寵壞小孩?

(A) 太在意小孩想要什麼東西
(B) 僅用金錢和物質表現親情
(C) 買生日禮物給小孩
(D) 和小孩的老師們爭論

> **解析**
> 首先要看懂題目中的spoil是「(因溺愛)而寵壞」的意思,由此概念出發,就能找出答案。男性提到如果父母的愛「以金錢和物質呈現」(money and material),就有可能寵壞小孩,正確答案為(B)。

Answer 4 (C)

在兒子成年之後,男性希望兒子怎麼做呢?

(A) 接管他的生意
(B) 兼職打工
(C) 對自己負責
(D) 從家裡搬出去

> **解析**
> 男性提到因為兒子成年,所以他希望兒子能「對自己更負責」(take more responsibility),正確答案為(C)。

Answer 5 (D)

男性的兒子這麼快就辭職的緣由可能是什麼?

(A) 他兒子不缺錢的事實
(B) 男性對兒子這份工作的態度
(C) 來自老闆的壓力
(D) 男性以前表達親情的方式

> **解析**
> 男性提到自己兒子找了一份打工,但只做了一個星期就辭職,他覺得自己現在正「付出代價」(suffer for my early actions),此處的early action指的是以前他使用金錢與物質的教養方式,正確答案為(D)。

中英文內容

短文 1

⊙慢速MP3 33-09　　◎正常速MP3 33-10

Some girls dream of a romantic proposal with the ring hidden in the dessert, and the man proposing on one knee in a fancy restaurant. However, I'm **not keen on such a showy proposal** because I think I would feel embarrassed in front of other people. Besides, what if the girl **wants to say no**? She would feel so **much pressure in such a situation**. And if she refuses, trust me, it would be the biggest humiliation for the man. Thank God my husband understands me well. He proposed to me when we went hiking. There was nobody else on top of the mountain. To me, this was the truly romantic way of proposing.

　　有些女孩會期望有個浪漫的求婚,男生把戒指藏在甜點裡,並在一家精緻的餐廳裡單膝下跪,向她求婚。不過,我並不熱衷於這種像在作秀般的求婚方式,因為在這麼多人面前,我應該會覺得很不好意思。而且,要是女生想拒絕呢?在這種情況下,她的壓力會很大。而且,相信我,如果她真的拒絕,那對男生來說簡直是丟臉丟到家了。謝天謝地,我丈夫很了解我,他是在我們去健行的時候向我求婚,那時山頂沒有其他人,對我來說,這才是真正浪漫的求婚。

短文 2

⊙慢速MP3 33-11　　◎正常速MP3 33-12

People always say love is unconditional and parents would do anything for their children. The flip side of this is that love **in the form of money and material** might spoil their kids. I used to be busy working, so I tried to make up for the lack of father-and-son time by buying my son a lot of presents, giving him ample pocket money, and saying yes to whatever he requested. Now, since he's turned into an adult, I hope he can start to **take more responsibility**. After all, we can't take care of him for the rest of his life. However, this is proving to be very difficult. He has begun a part-time job recently but quit after just one week. I feel I'm **suffering for my early actions** now.

　　人們總說愛是無條件的,父母會為孩子做任何事。從另一方面來看,以金錢和物質呈現的愛可能會寵壞他們。我曾經忙於工作,所以買給兒子很多禮物、給他足夠的零用錢,答應他的所有要求,藉以彌補他缺少的父子相聚時間。不過,現在他成年了,所以我希望他能變得更有責任感,畢竟,我們不能照顧他一輩子。不過,這件事很困難,他最近找了一份兼職工作,但才做了短短一個星期就辭職,我感覺自己現在正為了以前的行為付出代價。

喜怒哀樂 The Emotions

日常生活　娛樂活動　意見交流　特殊場合

MP3 34-01

下面將播放五組短對話，請仔細聆聽，再依對話內容答題。

Question 1

Based on the dialogue, why does the man cry?

(A) He had a serious argument with his family.

(B) Someone in his family just called him.

(C) Someone in his family passed away.

(D) He is missing his family back home.

Question 2

Why is the woman disappointed?

(A) Her brother defeated her in a math competition.

(B) She can't make her brother understand something.

(C) Her brother didn't need her to explain the math principle.

(D) She can't think of different ways to explain something.

Question 3

How does the girl seem to feel?

(A) She seems exhausted.

(B) She seems confused.

(C) She seems worried.

(D) She seems extremely happy.

Question 4

What does the man say the woman must do?

(A) Take a part-time job instead

(B) Look after her in-laws well

(C) Keep some time for herself

(D) Devote herself to her family

Question 5

Based on the dialogue, how is the boy feeling?

(A) He is shaking.

(B) He is furious.

(C) He is very sad.

(D) He is confused.

答案與解析 ～answer

Answer 1 (C)
根據對話內容，男性為什麼哭呢？

(A) 他和家人大吵了一架。
(B) 他的家人剛打電話給他。
(C) 他的家人過世。
(D) 他想念在家鄉的家人。

解析
一開始可聽出對話中的男性在哭泣，接著他解釋自己剛經歷了「喪親之痛」，關鍵字為bereavement，是喪失親人的名詞用法，正確答案為(C)。選項中的pass away為「過世」的講法。

Answer 2 (B)
女性為何感到很沮喪呢？

(A) 她弟弟在一場數學競賽中打敗了她。
(B) 她無法讓她弟弟理解某樣東西。
(C) 她的弟弟不需要她解釋數學原理。
(D) 她想不出其他方法來解釋某物。

解析
解題關鍵有兩處，最直接的是女性提到自己「用盡各種方式解釋數學原理，但她弟弟就是聽不懂」(just couldn't get it)；另一處線索在男性一開始問她陪弟弟做作業(assignment)的事，可知與課業教導有關，正確答案為(B)。

Answer 3 (D)
女孩看起來如何呢？

(A) 她似乎非常疲倦。
(B) 她似乎感到很困惑。
(C) 她似乎憂心忡忡。
(D) 她似乎非常開心。

解析
本題考的是片語over the moon，形容「欣喜若狂的樣子」，正確答案為(D)。如果聽不懂該片語，也可以從女孩後續的描述推測出被邀約對她而言是很開心的事，藉此剔除負面情緒的選項。

Answer 4 (C)
男性說女性一定要做什麼事？

(A) 找一份兼職工作
(B) 好好照顧她的公婆
(C) 留些時間給自己
(D) 全心投入她的家庭中

解析
女性一開始提到自己感到「筋疲力盡」(exhausted)，因此男性建議她要「安排專屬於自己的時間」，關鍵字為me time，表示「屬於自己的時間」，正確答案為(C)。

Answer 5 (B)
根據對話，男孩此刻的心情如何？

(A) 他在發抖。
(B) 他感到憤怒。
(C) 他非常難過。
(D) 他感到困惑。

解析
看到男生握拳顫抖的模樣，女孩忍不住問他怎麼了，此時男生說自己「氣得火冒三丈」(be fuming)，fume特別指的是「極端憤怒」，最接近的選項為(B)的furious(狂怒的)。

短對話 ❶ Conversation

Emma: What's the matter? Why are you crying?
艾瑪： 發生什麼事了？你怎麼在哭呢？
Tom: I'm sorry. There's been a **bereavement** in my family recently.
湯姆： 抱歉，我最近才經歷了喪親之痛。
Emma: I'm really sorry to hear that.
艾瑪： 我真的很遺憾。

短對話 ❷ Conversation

Zac: Why are you so defeated? Didn't you help your brother with his assignment?
柴克： 你看起來怎麼這麼沮喪？你不是去陪你弟弟做作業嗎？
Erin: I explained a math principle **in every way possible**, but **he just couldn't get it**.
艾琳： 我用盡所有方法解釋一個數學原理，但我弟弟就是聽不懂。

短對話 ❸ Conversation

George: You seem **over the moon**. What's the news?
喬治： 你一副欣喜若狂的樣子，怎麼了嗎？
Linda: Kevin just asked me out! I must get dressed up very nicely that day.
琳達： 凱文剛才邀我去約會！我那天一定要好好打扮。

短對話 ❹ Conversation

Cherry: I'm exhausted. I've devoted myself to the family. And now I need to look after my in-laws, too.
雀莉： 我感到筋疲力盡，我全心投入家庭，現在還必須照顧公婆。
Peter: You must make sure you have some **"me time"** as well.
彼得： 你得擁有「專屬於自己的時間」。

短對話 ❺ Conversation

Jenny: You're literally shaking with your fists clenched. What's wrong?
珍妮： 你緊握拳頭，全身顫抖耶，怎麼了嗎？
Warren: I'm **fuming**! My classmate accused me of stealing his idea for my project, but it's a pure coincidence!
華倫： 我氣得火冒三丈！我同學指控我偷了他的想法，用在我的報告中，但這純粹是個巧合！

長對話聽力實戰

MP3 34-04

請仔細聆聽下面的長對話，再依對話內容選擇正確答案。

Question 1

What could "hot and cold" mean in describing one's emotion?

(A) Being affected by what happens around

(B) Changing one's mood from one extreme to the other quickly

(C) Changing one's preference towards things quickly

(D) Being indecisive and unable to make up one's mind

Question 2

Generally, what impression does the man's girlfriend leave on people?

(A) Cheerful and extroverted

(B) Angry and moody

(C) Reserved and not talkative

(D) Outgoing but picky

Question 3

What reason does the man's girlfriend give for her bad mood?

(A) The man's inability to understand her

(B) Various bad habits the man has

(C) Insignificant things or no reason sometimes

(D) A problem with her finger

Question 4

How often is the man's girlfriend moody?

(A) On a weekly basis

(B) Every other day

(C) Whenever she feels like it

(D) About once a month

Question 5

What might be the cause for the man's girlfriend's moodiness?

(A) Some unknown mental illness

(B) Her menstrual period

(C) A serious problems in their relationship

(D) Hallucinations

答案與解析 ～answer

Answer 1 🔊 (B)

「冷熱無常」(hot and cold)是在形容什麼情緒？

(A) 被週遭發生的事影響

(B) 快速從一種極端的情緒轉變成另一種極端

(C) 很快就改變對事情的偏好

(D) 優柔寡斷，無法下定決心

 解析

解題關鍵除了可以從hot and cold字面上推測與「極端的狀態」有關之外，男性後面還提到女友有時會變得很情緒化(sometimes becomes moody)，由此可推測出這個用法是用來形容情緒的轉變，正確答案為(B)。

Answer 2 🔊 (A)

通常情況下，男性的女友給人什麼印象？

(A) 開朗又外向

(B) 暴躁又情緒化

(C) 保守又不多話

(D) 外向但很挑剔

 解析

男性提到女友個性變化無常(hot and cold)之後，女性感到訝異，說她印象中，男性女友「很活潑、外向」(bubbly and outgoing)，後面男性就說「通常是這樣沒錯」，正確答案為(A)。

Answer 3 🔊 (C)

男性女友對自己的壞情緒給了什麼理由？

(A) 男性無法理解她

(B) 男性的許多壞習慣

(C) 不重要的小事或毫無理由

(D) 她手指的問題

 解析

男性提到女友的情緒化似乎沒什麼特別原因，不是「微不足道」(trivial)的小事，就是女友根本說不出什麼問題，can't put one's finger on與手指毫無關係，真正的意思是「說不上來」，正確答案為(C)。

Answer 4 🔊 (D)

男性女友情緒化的頻率為何？

(A) 基本上每週一次

(B) 每兩天一次

(C) 只要她想，隨時都可能

(D) 大約一個月一次

 解析

解題關鍵在女性詢問這種情緒不穩定的狀態該不會是「按月」(on a monthly basis)發生，男性想了一下後發現「似乎如此」(I think it does)，正確答案為(D)。

Answer 5 🔊 (B)

男性女友變得情緒化的原因很可能是什麼？

(A) 不知名的心理疾病

(B) 她的生理期

(C) 兩人關係中的嚴重問題

(D) 幻覺

 解析

本題考的是單字menstrual(生理期的)，男性女友的狀態是「由月經引起的情緒波動」；由前文女性說不用擔心，下次只要泡一杯熱飲就沒事，也可以推測出並非嚴重的問題。

⊙ 慢速MP3 34-05　　◎ 正常速MP3 34-06

Jason: I need advice from a female. I just don't understand women.
傑森：　我需要女性的意見，我實在搞不懂女人。

Vivian: What's the matter?
薇薇安：怎麼了？

Jason: It's my girlfriend Megan. She can be **"hot and cold"** sometimes.
傑森：　是我的女友梅根，她的情緒有時還真變化無常。

Vivian: I've seen her once. I thought she's really **bubbly and outgoing**.
薇薇安：我見過她一次，我覺得她很活潑、外向啊。

Jason: **Generally, yes.** But she **sometimes becomes moody** and gets angry easily.
傑森：　通常是這樣沒錯，但她有時會變得很情緒化，很容易就發怒。

Vivian: Have you asked her what's wrong?
薇薇安：你有問過她是什麼問題嗎？

Jason: Of course. But the reasons are always **trivial**. Sometimes she just **can't put her finger on it**.
傑森：　當然有問，但原因都很微不足道，她有時甚至說不出是什麼問題。

Vivian: Doesn't this happen on a **monthly basis**?
薇薇安：這種情況該不會是按月發生的吧？

Jason: Umm...come to think of it, I think it does.
傑森：　嗯…回想起來，好像是這樣。

Vivian: Then it's nothing to worry about. Just give her some hot drink next time. I think she's just suffering from **menstrual mood swings**.
薇薇安：那就沒有什麼好擔心的，下次給她一杯熱飲就好了。我覺得她只是因為生理期而引起了情緒波動。

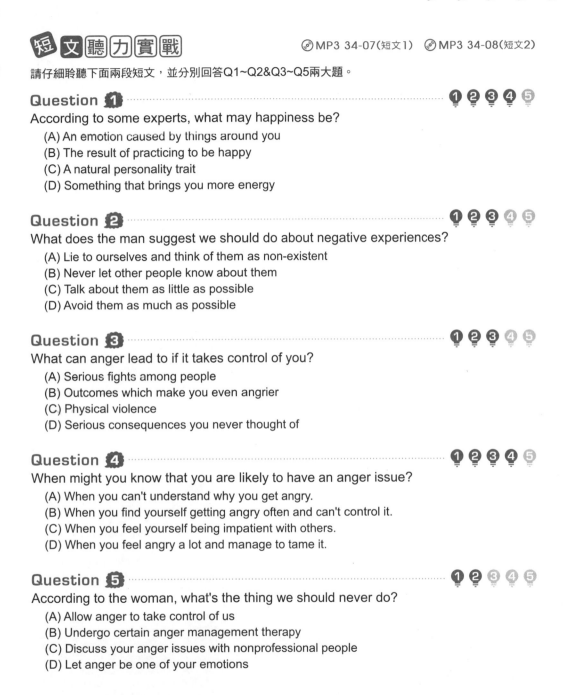

短文聽力實戰

MP3 34-07(短文1)　　MP3 34-08(短文2)

請仔細聆聽下面兩段短文，並分別回答Q1~Q2&Q3~Q5兩大題。

Question 1

According to some experts, what may happiness be?

(A) An emotion caused by things around you

(B) The result of practicing to be happy

(C) A natural personality trait

(D) Something that brings you more energy

Question 2

What does the man suggest we should do about negative experiences?

(A) Lie to ourselves and think of them as non-existent

(B) Never let other people know about them

(C) Talk about them as little as possible

(D) Avoid them as much as possible

Question 3

What can anger lead to if it takes control of you?

(A) Serious fights among people

(B) Outcomes which make you even angrier

(C) Physical violence

(D) Serious consequences you never thought of

Question 4

When might you know that you are likely to have an anger issue?

(A) When you can't understand why you get angry.

(B) When you find yourself getting angry often and can't control it.

(C) When you feel yourself being impatient with others.

(D) When you feel angry a lot and manage to tame it.

Question 5

According to the woman, what's the thing we should never do?

(A) Allow anger to take control of us

(B) Undergo certain anger management therapy

(C) Discuss your anger issues with nonprofessional people

(D) Let anger be one of your emotions

答案與解析 ~answer

Answer 1 ◀)) (B)

根據一些專家所言，快樂可以是什麼呢？

- (A) 由週遭事件引發的情緒
- (B) 持續練習快樂的結果
- (C) 一種天生的人格特質
- (D) 能帶給人更多能量的事物

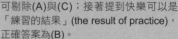

解析

解題的關鍵有兩處，首先必須聽出文章一開始提到情緒並非單純的「人格特質」或「受外界影響而引發的情況」，可剔除(A)與(C)；接著提到快樂可以是「練習的結果」(the result of practice)，正確答案為(B)。

Answer 2 ◀)) (C)

男性說我們應該怎麼面對那些負面經驗？

- (A) 欺騙自己那些事都不存在
- (B) 絕對不要讓其他人知道
- (C) 盡可能地少談論
- (D) 盡可能地避免

解析

直接與負面經驗(negative experiences)有關的答案，是男性提到要「盡量減少談論」(minimize the mention of)；在此句之前，男性有提到多往快樂的方面想，就能得到更多的正面能量，正確答案為(C)。

Answer 3 ◀)) (D)

當你被怒氣掌控時，可能會有什麼結果？

- (A) 人與人之間的激烈爭執
- (B) 讓你更加生氣的結果
- (C) 生理上的肢體暴力
- (D) 你從沒想過的嚴重結果

解析

解題關鍵在女性提到「被怒氣掌控」的話，可能會造成「無法想像的後果」(unthinkable consequences)。注意題目為「概括性的問題」，所以不能選如(A)(C)那樣過於侷限的情況，正確答案為(D)。

Answer 4 ◀)) (B)

你什麼時候能知道自己可能有憤怒方面的問題呢？

- (A) 當你無法理解自己憤怒的原因時。
- (B) 當你發現自己常生氣，無法控制時。
- (C) 當你感覺到你對其他人沒有耐性時。
- (D) 當你常生氣，且能控制住時。

解析

本題的關鍵在女性提到如果「經常性地」(regularly)感到一股「無法馴服的壞脾氣」(untamable temper)，那麼就有憤怒方面的問題。untamable為tamable「可制服的；可馴服的」的反義字，正確答案為(B)。

Answer 5 ◀)) (A)

根據女性所說，什麼是我們絕不應該做的事呢？

- (A) 讓憤怒控制你
- (B) 進行某些憤怒管理的療法
- (C) 和非專業人士討論你的憤怒問題
- (D) 讓憤怒成為自己的情緒之一

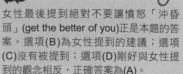

解析

女性最後提到絕對不要讓憤怒「沖昏頭」(get the better of you)正是本題的答案。選項(B)為女性提到的建議；選項(C)沒有被提到；選項(D)剛好與女性提到的觀念相反，正確答案為(A)。

 中英文內容

 短文 1
⊙慢速MP3 34-09　　◎正常速MP3 34-10

Being happy **is not merely** a personality trait or an emotion induced by external factors. As some experts suggest, happiness can be **the result of practice**. For instance, you may feel happy by actively listing the things that you are grateful for. The more you think of happiness, the more of this positive feeling you will receive. Also, practicing to **minimize the mention of negative experiences** is another tip. Thinking and talking about the positive things will not only bring you more energy, but also influence others. In the long run, you may be able to create a peaceful and great atmosphere around yourself.

快樂不僅是一種人格特質或被外部因素誘發的一種情緒。根據一些專家的說法，快樂其實可以是經由練習而得到的結果。舉例來說，當你主動列出那些讓你感謝的事情時，你會變得開心。你越常往快樂的那一面想，得到的正面能量就會越多。此外，盡量少談論負面的經驗也有幫助，多想想和討論那些正面樂觀的事情，這不僅能帶給你自己更多能量，還能影響周圍的人，最後你會發現周遭充斥的都是這種平和又安好的氛圍呢！

 短文 2
⊙慢速MP3 34-11　　◎正常速MP3 34-12

Anger is one of the natural emotions we have as human beings. However, when anger takes control of you, it can lead to **unthinkable consequences**. If you experience **untamable temper regularly**, then it is likely you have an anger issue and should undergo some kind of anger management therapy. Many people's social relationships with others can completely fall apart due to their anger issues. At work, colleagues and business associates might regard you as unprofessional if they can't reason with you rationally. When it comes to family or friends, they might fear your loss of control may lead to physical violence. So, you must remember this: **"never let anger get the better of you!"**

憤怒是人類的自然情感之一。然而，當你完全被怒氣掌控時，可能會造成無法想像的後果。如果你經常出現無法控制的壞脾氣，那麼你很可能有憤怒方面的問題，應該要進行一些憤怒管理的療法。許多人的人際關係會因為他們發怒的問題而完全瓦解。在工作上，同事和事業夥伴可能會因為無法跟你講道理，而覺得你不專業。在家人和朋友這一方面，他們則會擔心你的失控可能導致暴力行為。所以，千萬記得這一點：「絕對不要讓憤怒沖昏你的頭！」

Unit 5 閒話家常 The Daily Life

日常生活　娛樂活動　意見交流　特殊場合

短對話聽力實戰

MP3 35-01

下面將播放五組短對話，請仔細聆聽，再依對話內容答題。

Question 1

What does the woman say about her brother if he contacts her?

(A) He wants to chitchat with her.
(B) He wants someone to hear his complaints.
(C) He always brings bad news.
(D) He always has a request or wants something.

Question 2

Why doesn't the man like being tagged on Facebook?

(A) He doesn't like others knowing information about him.
(B) He doesn't like other people to see the pictures.
(C) Those who tag him are not his friends.
(D) He doesn't share his life on Facebook.

Question 3

What does the man find strange?

(A) People chat online when they can talk on the phone.
(B) People chat online when it's more natural to talk in person.
(C) The woman likes online chat rooms so much.
(D) People feel comfortable sitting next to each other.

Question 4

What is the man asking about?

(A) What to buy Ellie for her baby
(B) When Ellie's baby shower is
(C) When Ellie is supposed to give birth to her baby
(D) What they are due to help with the baby shower

Question 5

What is the man's suggestion to the woman?

(A) Hold a party to say goodbye to Jodie
(B) Expect Jodie's next trip to Taiwan
(C) Buy something for Jodie's farewell party
(D) Visit Jodie during the woman's holiday

答案與解析 ～answer

Answer 1 ◀》(D)
女性說如果她哥哥聯絡她的話，是怎麼回事？

(A) 他想要和她閒話家常。

(B) 他希望她聽他抱怨發洩。

(C) 他總是會帶來壞消息。

(D) 他總是有些要求想拜託她。

解析
女性說只要她的哥哥主動連絡，肯定是「別有目的」。after something是「有特別目地；追求某事/某人」的口語用法，正確答案為(D)。

Answer 2 ◀》(A)
男性為何不喜歡在臉書上被標記呢？

(A) 他不喜歡讓其他人得知他的資訊。

(B) 他不想讓其他人看到照片。

(C) 那些標記他的人並非他的朋友。

(D) 他不想在臉書上分享自己的生活。

解析
解題關鍵在最後一句，男性提到自己不喜歡「行蹤被人公開」，whereabouts指「行蹤；下落」(有關男性的「資訊」)，be made public則形容照片「被他人標記」。

Answer 3 ◀》(B)
男性覺得什麼事情很奇怪？

(A) 明明可以用電話聊，人們卻在線上聊天。

(B) 面對面聊天更自然時，卻選擇線上聊天。

(C) 女性這麼喜愛線上聊天室。

(D) 彼此坐在一起時，人們感到舒適。

解析
本題比較容易混淆的選項為(A)與(B)，請注意男性提到的「比鄰而坐」(sit next to each other)，在日常生活中，坐在隔壁的兩人不會特別用電話聯絡，因此正確答案為(B)。

Answer 4 ◀》(C)
男性在詢問什麼事情呢？

(A) 要買什麼給艾莉的小孩

(B) 艾莉的準媽媽嬰兒祝福派對是什麼時候

(C) 艾莉預計什麼時候生

(D) 準媽媽嬰兒祝福派對上，他們要做什麼

解析
解題時有兩個關鍵，第一個是a baby shower，指的是「準媽媽嬰兒祝福派對」，由此可知艾莉尚未生小孩；第二個解題關鍵為男性詢問的due date，因為話題圍繞著艾莉的生產，所以在此指的是「預產期」，正確答案為(C)。

Answer 5 ◀》(A)
男性給女性的建議是什麼呢？

(A) 舉辦派對向喬蒂道別

(B) 期待喬蒂下次再來臺灣旅遊

(C) 為了喬蒂的歡送會買東西

(D) 在女性放假的時候去找喬蒂

解析
a farewell party表示為了送別而舉辦的「歡送會」。如果沒有聽懂關鍵字farewell，也可以從女性一開始的話中得知喬蒂的假期將結束，合理推測她即將離開，正確答案為(A)。

中英文內容

⊙慢速MP3 35-02　　◎正常速MP3 35-03

短對話 1 *Conversation*

Bonnie: I knew it! Whenever my brother contacts me, he must be **after something**.
邦妮：　我就知道！只要我的哥哥聯絡我，一定別有目的。
Chris: Why do you say that?
克里斯：你為什麼這麼說？
Bonnie: Yesterday, he rang me up and asked me to do some translation work for him!
邦妮：　昨天他打電話給我，拜託我幫他翻譯東西！

短對話 2 *Conversation*

Kent:　I hate being tagged in others' photos on Facebook.
肯特：　我討厭在臉書上被標記在別人的照片中。
Eve:　Relax. That's just a way to share your life with your friends.
伊芙：　放輕鬆，那只是和朋友分享生活的一種方式而已。
Kent:　I simply don't like the feeling of my whereabouts **being made public**.
肯特：　我就是不喜歡行踪被公開的感覺。

短對話 3 *Conversation*

David:　Don't you think it's strange to see people **chatting online** while they're actually sitting next to each other?
大衛：　你不覺得明明坐在彼此身邊卻使用網路聊天很奇怪嗎？
Emily:　Well, some people seem to find it easier to communicate via technology.
艾蜜莉：有些人似乎覺得透過科技產品溝通比較容易。

短對話 4 *Conversation*

Kate:　Do you know Ellie is having a baby shower?
凱特：　你知不知道艾莉要辦個準媽媽嬰兒祝福派對？
Lenny: Oh, when is her **due date**?
藍尼：　喔，她的預產期是什麼時候啊？

短對話 5 *Conversation*

Mandy: How time flies. Jodie's trip to Taiwan is coming to an end.
曼蒂：　時間過得真快，喬蒂來臺灣的旅程就要結束了。
Luke:　How about we **hold a farewell party** for her?
路克：　我們幫她辦個歡送會如何？

326

長對話聽力實戰

MP3 35-04

請仔細聆聽下面的長對話,再依對話內容選擇正確答案。

Question ❶ .... ❶❷❸④⑤
What is the relationship between the man and the woman?

(A) They are university friends.

(B) They were classmates.

(C) They are mutual friends of the woman's husband.

(D) They are colleagues.

Question ❷ .... ❶❷③④⑤
What is the occasion in which the woman meets the man?

(A) A school reunion for former students

(B) A speed dating event for colleagues

(C) A farewell party for graduating students

(D) A family reunion for the woman

Question ❸ .... ❶❷③④⑤
Why didn't Mrs. Lin recognize the woman?

(A) Mrs. Lin's memory is not very good.

(B) The woman's outfit is different from what she normally wears.

(C) Mrs. Lin was in a hurry for some reason.

(D) The woman looks very different after all these years.

Question ❹ .... ❶②③④⑤
What did the woman do after secondary school?

(A) She traveled with her family to England.

(B) She went to England to get married.

(C) She went to England to study.

(D) Her family immigrated to England.

Question ❺ .... ❶❷❸④⑤
What's the reason the woman came back to her home country?

(A) To move back permanently

(B) To stay temporarily and visit her family

(C) To move there with her husband

(D) To find a new job

PART 7 人際互動

答案與解析 ～answer

Answer 1 (B)
對話中的男性與女性的關係為何？

(A) 他們是大學朋友。

(B) 他們以前是同學。

(C) 他們是女性丈夫的共同朋友。

(D) 他們是同事。

> **解析**
> 女性一開始詢問男性是否記得她，男性就說她是「六年級時坐他旁邊」(used to sit next to me in 6th grade)的同學，由6th grade可知是小學求學時期，因此不能選(A)或(D)，正確答案為(B)。

Answer 2 (A)
女性遇到男性的場合是哪裡？

(A) 校友們的同學會

(B) 同事間的快速約會

(C) 畢業生的歡送會

(D) 女性的家庭聚會

> **解析**
> 題目中的occasion問的是「場合」，解題關鍵在school reunion(同學會)，後面甚至提到他們以前的導師(our tutor)，除了(A)選項之外，其他不是缺少「重聚」的概念，就是少了「學校」的性質。

Answer 3 (D)
林老師為什麼沒有認出女性呢？

(A) 林老師的記憶力不怎麼好。

(B) 女性的服裝和她平常穿的很不同。

(C) 林老師當時忙著去處理其他事。

(D) 女性的外貌這些年來變了很多。

> **解析**
> 女性提到自己巧遇導師，但老師並沒有認出她(didn't recognize)，男性則說她似乎和他記憶中的模樣「有很大的不同」。be different from表示「區別；不同」，正確答案為(D)。

Answer 4 (C)
女性中學畢業後做了什麼？

(A) 和她家人到英國旅行。

(B) 為了結婚而去英國。

(C) 為了唸書而去英國。

(D) 她的家人移民到英國。

> **解析**
> 女性提到自己目前定居英國，男性問道她家人是否「移民」(emigrate)，女性否認，所以不能選(D)；她接著解釋自己中學畢業後就到英國念書，關鍵為after secondary school，正確答案為(C)。

Answer 5 (B)
女性回到自己國家的原因是什麼呢？

(A) 永久地搬回來住

(B) 為了看望家人所以回來一陣子

(C) 和她丈夫一起搬回來

(D) 為了找一份新工作

> **解析**
> 當男性詢問女性的丈夫是否有一同前來參加同學會時，她回答自己因為要「看望家人」(visit my family)所以獨自前來(came back alone)，正確答案為(B)。

 中英文內容

⊙ 慢速MP3 35-05　　◎ 正常速MP3 35-06

Tiffany: Hi, Jerry. Do you remember me? I'm Tiffany.
蒂芬妮：嗨，傑瑞，你還記得我嗎？我是蒂芬妮。

Jerry: Of course! You used to **sit next to me in 6th grade**.
傑瑞：　當然記得！你六年級時坐我旁邊。

Tiffany: This **school reunion** is making me very nostalgic.
蒂芬妮：這場同學會真是讓我感到懷念。

Jerry: Definitely. All the memories just come flooding back.
傑瑞：　就是啊，回憶一下子都湧上心頭了。

Tiffany: I just bumped into **our tutor** Mrs. Lin. She didn't recognize me.
蒂芬妮：我剛剛碰到我們的導師林老師，但她沒認出我。

Jerry: Well, you do **seem very different from what I remember**.
傑瑞：　你的確跟我記憶中有很大的不同。

Tiffany: I have kept in touch with Janet, but I don't see her much since I live in England now.
蒂芬妮：我跟珍妮特一直有連絡，但我們不常碰面，因為我住在英國。

Jerry: Did your family emigrate?
傑瑞：　你的家人移民過去嗎？

Tiffany: No. I went there to **study after secondary school**. I met my husband there, too.
蒂芬妮：不，我中學後去那裡讀書，我跟我丈夫也是在那裡認識的。

Jerry: I see. Is he with you today?
傑瑞：　原來如此，那他今天有跟妳一起來嗎？

Tiffany: No. He has work to do. I came back alone to **visit my family**.
蒂芬妮：不，他有工作要忙，我自己回來看望我的家人。

 短 文 聽 力 實 戰   ⊘MP3 35-07(短文1)   ⊘MP3 35-08(短文2)

請仔細聆聽下面兩段短文，並分別回答Q1~Q2&Q3~Q5兩大題。

Question 1

What does the woman's family prefer to do regarding gatherings?

  (A) Go to a fancy restaurant for dinner

  (B) Order from local takeaways

  (C) Cook and prepare dishes by themselves

  (D) Go traveling together

Question 2

What can be inferred from this article?

  (A) The woman doesn't like her family reunions much.

  (B) The woman's family enjoys cooking a lot.

  (C) The woman sometimes hopes to eat out.

  (D) The woman loves the way they hold gatherings.

Question 3

How may people feel when they count down on New Year's Eve?

  (A) They remember a lot of shopping they need to do.

  (B) They find excuses to stay up late.

  (C) They want to travel abroad to count down.

  (D) They feel a strong sense of hope.

Question 4

When did the man and his friends go to New York?

  (A) Just before the year 2000

  (B) After the year 2000

  (C) The year after the year 2000

  (D) On New Year's Day

Question 5

What did the man see on the TV screen in Times Square?

  (A) A concert for the New Year countdown

  (B) A live broadcast of countdown all around the world

  (C) The fireworks in his hometown

  (D) Tourists from around the world

答案與解析 ～answer

Answer 1 (C)
家族聚會的時候，女性的家人喜歡怎麼做？

(A) 去某間精緻的餐廳吃晚餐

(B) 從當地的外帶餐館點餐

(C) 自己下廚，準備餐點

(D) 一起外出旅遊

> **解析**
> 女性講到Unlike...開頭的句子時，提到很多其他家庭喜歡上餐廳吃飯，因為比較方便，但她家人卻寧願「在家下廚、吃飯」(cook and eat at home)，正確答案為(C)。

Answer 2 (D)
從本篇文章中可以推測出什麼呢？

(A) 女性沒有很喜歡家族聚會。

(B) 女性的家人非常喜歡下廚。

(C) 女性有時候會希望出去吃。

(D) 女性非常喜愛她家族聚會的方式。

> **解析**
> 本題的答案在文章的最後，女性提到自己希望「家族能一直以這種方式聚會」(continue having our family reunion this way)，可推測出她非常喜愛這種家庭式的溫馨聚會，正確答案為(D)。

Answer 3 (D)
跨年倒數會讓人們產生什麼樣的感覺呢？

(A) 他們會想到有很多東西要買。

(B) 他們找到熬夜的理由。

(C) 他們會想要出國參加倒數。

(D) 他們會有種充滿希望的感覺。

> **解析**
> 解題關鍵在男性描述大家聚在一起倒數時，會產生什麼氛圍，根據文章所說，會有股「充滿希望的感覺」(a great sense of hope)，正確答案為(D)。

Answer 4 (A)
男性和朋友們什麼時候去的紐約？

(A) 在2000年之前

(B) 在2000年之後

(C) 2000年後的一年

(D) 在過新年的那一天

> **解析**
> 男性提到自己很幸運，千禧年(Millennium)的時候能在紐約跨年，除了理解單字之外，男性也提到他們預定了飯店，在紐約觀光，然後在跨年當天到時代廣場慶祝，正確答案為(A)。

Answer 5 (B)
男性在時代廣場的大螢幕上看到什麼？

(A) 跨年音樂會

(B) 世界各地的倒數實況

(C) 他家鄉的煙火

(D) 世界各地的遊客

> **解析**
> 描述倒數的情況時，男性提到時代廣場的大螢幕播放「世界各地進行倒數的景象」，重點單字有broadcast(播放；轉播)與countdown(倒數)，正確答案為(B)。

中英文內容

短文1

⊙慢速MP3 35-09　　◎正常速MP3 35-10

Our family gatherings are always a delightful mix of chatting, eating lots of food and relaxing in the company of family. **Unlike many other families**, which tend to go to restaurants for convenience, my family prefers to **cook and eat at home**. When we have a gathering, each family prepares a dish in advance. Sometimes we bring the ingredients to cook together. After the meal, the youth will do the washing up. We don't need to be worried about when to leave since we are not in a restaurant. I just hope we **continue having our family reunion this way**.

　　我們的家族聚會一直以來都讓人很開心，大家聚在一起聊天、吃東西，並在家人的陪伴下放鬆。和其他為了便利性上餐館的家庭不同，我的家人反而喜歡在家下廚、吃飯。當我們聚會時，每一家都會提前準備一道菜，我們有時候也會帶食材來，一起下廚準備餐點，餐後年輕人則會負責洗碗。因為不是在餐館用餐，所以我們不用擔心散會的時間，希望我們家族能一直以這種方式聚會。

短文2

⊙慢速MP3 35-11　　◎正常速MP3 35-12

New Year's Eve has always been a special occasion for me. When people gather round and count down together, there is such a great sense of **hope**. I was lucky to have been in New York for the New Year going into the **Millennium**. My friends and I booked a hotel and enjoyed the sightseeing and shopping. On New Year's Eve, we went to Times Square to celebrate. As we watched the giant screen broadcasting **the countdown from around the world**, I had an indescribable feeling. The fireworks we saw that day were the most spectacular ones I had ever seen. Even now, I still remember that scene vividly. It is one of the experiences I'll never forget.

　　跨年對我來說一直是個特別的日子。當人們圍在一起倒數時，會有充滿希望的感覺。我很幸運，在千禧年的時候能在紐約跨年。我朋友和我訂了飯店，享受了觀光和購物，接著在跨年當天去時代廣場慶祝。當我們看著大螢幕上世界各地進行倒數計時的畫面時，我內心有股難以形容的感覺。那天觀賞的煙火是我所見過最壯觀的，就算到了現在，我都還清楚記得那一幕，那是我永遠不會忘記的經驗。

PART

社會議題

深度對談、意見交流，搞定專門領域，
聽力 K.O 沒問題！

Unit
1

氣候與自然 Nature

日常生活　　娛樂活動　　意見交流　　特殊場合

短對話聽力實戰

🎧 MP3 36-01

下面將播放五組短對話，請仔細聆聽，再依對話內容答題。

Question ❶　　　　　　　　　　　　❶❷❸❹❺
What is worrying the man?

(A) He finds it hard to decide what to wear when it turns cold.
(B) He only has one jacket for all types of weather.
(C) The trend of more extreme weather conditions
(D) The weather might suddenly change when he is in the office.

Question ❷　　　　　　　　　　　　❶❷❸❹❺
What advice does the woman give the man?

(A) Put on sunscreen when he goes to India
(B) Be aware of the sun and use sunscreen
(C) Use the highest SPF factor sunscreen
(D) Don't underestimate how much sunscreen can cost

Question ❸　　　　　　　　　　　　❶❷❸❹❺
What does the man think of the hiking trip?

(A) The scenery is not worth the work.
(B) It is a piece of cake for him.
(C) It is too difficult for him.
(D) It is beyond his expectation.

Question ❹　　　　　　　　　　　　❶❷❸❹❺
Why is the government bringing out a new policy on recycling?

(A) Many people still don't recycle correctly.
(B) Nobody in the city does recycling.
(C) People find it too bothersome to do recycling.
(D) Most people lack the knowledge about recycling.

Question ❺　　　　　　　　　　　　❶❷❸❹❺
What is the theme of the World Earth Summit?

(A) Certain substitute resources
(B) The ways to deal with pollution
(C) The sustainability of our environment
(D) Participation in a protest

答案與解析 ～answer

Answer 1 ◀》(C)
男性在擔憂什麼事情呢？

(A) 天氣變冷時，他不知道要穿什麼。

(B) 不管什麼天氣，他只有一件外套可穿。

(C) 極端天氣變化增加的趨勢

(D) 他在辦公室的時候，天氣就突然變化。

解析
詢問男性擔憂的事情時，重點要放在關鍵詞「極端天氣」(extreme weather)。對話一開始就點出他擔心極端天氣發生的狀況在「增加」，正確答案為(C)。

Answer 2 ◀》(B)
女性給男性的建議是什麼？

(A) 去印度的時候要擦防曬乳

(B) 注意日曬陽光並使用防曬乳

(C) 使用防曬係數最高的防曬乳

(D) 不要低估防曬乳的價格

解析
女性建議男性擦防曬乳，片語put on在此指「塗抹在身上」的動作；另外，對話中的Indian summer是指秋天裡變熱的那幾天，也就是我們常說的「秋老虎」，與印度完全無關，正確答案為(B)。

Answer 3 ◀》(C)
男性覺得這次的登山行程如何呢？

(A) 風景不值得他爬這麼辛苦。

(B) 對他來說非常容易。

(C) 對他來說太過困難。

(D) 出乎他的意料之外。

解析
解題關鍵在片語out of one's depth，表示「對某人的程度來說太難；一竅不通」，由此可知男性覺得這次的登山行程太困難。另外，也可以從女性的勸說推測男性想放棄，同樣能藉此剔除部分選項。

Answer 4 ◀》(A)
針對資源回收，政府為何要實施新政策？

(A) 很多人的回收仍然沒有做徹底。

(B) 該城市沒有人在做資源回收。

(C) 人們覺得做資源回收太麻煩。

(D) 大多數人缺乏對資源回收的認識。

解析
女性一開始提到政府要實施新的獎勵措施(incentives)，接著提到本題答案，這樣的措施是為了「鼓勵大眾將回收做得更徹底」，關鍵字為thorough(徹底的)，由此可推測出正確答案為(A)。

Answer 5 ◀》(C)
這屆地球高峰會的主題是什麼？

(A) 某些可取代的資源

(B) 處理汙染問題的方法

(C) 我們環境的永續經營

(D) 參加一場抗議遊行

解析
女孩邀請男孩參加地球高峰會議(World Earth Summit)，當男孩詢問主題時，她回答是關於「地球的永續發展」，關鍵字為sustainability，從動詞的sustain(維持)變化而來，正確答案為(C)。

短對話 1 *Conversation*

Danny: The **increase in extreme weather conditions** is very worrying.
丹尼：　極端天氣發生的頻率越來越高，真令人擔憂。
Penny: I know. It's particularly annoying when the weather changes all of a sudden.
佩妮：　對啊，天氣突然間就改變，實在很討厭。

短對話 2 *Conversation*

Kyle: 　I'm going to the beach since it won't be so hot in autumn.
凱爾：　我準備去海邊，因為秋天不會那麼熱。
Heather: Remember to put on lots of **sunscreen**. Don't underestimate **the viciousness of the Indian summer sun**.
海瑟：　記得塗上大量的防曬霜，別小看秋老虎的毒辣陽光。

短對話 3 *Conversation*

Dylan: Can we rest for a while? I think this hiking is **out of my depth**!
狄倫：　我們能休息一下嗎？這次的登山行程對我來說太困難了。
Wendy: Come on! Once we reach the top, you'll find it's worth it.
溫蒂：　拜託！一旦我們攻頂，你就會覺得很值得的。

短對話 4 *Conversation*

Tina: 　The local government is bringing out new incentives to encourage **more thorough recycling**.
蒂娜：　當地政府要實施新的獎勵措施，以鼓勵大眾的回收做得更徹底。
Derek: So what's their new initiative?
德瑞克：所以他們採取的新措施是什麼？
Tina: 　For those who use the specified trash bags, they can get the trash bags for free.
蒂娜：　如果你使用專用垃圾袋，就能免費拿新的垃圾袋。

短對話 5 *Conversation*

Vicky: 　I'm attending the World Earth Summit tomorrow. Do you want to join me?
維琪：　我明天要去參加這屆的地球高峰會，你想參加嗎？
Andrew: What exactly is the summit about?
安德魯：這個高峰會到底是在講什麼？
Vicky: 　They will talk about **the sustainability of the Earth**.
維琪：　主題是「地球的永續發展」。

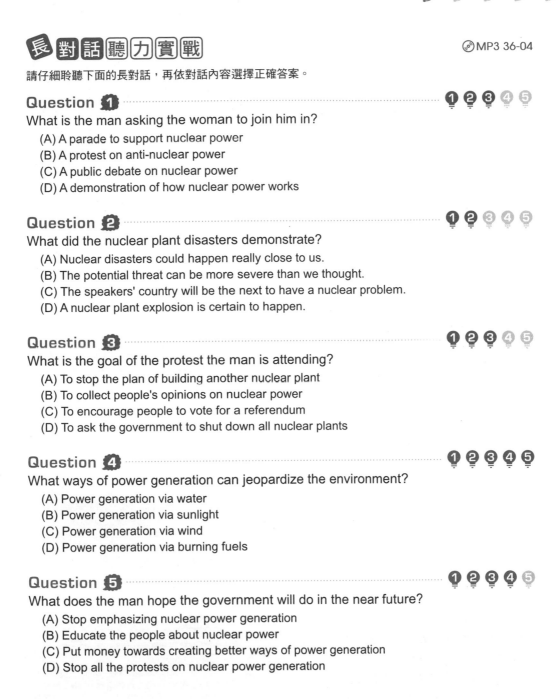

長對話聽力實戰

◎MP3 36-04

請仔細聆聽下面的長對話，再依對話內容選擇正確答案。

Question 1 ···· ① ② ③ ④ ⑤
What is the man asking the woman to join him in?

(A) A parade to support nuclear power
(B) A protest on anti-nuclear power
(C) A public debate on nuclear power
(D) A demonstration of how nuclear power works

Question 2 ···· ① ② ③ ④ ⑤
What did the nuclear plant disasters demonstrate?

(A) Nuclear disasters could happen really close to us.
(B) The potential threat can be more severe than we thought.
(C) The speakers' country will be the next to have a nuclear problem.
(D) A nuclear plant explosion is certain to happen.

Question 3 ···· ① ② ③ ④ ⑤
What is the goal of the protest the man is attending?

(A) To stop the plan of building another nuclear plant
(B) To collect people's opinions on nuclear power
(C) To encourage people to vote for a referendum
(D) To ask the government to shut down all nuclear plants

Question 4 ···· ① ② ③ ④ ⑤
What ways of power generation can jeopardize the environment?

(A) Power generation via water
(B) Power generation via sunlight
(C) Power generation via wind
(D) Power generation via burning fuels

Question 5 ···· ① ② ③ ④ ⑤
What does the man hope the government will do in the near future?

(A) Stop emphasizing nuclear power generation
(B) Educate the people about nuclear power
(C) Put money towards creating better ways of power generation
(D) Stop all the protests on nuclear power generation

答案與解析 ～answer

Answer 1 (B)
男性邀請女性和他一起參加什麼活動？

(A) 支持核能發電的遊行

(B) 反對核能發電的示威遊行

(C) 針對核電的辯論

(D) 展示核電如何運作的活動

解析

對話一開始，男性就詢問女性是否要一起參加「反核抗議」(anti-nuclear protest)，除了聽懂完整的關鍵字外，還能由anti-這個帶有「反對」意思的字首，推測出男性反對某物，如此也可得到正確答案(B)。

Answer 2 (B)
因核電廠而引發的災害展示出什麼？

(A) 核電災害可能離我們很近。

(B) 潛在威脅可能比我們想像的嚴重。

(C) 說話者的國家會是下一個受災區。

(D) 核電廠的爆炸一定會發生。

解析

男性在對話中提到俄羅斯與日本的核災例子，點出核災可能比我們想像中的更嚴重，關鍵句型為... than we imagined，正確答案為(B)。這裡要注意關鍵句中的can be more serious表示「可能性」，所以不能選(D)。

Answer 3 (A)
男性參加的示威遊行，其目的為何？

(A) 阻止新核電廠的建設計畫

(B) 蒐集大眾對核電的看法

(C) 鼓勵大眾投票支持公投

(D) 要求政府關閉所有的核電廠

解析

男性提到繞區遊行的目的，在於得到人民支持，以中止目前正在進行的「新核電廠的建設計畫」，正確答案為(A)。be planning使用現在進行式，表示現在正在進行的計畫。

Answer 4 (D)
什麼樣的發電方式會對環境產生危害？

(A) 水力發電

(B) 太陽能發電

(C) 風力發電

(D) 火力發電

解析

女性提到她希望很快能找到其他的發電方式，而且不會像火力發電(fossil fuel power)那樣對環境造成危害。片語do harm to sth./sb.表示「對某物/某人造成損害」，正確答案為(D)。

Answer 5 (C)
男性希望政府近期內會做什麼事？

(A) 別再強調核能發電

(B) 教導人民核能發電的知識

(C) 將預算投資在更好的發電方式上

(D) 停止所有反對核能發電的抗議活動

解析

男性最後提到風力或太陽能發電就是很理想的(ideal)方式，希望「政府未來能將資源投注在正確的方式上」。invest in表示投資，在此指將政府資源用來開發更環保、無害的發電方式上，正確答案為(C)。

中英文內容

⊙ 慢速MP3 36-05　　◎ 正常速MP3 36-06

Mason: Would you like to join me in our **anti-nuclear protest** this Saturday?
梅森：　你這個星期六要不要和我一起參加反核抗議？

Laura:　Absolutely. I'm a firm protester against the building of more nuclear plants.
蘿拉：　當然要，我堅決反對建核電廠。

Mason: Me, too. The long-term damage that comes after the short-term benefits can be really frightening.
梅森：　我也是，在短期利益過後的長期傷害很嚇人。

Laura:　Also, we must not overlook the potential threats it can cause.
蘿拉：　另外，我們也不能忽視核電的潛在威脅。

Mason: The nuclear disasters in Russia and Japan have demonstrated that **the damage can be more serious than we imagined**.
梅森：　俄羅斯和日本的核災就證明了核電的破壞可能比我們想像的更嚴重。

Laura:　And I feel so grateful yet sad to see the workers putting their lives at risk to monitor the reactor.
蘿拉：　看到那些工人冒著生命危險在監控反應爐，就讓我感到既感激又難過。

Mason: We are going to march around the block to gain more support for terminating **the new nuclear plant in planning**.
梅森：　我們打算繞街區遊行，取得更多人支持，以終止新核電廠的建設計畫。

Laura:　I hope we'll soon find other ways to generate energy without **doing harm to our environment** like that done by **fossil fuel power**.
蘿拉：　希望我們很快就能找到其他方式發電，又不像火力發電那樣會損害環境。

Mason: Technology utilizing wind and solar energy is truly ideal. I hope our government will soon start **investing in the right ways** of generating power.
梅森：　像是利用風力和太陽能的科技就非常理想，希望政府能很快開始將資源投資在正確的發電方式上。

短文聽力實戰

MP3 36-07（短文1）　　MP3 36-08（短文2）

請仔細聆聽下面兩段短文，並分別回答Q1~Q2&Q3~Q5兩大題。

Question 1
What climatic feature worsens Beijing's smog problem?

(A) Very infrequent rain
(B) Gradual industrialization
(C) Huge amounts of traffic
(D) Poor air quality monitoring

Question 2
What's the negative influence of the growth in traffic in Beijing?

(A) The sale of paper masks
(B) The release of a lot of carbon dioxide
(C) Little rain
(D) The decrease in the number of car owners

Question 3
What's the impact on animals due to global warming?

(A) They're under the risk of disappearing all together.
(B) They have to change their habitat every year.
(C) More and more get scared of human beings.
(D) They are being hunted by more and more people.

Question 4
What is the effect of global warming on polar bears?

(A) A rapid increase in the number of them
(B) A steady increase in the number of them
(C) A stable number of them
(D) A fast decrease in the number of them

Question 5
As more and more ice melts, what might happen to the polar bears?

(A) They might need to fight with each other for food.
(B) They might need to pray for food.
(C) They might need to travel longer distances for food.
(D) They might need to sleep less to get food.

答案與解析 ～answer

Answer 1 ◀)) (A)
什麼樣的氣候因素加劇北京的煙霧汙染呢？

- (A) 非常罕見的雨
- (B) 逐漸工業化的過程
- (C) 大量的交通流量
- (D) 空氣監測做得不夠好

解析
解題時首先要認清題目問的是「氣候因素」(climatic feature)，因為文章除了提到答案關鍵字it hardly rains(幾乎不下雨)之外，其餘都是人為因素，因此本題答案選(A)。

Answer 2 ◀)) (B)
北京汽車數量的增長帶來什麼負面影響？

- (A) 紙口罩的銷售量
- (B) 大量的二氧化碳排放量
- (C) 很少下雨
- (D) 車主數量的減少

解析
談到汽車數量激增的負面影響，除了「交通擁塞」(traffic congestion)之外，就是造成空氣汙染的「碳排放量」(carbon emission)，正確答案為(B)。注意選項(A)並非直接影響，而且紙口罩的銷售不能定義為「負面」。

Answer 3 ◀)) (A)
全球暖化對動物的衝擊為何？

- (A) 牠們有全數消失的風險。
- (B) 牠們每年必須改變棲息地。
- (C) 越來越多動物懼怕人類。
- (D) 越來越多人獵殺牠們。

解析
題目問的是對動物(animal)的影響，所以重點必須放在「瀕臨絕種」(become endangered species)的內容上，選項(A)的內容最接近。選項(B)有可能發生，但並非文中直接提到的事情。

Answer 4 ◀)) (D)
全球暖化對北極熊的影響為何？

- (A) 數量急速增加
- (B) 數量逐步增加
- (C) 穩定的數量
- (D) 數量快速減少

解析
談到北極熊的棲息數量(the polar bear population)，文中提到全球暖化是造成北極熊「急速減少」的主因，關鍵在a rapid decline，單字rapid意指「迅速的」，正確答案為(D)。

Answer 5 ◀)) (C)
當雪融得越來越多時，北極熊可能會怎樣？

- (A) 彼此為了食物爭奪。
- (B) 必須祈求有食物可吃。
- (C) 必須到更遠的地方找食物。
- (D) 必須少睡一點，以找尋食物。

解析
文章最後提到隨著雪融的情況惡化，北極熊遲早必須「游往更北邊以捕捉獵物」(swim further north...)，指出了地域的移動，符合這個概念的只有(C)。

中英文內容

短文 1　　　　　　　　　　　⊙慢速MP3 36-09　　⊙正常速MP3 36-10

In certain advanced and developing countries, rapid industrialization has made air pollution a serious matter. For instance, the air quality in Beijing has been decreasing as the country becomes more industrialized. **The smog in the city** is exacerbated by the fact **it hardly rains**. To make the matter worse, the number of cars on Beijing's streets has been multiplying at an astounding rate, which causes traffic congestion as well as contributes to **enormous carbon emissions**. The air quality monitor reading often suggests Beijing's air quality is "hazardous" to people's health. You may see some people on the streets wearing paper masks.

在某些先進國家和發展中國家，快速工業化使得空氣汙染成為一項嚴重的問題。舉例來說，北京的空氣品質就隨著它的工業化程度而不斷下降。因著北京幾乎不下雨的氣候，城市中的煙霧汙染更加嚴重。讓問題變得更糟的另一個原因是，北京的汽車數目以驚人的速度倍增，這項事實不僅導致交通擁塞，也成為碳排放量的主要來源。空氣品質監測儀器的測量結果往往顯示北京的空氣品質已達「危害民眾健康」的標準，在街上，你會看到一些人戴著紙口罩。

短文 2　　　　　　　　　　　⊙慢速MP3 36-11　　⊙正常速MP3 36-12

The extent of global warming is growing at a shocking rate. Not only do human beings suffer from natural disasters, but also many animals are becoming **endangered species**. An example of this is polar bears, which are under threat of extinction due to the climate change, rather than of being hunted. Scientists are blaming global warming as the main cause of **a rapid decline** in the polar bear population. As the situation worsens, more and more ice melts, which greatly affects the bears' habitats. Sooner or later, polar bears may have to **swim further north each year to reach their prey**. And this would put them in greater danger of drowning or starving to death.

全球暖化的程度正以驚人的速度上升。不僅是人類因為自然災害而受到影響，許多動物也成為瀕危絕種的物種。其中一個例子是北極熊，和被捕獵的數量相比，北極熊瀕臨絕種的最大原因反而是氣候變遷的問題。科學家們說全球暖化是北極熊數量急劇下降的主因。隨著氣候的惡化，北極冰融化，很快地，北極熊就必須年年游往更北邊以捕捉獵物，因此他們淹死或餓死的風險更大。

Unit 2 社會秩序 The Order

📺 日常生活　🎤 娛樂活動　✏️ 意見交流　🔖 特殊場合

短對話聽力實戰

🎧 MP3 37-01

下面將播放五組短對話，請仔細聆聽，再依對話內容答題。

Question 1

What's the woman's attitude towards the vagrants?

(A) She'd rather donate money online.
(B) She doesn't have the money for them.
(C) She doesn't think those people need help.
(D) She doesn't want to be tricked by dishonest people.

Question 2

According to the woman, what happened to Amy?

(A) She experienced an ATM crime and lost money.
(B) She was a victim of an ATM robbery.
(C) She gave the victims half of her savings.
(D) She lost her purse and a lot of money.

Question 3

What does the man say might have happened to the woman?

(A) She might be kidnapped.
(B) She might be a target for a ransom scam.
(C) She might have to pay some money for her son.
(D) Her son might ask her to transfer money.

Question 4

Why is the boy late for class?

(A) He was at the scene when a bomb exploded.
(B) He planned a bomb attack and carried out the plan.
(C) The police on the Underground carried out a body search on him.
(D) The bomb attack was serious, so all the trains were delayed.

Question 5

What does the man suggest the woman do?

(A) Donate to a charity with him
(B) Read more current comic books
(C) Donate her comic books to children in Gaza
(D) Read the news to know what's happening in the world

答案與解析 ～answer

Answer 1 🔊 (D)
女性對遊民的態度是什麼？

(A) 她寧願上網捐錢。

(B) 她沒有能給他們的錢。

(C) 她不覺得那些人需要幫助。

(D) 她不想要被人欺騙。

解析

當男性提到有些遊民可能是騙人的時候，女性說明了自己的態度，她不介意給錢，因此可剔除(A)；但是「如果被騙了，會感到不舒服」(uncomfortable)。單字con當動詞有「欺詐」的意思，正確答案為(D)。

Answer 2 🔊 (A)
根據女性所言，艾咪發生了什麼事？

(A) 她遭遇ATM詐騙事件，損失了很多錢。

(B) 她是ATM搶劫事件的受害者。

(C) 她給了受害者一半的財產。

(D) 她遺失了皮包和很多錢。

解析
解題關鍵在片語fall victim to，表示「成為…的受害者」，後面的單字scam則指「詐取；騙局」；接著說她損失了大半積蓄(savings)，正確答案為(A)。注意選項(B)的robbery指的是「搶劫」，與詐騙的意思不同。

Answer 3 🔊 (B)
根據男性所言，女性可能發生了什麼事？

(A) 她也許會被綁架。

(B) 她也許是綁架詐騙的目標。

(C) 她也許必須為了兒子付錢。

(D) 她的兒子也許會要求她轉帳。

解析

女性接到一通電話，說她兒子被綁架，ransom意指「贖金」。但請注意題目問的是男性認為發生了什麼事，因此重點要放在男性提到的may be a scam(騙局)，正確答案為(B)。

Answer 4 🔊 (C)
男孩上課為什麼會遲到？

(A) 他剛好在炸彈爆炸的現場。

(B) 他計畫了炸彈攻擊並加以實行。

(C) 地鐵站的警員對他進行搜身。

(D) 炸彈攻擊的規模很大，火車都因此誤點。

解析
男孩一開始就為了自己的遲到道歉，並跟著說自己在地鐵站「被搜身」(a body search)。注意之後提到的炸彈攻擊，是已經發生過的事件，並非男孩的親身經歷，正確答案為(C)。

Answer 5 🔊 (D)
男性建議女性做什麼？

(A) 和他一起捐款給慈善機構

(B) 閱讀新一點的漫畫書

(C) 將她的漫畫書捐給加薩的小孩

(D) 閱讀新聞以了解世界各處發生的事

解析

講到加薩被空襲的新聞，女性完全不清楚，所以男性建議她「多注意時事新聞」(read more on current affairs)，正確答案為(D)。注意漫畫書是男性建議「少看」的東西，別被(B)(C)混淆了。

短對話 1 *Conversation*

John: Do you know some vagrants on the streets begging for money could be frauds?

約翰： 你知道街上有些乞討的遊民可能是騙人的嗎？

Donna: Really? I don't mind giving them money, but it makes me **uncomfortable** knowing I **might be conned**.

唐娜： 真的嗎？我不介意給錢，但想到我可能會被騙就很不舒服。

短對話 2 *Conversation*

Jessica:Did you hear that Amy **fell victim to** an ATM scam recently? She lost nearly half of her **savings**!

潔西卡：你有聽說艾咪成了ATM詐騙的受害者嗎？她損失將近一半的積蓄！

Harry: Oh no! So what is she going to do now?

哈利： 哦不！那她接下來打算怎麼做？

短對話 3 *Conversation*

Anna: My God! I got a phone call saying my son is being **held for ransom**!

安娜： 天啊！我接到一通電話，說我兒子人被綁架要贖金！

Peter: Calm down. This may just be **a scam**!

彼得： 先冷靜下來，這可能是一個騙局！

短對話 4 *Conversation*

Henry: Sorry, I'm late. I was stopped on the Underground for **a body search**.

亨利： 對不起，我遲到了，我剛剛在地鐵被搜身。

Lisa: How come?

莉莎： 怎麼會這樣呢？

Henry: The police are on high alert because of the recent bomb attack.

亨利： 警方因為最近的炸彈客攻擊而處於高度警惕。

短對話 5 *Conversation*

Tony: The news on the recent air raid in Gaza is shocking.

東尼： 近期加薩被空襲的新聞真令人震驚。

Katie: An air raid? What's that all about?

凱蒂： 空襲事件？那是怎麼回事啊？

Tony: You should **read more on current affairs** and fewer comic books.

東尼： 你應該多注意時事新聞，少看點漫畫書。

長 對 話 聽 力 實 戰

MP3 37-04

請仔細聆聽下面的長對話，再依對話內容選擇正確答案。

Question 1

What was the public referendum held on last Thursday about?

(A) It was about Scotland's independence.

(B) It was about a riot in Glasgow.

(C) It was about the crowds' celebration.

(D) It was about the policy-making power.

Question 2

What news did the woman see?

(A) A riot took place in Scotland

(B) A warning of a riot in advance

(C) A riot that happened in Glasgow

(D) The Prime Minister's final decision

Question 3

What happened to the independence supporters after the vote?

(A) They asked for another referendum.

(B) Their actions were restricted during the riot.

(C) They were provoked by the oppositions' actions.

(D) They didn't take any action during the riot.

Question 4

What did the UK prime minister promise?

(A) To give more political power to Scotland

(B) To give more nuclear power to Scotland

(C) To make more policies for Scotland

(D) To change the power plant policies in Scotland

Question 5

What does the government seem to be doing about some serious issues?

(A) They seem to be making new laws related to issues.

(B) They seem to ignore the issues on purpose.

(C) They seem to be discussing the issues for a long time.

(D) They seem to be making policy adjustments.

答案與解析 ～answer

Answer 1 🔊 (A)
上週四舉辦的公投是關於什麼的？

(A) 關於蘇格蘭的獨立與否。

(B) 關於格拉斯哥的暴動。

(C) 關於大眾的慶祝活動。

(D) 關於決策權力。

解析

題目中的關鍵字為「全民公投」(public referendum)與「上週四」(last Thursday)。女性在對話中有提到那一場公投是關於蘇格蘭的獨立與否，只要抓到關鍵字「蘇格蘭」(Scotland)，就能選出正確答案(A)。

Answer 2 🔊 (C)
女性看到了什麼新聞呢？

(A) 蘇格蘭發生的暴動

(B) 事前對暴動的警告

(C) 格拉斯哥發生的暴動

(D) 首相最後的決定

解析

女性提到她看到有關發生在格拉斯哥(Glasgow)動亂的「新聞報導」(the news coverage on a riot...)，抓緊「地點」跟「看到的事情」，就能選出正確答案(C)。

Answer 3 🔊 (C)
在投票結束之後，支持獨立的人怎麼樣了？

(A) 要求舉辦另一次的公投。

(B) 在暴動期間被限制活動。

(C) 被立場相反者的慶祝活動激怒。

(D) 他們在暴動期間沒有採取任何舉動。

解析

男性説公投結束後，有群眾聚集在一起慶祝(gather to celebrate)，因此「激怒了獨立派的支持者」。aggravate在口語上有「激怒」之意，正確答案為(C)。

Answer 4 🔊 (A)
英國首相給予了什麼樣的承諾呢？

(A) 給蘇格蘭更多的政治權力

(B) 給蘇格蘭更多核子武力

(C) 替蘇格蘭制定更多政策

(D) 改變蘇格蘭當地的發電政策

解析

文中提到首相承諾「把更多的決策權力發放給蘇格蘭」，關鍵字為policy-making powers，此為政治權力的一項，正確答案為(A)。注意(C)並沒有給蘇格蘭更多權力的意思。

Answer 5 🔊 (B)
面對部分嚴重議題，政府似乎採取什麼行動？

(A) 為了這些議題制定新法律。

(B) 刻意忽略這些議題。

(C) 花很多時間討論這些議題。

(D) 針對政策做調整。

解析

解題關鍵在對話最後，女性提到政府似乎會「無視部分嚴重議題」(many serious matters)，關鍵片語為turn one's back on，表示「無視；不理會」，正確答案為(B)。其他三個選項都是積極處理的行動，所以皆不合適。

⊙慢速MP3 37-05　　◎正常速MP3 37-06

Brian:　Last Thursday was a monumental day for Scotland.
布萊恩：上週四對蘇格蘭來說是極具意義的一天。

Lauren: Because of the public referendum on **Scotland's independence**?
蘿倫：　因為蘇格蘭的獨立公投嗎？

Brian:　That's right.
布萊恩：對啊。

Lauren: I saw **the news** coverage on **a riot that took place in Glasgow**.
蘿倫：　我看到了有關格拉斯哥騷亂的新聞報導。

Brian:　Yes. After the vote, some crowds gathered to celebrate, and this action **aggravated the independence supporters**.
布萊恩：是的，在公投後，一些群眾聚集在那裡慶祝，這個舉動挑起了獨立支持者的憤怒。

Lauren: Thank God it didn't develop into a large-scale riot.
蘿倫：　謝天謝地，這件事沒有發展成大規模的暴動。

Brian:　Even though the referendum was not passed, the Prime Minister promised to **yield more policy-making powers** to Scotland.
布萊恩：雖然公投沒通過，但首相承諾把更多的決策權力發放給蘇格蘭。

Lauren: I hope we will have that much say one day.
蘿倫：　希望有一天，我們也能有這麼多的發言權。

Brian:　For independence?
布萊恩：關於獨立這件事嗎？

Lauren: And for many serious matters that the government seems to be **turning their backs** on.
蘿倫：　還有那些被政府無視，但很嚴重的議題。

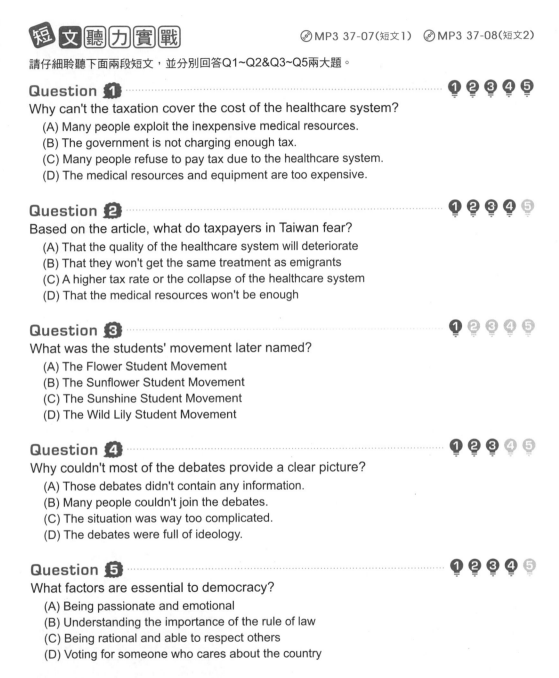

短 文 聽 力 實 戰   ◉MP3 37-07(短文1)   ◉MP3 37-08(短文2)

請仔細聆聽下面兩段短文，並分別回答Q1~Q2&Q3~Q5兩大題。

Question 1

Why can't the taxation cover the cost of the healthcare system?

- (A) Many people exploit the inexpensive medical resources.
- (B) The government is not charging enough tax.
- (C) Many people refuse to pay tax due to the healthcare system.
- (D) The medical resources and equipment are too expensive.

Question 2

Based on the article, what do taxpayers in Taiwan fear?

- (A) That the quality of the healthcare system will deteriorate
- (B) That they won't get the same treatment as emigrants
- (C) A higher tax rate or the collapse of the healthcare system
- (D) That the medical resources won't be enough

Question 3

What was the students' movement later named?

- (A) The Flower Student Movement
- (B) The Sunflower Student Movement
- (C) The Sunshine Student Movement
- (D) The Wild Lily Student Movement

Question 4

Why couldn't most of the debates provide a clear picture?

- (A) Those debates didn't contain any information.
- (B) Many people couldn't join the debates.
- (C) The situation was way too complicated.
- (D) The debates were full of ideology.

Question 5

What factors are essential to democracy?

- (A) Being passionate and emotional
- (B) Understanding the importance of the rule of law
- (C) Being rational and able to respect others
- (D) Voting for someone who cares about the country

答案與解析 ～answer

Answer 1 (A)
稅收為什麼不足以支付醫療資源的費用呢？

(A) 許多人過度利用不貴的醫療資源。

(B) 政府沒有收進足夠的稅收。

(C) 因為醫療系統，許多人拒絕納稅。

(D) 醫療資源與設備太昂貴。

解析

文章中提到臺灣方便的醫療體系同時也帶來財政負擔(financial burden)，財政負擔是結果，之後才敘述稅收之所以無法負擔的原因為許多人「濫用」(abuse)醫療服務，正確答案為(A)。

Answer 2 (C)
根據文章內容，臺灣納稅人會擔心什麼？

(A) 醫療的品質下降

(B) 他們無法取得與移民者相同的醫療

(C) 稅率提高或醫療體系崩解

(D) 醫療資源不足

解析

談完醫療資源被濫用的情況後，女性提到這樣會導致納稅人擔心「稅率調漲」與「醫療體系崩解」(collapse)。片語put up意指「調漲；調高」，正確答案為(C)。

Answer 3 (B)
文中的學生行為後來被怎麼稱呼？

(A) 花朵學生運動

(B) 太陽花學運

(C) 日光學運

(D) 野百合運動

解析

文章首先敘述了活動內容，接著提到這項活動之後被稱為「太陽花學運」(the Sunflower Student Movement)。關鍵在掌握name的動詞用法「命名」，正確答案為(B)。

Answer 4 (D)
為什麼大部分的辯論無法幫助我們理解事件內涵？

(A) 那些辯論裡面一點資訊都沒有。

(B) 很多人無法參與辯論。

(C) 事件的情況實在太過複雜。

(D) 辯論內容充斥著意識形態。

解析

男性提到了學運引起的辯論，並說這些辯論無法幫助我們理解事件內涵，其原因是當中「充斥著意識形態」(full of ideology)，正確答案為(D)。注意意識形態並不代表當中不具資訊，所以不能選(A)。

Answer 5 (C)
什麼是民主絕對需要的要素？

(A) 擁有熱情與情緒化

(B) 理解法治的重要性

(C) 維持理性並能尊重其他人

(D) 投票給關心國家的人

解析

文章最後提到民主絕對具備的兩項要素為「維持理性」(keep our rationality)和「尊重不同的想法」(be able to respect different voices)，voice在此指不同立場的發言，正確答案為(C)。

中英文內容

短文 1
⊙慢速MP3 37-09　　◎正常速MP3 37-10

　　Taiwan's healthcare system is really good since pubic healthcare resources are accessible to all citizens. However, the system also brings financial burden as the tax-generated funding is insufficient to cover the cost. Many people frequently **abuse** the relatively affordable **medical services**. Some Taiwanese emigrants abroad even come to Taiwan and benefit from the same discounted medical price even though they aren't paying taxes. Because of this, some taxpayers fear **tax rates will be put up** to help the government bear the cost, or even worse, that **the healthcare system will collapse**.

　　臺灣的醫療系統相當優秀，因為所有公民都能享有公共的醫療資源。然而，這樣的醫療體系也帶來了財政上的負擔，政府的稅收不足以支付醫療資源的花費。很多人經常濫用相比之下經濟實惠的醫療服務，甚至還有許多移居國外的臺灣人回來享有與納稅人同等的優惠醫療照顧，但是這些移民者根本就沒有繳稅。因為這樣的情況，所以納稅人擔心稅率可能會調漲，以幫助政府承擔醫療開銷，更壞的情況是連醫療系統都整個崩解。

短文 2
⊙慢速MP3 37-11　　◎正常速MP3 37-12

　　On March 18, 2014, a crowd of people, mainly students, climbed over the fence at the Legislative Yuan of Taiwan to occupy the premises. This action was related to the Cross-Strait Service Trade Agreement (CSSTA). Later, those students' action was named the "**Sunflower Student Movement**". No matter what the initial purpose of this movement was aiming at, it became controversial and aroused a lot of debates. Some people kept blaming the government and some emphasized how irrational those protestors were. If you look into the debates carefully, you'll find that most were **full of ideology** and thus didn't provide a clear picture of the issue. Democracy might not be easy to achieve, but **keeping our rationality** and **being able to respect different voices** are definitely essential.

　　2014年3月18日，一大群以學生為首的人，翻過柵欄佔領了臺灣立法院的議事廳，這次的事件與兩岸服務貿易協議(CSSTA)有關。這次行動被命名為「太陽花學運」。不論學運一開始的目的為何，它都變得很有爭議性，引起了各種辯論。有些人不斷責怪政府，有些人則強調抗議者的不理性之處。如果仔細研究，就能發現大部分的言論充斥著意識形態，無法幫助我們理解這個議題。民主或許不易達成，但維持理智與能尊重不同想法的胸襟是絕對必要的。

Unit 3

政治文化 The Politics

📄 日常生活　　🔊 娛樂活動　　✏️ 意見交流　　🚩 特殊場合

短 對 話 聽 力 實 戰

🎧 MP3 38-01

下面將播放五組短對話，請仔細聆聽，再依對話內容答題。

Question ❶ ·· ① ② ③ ④ ⑤

After hearing the man's words, what's the woman's reaction?

(A) She believes in politicians since the man said so.

(B) She thinks the economy will grow.

(C) She doesn't think politicians would care about social justice.

(D) She made a promise to her friend.

Question ❷ ·· ① ② ③ ④ ⑤

What is the woman going home for?

(A) For a business trip

(B) To vote in an election

(C) To visit her family members

(D) For a short holiday

Question ❸ ·· ① ② ③ ④ ⑤

Why does the man think it's unfair to hold elections on weekdays?

(A) Because most people have to work overtime.

(B) Because most companies don't let their workers vote.

(C) Because many voters won't vote after work.

(D) Because some voters cannot afford to take time off.

Question ❹ ·· ① ② ③ ④ ⑤

What do politicians often do to get elected?

(A) They blacken their opponents' name.

(B) They visit many families to leave a good impression.

(C) They promise something they can't do afterwards.

(D) They make lots of posters to promote themselves.

Question ❺ ·· ① ② ③ ④ ⑤

What damaged the reputation of the speakers' country?

(A) The rumors people spread about their country

(B) A corruption-related scandal that happened recently

(C) The government's way of making their promises come true

(D) The government's inability to handle certain cases

答案與解析 ～answer

Answer 1 (C)

聽完男性的話之後,女性的反應為何?

(A) 她相信政客就像男性說的那樣。

(B) 她覺得經濟會有所成長。

(C) 她不覺得政客會關心社會公義。

(D) 她向朋友做了一個承諾。

解析
男性首先提出自己對政客的看法,認為他們應該努力締造社會公義(social justice),此時女性反問他「講的真的是政客嗎?」重點不在於女性講了什麼,而在她「質疑締造社會公義」的態度,因此答案為(C)。

Answer 2 (B)

女生要回家的原因是什麼?

(A) 為了出差

(B) 為了選舉投票

(C) 為了拜訪家人

(D) 為了放個短期假期

解析
男性首先詢問女性回家是否為了「私事」(personal business),女性接著回答說她請假是為了「投票」(vote),除了vote之外,election(選舉)也是另外一個關鍵字,正確答案為(B)。

Answer 3 (D)

男性為什麼覺得週一至五舉辦投票很不公平?

(A) 因為大部分的人都要加班。

(B) 因為大部分的公司不讓員工去投票。

(C) 因為許多投票者下班後不會去投票。

(D) 因為有些投票者無法負擔請假。

解析
解題關鍵在男性最後提的What if...中的內容,他擔心那些請不了假的人無法參與投票。片語take time off表示「休假」,前面接cannot afford to表示某人無法休假,正確答案為(D)。

Answer 4 (C)

為了被人民選上,政客們通常會怎麼做?

(A) 抹黑對手。

(B) 拜訪人民,以留下好印象。

(C) 承諾一些自己之後做不到的事。

(D) 製作很多海報來宣傳自己。

解析
本題考的是「空頭支票」(empty promises)的用法,從字面上來看,「空洞的承諾」就是食言的一種形式,在選擇時,以關鍵字「承諾」(promise)去辨別也沒問題,正確答案為(C)。

Answer 5 (B)

什麼嚴重損害了說話者國家的聲譽?

(A) 針對他們國家而散播的謠言

(B) 最近發生的貪汙醜聞

(C) 政府兌現承諾的手段

(D) 政府在某些事件上的無能

解析
本題的關鍵字在launder這個字上,當動詞時有「採用不法手段洗錢」的意思,雖然單字難度很高,但由前面money(錢財)的形容,同樣也可以推知是與金錢有關的選項,正確答案為(B)。

短對話 1 *Conversation*

Lance: Instead of false promises of economic growth, politicians should try harder to create social justice.

蘭斯：　與其假意地保證經濟成長，政客應該更努力地締造社會公義。

Gina: **Are you sure you're talking about politicians**?

吉娜：　你確定你在講的是「政客」嗎？

短對話 2 *Conversation*

Ethan: Are you going home to take care of some personal business?

伊森：　你回家是為了處理私事嗎？

Sharon: No. I'm taking a day off to **vote** in the mayoral election.

雪倫：　不是，我請假是為了參加市長選舉。

短對話 3 *Conversation*

Mike: It's really unfair to hold elections on weekdays.

麥克：　把選舉日訂在星期一至五很不公平。

Sofia: Why?

蘇菲亞：為什麼？

Mike: What if some people **cannot afford to take time off**?

麥克：　那些請不了假的人要怎麼辦？

短對話 4 *Conversation*

Lisa: Politicians are so calculating.

麗莎：　政客們實在是太會算計了。

James: I agree. They often **give empty promises** before an election.

詹姆士：我同意，他們通常會在選舉前給很多空頭支票。

短對話 5 *Conversation*

Tim: The recent **money laundering scandal** has really damaged our country's reputation.

提姆：　最近那個洗錢的醜聞真是重創我們國家的聲譽。

Sally: Yeah. My German friend said he saw the news over there as well.

莎莉：　就是說啊。我的德國朋友說他們在那邊也有看到這則新聞。

長對話聽力實戰

請仔細聆聽下面的長對話，再依對話內容選擇正確答案。

Question 1

According to the woman, what is Grace still upset about?

(A) The party she supports didn't win any seats.

(B) She couldn't vote for the party she supports.

(C) There aren't any seats in the legislature's office.

(D) The party she supports is the minority in the legislature.

Question 2

What does "a fanatical political activist" mean?

(A) Someone who is concerned about politics very much

(B) Someone who is a big fan of a politician

(C) An active politician

(D) Someone who doesn't like to talk about politics

Question 3

What might Grace ask strangers she meets on the streets to do?

(A) Give her their autographs

(B) Put their names on petitions

(C) Sign up for her newsletter

(D) Write down their opinions about politics

Question 4

What do the woman's aunt and her family do when they meet?

(A) Talk about politics only

(B) Avoid talking to each other

(C) Try not to talk about politics

(D) Watch political programs together

Question 5

What does the man's family mostly talk about when they meet?

(A) Anything that they think of

(B) Something about their jobs

(C) Anything related to politics

(D) Popular movies

答案與解析 ～answer

Answer 1 ◀)) (D)
根據女性所言，葛瑞絲還很在意什麼事？
(A) 她支持的黨派沒有獲得任何席次。
(B) 她無法投票給自己支持的黨派。
(C) 立法機構的辦公室裡沒有任何椅子。
(D) 她支持的黨派是立法機關裡的少數。

解析
女性提到葛瑞絲支持的黨派沒有在立法機關(legislature)的選舉上「獲得半數的席次」，關鍵字為majority of seats(多數席次)，這並不代表該黨派一席都沒得到，所以不適合選(A)，正確答案為(D)。

Answer 2 ◀)) (A)
「政治狂熱分子」(a fanatical political activist)指哪種人？
(A) 極度關心政治的人
(B) 某位政治家的粉絲
(C) 一位積極的政治家
(D) 不喜歡談論政治的人

解析
要解讀這個詞彙，除了要能理解核心單字fanatical(狂熱的)外，也能從前後文得知葛瑞絲關心政治的程度，正確答案為(A)。

Answer 3 ◀)) (B)
葛瑞絲可能會請街上的陌生人做什麼事？
(A) 把親筆簽名交給她
(B) 簽署請願書
(C) 訂購她的商務通訊報紙
(D) 寫下他們對政治的看法

解析
當男性詢問葛瑞絲對政治的狂熱程度時，女性舉了一個例子，說葛瑞絲是那種會請陌生人幫忙「簽署請願書」(sign a petition)的人，重點單字為petition(請願書)，正確答案為(B)。

Answer 4 ◀)) (C)
女性的阿姨與家人碰面時，會怎麼做？
(A) 只討論政治
(B) 避免和對方交談
(C) 盡量不談政治
(D) 一起看政治節目

解析
提到政治立場可能會分化家庭感情時，女性提到自家的例子，說他們與阿姨見面時都會「避談政治」(avoid)，正確答案為(C)。注意選項(B)是指不交談，不符合本題的內容。

Answer 5 ◀)) (C)
男性家人聚在一起時，主要都在聊什麼？
(A) 任何話題
(B) 與他們工作有關的話題
(C) 與政治有關的話題
(D) 流行的人氣電影

解析
女性講完她家的例子之後，男性就說Mine is different.(mine在此指男性他家)，看得出來男性家人會談政治，之後他進一步說明他家「絕大部分的談話都與政治有關」。片語make up指「組成」，正確答案為(C)。

Judy:	My friend Grace is coming over tonight. Just don't mention politics in front of her.
茱蒂：	我的朋友葛瑞絲晚上會過來，記住，不要在她的面前提政治。

Andy:	Why?
安迪：	為什麼？

Judy:	She is still upset about the fact that the party she supports **didn't gain a majority of seats** in the legislature.
茱蒂：	她支持的黨派沒能在立法機關取得多數席位，她對於這點還是很介意。

Andy:	Is she **a fanatical political activist** or what?
安迪：	她算是個政治狂熱者之類的嗎？

Judy:	You could say that. She's the type of person who would ask strangers to **sign a petition**.
茱蒂：	可以這麼說。她是那種會請陌生人幫她簽署請願書的人。

Andy:	Differences regarding political viewpoints sometimes can even divide a family.
安迪：	政治上觀點不同有時足以分化一個家庭呢。

Judy:	Exactly! My aunt supports the opposing party to my family, so we **avoid talking about politics** whenever we meet.
茱蒂：	沒錯！我阿姨支持的政黨剛好和我家人的立場相反，所以我們每次碰面都避免談政治。

Andy:	Mine is different. Politics **makes up the majority of my family's conversation**.
安迪：	我家就不同，我們家人絕大部分的談話都與政治有關。

Judy:	It's not too bad when you support the same party.
茱蒂：	如果你們支持同一個政黨的話，就沒什麼問題啊。

🎧 MP3 38-07(短文1)　🎧 MP3 38-08(短文2)

請仔細聆聽下面兩段短文，並分別回答Q1~Q2&Q3~Q5兩大題。

Question ❶

What has become a frequent strategy for the candidates now?

(A) Deploying campaigns related to their vision

(B) Revealing their opponents' crimes or immoral behaviors

(C) Publishing their promises via tabloid magazines

(D) Exposing scandals about their own parties

Question ❷

Based on the reading, how do politicians feel while facing a political scandal?

(A) They will be upset if it's about themselves.

(B) They will try to stay calm when being interviewed.

(C) They will take it as a chance for publicity.

(D) They will refuse to talk to the tabloid magazines.

Question ❸

What does the man say is changing as the election draws closer?

(A) Commuter's routes to work

(B) The political candidates

(C) People's attitudes towards the election

(D) The atmosphere on the street

Question ❹

What do the candidates use a megaphone for?

(A) To play their recorded messages repeatedly

(B) To thank people who voted for them

(C) To attract attention for their speech

(D) To play music they like

Question ❺

With bigger budgets, what can the candidates do?

(A) They can hold another election when they lose.

(B) They can leave an impression on the public.

(C) They can get more publicity.

(D) They can change their campaign message.

答案與解析 ～answer

Answer 1 (B)

對候選人來說,什麼變成現在常見的策略手段?

(A) 利用造勢廣告宣傳願景

(B) 揭露對手的罪行或不道德的行為

(C) 刊登自己的承諾在小報雜誌上

(D) 揭露自己政黨的醜聞

> **解析**
>
> 題目中的has become問的是「轉變後的宣傳手段」,所以從以前就常用的造勢廣告不適合,可剔除(A);之後女性提到現在越來越多小報雜誌(tabloid magazines)揭露候選人的不法行為,與選項(B)reveal的意思最為接近。

Answer 2 (C)

根據文章內容,面對政治醜聞時,政客們有何感想?

(A) 如果醜聞與自身有關,他們會很沮喪。

(B) 被訪問的時候,他們會盡量保持冷靜。

(C) 他們會把這個視為宣傳的機會。

(D) 他們會拒絕小報雜誌的訪問。

> **解析**
>
> 女性雖然提到她認為報紙應該報導其他值得關注的事件,但這些醜聞事件對政客來說似乎都會變成「免費的宣傳」(free publicity),呼應文末的any publicity is good publicity,正確答案為(C)。

Answer 3 (D)

當選舉逼近時,什麼會產生變化?

(A) 通勤者上班的路線

(B) 選舉的候選人

(C) 大眾對選舉的態度

(D) 街上的氣氛

> **解析**
>
> 男性一開始就提到隨著選舉的逼近(draw closer),街道上的「氛圍」(vibe)也發生變化。接著提到無論到哪裡都可以看到各種海報、廣告看板和告示,正確答案為(D)。

Answer 4 (A)

候選人將擴音器拿來做什麼呢?

(A) 重複播放他們的訴求

(B) 感謝投票給他們的人們

(C) 吸引大眾來聽他們的演講

(D) 播放他們喜歡的音樂

> **解析**
>
> 題目中的關鍵字為「擴音器」megaphone,文中提到這個單字的地方,就是在說來「重複播放其選舉訴求」,關鍵字play(播放)可知並非候選人自己講話,可剔除(B)(C)。片語on a loop意指「重複」,正確答案為(A)。

Answer 5 (C)

如果擁有更多預算,候選人就能做什麼?

(A) 他們能在敗選之後舉辦另一場選舉。

(B) 他們能留給大眾深刻的印象。

(C) 他們能做更多宣傳。

(D) 他們能改變自己的政治訴求。

> **解析**
>
> 男性最後提到擁有較多預算(have much bigger budgets)的候選人自然能將金費用於宣傳(publicity)。注意選項(B)可能是多做宣傳的結果,但本題問的是「做些什麼」,所以最佳答案為(C)。

中英文內容

短文 1

⊙慢速MP3 38-09　　◎正常速MP3 38-10

　　Deploying campaigns regarding their vision is no longer the only strategy political candidates use. I have noticed the increasingly frequent **exposure by tabloid magazines** of alleged crimes or immoral behaviors. Often, the scandals are exposed by an anonymous citizen. Personally, I think newspapers should report the events that deserve more media attention. However, it is almost **like free publicity** for the politicians when they get interviewed on what they think of their opponent's scandals, or even their own scandals. As they say, any publicity is good publicity.

　　使用選舉造勢廣告宣傳願景不再是政治候選人使用的唯一策略。我注意到有越來越多的小報雜誌經常在揭露候選人涉嫌犯罪或不道德的行為。他們通常都會註明揭露這些消息的來源為不具名的公民。就個人而言，我覺得報紙應該報導更多其他值得關注的事件。不過，當政治家們被採訪，要求他們回應有關對手的醜聞，甚至是自己的醜聞時，對他們來說幾乎是免費宣傳的好機會。就像人們說的，不管形式為何，只要有宣傳，就是好宣傳。

短文 2

⊙慢速MP3 38-11　　◎正常速MP3 38-12

　　As the election draws closer, **the vibe on the street** is also changing. I see posters, billboards, and signs everywhere I go. When I drive to work, I often see candidates standing on their campaign vans, waving at the commuters passing by with a megaphone **playing their campaign message on a loop**. Even though I will not vote for someone just because I see or hear about him a lot, I must admit these people do leave an impression on me. It's like brainwashing! I sometimes feel certain candidates have an unfair advantage since they have much bigger budgets for **publicity**.

　　隨著選舉的逼近，街道上的氛圍也在發生變化。無論去到哪裡，都能見到海報、廣告看板還有告示。當我開車上班時，我經常看到候選人站在他們的競選車上面，對著經過的通勤者揮手，擴音器則不斷重複播放他們的政治訴求。雖然我不會因為常常看到或聽到某位候選人就投票給他，但我必須承認，這些人的確讓我留下了深刻的印象，簡直就跟洗腦一樣！有時候，我覺得某些候選人具備的優勢對其他人不公平，因為他們擁有更多的宣傳預算。

經濟現象 The Economy

🖥 日常生活　💡 娛樂活動　💬 意見交流　🏴 特殊場合

 短對話聽力實戰

🎧 MP3 39-01

下面將播放五組短對話，請仔細聆聽，再依對話內容答題。

Question ❶

What was the overall trend of the quarter's sales performance?

(A) It's impossible to tell.
(B) There was a serious decline at the end.
(C) There was a fluctuating trend with overall growth.
(D) There was a slight decline compared to last quarter.

Question ❷

What actions is the man's union going to take?

(A) Go on strike and hold a sit-in protest
(B) File a petition against their employers
(C) File a formal document to the government
(D) Try to get more union members

Question ❸

What does the man say many companies do?

(A) They pressure the government to amend the labor laws.
(B) They find ambiguity in labor laws that can be manipulated.
(C) They find labor laws ridiculous and don't follow them.
(D) They fire the employees who don't work overtime.

Question ❹

What would the woman do if she were in the man's situation?

(A) Sell her stocks in a bear market
(B) Not invest in the stock market
(C) Spread the investment risk
(D) Do more research on investment

Question ❺

Why is the woman worried?

(A) She lost a lot of money on her investment.
(B) She might lose money on her investment.
(C) A stock market crash is happening now.
(D) Her investment is not going to make a profit.

答案與解析 ～answer

Answer 1 ◀ᵒᵒ (C)
本季整體的銷售情況如何？

(A) 我們無法得知。
(B) 季末有嚴重的衰退。
(C) 有波動，但整體有成長。
(D) 和上一季相比，有些微衰退。

解析

解題關鍵在女性的回答，首先是在「開始時的虧損」(a loss at the beginning)，接著便逐漸「轉虧為盈」(recover)，季末的時候銷售則達到頂峰(a sharp sales peak)，整體而言有成長，正確答案為(C)。

Answer 2 ◀ᵒᵒ (A)
男性的工會將採取什麼行動？

(A) 罷工與靜坐抗議
(B) 連署與雇主抗爭
(C) 發正式公文給政府
(D) 試圖找更多人加入工會

解析

針對無薪水卻延長工時的作法，男性提到他草擬一份提議，要工會成員一同「罷工」(strike)與「靜坐抗議」(sit-in protest)，正確答案為(A)。

Answer 3 ◀ᵒᵒ (C)
根據男性所言，很多公司都怎麼樣？

(A) 給政府施壓，修改勞基法。
(B) 找出模稜兩可，能鑽漏洞的法律。
(C) 他們覺得勞基法很可笑，不會遵從。
(D) 解雇那些不加班的員工。

解析

女性首先提起一則過勞死的新聞，接著男性才說有很多公司「聲稱遵守勞基法，實際卻在鑽法律漏洞」，關鍵字為loop holes(漏洞)，正確答案為(B)。注意公司並沒有不遵守法律，所以不可以選(C)。

Answer 4 ◀ᵒᵒ (C)
如果是對話中的女性，她會怎麼做呢？

(A) 股市慘跌時賣掉股票
(B) 不要在股票市場投資
(C) 分擔投資風險
(D) 多研究投資的事情

解析

本題考了常見的俚語用法put all eggs in one basket，字面上的意思是「把雞蛋放在同一個籃子」，表示「冒很大的風險」，正確答案為(C)。另外也可以從女性不認同男性全投資在同一家公司的做法，推測她會分擔風險。

Answer 5 ◀ᵒᵒ (B)
女性為什麼如此憂慮呢？

(A) 她的投資虧損了很多。
(B) 她的投資也許將會虧損。
(C) 現在正經歷股災。
(D) 她的投資沒辦法賺錢。

解析

女性聽說(have heard)「股災可能將要來臨」，關鍵字potential為「潛在的」意思，所以不能選(A)(C)，因為這兩種都表示已經或正在發生的事實；選項(D)所使用的be going to句型暗示「相當肯定的未來」，最佳答案為(B)。

💬短對話 **1** *Conversation*

Glenn: Please summarize the financial report for this quarter.

葛蘭： 請幫我總結一下本季的財務報告。

Claire: We made **a loss at the beginning** of the quarter but things soon started to **recover** and we ended with **a sharp sales peak** towards the year-end.

克萊兒：我們季初虧損，但很快就轉虧為盈，接近年底時銷售達到高峰。

💬短對話 **2** *Conversation*

Susan: We should formally convey our dissatisfaction with the extended work hours without pay.

蘇珊： 我們需要正式表達對無薪延長工時的不滿。

Terry: I have started to draft a letter to the union members regarding **the strike** and **sit-in protest**.

泰瑞： 我已經開始擬一封信給工會成員，準備罷工跟靜坐抗議。

💬短對話 **3** *Conversation*

Ellie: Have you seen the news? An engineer died of extensive overtime work.

艾莉： 你看了新聞嗎？有一名工程師死於大量的超時工作。

Jack: Many companies argue they comply with all labor laws, whereas they actually exploit **loop holes** in the regulations.

傑克： 許多公司都聲稱他們遵守勞基法，但他們實際上都在鑽法律漏洞。

💬短對話 **4** *Conversation*

Keith: I have invested most of my savings in company A's stocks.

基斯： 我在A公司的股票上投入了我大部分的積蓄。

Rose: That sounds risky. I **wouldn't put all my eggs in one basket** if I were you.

蘿絲： 聽起很冒險，如果我是你，就不會這樣孤注一擲。

💬短對話 **5** *Conversation*

Leon: What's wrong? You look anxious.

里昂： 你怎麼了？看起來很著急。

Rosa: I've heard **a potential stock market crash is coming**. I'm worried I **might lose a lot** on my investment.

羅莎： 我聽說股災可能要來臨，真擔心我的投資慘賠。

Leon: I really hope it's just rumor.

里昂： 真希望這只是個謠言。

長對話聽力實戰

MP3 39-04

請仔細聆聽下面的長對話，再依對話內容選擇正確答案。

Question ❶
What might the man do about the Bali trip?
- (A) Ask the woman to go on the trip instead of him
- (B) Cancel his plans for the Bali trip
- (C) Reschedule the Bali trip to another time
- (D) Finish all his work before they go on the trip

Question ❷
Why is the man not sure if he's qualified for unemployment benefits?
- (A) He will need a formal notification from his company.
- (B) He hasn't been in the company for long.
- (C) He works on a contract basis.
- (D) He might be starting a new job soon.

Question ❸
Who should the man call to check his eligibility for benefits?
- (A) His company
- (B) An ex-colleague who got laid off
- (C) Certain charities
- (D) The Labor Bureau

Question ❹
What might the woman reconsider after hearing the man's words?
- (A) If she should also cancel the trip
- (B) If she should change the destination
- (C) If she should reconsider whom to travel with
- (D) If she should ask more friends to go together

Question ❺
What rumor did the woman hear about her company?
- (A) That she'll be laid off, too.
- (B) Her promotion is going to be canceled.
- (C) Her company will increase the employees' salaries.
- (D) There's a possibility her salary might be decreased.

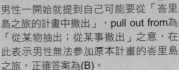

答案與解析 ~answer

Answer 1 (B)
關於峇里島的旅行，男性可能怎麼做？

(A) 要求女性代替他參加旅行
(B) 取消他去參加峇里島之旅的計畫
(C) 重新安排峇里島之旅的時間
(D) 在旅行之前完成所有工作

解析
男性一開始就提到自己可能要從「峇里島之旅的計畫中撤出」，pull out from為「從某物抽出；從某事撤出」之意，在此表示男性無法參加原本計畫的峇里島之旅，正確答案為(B)。

Answer 2 (C)
為什麼男性不確定自己是否符合失業給付的資格？

(A) 他需要公司發出的正式通知。
(B) 他在公司的時間沒有很久。
(C) 他是約聘人員。
(D) 他也許很快就會有新工作。

解析
女性聽到男性被裁員後，詢問對方是否能申請失業給付(unemployment benefits)，這個時候兩人開始討論申請的資格，男性不確定是否可以，因為他是「約聘員工」(contract staff)，正確答案為(C)。

Answer 3 (D)
若想確認領補助金的資格，男性應該要打給誰？

(A) 他的公司
(B) 被解雇的前同事
(C) 某些慈善機構
(D) 勞工局

解析
女性認為男性有資格領取補助金，關鍵字eligible有「法律上合格的」意思，接著建議男性打電話詢問勞工局(the Labor Bureau)，關鍵字bureau通常與政府機關有關，由此可知正確答案為(D)。

Answer 4 (A)
在聽完男性的話之後，女性可能會重新考慮什麼？

(A) 她是否也應該取消行程
(B) 她是否要改變旅程目的地
(C) 她是否要重新考慮旅伴
(D) 她是否應該邀更多朋友一起去

解析
聽到男性可能無法參加旅行，女性提到自己也應該重新考慮自己「是否應該去」(if I should go)，完整句型為if...or not，正確答案為(A)。

Answer 5 (D)
關於女性的公司，她聽到了什麼傳言？

(A) 她也將被裁員。
(B) 她的升遷將被取消。
(C) 她的公司將替員工加薪。
(D) 她的薪水有被調降的可能性。

解析
女性最後提到她聽到的「傳言」(rumor)，說他們的薪水將被減低(our salary is going to be cut)，cut在此指抽象的「減薪」，另外也可從關鍵字salary(薪資)剔除與薪水無關的選項，正確答案為(D)。

◉慢速MP3 39-05　◉正常速MP3 39-06

Michael: I might have to **pull out from the Bali trip** we were planning.
麥可：　我可能無法參加我們峇里島之旅的計畫了。

Judy:　Why?
茱蒂：　為什麼？

Michael: I just received an email from HR that I'm on the shortlist for being laid off.
麥可：　我剛剛收到人資部的電子郵件，我被列在被解雇的名單上。

Judy:　I'm sorry to hear that. You can apply for unemployment benefits, right?
茱蒂：　我很遺憾，你應該可以申請失業給付吧？

Michael: I'm not sure. I'm **contract staff**, and they won't ask me to leave before my current contract ends.
麥可：　不知道，因為我是約聘員工，而且在我合約結束前，他們不會炒我魷魚。

Judy:　I believe you are still eligible. Just call **the Labor Bureau** to check the requirements.
茱蒂：　應該還是有資格，記得打給勞工局問一下申請條件為何。

Michael: Thanks, I will. I might also try to negotiate with my company for more favorable terms.
麥可：　謝謝，我會的。我也許會試著與公司談一個比較有利的條件。

Judy:　But since you are unlikely to go, I might also reconsider **if I should go now**.
茱蒂：　但既然你不太可能去，我也許也該重新考慮自己是否應該去。

Michael: Why not? I thought many of your friends are going.
麥可：　為什麼不去？你不是有很多朋友要去嗎？

Judy:　Well, I heard a rumor that **our salary is going to be cut** soon!
茱蒂：　因為我聽到一個傳言，說我們很快就會被減薪！

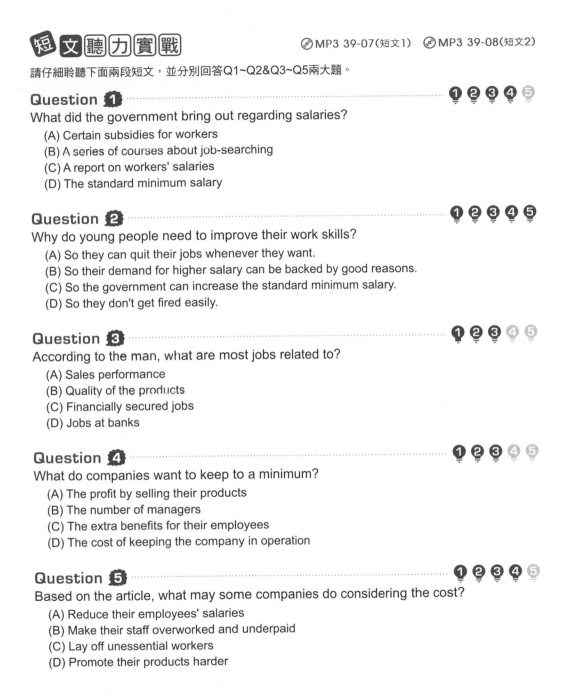

短文聽力實戰 　◉ MP3 39-07(短文1)　◉ MP3 39-08(短文2)

請仔細聆聽下面兩段短文，並分別回答Q1~Q2&Q3~Q5兩大題。

Question 1
What did the government bring out regarding salaries?
- (A) Certain subsidies for workers
- (B) A series of courses about job-searching
- (C) A report on workers' salaries
- (D) The standard minimum salary

Question 2
Why do young people need to improve their work skills?
- (A) So they can quit their jobs whenever they want.
- (B) So their demand for higher salary can be backed by good reasons.
- (C) So the government can increase the standard minimum salary.
- (D) So they don't get fired easily.

Question 3
According to the man, what are most jobs related to?
- (A) Sales performance
- (B) Quality of the products
- (C) Financially secured jobs
- (D) Jobs at banks

Question 4
What do companies want to keep to a minimum?
- (A) The profit by selling their products
- (B) The number of managers
- (C) The extra benefits for their employees
- (D) The cost of keeping the company in operation

Question 5
Based on the article, what may some companies do considering the cost?
- (A) Reduce their employees' salaries
- (B) Make their staff overworked and underpaid
- (C) Lay off unessential workers
- (D) Promote their products harder

答案與解析 ～answer

Answer 1 ◀))（D）
關於薪資，政府提出了什麼呢？
(A) 某些給員工的補助金
(B) 有關找工作的一系列課程
(C) 一份關於員工薪資的報告
(D) 最低標準薪資

解析
文章一開始提出了當前社會陷入了「剝削員工」與「對工資期待過高」的惡性循環，提到政府的解決方法是設定「最低標準薪資」(the standard minimum salary)，可由salary(薪資)這個字剔除(D)以外的選項。

Answer 2 ◀))（B）
年輕人為什麼需要改善自己在工作上的能力呢？
(A) 這樣他們隨時都能辭職。
(B) 這樣他們才有理由要求高一點的薪資。
(C) 這樣政府才能調漲最低標準薪資。
(D) 這樣他們就不容易被炒魷魚。

解析
女性講完公司可能長期不調漲薪資後(剝削員工的論點)，便開始介紹員工單純求調薪，卻不改善自己能力的問題(對薪資期待過高的論點)，並說自我進步將能成為調薪的理由。關鍵字justified指「有正當理由的」，正確答案為(B)。

Answer 3 ◀))（A）
根據男性所言，大部分的工作會與什麼有關？
(A) 銷售表現
(B) 產品的品質
(C) 在財務上有保障的工作
(D) 銀行類的工作

解析
男性提到現在大多數的工作都與「銷售業績」(sales performance)有關，片語be tied to表示兩物密不可分的關係，正確答案為(A)。注意選項(D)只是男性所使用的例子之一而已。

Answer 4 ◀))（D）
公司想將什麼維持在最低的程度呢？
(A) 銷售產品所得的利潤
(B) 經理的人數
(C) 給員工的額外福利
(D) 讓公司順利營運的成本

解析
題目中的重點用法在keep sth. to a minimum，表示「將某物維持在最低的程度」。男性在業績表現之後，提到公司也很重視將「營運成本」壓到最低，關鍵字為「營運的」(operational)，正確答案為(D)。

Answer 5 ◀))（C）
根據文章，考慮到成本，有些公司可能會怎麼做？
(A) 減少員工的薪水
(B) 讓員工超時工作但不加薪
(C) 解雇非必要的員工
(D) 更努力地推銷公司的產品

解析
講到營運成本時，男性接著舉例說有些公司可能會「解雇非必要的員工」，關鍵片語為「解雇」(lay off)與「非必要」(not essential)，選項(C)同時囊括這兩項概念，所以正確答案為(C)。

Our society is trapped in a vicious cycle of employee exploitation versus expectations regarding salaries. Since the government brought out **the standard minimum salary**, many employers use that as the benchmark. But this salary might not be increased for a long time. On the other hand, many fresh graduates keep voicing their concerns about low salary standards. However, they don't focus on how to improve their abilities, which would make them **more justified in demanding better pay**. I think there should be give and take from both the employers and employees. One should not exploit their staff, and the other needs to think about what they can contribute to companies.

我們的社會陷入了剝削員工與對薪水有過度期望的惡性循環中。自從政府規定了最低標準薪資後,許多雇主都將這個視為基準,但這樣的薪資可能會維持很長一段時間,都不調漲。另一方面,許多應屆畢業生不斷表達對低工資的憂慮,卻不把重點放在如何提高自己的能力,讓自己更有立場要求高工資。我認為雇主和員工雙方都應該互相遷就,一方不應該剝削員工,另一方則必須思考他們能為公司帶來什麼貢獻。

Ever since the financial crisis in 2008, many companies have been much more cautious about hiring new staff, which makes the job market quite unpromising. Nowadays, most jobs are tied to **sales performance**. For example, if you work in a bank or life insurance company, you will have to work hard to promote credit cards and insurance products. This kind of requirement will become one of the criteria used to evaluate executives. Furthermore, keeping **the operational cost** to a minimum is becoming more and more important to most companies. Therefore, some may even **lay off those who are not essential** at work.

自從2008年的金融危機以來,許多公司在雇用員工方面的態度變得更加謹慎,使就業市場更加慘淡。如今,幾乎所有的工作都與銷售業績息息相關。舉例來說,如果你在銀行或壽險公司工作,你就必須努力推銷信用卡和各項保險產品,這類型的業績表現將成為審視主管績效的標準之一。除此之外,將營運成本維持在最低的程度對大多數公司來說變得越來越重要,因此,有些公司甚至會解雇那些非必要的員工。

Unit
5
教育和教養 Education

🗣 日常生活　🎤 娛樂活動　✏ 意見交流　🚩 特殊場合

短 對 話 聽 力 實 戰

◉ MP3 40-01

下面將播放五組短對話，請仔細聆聽，再依對話內容答題。

Question 1

What is the topic the speakers are talking about?

(A) The way to get into some private schools

(B) The ever-changing education system

(C) The difference between options and limitations

(D) The purpose of educational reform

Question 2

What does the man find hard?

(A) To be responsible in teaching

(B) To teach his students one thing when their parents do the opposite

(C) To believe the children are capable of doing things

(D) To convince the parents to pay for private lessons

Question 3

What example does the woman mention to the man?

(A) She insists on doing laundry for her daughter.

(B) She can't be independent when she is with her mom.

(C) Her mom does housework for her even though she's an adult.

(D) She can't let go of her teenage daughter.

Question 4

What advice does the man give the woman?

(A) Not interfere in her son's business so much

(B) Talk to her son's teacher in private

(C) Get involved when the pushing gets to the next stage

(D) Go and talk to the teacher together with her son

Question 5

How does the man sometimes feel as a teacher?

(A) Lost and confused

(B) Disrespectful and naughty

(C) Furious and sad

(D) Discouraged and disappointed

答案與解析 ～answer

Answer 1 (B)
說話者在談什麼話題呢？

(A) 進入某些私立學校的方式
(B) 不斷改變的教育體系
(C) 選擇與限制的不同
(D) 教育改革的目的

解析

女性一開始就提到「教育體系」(the education system)，而男性也順著她的話往下說體系當中有很多限制，所以兩人在談論的話題是教育體系本身，而非學校、規定內容或教育改革的原因，正確答案為(B)。

Answer 2 (B)
男性覺得什麼很困難？

(A) 在教學上有責任心
(B) 在學生父母作法相反的情況下教導學生
(C) 相信孩子們有能力完成許多事情
(D) 說服學生父母繳私人課程的學費

解析

男性一開始就提到要教孩子「獨立和負責」(independent and responsible)是很難的一件事，原因是父母「不能放手」(can't let go)。「獨立自主」的態度與「父母管控」會有不同的影響，所以正確答案為(B)。

Answer 3 (C)
女性舉例時和男性講了什麼？

(A) 她堅持幫女兒洗衣服。
(B) 和母親在一起時，她無法獨立自主。
(C) 就算她已成年，母親還是幫她做家事。
(D) 她無法放手讓正值青春期的女兒獨立。

解析

男性要談的是對孩子很難完全放手的教養心態，此時女性舉自己的例子，說與丈夫回娘家時，衣服都是她母親洗的。要表達的是已經成年結婚的她，在母親眼中依然是需要幫忙的人，正確答案為(C)。

Answer 4 (A)
男性給了女性什麼建議呢？

(A) 別介入太多她兒子的事情
(B) 私底下與她兒子的導師談談
(C) 當推擠事件變嚴重的時候再介入
(D) 和她兒子一起去找導師談

解析

一聽到女性打算採取的行為，男性就勸她「不必什麼都插手」，關鍵片語get involved in意指「涉入」，與選項(A)中interfere(介入)的意思最為接近。注意選項(D)不適合的地方在，男性是勸女性先讓兒子自己處理，而非陪同處理。

Answer 5 (D)
身為老師，男性有時會有怎樣的感受呢？

(A) 迷惘且困惑
(B) 失禮且調皮
(C) 暴怒且難過
(D) 沮喪且失望

解析

本題考的是單字(disheartening)的意思，hearten與「心」有關，當動詞時有「鼓舞」之意，由此可知加上否定字首的disheartening的意思為反面的「令人沮喪」，正確答案為(D)。

⊙慢速MP3 40-02　　◎正常速MP3 40-03

短對話 **1** *Conversation*

Jill: **The education system** seems to be constantly changed.

吉兒：　教育體系似乎一直不斷在改變。

George: Tell me about it. There are so many options and limitations.

喬治：　就是說啊。現在的制度提供許多選擇，但也有很多限制。

短對話 **2** *Conversation*

Andrew: As a teacher, I find it hard to teach my students to be **independent and responsible**.

安德魯：身為老師，我覺得教孩子獨立和負責是很難的一件事。

Elsa: Why is that?

艾爾莎：為什麼呢？

Andrew: Because some parents just **can't let go** or believe these kids are capable.

安德魯：因為有些父母就是不放手，或相信孩子有能力做到。

短對話 **3** *Conversation*

Dan: It is hard to let go and let your kids be completely independent.

丹：　　要放手讓孩子完全獨立真是難啊。

Susan: Tell me about it. My mom still **does our laundry** when my husband and I go home.

蘇珊：　就是說啊，當我先生陪我回娘家時，我媽還是會幫我們洗衣服呢。

短對話 **4** *Conversation*

Vivian: I need to talk to my son's teacher. He said a classmate pushed him.

薇薇安：我得跟我兒子的老師談談，他說同學推他。

Ted: I think it's best to let him handle it. We **don't have to get involved in everything**.

泰德：　我覺得最好讓他自己處理，我們不必什麼都插手涉入。

短對話 **5** *Conversation*

Anthony: It can be **disheartening** being a teacher sometimes.

安東尼：　有時真的覺得為人師長很令人沮喪。

Debbie: Why? What happened?

黛比：　為什麼？發生什麼事了嗎？

Anthony: Many students don't have respect for teachers. They don't even look you straight in the eye when you're talking.

安東尼：　很多學生都不尊重老師，你在講話的時候，他們甚至不正眼看你。

長 對 話 聽 力 實 戰

MP3 40-04

請仔細聆聽下面的長對話，再依對話內容選擇正確答案。

Question 1

What does the woman ask the man to do for her?

- (A) Attend the meeting her son's school is holding
- (B) Take her son to school for the meeting
- (C) Change her work shift for this week
- (D) Tell their boss she can't go to work this week

Question 2

What does the woman say the meeting is about?

- (A) The actions taken in response to the new exam system
- (B) The measurements for the graduates
- (C) Students' performance on their exams
- (D) The assignments for the students this semester

Question 3

What has the new exam system brought?

- (A) Many more exams
- (B) Confusion and more stress than before
- (C) Higher university entry rates
- (D) A lot more courses for students

Question 4

What does the school think it will accomplish by rearranging the lessons?

- (A) Help the teachers go home earlier
- (B) Help deliver a fuller curriculum
- (C) Help the students take fewer exams
- (D) Reduce the number of non-core subjects

Question 5

According to the man, what action won't be helpful to anything?

- (A) Holding meetings with students' parents
- (B) Rearranging all lessons every semester
- (C) Placing less importance on lessons like art
- (D) Putting greater importance on non-core subjects

答案與解析 ～answer

Answer 1 ◀)) (C)
女性要求男性替她做什麼事？

(A) 參加她兒子學校舉辦的會議

(B) 帶她兒子去參加學校的會議

(C) 調換她這星期的工作排班

(D) 告訴他們老闆，她這週無法去上班

解析
本題關鍵在對話一開始的Can you...?此為女性要求男性替她「重新排班」(rearrange my shift)，正確答案為(C)。注意後面說的學校會議，只是需要重新排班的原因，並非要求。

Answer 2 ◀)) (A)
根據女性所言，這場會議與什麼有關？

(A) 對應新式考試制度而採取的行動

(B) 為了畢業生而採取的措施

(C) 學生們在考試方面的表現

(D) 學生本學期的作業

解析
當男性詢問會議與什麼有關(be about)時，女性回答是為了新式考試制度(for the new exam system)而辦的。重點放在「制度」(system)與「措施」(measure)，正確答案為(A)。

Answer 3 ◀)) (B)
新式考試制度帶來了什麼影響呢？

(A) 更多的考試

(B) 讓人混淆與比之前更大的壓力

(C) 更高的大學入取率

(D) 學生們必須上更多課程

解析
談到新式制度，女性覺得「令人混淆」(the confusion)與「更多壓力」(extra stress)，正確答案為(B)。要注意選項(D)的內容是學校採取的措施，並非新式制度本身的規範。

Answer 4 ◀)) (B)
學校認為重新排課會帶來什麼效果？

(A) 幫助教師早點下班回家

(B) 排入更多課程

(C) 減少學生的考試數量

(D) 減少非核心課程的數量

解析
解題時要認清題目問的是「重新安排課程」(rearrange the lessons)的效果，選項(D)所談的是學校會採取的另外一項措施，所以不能選。真正的答案在「排更多課程」(deliver a fuller curriculum)，正確答案為(B)。

Answer 5 ◀)) (C)
根據男性所言，什麼樣的措施不會有任何幫助？

(A) 和學生們的家長開會

(B) 每學期重新安排課程

(C) 減少像美術這種課程的重要性

(D) 增加非核心課程的重要性

解析
本題要著重於男性的反應，對話最後他提到「減低美術課的重要性」不會有任何幫助，代表他不認同學校的作法，正確答案為(C)。

中英文內容

⊙慢速MP3 40-05　　◉正常速MP3 40-06

Sandra: Can you **rearrange my shift for this week**? I need to attend a meeting my son's school is holding.
珊卓：　你能幫我重排我這星期的班嗎？我必須參加我兒子學校舉辦的會議。

George: Sure. So what is the meeting about?
喬治：　沒問題，是關於什麼的會議啊？

Sandra: It's about **the measures** the school is going to take **for the new exam system**.
珊卓：　是關於學校針對新式考試制度而採取的措施。

George: I thought we can only follow the rules they announced.
喬治：　我以為我們就只能遵守政府宣布的規定。

Sandra: That's basically right. But with all **the confusion and extra stress**, we should do something about it.
珊卓：　基本上是如此沒錯，但這些規定實在讓人混淆，又帶來更多壓力，所以我們必須做點什麼才行。

George: I can explain it to you. I spent a whole week reading on it!
喬治：　我可以解釋給你聽，我花了整整一個星期讀這方面的資訊呢！

Sandra: Also, the school will rearrange the lessons, which might **help deliver a fuller curriculum**.
珊卓：　另外，學校也將重新排課，幫助老師排更多課程。

George: That sounds stressful for the poor kids.
喬治：　那聽起來壓力好大，孩子們真可憐。

Sandra: They will also decrease the amount of homework in non-core subjects like art.
珊卓：　他們也將減少非核心科目的作業，像美術這類的課。

George: I don't think **giving art less importance** will solve anything!
喬治：　我不認為減少美術課的重要性能解決什麼事！

短文聽力實戰

⊙MP3 40-07(短文1)　⊙MP3 40-08(短文2)

請仔細聆聽下面兩段短文，並分別回答Q1~Q2&Q3~Q5兩大題。

Question ❶

Based on the article, what is the most important thing in education?

(A) A distinctive teaching method
(B) What and how teachers deliver in class
(C) The support parents provide
(D) The great effort students make

Question ❷

What can be inferred from the article?

(A) Parents' role in education may be greater than schools.
(B) A special teaching method won't help students.
(C) Taking exams is the best way to know the students' level.
(D) The speaker criticizes some parents a lot.

Question ❸

Apart from graduation rate, what does the ranking report consider?

(A) The money students spend to graduate
(B) The value of loans that students borrow to get an education
(C) The average expense spent on students
(D) The average tuition fee

Question ❹

What does Finland's education system allow the teaching to be?

(A) Flexible within the overall specifications
(B) Free without any principles
(C) Inefficient if teachers don't like it
(D) Decided by students alone

Question ❺

What do students in South Korea need to do for exams?

(A) Find internships to gain more experience
(B) Do more extracurricular reading
(C) Join study groups for discussion
(D) Remember a huge amount of information

答案與解析　～answer

Answer 1 🔊 (C)
根據文章內容，教育中最重要的事是什麼？

(A) 獨特的教學方法
(B) 老師上課的內容與教學方法
(C) 父母給予的支持
(D) 學生自己付出的努力

解析

解題關鍵句在女性談到學習效率時，提到「沒有什麼比父母的支持更重要」。nothing beats...的句型表示「後者提到的內容比任何事都重要」，正確答案為(C)。

Answer 2 🔊 (A)
從文章裡可以推測出什麼結論？

(A) 父母在教育中的角色可能比學校更重要。
(B) 獨特的教學方法無法幫助學生。
(C) 考試是了解學生程度最好的方法。
(D) 針對某些家長，説話者批評了很多。

解析
本題問的是文章主要談的內容，即「父母在教育中的重要性」。一開始雖然提到獨特的教學方式，但女性並沒有去評估這些教學方式的效果，所以不能選(B)；選項(D)只是稍被提到，但女性沒有花很多篇幅批評。

Answer 3 🔊 (C)
除了畢業率之外，該排名報告考慮的因素還有什麼？

(A) 學生為了畢業所花的錢
(B) 學生為了受教育而借的貸款
(C) 在學生教育上的平均花費
(D) 平均的學費

解析

一開始介紹報告內容之後，男性開始説明這項排名的基準包含「花在每個學生教育上的費用」(education expenditure on each student)與畢業率(graduation rates)。依前後文可知與學生繳納的錢無關，正確答案為(C)。

Answer 4 🔊 (A)
芬蘭的教育系統容許什麼樣的教學方式？

(A) 在整體規範中保有彈性
(B) 完全不受任何原則拘束
(C) 當老師不喜歡的時候亂教
(D) 僅照學生的想法決定

解析
男性提到芬蘭教育容許「老師不完全遵照國家的教綱」，關鍵在loosely based on，loosely有「鬆散地；大致上地」意思，最佳答案為(A)。

Answer 5 🔊 (D)
南韓的學生為了準備考試必須做什麼呢？

(A) 為了取得更多經驗去實習
(B) 閱讀更多課外讀物
(C) 加入讀書會，互相討論
(D) 背誦大量的資訊

解析

提到南韓學生的應試準備，文中提到他們「必須背很多資訊」。句型be meant to表示「應該」，後面則接解題關鍵memorize a lot of knowledge，正確答案為(D)。注意(B)雖然也與資訊有關，但僅提到「閱讀」，所以不宜選。

中英文內容

短文 1

◎慢速MP3 40-09　　◎正常速MP3 40-10

　　Many distinctive teaching methods have been proposed over the last few centuries, including the Montessori system and Rosetta Stone learning. However, when it comes to the efficiency in learning, **nothing beats the support the parents provide**. Some parents tend to blame the teachers for not doing a good job, but rarely think about how much support they give to their children. What and how teachers deliver in class is undoubtedly important. However, learning **should not be limited to schools**. It is only **through appropriate demonstration by the parents** can students truly comprehend the knowledge they have acquired.

　　在過去的幾個世紀，有許多獨特的教學方法已經被提出來，包括蒙特梭利系統(Montessori system)和羅塞塔石碑學習系統(Rosetta Stone learning)。然而，當我們談到學習的效率時，沒有什麼比父母提供的支持更重要了。有些父母會傾向責怪老師沒有教好，卻沒有想想自己給了孩子多少支持。老師上課傳授的知識內容與教學方法固然重要，但學習不應該僅限於學校內，只有透過父母適當的示範，學生才能真正理解所學的知識。

短文 2

◎慢速MP3 40-11　　◎正常速MP3 40-12

　　The latest global report on education systems shows that South Korea tops the rankings in 2014. The major factors they consider include **education expenditure on each student** and graduation rates. The result is very interesting when you compare it to last year. The previous winner, Finland, allows teaching to be very **loosely based on its national curriculum**. Students in Finland don't need to take a lot of tests. In contrast, students in South Korea are meant to **memorize a lot of knowledge** for exams. Despite South Korea topping the rankings, some scholars argue that there are many other factors that should be involved in the quality of education.

　　一份有關全球教育體系的最新報告顯示，南韓在2014年的排名第一。該報告評估的主要項目包含學生教育的單位成本和畢業率。如果把這個結果和前一年比較，就會發現一件有趣的現象。之前排名第一的國家芬蘭，在教學上允許老師不須完全遵照國家的教綱，芬蘭學生也不須要參加很多考試。另一方面，南韓的學生則必須為了考試而背很多資訊。儘管南韓的排名高居第一，部分學者認為還有許多其他因素也應該被納入考慮才對。

好康大補帖 ～自學急救 must-see 網站

優質影片訓練網站

TED: Ideas worth spreading

http://www.ted.com/

這個網站蒐集了許多很棒的演講內容，在觀賞影片時能選擇字幕（但並非每部影片都附上多種語言字幕），想自我訓練的人可以看無字幕版。更棒的是，每個影片都會附上完整的英文內容（transcript)，而且會隨著演講者講到的句子，一句句標註出來，所以聽不懂的學習者可以跟著文字邊聽邊讀，甚至記錄自己不懂的單字與片語。

自學實用度 ★★★★★　　　　　　**內容難度** ★★★★☆

VoiceTube

https://tw.voicetube.com/

蒐集了種類廣泛的各式影片，每部影片會附上中文 / 英文字幕（有的只有英文字幕）。影片右邊的英文內容，會隨著說話者一句句標註。最方便的是，網站結合 Dr. Eye 的字典系統，所以只要在 transcript 當中點一下，就會立即跑出字典翻譯喔！

因為使用免費會員制，所以每部影片都有「單字」、「筆記」、「佳句」的功能，查過的單字會自動列在「單字」中；也可以針對影片寫筆記 & 記錄佳句，打造個人化的學習環境，非常方便。

◎特別註明：使用前須先註冊會員（註冊是免費的）。

自學實用度 ★★★★★　　　　　　**內容難度** ★★★☆☆

基礎綜合型訓練網站

⌗ elllo

🖥 http://www.elllo.org/

　　包含 Views（對話 MP3）、Video（影片）、Mixers（不同人針對單一主題的短評）、Game（互動遊戲）四大類型，是資源很豐富的綜合型網站。資源旁邊都會註明內容難易度 & 說話者是哪一國人，提供有口音方面考量的人參考。

◎特別註明：影片（Video）因為上傳自世界各國人士，所以都只是個人講話的錄影，主題也多半比較生活化，講求內文專業度的人，請自行斟酌再使用。

自學實用度 ★★★☆☆　　　　　　　　　　**內容難度 ★★☆☆☆**

反轉對新聞英語的恐懼

⌗ BBC Learning English

🖥 http://www.bbc.co.uk/learningenglish/

　　綜合型的學習網站。一方面提供影片，循序漸進地介紹單字、片語、短文；另一方面還提供自我測驗的聽力小短文，讀者可按進度，一堂接著一堂練習。

　　以學習為導向，會附上完整的英文內容、單字／片語的英英解釋，甚至還有文法介紹，內容很豐富。

◎特別註明：BBC 以「英式英文」（British English）為主，所以會學到美國人不常用的單字與片語，有特殊考量的學習者還請自行斟酌。

自學實用度 ★★★★★　　　　　　　　　　**內容難度 ★★★☆☆**

VOA Learning English

http://learningenglish.voanews.com/

　　「美國之音」的學習版，裡面會用慢速朗讀新聞，並會隨著主播的速度同步跑英文字幕喔！

　　對新聞有恐懼的學習者也不用擔心，因為裡面包含的主題相當廣泛，並分成 Level One~Three，可按照自己的程度選擇。每篇文章還會附上慢速朗讀版的 MP3（可下載）、完整的英文內容、以及單字的英英解釋。

　　附上官方頻道，https://www.youtube.com/user/VOALearning English。聽新聞累了嗎？推薦輕鬆的 English in a minute，一分鐘掌握美國人的慣用語！

自學實用度 ★★★★☆　　　　　　　　**內容難度 ★★★☆☆**

VOA News

http://www.voanews.com/

　　「美國之音」的標準速度版。如果 VOA Learning English 的速度對你來說沒什麼問題，也不排斥新聞的話，恭喜你！可以進入 VOA News 聆聽正常速度的新聞了。

　　雖然不是每篇文章都有影片，也不像 VOA Learning English 那樣會放上完整的英文內容，但影片旁邊都會附上大意摘要，可藉此加強學習效果。

自學實用度 ★★★☆☆　　　　　　　　**內容難度 ★★★★★**

🎧 CNN Student News

🔗 http://edition.cnn.com/studentnews/

　　為了美國中學生而做的節目，週一至週五將新聞做成 10 分鐘的簡報，因為是為了中學生而設計的，所以報導內容不帶評論，盡量以中立的角度敘述新聞，不管是自學還是做教材都很適合。

　　進入網站之後，請點進 Show Archive 的內容，裡面會以「日期」作檔名，為新聞簡報的影片檔，也提供完整的文字（transcript）。不過，CNN 特別註明，不保證文字與最終上傳的影片一模一樣，發現有些微出入可別驚訝喔。

◎特別註明：影片下方會有 Story Highlights 的區塊，註明新聞的重點，對聽力沒把握的讀者可先閱讀後，再觀賞影片。

自學實用度 ★★★★☆　　　　　　　　　　**內容難度 ★★★★☆**

👤 檢測實力的線上聽力題庫 👤

🎧 Randall's ESL Cyber Listening Lab

🔗 http://www.esl-lab.com/

　　如果想要訓練多益等檢定考的聽力測驗，這個網站非常實用！進入網站之後，會有 Easy（初級）、Medium（中級）、Difficult（高級）三大區塊，點進適合自己的程度就能開始練習。

　　決定「程度」與「選題」後，就可以從 Listening Exercises 開始自我測驗。答題完成之後，可點選 Final Score 的按鍵來確認自己的得分。另外，底下會提供 Quiz Script（英文內容），讓學習者重複聽的同時，跟著文字理解。

自學實用度 ★★★★★　　　　　　　　　　**內容難度 ★★★★☆**

OM Listen

http://www.ompersonal.com.ar/omlisten/contenidotematico.htm

　　進入網站後，一樣有難易度的分級，分為 Elementary（初級）、Intermediate（中級）、Advanced（高級）三部分。點進題目之後，同樣也有選擇題可練習，比較可惜的是，OM 並沒有直接確認分數的設計，必須點進「Check Here」看答案及英文內容，需要對照兩個視窗，與 ESL-Lab 相比，比較沒那麼方便。

自學實用度 ★★★★☆ 　　　　　　　　　　　**內容難度** ★★★☆☆

 專業的學術英文也能訓練

MICUSP Simple

http://micase.elicorpora.info/

　　MICUSP Simple 並非聽力訓練的網站，而是蒐集了許多專業學術文章的英文網站。補充在這裡，是希望能讓那些有特殊需求的學習者，找到訓練專業英文的資源。

　　進入網站之後，會出現一個圖表，每個圖表下方就是各個專業領域的分類，例如：BIO（Biology 生物學）、ECO（Economics 經濟學）…等等，點進之後就有文章可供閱讀，不僅能成為研究人員的資料庫，同時還能學會專業的英文用字。

◎特別註明：因為文章涉及專業領域，所以就算一時半刻看不懂也不用灰心。
　　　　　　普通學習者只需把這個網站視為學習進階單字的資源即可。

自學實用度 ★★☆☆☆ 　　　　　　　　　　　**內容難度** ★★★★★

383

國家圖書館出版品預行編目資料

一聽忘不了!兩段速英語精聽精練 / 張翔 著. -- 初版.
-- 新北市：知識工場出版 采舍國際有限公司發行，
2017.11　面；　公分. -- (Master；04)
ISBN 978-986-271-790-5(平裝)

1. 英語　　2. 讀本

805.18　　　　　　　　　　　　106015636

 知識工場 · Master 04

一聽忘不了! 兩段速英語精聽精練

出 版 者／全球華文聯合出版平台·知識工場
作　　者／張翔　　　　　　　　　印 行 者／知識工場
出版總監／王寶玲　　　　　　　　英文編輯／何牧蓉
總 編 輯／歐綾纖　　　　　　　　美術設計／蔡瑪麗

郵撥帳號／50017206 采舍國際有限公司（郵撥購買，請另付一成郵資）
台灣出版中心／新北市中和區中山路2段366巷10號10樓
電話／（02）2248-7896　　　　　　　傳真／（02）2248-7758
ISBN-13／978-986-271-790-5
出版日期／2017年11月初版

全球華文市場總代理／采舍國際
地址／新北市中和區中山路2段366巷10號3樓
電話／（02）8245-8786　　　　　　　傳真／（02）8245-8718

港澳地區總經銷／和平圖書
地址／香港柴灣嘉業街12號百樂門大廈17樓
電話／（852）2804-6687　　　　　　　傳真／（852）2804-6409

全系列書系特約展示
新絲路網路書店
地址／新北市中和區中山路2段366巷10號10樓
電話／（02）8245-9896　　　　　　　傳真／（02）8245-8819
網址／www.silkbook.com

本書採減碳印製流程並使用優質中性紙（Acid & Alkali Free）通過綠色印刷認證，最符環保要求。

本書為名師張翔及出版社編輯小組精心編著覆核，如仍有疏漏，請各位先進不吝指正。來函請寄
mujung@mail.book4u.com.tw，若經查證無誤，我們將有精美小禮物贈送！

nowledge. 知識工場
Knowledge is everything！

知識工場
Knowledge is everything！